For Laurinda
Enjoy!

LEE FRENCH

DAMSEL IN DISTRESS

a novel of Llauris

Published by Tangled Sky Press
www.tangledskypress.com

First printing, March 2014

Damsel in Distress is a work of fiction. Names, places, and incidents are either products of the author's imagination or used fictitiously. Any resemblance to actual persons, living or dead, events, or locales is purely coincidental.

ISBN: 978-0-9911965-4-8

Acknowledgments

I wish to thank Erik, Bob, Gwen, and Anastasia as the persons most directly responsible for shaping this tale. Kelly, Liz, and Dana provided support, as they always do. I also want to thank Kris, not just for being a fabulous person, but because her work with STAND! For Families Free of Violence in Concord, CA inspired me to believe this is a kind of story that should be told.

Finally, Catherine Jeltes is the person responsible for the beautiful stone on the cover. I found it in her Etsy store, galleryzooartdesigns, and had to have it for this book.

Author's Note

This novel contains a depiction of domestic abuse. Some readers might be disturbed by it. Although the story is entirely fictional, the abuse is based on real accounts of real women. I've done my best to keep the 'on screen' brutality minimal and to not sensationalize or glorify it.

I believe that silence is the greatest ally domestic abuse has in the world. It's my hope that stories like this one - of fantasy and adventure and magic - can shed light on the subject for people who otherwise wouldn't think about it very much.

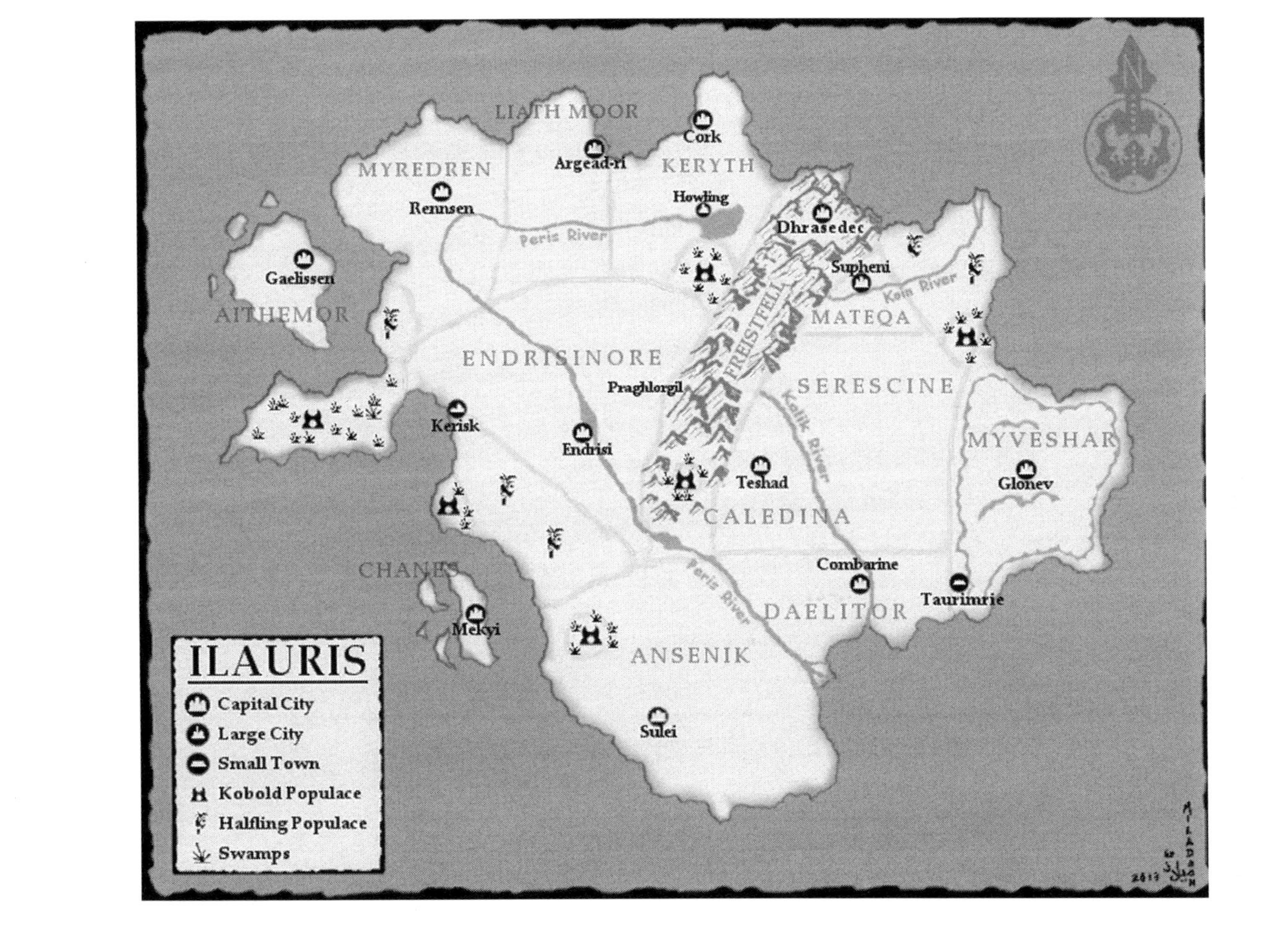
ILAURIS
Capital City
Large City
Small Town
Kobold Populace
Halfling Populace
Swamps
LIATH MOOR
MYREDREN
KERYTH
Cork
Argead-ri
Rennsen
Howling
Dhrasedec
Peris River
Gaelissen
AITHEMOR
Supheni
Koin River
MATEQA
FREISTFELL
ENDRISINORE
Praghlorgil
SERESCINE
Kerisk
Endrisi
Kalik River
MYVESHAR
Teshad
Glonev
CALEDINA
CHANES
Combarine
Taurimrie
Mekyi
DAELITOR
ANSENIK
Sulei

Preface

The story contained herein is a fictionalization of my collected notes regarding the Sword of Kailesce (pronounced 'Kī -less'). While I have done what I can to ensure the facts of this account are true, much liberty has been taken, especially with dialogue, some of which I do not remember taking place despite being there. Likewise, I cannot say with certainty what anyone felt at the time, nor can the author, and I would like to hope some of the early events are exaggerated. Further, I find the characterization of myself to be entirely inaccurate. I do not 'bounce', and never have. I also do not fill the air with idle chatter for hours on end. 'Prattle', indeed.

In fairness, it is true that I do prefer books to men.

-Evi Narien, Archive of Ar-Toriess

Prologue

"This is the place." The ball of maroon light floating over Keric's head provided enough illumination for him to study the old stone doors. The runes carved into them were in one of the old languages, and he had to refer to his translation scroll to make sure he had them all correct. If this wasn't the right cave, someone went to a great deal of effort to make it appear as if it was. The guardians they already defeated on the way certainly left their mark in the form of blood spatters on their clothes and minor injuries in their flesh.

Behind him, Jason scratched with his pencil on the map he'd been drawing of this labyrinth. It was full of twists and turns, dead ends and black pits of doom. Keric would draw the map himself, but he needed both hands free to protect the pampered nobleman's son from meeting an untimely death in some trap or at the hands (or claws) of a hungry denizen of the dark. So far, he'd done as good a job as he'd been paid to. "Can you open it?"

"Just a minute." Keric's eyes flared with a maroon glow as he invoked his power to see magical auras. The doors were sealed, he could see the patterns in the Aether bleeding through along the crack in the middle. "It's warded. I'll need to study it for a while."

"Or," said a voice from behind them, "we could work together and be out of here in no time at all." The owner of the voice stepped into the light. It was an elf man, which surprised Keric. He hadn't seen one this far north in years.

Jason crossed his arms, standing straight and tall enough to loom over the shorter, more slender elf. "And why would we want to do that?"

The elf clasped his hands behind his back and rocked on his heels, looking pleased with himself. "I have the key to these doors, for one. For another, after everything I've had to deal with to get this far, I'm really not in the mood to kill you both."

With a threat now issued, Keric gave the elf his full attention. The man didn't look terribly dangerous, and wasn't any more magical than any other member of his race. What he did have, though, was a deceptive sort of grace to all his movements, the kind that spoke of a cobra lying in wait to strike his prey. In his years as a mercenary, Keric had seen men like that before, and all of them were deadly with a blade when they chose to be. This one carried two weapons in plain sight and probably had more hidden away.

Jason regarded the elf with obvious skepticism. "All you're proposing to save me is time. My mage can handle the doors."

The elf's eyes darted from Jason to Keric and back, comprehension flickering across his features. A calculating smile replaced it. "Are you sure about that?"

The question was passed to Keric, and he shrugged. "It's hard to say for sure. It does have a keyhole, and we don't happen to have the key. I might be able to trick it, but it would be significantly easier to just use the proper key. We'd save a lot of time." Since he was being paid by the day, there was an obvious benefit for his employer to take the elf's offer. Besides, Jason was the type of man who'd rather be bedding young women than tromping around in dank caves and fighting strange creatures.

Jason nodded and turned back to the elf. “What are you proposing?”

“We open the doors together and fight whatever might lie in wait inside, and I take half the treasure.” The elf held up his hands to suggest he had no plan to stab them both in the back at the first chance. “I'd rather have it all, but I can see the value of teamwork. Besides, if my sources are accurate, there's more than enough to share.”

Just like he knew Jason would, the man nodded without delay. This wasn't about the money, not for him. It was about glory and glamor. The young man wanted a sword to prove his worth to the High King and his father, and a heroic tale to go along with it. His eyes were on a true title, not the mere Earldom his father commanded. To get that, he either had to marry some girl he couldn’t stand or perform an act of greatness for the kingdom. Where he got the idea that retrieving this blade would fit the bill, Keric had no idea. He also didn't care. So long as he got paid, the rest was unimportant.

“I accept. I'm here for a particular artifact, though, and I insist upon taking it as part of my share.”

“That's fine. I don't care what I get, so long as I can sell or spend it.” The elf offered his hand to shake with Jason. “You have a deal. My name is Inderion.”

“Jason. This is Keric.”

“Well met. Here's the key.” Inderion tossed the key to Keric, who used his power to catch it.

Plucking it with his hand from where magic held it in the air, he slid it into the matching hole on the wall next to the left door and turned it. A series of clunks and clangs announced the turning of gears and other mechanical parts. The glow of magic faded from the cracks, and he pushed the doors open. The chamber beyond it surprised him; he expected a dank cave with debris they'd have to sift through for hours. Instead, they found a white marble tomb with a shaft of blue light slashing through it from above to illuminate a slab coffin.

The most unexpected part was the overwhelming amount of magic present in the room. Keric had to shut his eyes and turn away, dismissing the enchantment that let him see the Aether pulsing through the air. "So much power," he breathed. Even without seeing it, he could feel it thrumming through his veins, calling to him. All he had to do was reach out his hand and take as much of it as he needed. It was a trap, of course. Only an untrained fool would open himself up to this. He'd burn to ashes in seconds trying to channel it.

"Is it safe?"

Keric cracked his eyes open to fix Jason with an annoyed glare. "Yes." In a manner of speaking.

That was all the reassurance Jason needed (or, probably, wanted). Inderion followed a few paces behind him, and Keric only paused long enough to take a deep breath before bringing up the rear. Jason went straight to the coffin, while Inderion peered all around, poking at the tiles on the walls and floor. Ignoring all of it, Keric rubbed at his temple with two fingers, thinking he probably should be getting paid more for this.

Without preamble, Jason pushed at the lid of the coffin. The slab was heavy, but he was strong and had it shoved far enough to expose a sliver of the inside before Keric thought to stop him. Just as he reached out and started to say something, a blue mist issued up from the darkness within, threatening to fill the room. Inderion and Jason both drew their blades. Keric muttered a phrase to summon up power to protect them, making the red crystal topping his staff give off a dull glow.

The three men moved together, facing the blue mist that resolved into a shape vaguely resembling a woman. Only her eyes had detail, the rest was indistinct. Those eyes, they were pools of molten silver, reflecting everything. “Who dares to disturb this crypt?” Her voice echoed in Keric's head, bouncing around his skull like a confused bird. The feel of it made his jaw go slack and his eyes go wide. It struck him to the core, reverberating in the same way that magic did. Was this a manifestation of the Mother Goddess?

“I dare.” Jason's voice held even more arrogance than usual, probably hiding terror behind a facade of bravado. “I will have the Sword, and you won't stop me.” He struck a defiant pose, holding his blade like he meant to stab her if she proved hostile or difficult.

Keric bowed his head as he touched his heart, then his forehead, then his lips, the formal sign of obeisance to Her. At the same time, he withdrew his magical protections from Jason, keeping them on only himself. Whatever She might do to his employer, Keric wanted to be clear he was neither a fool nor an idiot, and they shouldn't be lumped together. Out of the corner of his eye, he saw Inderion drop to one knee and bow his head. He wasn't sure what elves did to honor their own goddess, but this was probably his form of politeness for one other than Mysariel.

The mist form spread her arms. “So be it.” She flew apart, the mist settling into two shapes, each the size of a man. Their forms became solid, grotesque mockeries of men. Twisted and gnarled, they leaped at the three interlopers. One hit Keric's shields, sliding to the ground with a snarl just a foot in front of him. The other charged Inderion, who lunged behind Jason to evade it. The things were fast, moving in a blur Keric had no hope of dodging. He was a mage, not an acrobat.

He raised his staff and spun out threads of power at the closer one, holding onto hope that Inderion and Jason could at least keep the other busy for now. His will stabbed through the thing's body, making it jerk with uncontrollable spasms. Stupid boy. Jason should have known better than to goad a goddess. As he held the creature with his power, he marveled at its stamina. An average man could only withstand a few short seconds of this effect before being burnt to ashes, yet this thing almost seemed to be enjoying it.

Concerned that his magical attack wasn't doing what he expected, he cut it off and watched to see what it did next. It dropped to all fours and shook its head, then reached out with a deformed hand, stretching long, bony fingers tipped with thick claws toward him. The movement was too slow to be an attack, until he realized what it was doing. Its claws sank into his shields and pulled them, ripping them away as easily as a blanket thrown over his head.

His heart thudded in panic and he swiped his staff at the creature, only to have it knock the wood out of his hands and send it clattering across the floor. He didn't need the staff to shape his power, it was more like a security blanket than anything else. One he no longer had access to. Throwing power out to keep it from slashing his chest open, he thrashed his arms about, trying to dislodge it.

It didn't do what he expected. Instead of plunging its claws into his body, it plunged them into his aura. His body bowed from the shock and he screamed. In that moment, he understood it meant to eat his connection to the Aether, which would make it more powerful and leave him as nothing more than an ordinary mortal, a husk of himself. If it left him alive, that is, which was far from certain.

Jason appeared beside him a the creature stuffed its first bite of his aura into its gaping maw and stabbed it through the neck, angled so his blade plunged through its body without stabbing Keric. Thick blue ichor flooded out of its mouth and neck, drenching him and flowing into his own mouth. He gagged on it, feeling his aura still drawn away from him. Rolling to his side, he coughed and spat while flailing his arms wildly in the air to try, somehow to grab at his aura before it left him completely.

Beside him, Jason staggered back a step, gasping and pulling his sword with him. Keric could feel his aura going with his employer, and he understood what was happening. "Drop the blade," he hacked out, wiping the blue ichor off his face with his sleeve. The stuff created a conduit between them, sending his aura of power into the sword.

Instead of doing as he was told, Jason stood there with a stupid, stunned look, gripping the blade so hard his knuckles went white.

His mouth opened and shut, gaping like a twit. Inderion stepped up and kicked the blade, breaking Jason's grip and sending it skittering across the floor to where Keric's staff lay. Too late, but not in the way he expected.

Keric invoked his power to see magic again, relieved to find that working. The room still had a disturbing amount of power, but he squinted to see what was really going on. He stared at Jason and thought seriously about the killing the man on the spot. Pay be damned, he didn't want to spend the rest of his life with his aura tied to this ass. Yet, that's exactly what happened. The blade acted as a bridge, and now he was tied to Jason. For the rest of his life.

"What happened?" Inderion wiped his blades on his pants and sheathed them.

Keric shook his head and got to his hands and knees. "Magic stuff."

Jason took a few deep breaths. He rubbed his face with both hands, leaving a smear of the blue stuff on his cheek. "It was a rush."

"That's great." Inderion nudged one of the corpses with his boot. It didn't react. "Where's the gold?"

"Keric, check in the coffin." Although Jason actually said it like a request, Keric felt compelled to do it. His heart sank to his boots. This connection meant he was under Jason's control. Over time, it might weaken, but he was bound to this ass for now, and forced to do his bidding.

Getting to his feet, Keric staggered to the coffin, catching himself on it. His legs felt like jelly and his head throbbed with the start of an ache behind his eyes. What he should be doing was sitting and resting. Instead, he stared down at the slab still covering all but a tiny slice of the coffin and put his hands on it. He shoved at the slab, finding it – as expected – much too heavy for him to budge even an inch. “I need help to do this,” he grunted, his voice rough.

The other two men helped, and they shoved the lid until it fell off the other side. Inside the crypt, a skeleton lay with nothing but a sword clutched in its hands. Except, even in his current condition, Keric could see the sword was a flimsy knock off. The half-rusted blade had a dull blue rock set into the pommel, not a brilliant blue stone like the legend said. Jason reached out and touched it. The blade disintegrated into a pile of dust, the rock falling into the ribcage with a clunk.

Jason swore colorfully while Inderion shoved himself away from the coffin and kicked out in frustration. Keric, on the other hand, giggled, unable to restrain himself. All that work and pain and struggle, not to mention getting bound to Jason, for nothing. Slumping over the edge of the coffin, he stared at the skeleton, lying there so peacefully. His giggles subsided while the other two men shouted and beat out their anger and annoyances.

“What an incredible decoy you are. Amazing, even. I'm in awe of your guardian.” As he spoke, he reached down and shoved the ribcage aside to grab the rock, disturbing the whole skeleton. The skull rolled to the side, revealing a folded piece of leather. He picked it up, finding the softness remarkable given how long this place must have been sealed. It had a flap, which he opened. Inside was a folded piece of oiled parchment. He drew it out carefully, then unfolded and read it.

The language, older than he was used to deciphering, would take some time to translate properly, but he got the gist: riddles. Clues. There would be a lot of work involved if Jason really wanted to pursue this, but it could still be done. If he was reading this right, the thing was actually broken into pieces and they'd have to hunt them all down, then figure out how to put them back together. It could take years. If he was lucky, he'd find a way to break free of Jason in the course of it.

"Gentlemen," he said. Both men had wound down, now just standing and glaring, so he didn't quite have to shout to be heard. They turned and directed those glares at him. "I believe I've found a map, of sorts."

Chapter 1

Staring at the full length mirror, the little girl stood completely still while her dress was buttoned up. Not doing so would only earn her a swat on the rump, she already knew this. Her dress for this occasion was a simple blue silk gown, embroidered in a lighter blue with flowers around the hems, waist, and collar, with a white lace pinafore, white silk socks and blue slippers completing it. The color, sky blue, was a shade she liked well enough, one that matched her eyes. It was, of course, chosen for that reason.

"The buttons barely meet," her mother said disdainfully. "Sabetia, you're getting fat. No lunch for you today and your meals will be smaller."

The girl did everything she could to hide her reaction to this pronouncement. It wasn't fair and she'd starve like that!

Sabetia's new maid, a plain girl in her late teens, frowned as she tugged the buttons together in the back and fastened them. "Madam, she's only seven. More like she's growing into the fine young lady she'll become in a few years. This isn't fat, I think-"

"I did not hire you to think," her mother snapped. Sabetia couldn't help herself – she flinched when her mother's hand flew up to lash out. No blow came, though, and when she opened her eyes and straightened before incurring a scolding, she was surprised to see Myra hadn't been hit, either. "I hired you as a favor for a friend who thinks highly of your father. By all means, continue, if you want to find yourself looking for a new position with the very unpleasant referral I will give you."

The maid blinked a few times, then firmly shut her mouth for a few tense seconds while her fingers continued to work with the buttons. "Yes, Madam," she finally replied. "I understand."

"Good. Make sure you do something attractive with the curls. Her nursemaid had no idea what to do with them." Her mother crossed her arms and went back to watching the maid like she expected something to go wrong.

Myra nodded and reached for the pinafore, then draped the halter neck over Sabetia's head. "Arms up." Sabetia complied, sticking her arms straight out with her hands held precisely, palms down. The delicate cloth was wrapped around her and tied in the back. When the maid tapped her arm, Sabetia lowered both and stood as straight and tall as she could again. "We could-" She bit off what she was going to say with a nervous glance at the older woman. "That is, would you like anything in her hair? Or just let the curls hang loose? She does have beautiful hair."

Her mother, whose hair was exactly the same shade of burnished gold and formed exactly the same corkscrews, preened with the compliment she obviously took for herself. "We aren't common peasants, make sure she doesn't look like one." Despite her pleased smile, the words were delivered with a sharp, venomous bite. She started to say something else, but a solid knock on the door interrupted her, making her mouth go thin. Before any of them could say anything or move even a step towards it, the heavy oak doors flew open.

Sabetia didn't dare turn to look until she heard a booming voice she knew well. Grandmother Kayles was her favorite person in the world, even more than the cook's assistant who sneaked her treats sometimes. "How is my favorite granddaughter?" Her voice always held joy and happiness, and she would never, ever swat Sabetia, not even for the most flagrant impertinence.

Knowing she could now move and get away with it, Sabetia's face lit up and she ran for her grandmother, jumping into her wide open arms. The old woman didn't care if the little girl crinkled the velvet of her gown and scooped her up into a warm, welcoming hug. "Hello, Grandmother Kayles," she said happily, her small voice quiet so as to not annoy her mother. "I'm so happy you're coming with us."

"I'm happy about that, too. Angelica," Grandmother's attention turned to her daughter-in-law and held sharp rebuke, "what are you feeding her?" She settled the girl onto her hip. "She's too light. A little girl her age should be heavier than this. I should nearly break my back trying to lift her."

Without looking, Sabetia could tell Angelica's mouth still drew down into a frown, but her mother would make an attempt to hide much of her scorn in deference to a source of wealth she intended to collect upon the old woman's death. "She eats well enough," was all she said in response.

Grandmother's free hand – she needed just the one arm to hold Sabetia on her perch – waved Angelica off. "Go tend to your own and my son's preparations, I'll see to Sabetia." It was a command, one not to be refused lightly.

"As you wish, Breanne." Angelica gave the older woman a light curtsy and swept out of the room. Sabetia saw the daggers she glared at Grandmother's back while pushing the bedroom doors shut behind herself and tried very hard not to react to it. As soon as the doors were closed, Grandmother set her down and left a hand on her shoulder. "What's your name?"

"Myra, Madam." The maid gave Grandmother a polite little dip.

"Well met, Myra. Let's put some flowers in Sabetia's hair, shall we?" The corners of Grandmother's eyes crinkled up in pleasure at Sabetia's squeal of delight.

"Can we, please," she begged Myra, her eyes wide and hopeful.

Myra smiled in relief. "That's what I was trying to suggest to your mother." She went to Sabetia's new desk with the second mirror, where cosmetics would be stored in a few years, and pulled open one of the drawers.

"Angelica doesn't take kindly to suggestions," Grandmother sneered. "Fortunately, I'm old and rich, so she listens to me. If you want to leave this position with a good reference, I recommend being highly deferential and doing exactly what she says without argument. Whenever you see or hear her doing something unpleasant to Sabetia, you can tell me. I'll deal with it."

"Yes, Madam. I have a feeling I may be doing so often. Just before you came in, she decided to restrict Miss Sabetia's diet."

"She said I can't have lunch," Sabetia pouted. "She said I'm too fat."

Grandmother sighed with great annoyance. "I see. I'll deal with that. In the meantime," she beckoned Sabetia to come with her to the chair at the desk where she sat and pulled the girl into her lap.

From behind her back (Sabetia had no idea where it really came from, but often suspected Grandmother had some small amount of magic), Grandmother produced a small box wrapped in shiny blue paper with a lavender silk bow tied to the top. "I have a gift for you."

"For me?" Sabetia sucked in a breath of pure joy, taking the lovely box in her small hands and drinking the sight of it. She rarely received presents, and they were never decorated so wonderfully. For her birthday, her mother let her have cake, and her father typically gave her something too big or oddly shaped for proper wrapping. The white painted desk with its large, ornately bordered mirror was her last birthday present, given to mark her transition from young child to older child. Myra was also part of this change; she was a big girl now.

"Of course for you. Your father disapproves of gifts from me, for the most part. He says you should not be spoiled." Something in her tone made Sabetia certain the old woman thought that ridiculous. "This, though, is something he won't dare object to. Go ahead, child, open it."

As Sabetia reached over and kissed Grandmother lightly on the cheek, Myra set a tray on the desk, one with freshly picked little white flowers laid out next to a cord to thread through her hair. Grandmother jostled her lightly to make it possible for Myra to tend to her hair while Sabetia opened the box. Inside it, she found a lavender velvet bag with a lump inside. Only Grandmother cared that Sabetia liked light purple better than blue.

Drawing out the bag reverentially, she squished it, feeling the fabric crinkle on her fingers, smooth and pleasant. "What is it?" She turned to her Grandmother to see the old woman gazing at her fondly. Her father looked at her like that when he wasn't too busy to take a moment for her.

"The bag holds a secret, Sabetia. Inside is a precious thing, something your great grandmother gave to me to safeguard for you before she passed. You see, my darling child, this is an heirloom of the Kayles family, one for women only."

Turning the bag over in her hands, she stared at it again, now in wonder. "What's an 'heirloom'?"

"It means that women of the Kayles family have possessed it for a very long time. Your great-grandmother got it from her grandmother, who got it from her grandmother, and on, for a very long time. So long, in fact, that I can't say how long ago it was made. Open it up, dear, it's yours to keep now."

Myra's ministrations as she threaded her curls up and deftly wove the tiny flowers in didn't distract Sabetia in the slightest. Her attention focused completely on the bag, on the mystery it represented. Carefully, she untied the silken cord holding it shut and eased the cinching open. Upending the bag, she poured the contents into her hand. It was a brilliant blue stone with silver streaks and dark patches, shaped like a teardrop and almost as big as a walnut. A delicate golden wire basket held the stone on a thin gold chain. "It's beautiful," she breathed, afraid loud noises would harm it somehow.

"No, Sabetia, you're beautiful. This is just a pretty rock." Lifting the gift from the girl's hand, Grandmother put the chain around her neck, fastening and straightening it. "It has a story, one that you'll need to tell your daughter or granddaughter someday, so listen well."

She waited for Sabetia to nod, eyes wide with wonder again, giving her grandmother her rapt attention. "Once upon a time, there was a great hero, a swordsman who lived long ago, before even the time of Clynnidh, before we knew of the bounty of the Mother Goddess and when men were savages. He was a noble adventurer, the kind of person that roams about righting wrongs for the mere sake of doing so.

"Many are the stories of him, I'm sure, but I only know the one. He stalked a demon plaguing the land. It made a pact with a sorcerer to escape the Hells and managed to kill its controller, leaving it free to wander and pillage. Many were killed and harmed before the hero learned of it, but once he did, he hunted it. It was tricky and clever, but he was strong and brave. When he caught up to it, many lives were taken or shattered already, and he fought it to put an end to its horrible reign of terror. The battle was epic, grand, a thing to be a tale in itself. The final killing blow pierced the demon's heart, but it held a horrible secret.

"You see, the demon knew it was going to die as soon as the sword touched its flesh that final time, and it had a moment to react. That wasn't enough to save itself, but it was enough to utter a final curse, one that made its shell explode. The explosion shattered the sword, flinging one of the shards into the hero and killing him. The rest of the shards were flung far away by the force, to be buried in places far, far away, save the one," she tapped the pendant that now hung halfway down Sabetia's chest, "left in his heart. We keep it safe for him, because the demon could not be killed forever, such things cannot be. But," she lifted a finger to emphasize a point, "they can be contained. Just as the demon made a wish with its last breath, so did the hero. He wished for the demon to be imprisoned in the sword. But, it was broken, and the only piece to fulfill his wish was the handsome jewel set into the pommel.

"Should the pieces of the sword ever be brought together again and reforged, the demon will be released. And now, Sabetia," Grandmother fixed her with a very direct, serious gaze, "you are being entrusted with the safekeeping of the jewel. You must never let anyone take it from you. Do you understand? This is a weighty responsibility I place on your shoulders."

Her mouth hanging open in awe at the tale, Sabetia nodded. "I will keep it safe," she said solemnly. "I promise."

"Good girl," Grandmother said with a nod of satisfaction. "Now, take a look at what Myra's clever hands have done with your hair."

Sabetia turned obediently to follow Grandmother's pointing finger. At the sight, her eyes widened in delighted surprise. Her curls were bound up all around by a halo of tiny white stars, like a tiara fit for a princess. "Oh, Myra, thank you!" She smiled joyfully and jumped off Grandmother's lap to hug Myra.

"You're welcome, Miss Sabetia," Myra said warmly, "but mind you don't jostle it much or it'll come undone."

Letting go immediately, Sabetia ran to the larger mirror and twirled around, watching herself. Not even the High Princess would look so fine! Her father was the Weavers' Guildmaster and her mother was the Needleworkers' Guildmistress – together, they had access to everything the High King did, and knew firsthand what the Royals would be wearing, as they provided it themselves. She laughed at the idea of being mistaken for the High Princess Caitlin, a girl only a year older than herself.

"That is how a child should sound." Grandmother grinned and stood, smoothing her skirts. "Myra, are you accompanying us today?"

"No, Madam," Myra bobbed a shallow curtsy. "I haven't been with the household long enough, so the Madam said."

Grandmother snorted. "She's afraid you'll embarrass her by being uncouth, no doubt." Sabetia stopped twirling, curious what 'uncouth' meant. If it was something her mother didn't like, she thought it was a good thing to know. This wouldn't be the time to ask, though, as Grandmother held her hand out for Sabetia, and she rushed to take it. "Very well. I will be your guardian for today, my dear. Come along, your mother will be tapping her foot if we take much longer."

"Goodbye, Myra. See you tonight," Sabetia said politely as she was led away. Myra waved to her with a smile, the girl waved back, and then they were off. Grandmother set a quick pace; Sabetia had to hurry to keep up.

"It's important to remember that this is a solemn occasion, Sabetia. We're going to a funeral, not a party. No one expects a child to be dour or solemn, but keep your merriment quiet."

"Yes, Grandmother." They walked together down the wide hallway connecting Sabetia's room to the main part of the house. She had her own play room, bathing room, privy, wardrobe, and bedroom, with Myra's rooms alongside them. Another sturdy oak door opened into the main entry, and a servant opened the front door for them. Outside, a carriage waited with the door open. A man stood at the ready to shut it behind them as they climbed in, Sabetia first. Her parents already sat inside, and she took the seat opposite her father.

His clothes were handsome today, rich brown and maroon finery with embroidered shapes. It made his graying brown hair and full beard seem more stately than usual, his light blue eyes more alive. Or, perhaps, that was because he actually looked at Sabetia and smiled at her, instead of reading papers of one kind or another. "You look very nice, Sabetia." The warm approval in his tone made her smile wider.

"Thank you, Papa," she answered dutifully. The carriage started to move, rocking and swaying as it trundled along.

Her mother sniffed with disdain. "That maid needs to learn propriety. She's done up her hair like a noble."

"She's a child, Angelica." Her father kept his eyes on Sabetia, making it seem like he took her into his confidence. "No one will be offended. I don't recall giving you a pendant that fine, though. Where did it come from?"

Grandmother reached over and patted Sabetia's leg. "I gave it to her. She is to be allowed to keep it."

With a deferential nod, he said, "Yes, mother, of course."

"She's not old enough to be trusted with things of such value," Angelica said. It wasn't quite snippy, but her tone gave a sure sign that she was annoyed.

A light blush colored Sabetia's cheeks as she spoke up, hoping to mollify her mother, at least a little. "I promised to be very careful and take good care of it."

Angelica and Grandmother stared at each other in some kind of battle of wills. The space inside the carriage grew tense, and Sabetia turned away from the two women to find her father still looking at her. Silently, he offered her his hand, which she took happily and climbed into his lap. It wasn't something that happened very often, and she enjoyed it while she could. He wrapped his arms around her and took a deep breath, smelling her hair and flowers.

"Oh, honestly, Travin, she's not a baby anymore." The battle was over, and Angelica waved irritably at her daughter. She must have lost, because Grandmother looked satisfied. "Don't treat her like one."

Travin sighed and squeezed Sabetia once more before pushing her off to sit in her own seat. "Yes, dear."

Angelica narrowed her eyes and growled, "Don't use that tone with me."

Grandmother laughed, it was rich and rolling and hearty. "I hope you'll behave better in front of the High King and his family, lest they decide you're uncultured swine."

Turning away from everyone in the carriage, Angelica glowered out the window in the carriage door. Sabetia didn't want to be drawn into an argument, so she did the same out the window on the other side, only without the glowering. Instead, her eyes watched with excitement as they passed through the streets of Rennsen. She didn't leave the estate very often; this was a treat. Their manor sat on the west side of the city, nestled among others of similar size. To get to their destination today, they passed through a section with much smaller houses, all crammed together with no front gardens but still very nice to look at, in many different colors.

There were also businesses, ones with brightly painted signs showing what they offered in pictures and words. Sabetia could read well enough to understand them all. Her mother said she needed to be able to read to run a household. That was what she would do someday. She'd be married to whoever her father arranged it with, then she would have babies and manage servants and keep track of expenses and such things. It sounded like a lot of work, but it was what she was being trained for, and refusing was not an option.

They also passed through a part of town with buildings that had so many windows she didn't know what they were for. With no signs, she guessed they must be houses for people who didn't like to look at nice things, but didn't really understand why the windows had no glass. The people on the street here didn't look like regular people, either. They wore drab clothing, their faces seemed less cheerful, more haggard. Some dressed in what she would call rags. "Papa, what's wrong with that woman?" She pointed to one in particular who hobbled with a cane and had strange growths on her face, purplish globs of flesh she'd never seen the likes of before.

Travin reached over and pulled the window shade down, cutting off her view. "Don't think about it, Sabetia. Those people aren't worth worrying over. They're filthy and should be swept off the streets."

Looking to Grandmother for confirmation, she found an expression she didn't understand: it was strangely closed off. "There's nothing we can do for them," Grandmother said after a few long moments. “It's best to put them out of your mind.”

Confused, Sabetia's eyes slid to the other window, but her mother drew the shade over that one, also, leaving them with only dim light provided by the ventilation slats overhead. “But why are they like that?”

“They're nasty, dirty people with no money,” Angelica sneered. “They sleep with rats and have fleas and diseases. The High King can't rid the world of them, so he lets them stay in the city. They work in the sewers and other places beneath us.”

“Someone has to do those jobs,” Grandmother said more gently, but with her expression still strangely stony. “Their lives could be made better, but they don't want help, they want the dignity of paying work and standing on their own two feet.”

Although she didn't truly understand, Sabetia nodded and looked down at her hands, clasping them together in her lap. Her father put his hand on both of hers and squeezed them, his eyes on her so intently she could feel it. “What matters is that you'll never have to deal with them, not so long as I live.”

She nodded again and went quiet, unable – and unwilling to try – to explain why everything they said made her uneasy. The carriage trundled along and she tried to put it out of her mind, but the sight of that woman, her face wrinkled and weathered much worse than Grandmother's, stayed with her, kept pressing on her. Were some of those crinkles from pain? Did those growths hurt, or were they normal? Could she have made that woman smile by twirling for her like she did for Grandmother?

The carriage remained silent save for the groaning of the wood as it trundled along and the clopping of the horses' hooves as they pulled it. When it stopped, the servant man opened the door again and helped Grandmother out, then Angelica and Sabetia. Her father climbed out of the carriage on his own, as was proper for a gentleman. He offered his arm to his wife, who took it without comment and started walking with him. Grandmother took Sabetia's hand and they followed.

It was a Temple, but not the one at the Royal Palace. Sabetia vaguely remembered visiting that one a few years ago when they went to pay their respects to the newest member of the High King's household, the High Prince Aldan, who would probably be High King himself someday. As Grandmother put it, he would take the throne so long as he didn't anger too many nobles or prove himself to be horribly stupid.

This Temple to the Mother Goddess was a single room, one with a high ceiling meeting at point in the middle and wondrous murals painted on the walls, of stories she knew about Clynnidh, the First Disciple. The windows letting in outside light had been stained to fit into the images. Most of the floor in the wide hall held curved benches arrayed around a platform in the center. The Royal Temple was a lot like this one, just with a special box for the Royal Family to sit in and places for their guards, and it was much bigger, with the artwork on hanging canvases instead of directly on the walls.

The line of people come to pay their respects to the survivors of the dead man snaked through the benches – it would take a while to reach the front. Sabetia stood still as she'd been warned to do, staying with her Grandmother and keeping quiet. Other children didn't follow suit, she noticed, some of them shrieking and laughing and running around while their parents did nothing to stop them. Grandmother's firm grip kept her from considering any attempt to join them, even though her mother's presence was more than enough to do so on its own. It was frightfully boring, though. She amused herself by following the lines of the murals with her eyes, playing over the stories in her mind.

Clynnidh was such a fantastical woman, who single-handedly brought the truth of the Mother Goddess to the savage men of the lands. She raised the Isle of Niwlynys from the depths and shrouded it in a veil of mystery and secrecy. She founded the Bratikren, the order of nobility and authority from which men drew their power to rule. She was also part of the Middyn's counsel and helped him form the Order of Middyn, the wandering sages and scholars and musicians (usually called 'bards') who spread the tales of the past. Surely, if the High King was going to be here as her mother said, a bard would be here to speak. They were supposed to be eloquent and brilliant, and she'd never seen one before.

As they got closer to the platform and altar, her mother startled her out of her musings by pushing a flower into her hands. It was a white daisy, the center purple and dotted with tiny flecks of bright yellow. This was the most wonderful flower she'd ever seen. Their glorious gardens had nothing like this.

Her mother favored roses and exotic plants, ones that were difficult to get and to grow, especially magical varieties. One glowed in the dark, another had petals that burned with what looked like real fire. Even so, with all the fine types to be found there, this simple one with so many long, thin petals enchanted her. Lifting it to her face, she took a long, slow breath in through her nose. Its scent was subtle, barely there, but it smelled alive in a way none of those fancy flowers did.

Grandmother bent down and whispered, "When we reach the platform, you curtsy and then we will place the flower on the altar." She didn't have one herself, so this was a special treat for Sabetia.

Except she didn't want to give up this flower. It seemed a gift from the Mother Goddess especially for her. Why else would her mother have chosen it for her? Without some kind of prodding, her mother's natural choice would be whatever was most ornate. Instead, she selected this incredible piece of simple perfection. Maybe she could pretend to set it down without doing so, hiding it under her dress. Yes, that was the answer. She felt a mild heat burning her cheeks and knew she blushed just a little. A furtive glance around told her no one noticed.

The line moved slowly forward, and she finally could see the man standing in front, accepting the wishes of those who waited in line. He was an adult, but not by a lot – he still looked young and fit. His black hair and close cropped beard framed a face with strong lines and dark eyes. He was pleasant to look at, aside from how serious he seemed. He wore a black suit made of fine fabric and fitted to him perfectly, with polished black walking boots. The way he moved, something in his gestures and bearing, cast him as so sad and unhappy. Sabetia wanted to hug him, but she knew she'd get into trouble for doing any such thing, let alone breaking away from Grandmother.

She looked from him to her flower and back again a few times, coming to the conclusion he needed it more than she did. Her parents stepped up onto the dais with him. Angelica lowered into a deep curtsy, Travin bowed. The sad man nodded to both of them and murmured something. Then she and Grandmother stepped up and both curtseyed. This time she heard what he said, "Thank you for coming". Instead of moving off like her parents did, to place the flower on the large pile already there in front of the cloth wrapped corpse on the altar, she resisted Grandmother's pull to lift the flower up, presenting it to him.

"You should have this one," she whispered, aware her cheeks blazed bright pink and ignoring the insistent tug of Grandmother's hand. "He has enough already."

The man blinked as if coming out of a daze and focused on the flower. His hand moved and he took it, then he looked at her. She watched his eyes search her face then take all of her in. Looking around after that, he spotted someone, but Sabetia didn't turn to see who it was. "Madam." His voice had a little bit of a croak in it; he probably hadn't spoken beyond the soft murmurs for a while. He cleared his throat and frowned, giving his attention back to Sabetia. "What is your name, girl?"

Her blush burned more fiercely, all the way to her ears. "Sabetia Kayles, my Lord."

"Thank you, Miss Sabetia Kayles," he said politely, nodding to her. "You are a rare and beautiful gem."

This time, when Grandmother tugged at her hand, she obeyed and followed her off the platform. Glancing back, she saw him still looking at her, then watched as he lifted the flower and smelled it, getting a very small smile. That was all she wanted, all she truly meant to do. It warmed her heart to see it, and her blush receded. No one said anything as they kept going, heading for the closest empty space they could find on a bench. The inner circle was already filled, as with the next three circles. Just as her mother urged her father to one in the fifth row where they'd sit with a view of the dead man's feet, a man cleared his throat and all four of them turned to look.

It was High King Kaidyn himself, in rich red and gold fabrics provided by her parents. He was a younger man than Sabetia's father, still hale and hearty with many years ahead of him. Beside him, holding his hand, stood High Princess Caitlin, in a purple gown much finer and more ornate than Sabetia's, but with her straight brown hair held back only by a golden headband and no flowers. No one would ever confuse the two girls, Sabetia noted with disappointment, yet she felt a thrill to know that her own hair looked more regal. Everyone around him, upon realizing who he was, bowed or curtseyed in whatever way they could.

"Excuse me, Master and Madam Kayles. Caitlin," he gestured fondly to his daughter as if there could be any doubt who he meant, "would like to meet Miss Sabetia."

Caitlin smiled politely and extended her delicate pale hand. "Hello, Miss Sabetia." Her voice was clear and calm and confident. "Your hair is really pretty."

Unable to believe what was happening, Sabetia simply followed suit, taking Caitlin's hand in her own like she'd been taught to, clasping it lightly. "Thank you. It's..." Was she supposed to say 'an honor', or 'a pleasure', or something else? The blush that colored her cheeks must have been bright crimson. “An honor,” she finished uncertainly, stifling down a nervous gulp.

This earned her an indulgent grin from the High King, who crouched down to be eye to eye with her and extended his hand. “That was a very nice thing you did for a young man in mourning, Miss Sabetia. If it's alright with your parents, I would like to extend an invitation to you and your tender to sit with us.”

“This is my grandmother,” Sabetia blurted out as she offered him her hand, but she tensed immediately after, expecting to be swatted for her outburst.

Instead, Grandmother Kayles and the High King both laughed. “We would be honored to accept your invitation,” Grandmother said graciously.

“Excellent.” The High King squeezed Sabetia's hand and let go, nodding his head in satisfaction, then Caitlin took her hand instead. The High Princess led her away, and they passed faces staring at her with varying degrees of shock or jealousy. They stopped at a seat in the innermost circle, where they could watch the rest of the well-wishers being greeted and delivering their flowers. Grandmother followed on the High King's arm at a more sedate pace. The two adults spoke quietly together, then Grandmother settled next to Sabetia while the High King sat next to his daughter. On his other side, the High Queen and High Prince Aldan were already seated.

Sabetia had no idea what to say. Here she was, sitting next to the High Princess and the rest of the Royal Family! Grandmother put a reassuring hand on her shoulder, a warm, grounding presence that let her at least look around without feeling starstruck. Everyone else in the inner circle wore clothes just as fine as her own, the same for the second circle. Beyond that, she could really only see colors, except that she found her mother watching her, even through the line of those still waiting to offer their condolences, even through the sea of those already seated between them. Angelica mouthed something at Sabetia. She had no idea what her mother said, but nodded demurely anyway. More than likely, she was being reminded not to do anything rude or silly.

"It was his father that died," Caitlin whispered into her ear. A low buzz of chatter all around gave the illusion of privacy. "His mother killed him. My father had her hanged."

Surprised by this, Sabetia blinked and stopped thinking about her own mother. Whispering back, she asked, "Why did she do that?"

"I don't know," the other girl confessed. "No one will talk about it around me. But he was the Earl of Venithys." She hooked her ankles together and swung her feet back and forth as if she couldn't stand to sit this long. If Sabetia did that, she had no idea what her mother would do to her. Something worse than caning, probably.

"Where's that?"

The Princess clearly enjoyed knowing things Sabetia didn't and telling her. "This is Venithys, here. Earl is the title you buy. No one knows if the son is going to buy it or not except my father. He won't tell anyone yet." Though her understanding of the nobility was probably more limited than Caitlin's, Sabetia did know how the various titles worked. Myredren was ruled by the High King. Under him were the Kings of Liath Moor, Aithemor, and Keryth. Dukes were next, then Earls, then Barons and Counts. Earls weren't really the same as the rest of the titles, as one didn't earn it through lineage or deeds. The Bratikren chose amongst themselves who gained the titles and who didn't, except for the Earls.

Sabetia nodded her understanding of the news and glanced at the High King. "Will he announce it today?"

"You two are worse than a pair of gossiping old hens," Grandmother chided with a chuckle.

"Yes," the High King added, "I will. This, however, is a place for quiet contemplation, ladies. You can speak as much as you like outside, after the service."

"Yes, Father." Caitlin sighed, and where he couldn't see it, she made a face, rolling her eyes around and sticking her tongue out. It made Sabetia cover her mouth to stifle a giggle, which made Caitlin do the same. The High King ignored them, which surprised Sabetia. Angelica would give her a sharp swat on the bottom for that sort of thing. Grandmother more predictably shushed them both without sharpness. What surprised her even more was how Caitlin took her hand again, keeping hold of it and smiling, her feet still swinging back and forth.

All through the greetings, the new Earl of Venithys held onto Sabetia's flower. Well before the line finished, he lifted it up and sniffed it again, then shook his head and stalked off the platform, apparently unwilling to continue any longer. He took a seat left open for him next to High Prince Aldan and the High Queen with a heavy sigh and stared at the flower. Caitlin leaned out to watch him, Sabetia followed. They watched as his expression hardened. She thought he looked like he was refusing to cry. The High King reached an arm out and pushed both girls back without looking while guards dispersed the rest of the line.

A man in scarlet and black finery hopped up onto the platform, spreading his arms to make sure everyone understood him to be the center of attention now. He was an older man with fully gray hair, his face tanned and creased enough to suggest he spent much of his life outdoors, but not so much to say he had a hard time of it. "Lords, ladies, and gentlemen, we all know why we have gathered in this solemn place." Although the Temple surely was designed to make it easy to be heard, his words felt as if they danced on the air, slipping and sliding through the room to carry without him speaking any louder than a normal conversation.

"The Earl Adam Brexler was a good man, he saw to the prosperity of every soul in Venithys. Let no one speak ill of the man who sponsored the paving of streets he did not need to as part of his duty, of the man who created the public garden not far from here, of the man who hired the artists whose work graces these very walls." As he spoke, he moved about the dais, skirting around the body and flowers. He faced the High King most of the time, but also addressed the rest of the assembly. "His life's work was to see to the enrichment of others, to bring out the best in all of us by showing what a great man does with his wealth for the betterment of all. Today, we celebrate this man, his life cut shorter than it should have been."

He gestured in one direction, where a woman dressed all in white paced down one of the aisles between the benches. She had to be a Disciple of Clynnidh, probably the Matron in charge of this Temple.

Her clothes were simple, just a formless, high neck gown with a hood over her head, leaving her hands and face as the only exposed flesh. The heavy cloth dragged on the floor, making Sabetia wonder how it stayed so incredibly clean and white. If she ever wore such a thing, it would be dusty brown within minutes.

The man in scarlet, who must be a member of the Order of Middyn, offered the woman a hand as she stepped up onto the platform, then bowed to her. “Matron Aila has prepared the body already, it will be delivered back to the earth from whence it came this evening. Please be silent for her invocation.” He stepped back to give her the stage, but remained on the platform with her.

“Blessed be the Mother Goddess, Blessed be the Saint Clynnidh.” The word 'Amen' rippled through the crowd as everyone intoned it in reaction. “This place is sacred in the eyes of the Mother Goddess who holds us all to her breast.” The Matron's voice rang out stronger and louder than the bard's, more direct and forceful. Where listening to him felt like being spoken to personally, listening to her felt more like being ordered to obey. Sabetia found the woman's speech so much more familiar, she preferred it and listened, enthralled by the words. “She is the Creator, the Destroyer, the Earth, the Sun, the Moon, and the Stars. She is warmth and frost, in heat or cold. She is softness and light, pain and darkness. We are Her children, each and every one of us, and we call upon Her to guide this soul to his rightful rest.”

Sabetia had never been to a funeral before, so she was surprised when the woman stopped there and threw her head back and arms out in supplication. Her hood stayed in place, clipped there somehow, and she remained like that as the bard behind her began to sing. The melody was strange, as were the words. It sounded like a hymn in Nyddhish, but with an odd, difficult to understand accent.

The simple, sad song rolled over the crowd. Even though many of the words made no sense to her, Sabetia grasped what it said: everything lives and everything dies. She never met this man and only knew his name because the bard said it, yet she found herself moved by the song, a tear sliding down her cheek. The High Princess sniffled beside her, having stopped fidgeting sometime in the middle of the hymn. Grandmother reached up to wipe her own tears away. If everyone else cried, there was no shame in it, and she didn't try to stifle it down.

The last note quivered in the air like a plucked harp string for several seconds after the bard closed his mouth. When it faded, the spell it had wrought on the crowd broke. Sniffles echoed around the chamber. Movement marked many people daubing at their eyes and cheeks. Grandmother handed Sabetia a handkerchief, using another one on her own face. Before anyone could start talking, the Matron's head raised up and her arms drifted back down to her sides.

"We mourn together the hole this departed soul leaves in our hearts, there is no shame to that. Know he is at peace and in the bosom of our Holy Mother." She paused for a moment. "The body will be buried in the garden generously donated to the realm by the Earl, this evening at dusk. Any who wish to attend are welcome." She bowed towards the High King, who stood up and paced to Jason, putting a hand on the younger man's shoulder. Jason, who didn't look up and still clutched the flower in his hand, shook his head as if he'd been asked a question, which prompted the High King to pat that shoulder and let go, then go to the platform and step up onto it.

"Allow me to make an announcement before the assembly disperses. The late Earl's son, Jason, has elected to take up the title vacated by his father. Let it be known he is, today, the Earl of Venithys until the day he shall die. Let there be no aspersions cast upon his character by the actions of his relations, for they are not his burdens to bear." Taking the Matron's hand, he helped her step down while doing so himself, a signal to the assembled crowd that the service was over.

Caitlin jumped up, eyes bright, and pulled Sabetia with her. Surprised, she stumbled a little, but gained her footing before the High Princess dragged her off and before Grandmother could prevent it. The two girls ran for door, ducking and weaving through the crowd, and kept going when they reached sunshine. Sabetia knew she wasn't supposed to run outdoors in her slippers, they were too fragile for that and would rip or snag on nearly anything. She did it anyway, finding joy in the careless race with her new friend.

They darted across the street and around the corner, with enough speed to suspect some villain chasing them. Sabetia didn't dare look back to see if that was the case – they went so fast she might trip just for doing so. When they reached trees, Caitlin plunged into them, into what must be the park spoken of earlier. It had stone paths, but Caitlin ran across the grass until she stopped suddenly. Sabetia ran into her, and they both tumbled into a hole in the ground. Both girls shrieked in surprise, then squealed in pain as they hit the bottom in a heap.

For a moment, both were too stunned to do anything but lie there, panting, then Caitlin moaned with pain. Sabetia scrambled to get off her new friend, then immediately checked Caitlin over for any serious injury. Despite the heady rush of their flight, reality crashed down, and she knew she would be in trouble when they got out, very serious trouble. If the High Princess was genuinely injured, she might be whipped.

It was her ankle. Sabetia picked it up gently and rubbed it. She opened her mouth to ask if it hurt, but Caitlin's groan made the question unnecessary. "It's not broken," she assured the other girl. She had no idea how she knew that, she just knew it was true. Holding it up was an equally mysterious impulse, but she did it anyway, somehow knowing it was the best thing to do.

"Are you okay?" A boy's high voice came from above. Sabetia turned to look, still holding Caitlin's foot up. He was a little older than them, maybe eleven or twelve, and not dressed for a funeral. His clothes were simple, but the fabrics weren't common or cheap. Everything he wore – vest, shirt, pants – was made of high quality cotton, dyed black. His shoes marked him as respectable without being wealthy. He was just a concerned boy, one with dark blue eyes and a messy mop of light red hair.

"Yes," she nodded, "I'm fine, but she hurt her ankle." No one would know where to look for them. At this moment, her mother probably shrieked at guardsmen to find her, now. Her father would beg them, perhaps even offer a reward.

"We should go back to the Temple," Caitlin said, her voice just as pinched with agony as her face.

Again sure she was right, Sabetia scolded her. "We're stuck in a hole, and you can't walk on this." As soon as she said it, she realized she shouldn't take that tone with Royalty and blushed at her boldness.

"I can help." The boy grinned mischievously. "Promise I won't even pick your pockets."

"Don't be dumb," Caitlin snapped. "Do these dresses look like they have pockets?"

The boy laid down on the edge of the hole and reached his hand out. "I'll pull you up, come on."

"You go first," Sabetia said. She helped Caitlin up and pushed while the boy pulled. When she was out, the boy reached back down and pulled her up. "You ladies from around here? Can't recall seeing you in these parts before."

Caitlin pouted where she sat, fingering a tear in her dress. "No."

"We were at the funeral," Sabetia explained, dismayed the boy wasn't and didn't realize that for himself.

"I guess that explains the dresses." He smirked. "Aside from the grass stains, anyway."

Sabetia looked down at her dress and blushed harder. Between a rip here and the green smear there, the pinafore was probably ruined. So were the slippers, and she felt sweaty and dirty. Her hair was definitely messy now, too. "My mother is going to beat me," she whimpered.

"Nothing good comes from falling into a grave." The boy grinned, like it was the grandest joke he could imagine.

Falling into a sulk, Caitlin crossed her arms. "Go fetch a guard."

"Don't be a baby." He offered Caitlin a hand. "Come on, I'll help you walk back to the temple."

Caitlin huffed out a breath, then stuck her hands out. At the boy's gesture, Sabetia took one hand while he took the other. Even though he didn't look very strong, he slipped under her arm and took most of her weight on his shoulders. All Sabetia really felt capable of doing was holding Caitlin's hand to keep her company.

"I'm not a baby," Caitlin said as she hopped along with him.

"'Course not. Got up, didn't ya? Baby woulda sat there, waiting for someone else to do something."

"You there, unhand the Princess!" A guardsman hurried up the road as they reached the edge of the park. His command felt so imperative Sabetia immediately did as she was told. Fortunately, the boy didn't, and Caitlin put up the hand Sabetia no longer held to ward him off.

"It's okay. He's helping me," she called out. "I think I twisted my ankle."

The guard ran up. "As you say, Highness." He scooped the girl up, away from the boy, who put on a good show of being innocent.

"See? Didn't do anything, just helping out like a good citizen and all." He smiled and held one hand out and open. "I hope you're okay, Highness," he said politely, even offering a small bow.

Ensconced in the guard's arms, Caitlin looked over his shoulder and blew the boy a kiss. "What's your name?" she called out.

Shocked by all of this and knowing she needed to return with the High Princess, Sabetia followed the guard in silence. She heard the boy shout "Connor" in response. It sounded like he was grinning, and when she glanced back, his attention turned to something of great interest in his hands. Reaching up, she checked to make sure her pendant still hung around her neck, which it did. Since she had nothing else of value, he must have taken something from Caitlin, which didn't really concern her.

The punishment for this would be horrific. She dropped her eyes to the ground, hoping her mother would let Caitlin take the blame. Angelica couldn't do anything to Caitlin, after all.

Chapter 2

The mirror showed a young woman standing with her hands gripping the post of her bed, one that didn't feel ready for what she would face tonight. Myra stood behind her, pulling on the laces of the corset she didn't want to wear at the direction of her mother. Angelica was never satisfied with how tight it got. Sabetia let out her breath, unable to hold it any longer. The corset cinched more than she would be able to stand for long.

"There we go," Angelica snapped. "Finally. Tie it off."

"I can't breathe," Sabetia gasped.

Her mother sneered at her. "You should have thought of that before you ate those pastries. How you expect me to make you desirable to a man when you insist upon stuffing your face every time I turn my back is beyond me."

Myra stayed silent. She was good at that now. Sabetia closed her eyes and willed herself to stay conscious as her maid tied the laces. The longer it stayed like this, the more she noticed how it hurt to have her breasts bound so they plumped out like overripe melons. "It's too tight," she whimpered.

A rap on the back of her head pitched her forward hard enough to hit the post painfully. "Enough," Angelica snapped. "No more whining. I have other things to deal with." Directing her attention to Myra, Angelica looked down her nose. "Everything is laid out. If she isn't wearing it all exactly as I directed, you'll both be caned in the morning."

"Yes, Madam," Myra said obediently, tucking the laces into the corset. Angelica swept out of the room, not bothering to shut the doors behind herself.

"I'm going to faint," Sabetia whispered. Behind her, Myra sighed and loosened the corset. She sucked in a great lungful of breath and yanked at the stupid thing to let herself free.

"You have to wear it. You heard her."

Swinging herself around, she dropped down to sit on the edge of her feather mattress in her chemise, drawers, and stockings, the corset still on but held in place by one of her hands. "I know." Angelica meant it when she issued those threats. After that funeral almost eight years ago, she started doing it. 'Get that dress dirty, and I'll whip you.' She didn't believe it the first time, then it happened. "Just give me a minute."

Myra nodded. "At least she was willing to leave it to me this time." She rubbed her face with both hands and looked up. "If your Grandmother was still with us, Goddess rest her soul, you wouldn't have to put up with this."

Not wanting to dwell on Grandmother Kayles's death nearly two years ago, Sabetia sighed. "This party is making her crazy." She took in another deep breath, then stood up and grabbed the post again. "It only has to be tight enough for the dress to fit. That's all."

"I'll do what I can," Myra promised. Without Angelica directing, she tied the corset off well before it got uncomfortable. "We'll just try the dress like this, and tighten it if we need to." Myra turned and picked up the next layer, a thick underskirt meant to give her dress volume. That layer would fit no matter what, it had long strings and wouldn't be seen by anyone.

Sabetia stepped into the skirt and stood still while Myra tied it off around her artificial waist. "Do men really like breasts so much as to warrant this effort?"

Myra chuckled, picking up the first of two layers that would actually be seen. "Yes, they do. I've had a man buried in my bosom a time or two, and let me tell you, they can be quite obsessed." This was a full dress in light blue crushed velvet to match her eyes, trimmed with embroidery and feathery lace. It buttoned up in the back and had long sleeves, a skirt that reached the floor, and a simple circle waist. This one went over her head, which Sabetia facilitated as much as she could.

"You never wear a corset, though, so it stands to reason they don't care one way or the other, so long as you have them." She cringed, waiting for Myra's verdict.

"It looks like this is fine. I don't know why your mother is in a tizzy about cutting off your air. And I agree with you, but there will be noblemen at your party tonight, and they demand this sort of thing." Pacing around in front of Sabetia to settle the dress properly, she tsked. "Poor Sabetia, if you were poor, you could let them droop as much as you want. But, you're not, so you have to give the rich men what they want."

"How about being thin? Do they care about being thin?"

Myra rolled her eyes. She was a stout woman herself, full of plenty of curves. "I don't think they really give a hoot so long as you let them have at your boobs and between your legs."

Sabetia blushed light pink and stammered, not managing to offer a coherent word in response.

"Don't worry about it, Love. The ones that care so very much aren't worth having anyway." Myra picked up the last layer, a gauzy, opalescent sleeveless overgown. The fabric was expensive and frivolous, something no one in their right mind would waste money on. Except Angelica Kayles, who had it specially made for this party, which was to be Sabetia's introduction to the world as a woman.

At this event, during which she would make her first impression on whatever young men had been goaded into showing up, she was to be showcased as spectacularly as possible in the hopes they wouldn't have to do this again. If there were no marriage proposals after tonight, she would be beaten so horrifically as to make all previous beatings pale in comparison. A myriad of thin white scars across her lower back attested to the earnestness with which Angelica carried out her threats.

When Myra stepped back to admire her handiwork, she covered her mouth with a hand. The smile behind it shone in her eyes, bright with tears on the verge of spilling. "You're so lovely. As a girl, you were beautiful, but now, you're radiant. And we haven't even done your hair yet."

Sabetia took Myra's hand in her own and squeezed it. "I'm glad you're still here with me. Will you come when I get married?"

"With the alternatives of staying on here or looking for a new job?" Myra snorted and grinned. "Yes, of course. I wouldn't leave you for anything. I would've left years ago if that wasn't the case."

"I'm glad you didn't."

"Stop it." Myra waved at her face. "I'm going to cry, and then you'll cry, and we'll be a big mess. It'll take too long to fix that. Besides, it's not as if you'll be carted off in the night and this is our last chance to say goodbye or something."

Sabetia hugged her best friend, but not so tightly as to risk harming the dress. "And here I thought I was being set out so I could be snapped up."

"Well, you are." Myra let go and guided her to the white desk she still had so they could apply powders and creams and things.

Sabetia sat and helped by holding up containers, arranging the towels to protect the dress, and then staying still. "High Prince Aldan is supposed to be coming."

"He's a bit young for you."

Sabetia giggled. "I know that, he's only eleven. But if he's here, Caitlin might be, too." In the years since that funeral, she saw Caitlin once in a while, and they stayed friends. The High Princess moved in different circles and had a coterie of noble daughters around her now, but they still had that connection, that shared bit of wild abandon. Any time she could, Caitlin made a point to see her, it just wasn't possible very often.

"She's been snapped up, hasn't she? I thought I remembered hearing that."

"Yes, by Royal Prince Quinn of Aithemor."

"It'll be harder to see her then. That's a long journey, and part of it has to be on a boat."

Instead of answering, Sabetia sighed. They weren't great friends by any measure, but she always knew she could count on Caitlin for companionship when she really needed it. "She's not leaving for another few months, at least. Weddings in the High King's family take time to prepare for."

"There's that. And you'll go, of course. So, you can see her off."

"Yes, there's that. I suppose we can always write letters."

"There you go. That'd be nice. I'm sure she'd be happy to 'chat' like that with you. I'm also sure her father will demand she visit from time to time, and you can ask her to visit with you then."

"Assuming I'm still in the country, let alone Rennsen." Sabetia shook her head to stave off depression. Myra tapped her shoulder to make her stop. "Sorry. I just wish this could wait another year, I guess."

"You're lucky your mother didn't try to marry you off already. Asking her to wait two more months until your fifteenth birthday was even too much for her, let alone sixteen." She paused long enough to fix the last skewer holding her hair up. "It seems like you turned eight just yesterday." The last word turned into a wistful sigh, and she pulled her hands away to let Sabetia really look at herself.

The young woman in the mirror didn't feel like it could possibly be her. She looked like a sophisticated courtier, her hair in an elegant arrangement with long corkscrews framing her face. Strands of tiny blue teardrops dangled from holes in her earlobes. Grandmother's pendant perched just above her cleavage, calling attention to it. The biggest difference came from the powder all over her face, covering the light spray of freckles on her nose and cheeks. Red paste painted on her lips completed the facade.

Everything, from the top of her head to the tips of her toes, was what her mother wanted. The only thing they dared to change was the tightness of her corset. Angelica was just being mean with that anyway, since the dress fit just fine like this. If Sabetia had her way, though, she wouldn't wear one at all. She didn't, normally. While her breasts were a handful each, she didn't need more than her clothes to corral them, and no one but her mother ever looked askance at her. She knew for a fact that Caitlin only wore a corset for special occasions, and also hated them.

She pulled the towels off and set them on the desk to go to her full length mirror and stare at herself. "This is just who she wants me to be," she murmured. Desperately, she wanted to have some say over her life, some tiny thing she could control. Anything. Her underwear wasn't even left up to her, and Angelica couldn't see that.

In the mirror, she saw the reflection of the pretty little shoes Angelica demanded she wear. They were light blue with embroidery around the edges and a thin heel. The heels made no sense to her. So far as she could tell, they did nothing more than make her feet hurt after wearing them for a while. An inch of height wasn't worth that.

"I'm going to wear slippers," she announced to Myra and the room. "I have slippers this color, and the dress is so long, no one will ever notice I'm not wearing those hideous things."

Still over by the desk, Myra frowned and took a deep breath. "If she does notice, we'll both be for it."

Sabetia slumped where she stood and stopped her hands halfway to covering her face and mussing her makeup. "I'm sorry, I forgot. This isn't just about me, it's about you, too. I just-"

"I know, Love, I know." Myra went quiet. A few seconds later, she left the room at a brisk walk.

"I'm the most ungrateful, selfish person," Sabetia told herself softly. Straightening again, she stared at the shoes. They didn't care in the slightest, because they were shoes. If this was a fairy tale, the shoes would sprout mouths and start talking. Maybe they'd magically make her feet never hurt for the whole night. That seemed like a greater benevolence than she deserved from the Mother Goddess right now.

Myra reappeared in the doorway, bustling in with the light blue slippers in hand. She dropped them at Sabetia's feet. "I'll hide the shoes. If you don't tell, neither will I."

A lump formed in Sabetia's throat and her eyes threatened to water. "I'll try my very hardest to make sure she doesn't notice."

"I know you will, Love." Bending over, she picked up the offending shoes and tucked them under an arm. "Now go on and have as much of a good time as that crone will let you."

Breathless with gratitude, Sabetia kissed her cheek before hurrying off. It didn't matter if her mother figured out the corset was looser, because the dress fit. What did matter was if she presented herself late, looked out of breath, or appeared to be enjoying herself. Until the party started. At that point, she better appear to be enjoying herself. Pausing at the doors to her wing, she breathed a few times in and out, then opened them and stepped cautiously out.

As she already knew, the entry was bedecked in flowers and enchanted candles. Her father spared little expense for this, hoping to make certain everyone knew of his wealth. All this money would someday be Sabetia's, and therefore, her husband's. He and his wife had enough of a reputation that Sabetia would be matched with someone. What they wanted was to make the best possible match, hopefully with nobility. With their daughter married into the nobility, they would have new access to parties and other events. Instead of just selling those people their finest cloth, they would step up to the honor of attending.

None of that was about Sabetia, of course – her opinion didn't matter in the slightest. She paused to smell some of the flowers, finding the rose musk delightful. Nothing could ever compare to that one daisy, but it was still nice. Lest her mother find her tarrying, she didn't stop long, and hurried on her way to station herself in the main receiving room. There, she would greet everyone on their way through the house to the back garden. It would be easier for them to all just go around the house, but then Angelica couldn't show off all her decorating prowess.

"Sabetia, you're beautiful." As always, a compliment from her father gave her a glowing smile.

"Thank you, Papa." She hurried to his side and kissed his cheek. Lately, that felt awkward, and something about the way he hugged her wasn't right. His hands lingered too long, then he pulled them back abruptly.

He coughed and clasped his hands uncomfortably behind his back. "Are you excited?"

"Yes, I am." Eager for another compliment from him, she twirled around with her hands up over her head.

A wistful smile perked the corners of his mouth, then he looked away from her, eyes darting around for something else to rest on.

"I'm glad to hear that." Pointing to the door that led to where his liquor was kept, he walked there hastily. "I'm a little nervous, myself. Just going to loosen up a bit. Back in a few."

She sighed, disappointed he said nothing about her dress. At least his nerves meant this was important to him, which boded well from her mother's perspective. So long as Angelica was happy, everyone else had a chance to be, too. She walked around the room, enjoying the flowers and candles, shifting a few of them while she waited.

"Stop touching that," her mother's voice snapped from behind her.

Sabetia yanked her hands away from a vase, having just centered its floral design. "Yes, Mother, I'm sorry. I was just keeping my hands busy."

"Turn around, let me see how we did."

Following the command, Sabetia took a few steps towards her mother and turned slowly with her arms out. When she stopped, she saw a very mild scowl accented with an upraised eyebrow. It could have been worse.

"I see Myra loosened the corset," Angelica sniffed.

Sabetia lowered her eyes. "The dress looked funny."

Angelica took a deep breath and sniffed disdainfully. "Stand up straight. It looks fine, I suppose. Nothing for dinner for you tonight."

"But it's my party!"

Angelica crossed the room so fast Sabetia barely saw her move. Even through four layers of clothing, the swat to her rump stung. That would have gone across her face if she could do it without leaving a hand print, and it would have hurt much more. Angelica's nostrils flared and her jaw clenched.

"I'm sorry, Mother." Head dropped down, Sabetia clasped her hands to stop herself from rubbing her bottom. "If a gentleman offers me something, I won't refuse it."

Waving that off, Angelica breezed past her, heading straight for the vase Sabetia just left to fiddle with it. "Don't be stupid, of course not. If a nobleman tells you to eat lard off his ass, you will agree."

The very idea made Sabetia blush bright pink. "Yes, Mother."

When Angelica left the vase alone, it was exactly as Sabetia set it. "Guests should begin arriving shortly. You will say...?"

Clasping her hands together in front of her (this was supposed to keep her from knocking anything over), she mustered the brightest smile she had at the moment and said, "Hello, I'm so pleased you came tonight. I look forward to dancing or chatting with you later this evening. Depending on if it's a man or a woman."

Angelica watched skeptically, but nodded with satisfaction. "I'll let you know when you can stop doing that and go into the gardens."

"Yes, Mother." That was all she ever really wanted to hear anyway.

Travin opened the door with a drink in his hand, saw his wife, and stood there awkwardly for a moment. "Are we ready, then?"

"Are you drunk already?"

"He just went in there a few minutes ago," Sabetia pleaded, hoping to avoid a fight. To help, she put herself physically between them, knowing that would redirect her mother's anger back to her.

Setting his drink aside, Travin rolled his eyes. "No, I am not drunk. Do you hear me slurring my words?" He walked steadily to Sabetia and put his arm around her shoulders. "Maybe you should have a finger or two. It would take the edge off."

"I do not need to 'take the edge off'," Angelica snarled. Rather than pursue the matter, she spun around and stalked out of the room, towards the front entry where she would greet their guests.

"Yes, dear, you really do," Travin muttered. His hand squished Sabetia to him a little more than was strictly comfortable, then he let go and stepped away, averting his eyes from her. "You'll be fine. I'll be right out there," he pointed at the entry, "with your mother. If you get tired or anything, just let me know."

"Thank you, Papa." She would do no such thing, because if she did, her mother would be neither amused nor sympathetic. "This will be a very good party."

"It better be." He took a deep breath and headed out to his wife, where there would probably be a short, vicious argument, then they'd both plaster on very fake smiles and welcome everyone to their happy, spacious, impressive home. Sabetia watched him go, wishing they could just skip this part and go straight to the dancing. At least while she was dancing, she could ignore her stomach. Lunch had been paltry, on her mother's orders: a small cup of cooked vegetables, a small slice of bread, and a small wedge of hard cheese. Always, everything was small. It wasn't really enough, and her stomach would undoubtedly start growling at the most embarrassing time possible.

Just a few minutes of brooding later, she heard a commotion at the front door, then people started coming through. She smiled as genuinely as she could, clasping hands and telling them all how happy she was to see them, despite never having met most of them before. Every man she met, young or old, married or not, let his eyes rove over her body, obviously approving of what he saw. Some let their gazes linger longer than others, but all of them made her feel like a piece of meat in a butcher shop window.

Until the Earl of Venithys walked in. He entered the room looking back at the entry, and his expression was something like confused when he turned to see her. She recognized him immediately, of course. He hadn't changed much since the funeral, just gotten a few wrinkles and a little more life on him. She, on the other hand, was no longer a child. He must have recognized her mother, but couldn't place her.

"My Lord Earl of Venithys, I'm honored you've come." She curtseyed for him, dipping down as low as she understood he was entitled to, until her knees were half bent.

"Miss Sabetia, I'm pleased to be here." He took her hand as she straightened and kissed the back. By then, her hand had been kissed so many times, she didn't think much of it, but tiny shivers danced down her spine. "It's embarrassing that I feel we've met before, but I can't think where."

He brought out the first genuine smile she'd had since this ordeal began. "It was at your father's funeral, Goddess rest his soul, my Lord. I gave you the flower."

Obviously stunned, he blinked and looked her over. "Surely not. That was a little girl. A sweet one, to be sure, but just a girl. You,

you're a woman, a beautiful one at that."

She giggled. "My Lord, as it turns out," she stepped closer to take him into confidence, "girls grow up to become women."

For a moment, he kept staring, then he barked out a laugh. "I suppose they do, Miss Sabetia."

Her stomach aflutter, she beamed at him. "I could give you another, if it would make it easier to remember me this time."

"I can't possibly imagine forgetting such a lovely vision."

Much to Sabetia's horror, the flutter turned to a gurgle and her belly growled with hunger. She blushed instantly, scarlet to her ears. The makeup covered it a little, but not remotely enough to hide it all. "Oh, excuse me, my Lord," she mumbled, not sure what to do.

"This sort of thing makes me hungry, too," he confided. Offering his arm, he gestured towards the door to the back with the other. "May I conduct you to your party and the delicacies to be found there, m'lady?"

Sabetia glanced at the front door, but her mother had said – colorfully – to do whatever a nobleman wanted her to. She slipped her arm through his and brightened her smile back up. "With pleasure, my Lord."

"I'm stealing away your daughter," he called towards the front door, then whisked her away before either of her parents could object. Out through another sitting room displayed to perfection, they found the back door standing open, plenty of guests already wandering through the garden. Servants moved through the crowd with trays carrying glasses. Tables along one side of the immediate courtyard stood laden with finger foods of an astounding variety.

The courtyard was draped in the same flowers and candles as the house, and a string ensemble played unobtrusively off to one side. Beyond the courtyard, paths wound through Angelica's gardens.

Jason took her directly to the food, not pausing for even a moment in the doorway for a grand entrance. Only a few people nearby noticed them coming through, and none tried to stop them. The moment they reached the table, he picked a cracker with something red and white smeared on it and stuck it into her mouth. He seemed amused by doing that, and she was so hungry she'd eat nearly anything, so she grinned and crunched it up. When she swallowed it, he already had something else in hand and popped it into her mouth before she could say a word.

"I could get used to this," he chuckled, watching her. She wanted to agree, but he kept her mouth full. Getting into the game, she opened her mouth for him for a sixth time. Instead of more food, he touched a finger to her lips. "I think that's enough for now." Something about the way he said that, with a low rumble in his voice, frightened her just enough that she couldn't breathe. Or was that fear? It was, but it wasn't. She had no idea what it really was. "My dear Miss Sabetia, are you cold? You seem to be shivering."

"I..." Nothing followed that. Her mouth stayed open, no more sound came out. Her eyes stuck on his, trapped, unable to tear themselves away. Vaguely, she noticed her heart beating much faster than it should, and her breaths came short and sharp.

"I could get used to this, too." He bent and kissed her, his arms wrapping around her and holding her still. She had no idea what to do, but he definitely did. When he broke it off, her knees were weak and she had to gasp for air.

"Should we turn this into a Handfasting celebration, my Lord?" Angelica's dry voice pushed into the moment.

Jason held Sabetia up still, his eyes only for her. "If Master Kayles is amenable, then yes, we should."

"Master Kayles will be delighted by the news," Angelica purred. "Shall we set a date now, or would you like to merely scoop her up and take her to a Temple now?"

He grinned. "I'll go speak with your husband now, Mistress Kayles. This is something to be arranged between men."

"Of course, my Lord." She was mildly annoyed, Sabetia could tell by the set of her shoulders and tightness around her mouth, but Angelica dipped into a shallow curtsy and gestured for him to accompany her. "Sabetia, come."

Her head whirled. Just like that, she would be married to a wonderful man, one that would leave her head spinning and knees weak. When he let go of her to walk with Angelica, she stumbled a few steps, lost in a daze. The lights all around disoriented her long enough to fall behind while she got her feet under herself again. By the time her wits settled about her again, Jason and her mother were gone, already inside, and people stared at her.

"Sabetia!" High Princess Caitlin swooped in and put an arm around her shoulders. "I love your dress," she said with a giant smile. Her brown hair was wrapped up into an elegant and complicated arrangement on top of her head with barely curled tendrils hanging down over her ears. The dress she wore wasn't as nice as Sabetia's but it was close, all in purple silk with gold trim. "I must get some of this fabric, what is it?"

"It's called whisperweb." Sabetia blinked, still dazed and offering no resistance when Caitlin pulled her away.

"Wow, he really rang your bell. I guess you're getting married soon, too. Everyone saw that, by the way. He kissed you and it went on so long." She led them out into the gardens, wandering among the flowers, a buzz of chatter in the background. "I guess he's a pretty good kisser?"

Sabetia sighed happily. "It was *wonderful.*" She took Caitlin's arm and leaned into her friend. "I got all warm and couldn't think, it was incredible. And that's only kissing! Oh my gosh, I can't wait to find out what the rest of it is like. Caitlin, he's...he's just..." She trailed off into a coo.

Caitlin giggled. "He's handsome, mature, and apparently knows what he's doing? I'm jealous. I haven't even met Quinn yet. For all I know, he's an ugly, drooling idiot." Leaning in, she said quietly, "My father says he's fine, actually, but I can't speak to his...experience, if you know what I mean."

The giggling spread to Sabetia as she realized what Caitlin meant. Obviously, Quinn had been through the ceremony all Bratikren went through, losing his virginity to a Disciple. Who knew what he'd done since, though. "Aren't you going to be Handfasted first?"

"Yes," Caitlin nodded wistfully. "It's more of a formality for us, but yes. He's coming for the ceremony in two weeks, so I guess he's probably already on his way. After that, he'll stay at the Palace with us, and then-" She deflated a little. "Then I'll go home with him after the wedding."

"I'm going to miss you," Sabetia squeezed Caitlin's hand fondly. "Maybe we can come visit. The Earl probably won't mind taking a trip to visit a future King and his new wife."

"I hope you can." Caitlin squeezed her hand back and leaned her head on Sabetia's shoulder. "I know we're not as close as we could be, but you're the most honest friend I have, and the only one I have a real secret with."

"I wonder what happened to that boy."

"Connor, I remember." They shared a dreamy smile. "I'm just going to imagine he's the one who'll rescue me if it turns sour with Quinn."

"I can't see how it could ever turn sour with Jason." Sabetia gazed off into the darkness, the memory of the kiss overpowering everything else. Her hand reached up and brushed her lips. The sensation made her shiver again.

"Well, just in case," Caitlin grinned, "he can be your fantasy rescuer, too." Both girls went quiet for a few seconds, then she said, "Jason is an Earl, that's a high rank. And we're both getting Handfasted about the same time, so we could both be getting married at the same time. Maybe, if you wanted to, we could do it together."

"Really?" Stunned, Sabetia blinked several times. "Don't you want to have your day all to yourself?"

Caitlin put an arm around Sabetia's shoulders and hugged her. "I don't care about that. I want to see your dress when you get married, because it's probably going to be incredible, even more than mine, and I want to have someone there with me who really understands.

My mother doesn't, that's for sure. If we do it at the same time, then we're sure to be able to share the day!" Her big brown eyes found Sabetia's and pleaded with her. "You're the only person I know who's getting married around the same time, and doing this will mean we'll have to meet a hundred times until it happens, to do whatever you do before a wedding."

The High Princess was begging her, a commoner, to share her wedding with her. There was only one right answer. "Of course! It'll be fun, and wonderful. I can't even imagine getting married in the Palace Temple." She hugged Caitlin back, delighted by the idea.

Her mind turned to fantasies of planning the event, with flowers and ribbon and candles. She tossed fabric in the air and danced under it with Caitlin, laughing, while her mother stood by, unable to stop them because it was the High Princess. Time slipped past with them just sharing the space, no need for words. It was a pleasant, companionable quiet, only broken when someone came looking for them.

"As much as it pains me to disturb you, High Princess, Miss Sabetia is neglecting her other guests." Jason's voice flowed smooth, like fine silk, and with nothing more than her name coming from his lips, she felt warmth stirring in her core. "This is her party, after all."

The two young women turned together to look at him. He had a pleasant smile on his face and bowed as soon as they could see him. "My Lord Earl." Caitlin stood up and acknowledged him with a slight nod of her head. "You're quite right. I'm monopolizing all of her time, how rude of me."

Sabetia also stood, blushing and smiling joyfully. "You've stolen my sense, my Lord," she told him with a small curtsy.

"I've never been accused of stealing before, but I'll happily suffer the sting in this case." He moved close enough to take her hand. "Please excuse us, High Princess, I'll need to have a word with Miss Sabetia before returning her to her celebration."

"Of course." Without bothering to hide it from Jason, Caitlin waggled her eyebrows and walked away with a smirk.

Jason grinned and took Sabetia's small hands in his own larger ones. "After this party, I'm taking you to a Temple. We'll be Handfasted, then we'll retire to my estate. Your maid is packing your things as we speak. She mentioned she'd prefer to come along with you, and I've hired her. Assuming all goes well, we'll marry on your birthday."

She was taught to want this, and she beamed up at him, pleased beyond words that she wouldn't have to deal with her mother anymore. "As you wish, my Lord."

"This is precisely as I wish, yes. Your father was eager to make this arrangement, and you will have a very comfortable life for it. I'll keep you in silk and velvet, and feed you only the best." The way he looked at her, he clearly expected her to make some sort of pledge in return.

What did he want to hear? "And I'll bear your children, my Lord, and..." A fierce blush spread across her face. She fought to keep her eyes on his. "And, ah, satisfy your...needs?"

He grinned. One hand reached up to brush her cheek with two fingertips. "Yes, you will."

It was the first thing he said that bothered her, but she pushed it aside as nervousness. Tonight, she would learn something new, something exciting and wonderful. No matter what her mother said, about it being her duty to be endured, she couldn't believe it would be like that with Jason. She wanted to say something to this man who she would spend the rest of her life with, but when she opened her mouth, she couldn't think of anything and merely stood there.

His hand reached under her chin and pushed her jaw up. "There's no need for pretty words, not with such a face. Come, let's announce it. All you need to do is smile and stay by my side. Yes," he said encouragingly as she did as he asked, "like that. This is what you want, show them."

It *was* what she wanted, she told herself. Following along in his wake, her hand held securely in his, the world sped past in a blur. He made the announcement. People congratulated him and wished her well. Sabetia's parents and Caitlin were very excited about it. Everyone else was polite. She smiled and didn't say anything but 'thank you' for a while. Very little registered until she sat in a strange carriage next to Jason. He set his hand on her thigh and squeezed.

In the near-darkness of the carriage, she could barely see him, but did feel the warm weight of his hand in a place no one ever touched her before. It made her both scared and excited at the same time. What, exactly, would he do with that hand? Too flustered to think coherently, she focused on not doing anything to annoy Jason. Her mother's favorite rule, 'Don't speak until spoken to', seemed to apply. The short ride passed in silence.

When the carriage stopped, Jason conducted her inside, then left her waiting with his guards while he roused the Disciple who tended the place. Matron Aila, the same one Sabetia remembered presiding over the funeral, accompanied him out in a plain beige robe, weariness clinging to her. The Disciple smiled when she saw Sabetia and walked right up to envelop her in a warm embrace.

While there she whispered into Sabetia's ear, "If you're willing, nod now. If you're not, shake your head."

Did she meet many unwilling brides-to-be? Perhaps it was the time of day. Being asked to do this late at night probably wasn't usual. Sabetia nodded her head and smiled.

"I'm very happy for you, Sabetia." Matron Aila held her out at arm's length and looked her over. "How old are you, dear?"

"Fourteen," she answered dutifully. "My birthday is in two months."

"My Lord Earl, she's almost sixteen years younger than you."

"That hardly matters," he waved off the complaint. "She's old enough and willing." He produced a sealed letter, the wax had her father's stamp. "We have her parents' blessing."

Matron Aila pursed her lips as she took the letter and broke the seal. "I don't generally approve of girls this young being married off, my Lord." Scanning the letter didn't change her expression.

"I've found what I'm looking for, Matron. I refuse to allow her to slip away just because she's a little young. Besides, look at her." He certainly did, but the Matron's eyes only flicked away from the letter briefly. "There's nothing childish about her. And weren't you just chiding me the other day for failing to find a wife?"

"I meant someone a little older. Fourteen, my Lord? Really?"

The way she scoffed made Sabetia's smile falter. She wanted to say something again, but the Matron had authority here.

The Matron sighed heavily. “She's wilting. I'm aware that she's technically old enough, but that doesn't mean I approve.”

“I didn't come here for your approval, Matron.” He lifted his chin. It was the first time Sabetia thought of him as arrogant, but perhaps it was more stubbornness. “I came for the Mother Goddess's. Ask Her, let Her decide whether to bestow Her Blessing or not.”

His request made the Matron scowl, and she pushed the letter back into his chest. “Fine,” she threw up her hands in surrender. “Let the choice be Hers, and let the consequences be on your head. You,” she pointed firmly at Sabetia, “I want to see you tomorrow morning, to talk.”

“Yes, Matron,” she said immediately and obediently. For some reason, that annoyed the Matron more, but she stalked away.

“Come, let's do this so you can go deflower her as soon as possible.” The Matron's words were so acidic and dry they made Sabetia flinch.

Jason put his arm around Sabetia and pushed her along. “This is because I woke her,” he explained softly. “She's cranky, that's all. I want you, Sabetia, never doubt that. You. No one else.”

If she said the same back, it wouldn't be true. Such conviction in him; she couldn't match it, no matter how much she wanted to. “I have no doubts,” she breathed back at him, thinking it might be a lie. He swept her off her feet, and she barely had a chance to meet anyone else. A swirling flutter of 'what if' questions circled in her mind, making her less certain.

"Of course you don't," the Matron grumbled. She stepped onto the platform and went to the altar. "Come up, let's do this." When they both stood before the Matron, she directed them to place one hand each on the altar, next to each other. "This is simple and painless. When it's done before a congregation, I ask if anyone present objects. Tonight, we will ask the Mother Goddess herself if She objects instead. Will your men there act as witnesses? Come closer, gentlemen," she called without waiting for an answer. "I need three of you. Stand there and keep quiet." At her command (and a nod from Jason), three of his four men approached and stood just off the platform, facing them, straight and tall, still and silent.

Matron Aila reached across from the other side and put her hand over theirs, touching both and the altar. "Hear me, Mother Goddess, hear the words of one of your Disciples. These two souls wish to join in Handfasting to ensure they are compatible before marriage. In the absence of members of the community to voice their concerns, I call upon you, in all your wisdom and benevolence, to let it be known whether this joining is acceptable in your eyes before it can be proven so in body."

She spoke more words in that other language, the words that seemed familiar but weren't, and Sabetia felt a tiny jolt hit her hand, running through her whole body until it reached her toes, her ears, all her fingers. Something sparked in her belly, low and strange. It took everything Sabetia had to not jump and back away from the altar to make the sensations go away, but she did it. Her hand was already spoken for, by this man, and she was willing. If this was some kind of test, she meant to pass it no matter what doubts might have surfaced since she agreed to it. Now that she was free of her mother, she could never go back, and there was no other choice.

"So be it." Matron Aila's voice cut through everything and the sparking sensations stopped when she pulled her hand away. "The blessings of the Mother Goddess upon you. May you be fruitful that you may be wed as soon as possible. I declare you handfasted, these men will bear witness." Though Sabetia always thought something like this was an occasion for joy, the Matron didn't look happy, she looked surly. "Be off with you all. I need my sleep."

Jason smiled possessively and picked Sabetia up. "You did well, and my birthday gift to you will be becoming the Lady of Venithys."

Being carried off like this warmed Sabetia all over and she giggled in delight. Back in the carriage, he pulled her onto his lap and held her close, which she liked. It reminded her of her father, before he grew strange around her. As with him, she craved the attention and approval.

The ride from the Temple took barely any time at all, and she got her first look at his estate while being carried inside it. Servants opened doors for Jason and he didn't stop until he reached a bedroom that must be his. Setting her down on her feet next to the bed, he didn't let her see much of the room before kissing her again.

That first kiss had been sweet and hesitant. This one was hungry and demanding. He devoured her, making it impossible for her to think anymore, which she didn't want to do anyway. His arms wrapped around her, making it impossible for her to get away, which she didn't want to do anyway. When he broke it off, it was to start undressing her. Though his every movement spoke of impatience and need, he took care with the dress, pulling off the outer layer without tearing it, then circling around behind her to undo buttons, one by one.

"Sabetia, you'll wear that layer again, the thin outer one, for our wedding. Tend to it in the morning before you're taken to see Matron Aila."

"Alright," she answered breathlessly.

His heated hands slid under the blue layer, stripping it off her with the same care. "I like it when you call me 'my Lord'. I command that you only ever call me that in this room."

"Yes, my Lord." It took him a few minutes to make it so, yet it seemed she stood before him in just her corset and underclothes all of a sudden.

"I don't want to see you in a corset ever again. Is that understood?" With that piece of clothing, he didn't bother being gentle. He yanked the laces loose and ripped the thing from her, then tossed it across the room.

She couldn't breathe, only nod to show him she understood.

"Say it, Sabetia." His mouth was suddenly an inch away from hers. "Say it or I won't kiss you again."

"Y-yes, my Lord."

His lips brushed against hers so lightly she might have missed it. "That's good, Sabetia. I would rather see you without these things as often as possible, too. Wear your dresses by themselves."

"Yes, my Lord," she managed to mumble out.

He kissed her hungrily again and tore her chemise off.

Chapter 3

Sabetia examined her reflection in Jason's full length mirror, trying to understand how such a profound difference inside could cause no change at all on the outside. His robe, fluffy and white, made her look like a child playing dress-up. It was also the only thing she had to wear until Myra arrived with her clothes. Even if it wasn't far too fine a garment, her party dress wouldn't fit properly without the corset. That thing still lay on the floor in a crumpled pile where he tossed it, the laces torn so she couldn't wear it even if she wanted to, which she didn't.

Last night was the most wondrous she'd ever had. Jason did things to her she never imagined could be done. His hands, his mouth... Her poor mother. Maybe her wretched unpleasantness stemmed from her father being inept in bed. The thought made her giggle.

Jason stepped into view behind her with a satisfied, possessive smile firmly on his lips and his eyes on her. One of his hands reached into her hair, grabbed, and pulled her head enough so he could kiss her with a soft, light touch of his lips on hers. "You need a robe that fits you better so you can meet the staff." His nose brushed hers as he let go of her hair to wrap an arm around her waist, staying behind her and directing his attention to her reflection.

She snuggled into his embrace, delighted by his affections. "I have one, Myra will bring it."

"Not necessary." From behind his back, he pulled a wad of blue cloth out and let it hang from his hand. The bundle became a shimmering slip of a robe, one that would reach just past her knees. "I want to see you in this as often as possible." His hand pulled on the tie holding his robe shut around her and he managed to get it to fall from her shoulders with one smooth movement, leaving her naked in his arms. By reflex, her hands moved to cover herself, but he grabbed one to stop her. "Sabetia," he murmured into her ear, a rough whisper of desire, "I would have you bared as much as possible. In this room, unless there's a reason to be otherwise, you wear nothing at all. Outside this room, you wear this robe unless you need to be dressed."

She looked up at him, not sure if he was serious. His expression dispelled any doubt, and she felt compelled to protest. "Jason-"

He shushed her with a finger on her lips. "Try it for a few days. You'll see. It's freeing and you'll like it." Letting go of her, he draped the new robe over her shoulders. The fabric was so thin and smooth, it felt like wearing nothing at all. His hand swiped slowly across her neck to free her hair, sending shivers down her spine at the same time as it warmed her womb. The kiss he planted on her neck reminded her of all the other kisses he'd put on other parts of her, and she let out a tiny moan. "I see we won't be leaving the room for a while after all."

Sabetia had no idea how much time passed with them in the bed again, all she knew was that when he rolled off of her, he patted her bare bottom hard enough and low enough to make her wince. He left her lying on the bed to catch her breath and too well spent to want to get up again. Even more, she wasn't even willing to roll onto her back or pull a sheet up to cover herself.

“All mine,” Jason chuckled, promises of wicked things in his tone. The bed shifted as he got back onto it and ran his hands up her legs.

“Please, no more right now,” she gasped as he slid them up her body. “I hurt.”

Pulling his hands away, he sat on her calves and sighed with disappointment. “You're young, you'll heal quickly. I can restrain myself until tonight.”

She squealed with surprise and pain when he swatted her sharply on her bottom. “Jason, please,” she begged.

That chuckle came again, but he leaned down and kissed where he just smacked her, then crawled off her legs. “Up with you. It's time to meet the staff and guards.” He got off the bed, and a few moments later, as Sabetia still lay there, not ready to move yet, he draped her robe over her body. “Come, my flower. The world won't wait forever.”

The new pet name made her cry. She was his flower. No one else's, only his. She only ached now because he wanted her so much he couldn't keep his hands off of her. No one ever wanted her so badly, so much it hurt. Her little sobs seemed deafeningly loud, and Jason crouched down where he could stroke her hair and look into her eyes.

His voice was so soft and gentle. “What's wrong, my flower?”

“Nothing,” she hiccuped out.

For a few long moments, he let her cry, then he pulled her into his arms and sat with her across his lap, the robe covering her, his plain shirt and pants keeping her from touching his skin. “It's easy to forget how big a change, how momentous this is for you. You've become a full woman now, and will be a wife soon, then a mother."

The soothing words struck at the entire reason for her tears and she nodded, clinging to him. Her mother never managed to understand half so well. There was more to it than that, and she struggled to find the words to explain. "You want me," she whispered.

He smiled at her, the sweetest thing she'd ever seen. "Yes. I want you, and only you. I want you more than I have ever wanted anything else before, and I can't imagine ever wanting anything else so much." He bent and kissed her forehead lightly. "Come, my flower. You can rest later. Now, meet the people who will serve you and protect you. You also need to eat."

As if her stomach heard him, it rumbled with hunger. She could ignore that if she had to, but the idea of him feeding her again, as he had last night, made her eager. With his help, she got to her feet and wore the robe properly. It felt strange to meet people while dressed in so little, but she had nothing else. Before they left the room, he wiped her face and kissed her forehead again, then offered her his arm and guided her out into his house. On the way in, she saw nearly nothing, all she knew for certain was that it had stairs, because he carried her up them.

His bedroom- No, *their* bedroom. Their bedroom was the largest part of the top floor of the house. The rest of the floor had the usual rooms, along with several guest rooms. He guided her to the closest of them, it was empty and plain white. "We'll use this room for the nursery," he told her when she gave him a quizzical look. "You may decorate and furnish it as you please, whenever you wish."

"Oh, thank you," Sabetia breathed, overjoyed to have so much freedom for something, anything. She padded into the empty space, trying to imagine what it should look like. Never having had so many choices to make at once, she wasn't sure where to start, but perhaps colors would be the thing. For a moment, her face fell, but then she thought of something that made her brighten back up: Myra would know what to do. Her maid would arrive today or tomorrow, and they'd figure it out together.

Secure that the problem would be solved, she returned to Jason's side to be led to the stairs down. Below, she heard boots and shoes on the wood flooring, it sounded like people hurrying about. They turned the corner of the stairs to find several women and men arranging themselves at the bottom. The women all wore black frocks with white aprons and white hats covering their hair. Most of the men wore matching black suits with white shirts. One wore a plain suit that made him look respectable, but not part of the household. The other odd man out was dressed like a guard in more utilitarian pants and shirt, with a sword belted at his waist.

"This is Sabetia," he announced to the assembled servants, "she will be my wife in two months." A strange little thrill ran through her at his words. "Her personal maid will arrive with her things soon." They reached the bottom step and he named off each servant for Sabetia. The women curtseyed and the men bowed. When he reached the two men not in uniform, he stopped walking. "This is Keric," he indicated the man in the suit. Behind them, the servants discreetly slipped away to tend to their duties again. "He's my house mage."

Keric took her hand and bowed over it without kissing it. "My Lady, it will be a pleasure to serve you as well as the Earl."

Sabetia's parents didn't have a house mage. Only the wealthiest nobles did. Most mages, so she thought, preferred to remain unattached to an individual household, and could command staggering fees for their services. "I didn't know you had one," she told Jason.

"It isn't exactly something I want known. Part of his job is to be a surprise defense at need."

Keric put up a hand. "Not that the estate is under attack all the time," he reassured her, probably in response to the icy little spike of fear she must have shown. "My Lord Earl is a wealthy man, and there are always thieves who think they will be the ones to sneak in and steal something of value. That's why I'm here. Not to repel an endless series of assassins."

"Oh, that's..." Sabetia wasn't sure what to say. She finally settled on, "comforting".

Both men were clearly amused by her reaction. "You grew up wealthy, I'm sure your father took precautions, but being nobility changes things. Along with a house mage," Jason gestured to the man with the sword, "you also now have a personal guard. This is Darius, he is responsible for your safety any time you leave the house. I expect you to let him observe your habits so he can effectively protect you. If he tells you to do something, you will do it."

Darius didn't take her hand, he merely bowed, stony faced. The man was a hulking brute, he towered over her by more than a foot. Despite being the same height as Jason, he made her feel small and weak and vulnerable just by standing there. There was nothing particularly interesting or handsome about the man – she thought him too imposing and remote for that, even if his features were arranged well and his light hair suited him. At a guess, Darius was probably a few years younger than Jason, maybe in his middle twenties.

"Thank you." She had no idea what else to say.

Jason nodded to the man, he nodded back and shifted in a way that seemed like relaxing. "Come, let's get you fed, then you can do as you please. The cook guessed what you might like for breakfast, but if you tell us what you like, you can have anything you want after this."

"Anything? Anything at all?" Sabetia blinked and forgot all about Darius.

"Yes, of course." His mouth curled into a smirk that made her blush light pink. "I'll make sure you get enough exercise."

It took her just a moment to understand what he meant, then she shivered a little. "Yes, my Lord," she breathed, moving a little closer to him and holding tightly onto his arm.

"Having heard you address me both with my name and as your Lord, I have to say I still prefer the latter. I would have you call me that all the time, I think." They arrived in his informal dining room. It had a small round table, with only four chairs around it. One wall was the largest sheet of pure, perfect glass she'd ever seen. It must have been fifteen feet long and ten feet high, offering a view into a paved courtyard full of leafy plants in borders and pots. Only a few flowers stood out in white and yellow here and there, and the metal chairs looked disused.

The moment she saw the glass, she let go of him to walk right up to it, ignoring the table laden with covered plates on a plain white tablecloth. "Do you never sit outside, my Lord?" His request was no hardship; he was already being so good to her that she had no reason to refuse.

"It's difficult to work out there. Whatever you might think about wealthy noblemen, I ordinarily spend several hours a day dealing with my various business and investment interests." The scrape of one of the dark wooden chairs on the tile floor announced he expected her to sit. "If you'd like to change the gardens, feel free. I have little interest in all that, and employ a gardener to keep them tidy merely for appearance's sake."

Eyes wide with delight, Sabetia clasped her hands to her chest and made a small sound of pure joy. First the nursery, then the food, now this. "Thank you, my Lord!" She ran to him where he stood beside a chair waiting for her and threw her arms around him, hugging him tightly. "Such wonderful gifts you've given me."

He took her head gently in his hands and pulled her away enough to kiss her lightly. "Sit, my flower, and let me feed you."

With that as enticement, she sat obediently and primly with her hands in her lap. He grinned and sat beside her, uncovering the plates to reveal a wide variety of foods, the likes of which she was never, ever allowed to have at her parents' house. So many pastries and so much cream and butter and syrup and even chocolate! Her mouth watered and only the fact he dipped his finger into some of the cream and offered it kept her from greedily sampling everything until she burst. Under his instruction, she learned how to use her tongue for him. He wiped a chocolate covered strawberry over her lips and watched her lick them clean. When he seemed to be on the edge of tearing her robe off, he switched to actually feeding her: wedges of waffle, pieces of pancake, bits of muffin, slices of cake, and more.

There was far too much food, she knew that. Even though she wanted it all, she also knew stuffing herself silly would only make her sick. When she just barely started to feel full, she sat back and put up a hand to tell him she didn't want any more. He nodded and set the next bite back down.

"I never want you to be hungry, my flower. Whenever you want food, you only need to ask for it."

"Thank you, my Lord," she said after swallowing the last bite. "I'm full now."

"There's something else I want you to put into your mouth, my flower. Kneel for me, on the floor, and we'll see how well you learned with my finger." He pointed to where he wanted her to be, right in front of him. Having no idea what he might mean, she obeyed, keeping her hands to herself. "I said I would restrain myself to let you recover, and I meant that, but I want to show you how you can always thank me, no matter how sore you may be."

Where she knelt, her eyes naturally strayed to what was right in front of her: the bulge in his pants. Did he mean...? Never mind. If he wanted her to do something, she would do it. Jason was so good to her already, it was only fair she do whatever he asked of her. She took a shaky breath and nodded. "As you wish, my Lord."

In no way would she ever have thought on her own to do what he wanted. Even though he'd done this to her already, it simply didn't cross her mind that she should do it back to him. It wasn't the most enjoyable thing she'd ever done, either, and the only pleasure she got from it was seeing him watch her with startlingly intense desire. Like he said, he wanted her, not anyone else. No reason to doubt that anymore.

At the end, she almost choked, but he didn't care by then. He sagged back in the chair while she leaned away and reached for a napkin. That cup of juice was welcome, and she drank half of it down right away. "Well done," Jason said between panting breaths. "You have a clever little tongue, my flower."

At least he was pleased. Sabetia sat back down in her chair, wiping her mouth off over and over, trying to decide if that was better than him taking her while she was still sore. Her mother's explanations left her unprepared for his appetite; she had no idea a man could want so much. Maybe it would be better if she let him...toughen her up, so to speak, rather than doing that for him again and again.

Movement outside caught her eye, and she got up to see, glad for the distraction. Two large dogs ambled into sight, chocolate brown ones. Sabetia didn't know much about dogs, but these looked very normal to her. One passed by the window without looking, the other paused and tilted its head as if to say 'who are you?' to her. She waved and the dog turned away, not so interested after all.

"Come, we'll go and meet them." Already, Jason seemed to have recovered. By the time she glanced back, his pants were back in order and he held out a hand for her. "I take them with me when I leave the city. Excellent deterrents for thieves and other attackers."

"That seems to be something you're very worried about." She took his hand and followed in his wake as he led her to the nearest back door.

"Prevention is preferable to justice, if you ask me. You'll find that a common view in the upper nobility." The air outside was just cool enough for Sabetia's robe to be too thin for comfort, and she huddled behind him for warmth. Thankfully, Jason didn't go far past the door before whistling and calling out, "Sword, Shield, come!" Within seconds, the two dogs ran up and stopped in front of him, staring firmly at their master. He took a small step to the side and gestured to Sabetia. "Greet." To her, he said, "Offer them your hand."

She did as she was told and the dogs both moved in, sniffing her hand. "How do you tell them apart?" All she saw was two brown dogs that looked exactly the same.

"Shield has a notched ear." He scratched one dog on the head, pulling up the ear to show her where it must have been cut or torn at some point. "If they ever growl, back away slowly and don't run. Come to me and I'll handle it. Darius also knows how to handle them." No longer satisfied with just her hand, the dogs moved in closer to sniff her all over, but Jason pushed them off. "Go play," he told them, and pretended to throw something. Both dogs took off running like they would catch it. "They won't take orders from you, don't bother trying."

"Yes, my Lord." In reaction to her saying that again, she noticed the corners of his mouth twitch up. "I'm a little tired." Did she need to ask permission to go lie down, or was informing him alright? She left a short pause before deciding to try the middle ground. "Do you mind if I go take a nap?"

"No, go ahead. I have work to do anyway."

She couldn't guess if that was right, but at least it wasn't wrong. Giving him a quick smile, she went back inside and made her way upstairs, falling asleep in the bed almost instantly. When she woke, it was to someone jostling her just enough to be annoying and she made a small noise of protest.

"About time you woke up, Love."

"Myra!" Sabetia smiled broadly at her maid and jumped out of bed to give her a warm hug. "When did you arrive?"

"Not long ago." She returned the embrace wholeheartedly. "Your things have been put away already. I guess he wore you out, then," she said with a waggle of her eyebrows and a lascivious grin.

She gave Myra a playful tap on the arm. "Yes, he did. Completely."

"Well, it's time to get up, because there's a Matron here for you. I heard her say you were supposed to go see her this morning, and when you didn't, she got worried and came to make sure you were alright. His Lordship told her the problem was you didn't have clothes. 'A regrettable oversight', he said," Myra chuckled, "but I'm sure he's got no regrets."

"No, I don't think so," Sabetia agreed. "Where are my clothes?"

"Don't bother, Love, the robe is good enough. Come on." Myra hustled her out without letting her do more than rewrap and tie her robe. “Don't fuss, she knows what kind of a night and day you've had.”

Myra led her to a sitting room, something this place had several of. This one was all brown and forest green, comfortable in a masculine sort of way. Jason stood just inside the door, Sabetia thought he seemed relaxed and calm. “All I'm saying is that your concerns, while understandable, are unnecessary.”

Sabetia had a thought to lurk and eavesdrop as she often did to gauge the mood of her parents before announcing herself, but Myra chivvied her inside, even knocked on the door to get Jason and the Matron's attention. “Hello,” she said shyly, walking in. Her cheeks flared with a light blush.

“And here she is to tell you herself.” Jason took her hand and kissed it, then used it to pull her around and farther inside. “Matron Aila would like to speak to you, just be honest. I'll be in my office.”

It felt like being abandoned, the same way it felt when her father started pushing her off his lap for no real reason. “You aren't staying?”

Jason smirked without amusement. “No. You'll be fine.”

“I wish to speak with you alone, Sabetia,” Matron Aila said. Patting the cushion next to herself, she clearly wanted Sabetia to sit there, so she did. As soon as Jason closed the door behind himself, not looking back, Matron Aila put a hand on Sabetia's knee and said very seriously, “Has he hurt you at all?”

Oh, now she understood. “No, not at all. I am a little sore, but not hurt.”

"Soreness is normal," the Matron confirmed. "Especially if he's as virile as he looks. Has he made you do anything you didn't want to?"

Her mind immediately went to what happened in the dining room, but it wasn't really that awful. She didn't like it, but that wasn't the question. "No, nothing bad."

Matron Aila looked her over critically, skeptically, an eyebrow arching upwards. "Really? Nothing he's done or asked you to do has made you uncomfortable?"

This felt like a test of some sort, like if she lied, she'd be taken away and forced to go back home to her parents. It would be best if she explained as much as she could, she thought. "He's been nothing but gentle with me. I'm not sure how much I like some of the things he wants, but this is all so new."

Her answer seemed satisfactory to Matron Aila, who nodded. "Very well. You understand you'll most likely be pregnant within a few weeks?"

"Yes, I understand. My mother explained."

"Alright. If, for even a moment, you have any regrets, misgivings, or concerns, you come see me. Right away. I don't like that you're so young, and I've made that quite clear to him, and now to you. I'd rather see you sixteen before all of this."

Sabetia took the Matron's hand in both of hers. "I'm fine," she said firmly. "Thank you for your concern."

It didn't seem this was the outcome Matron Aila really wanted, but she accepted it anyway. "So be it. I hope you're as ready for this as you think you are." She stood up and left Sabetia alone there, telling herself that she was, in fact, ready for this. What better man could be found? He had money and a title, treated her well and wanted her. So resolved, she stood up and found Myra lurking just outside the room.

"She didn't drag you out by the hair, so I guess it went well," Myra said cheerfully. "How about we get you dressed for dinner?"

She looked down at herself and was about to agree when she remembered what Jason said. "I'm dressed enough for dinner without company, but I think I'd like a bath." The bathing room had running hot water, just like her parents' house. Used to the luxury, she didn't linger too long. It helped with her tender parts, something she kept in mind and took advantage of several times over the next few days.

Jason's appetite for her was voracious, and his seemingly bottomless well of desire for her exhausted her. On the fourth day, she finally found herself awake, bathed, fed, and left alone while Jason tended to business matters. Myra helped her put on a dress against the autumn chill and Darius came with her as she took the chance to stroll through the gardens. Because she wanted to, she wore her blue pendant.

The courtyard was a good example of the design of the grounds. Plants were green with very few flowers among them – it had a lot of evergreen shrubs and shade trees. Stepping stones surrounded by small, smooth stones formed the walkways between raised bed. The gardeners did their job well, just without inspiration.

"The Earl said I can redo whatever I wish out here. Do you think he meant it?" Up to now, she spent very little time with Darius, having barely left the bedroom. She looked back at her hulking shadow, genuinely wanting to know what he thought.

Darius nodded curtly, his attention on the surroundings rather than her. "If that's what he said, then yes, he meant it. My advice would be to make gradual changes, and not do anything to bring a lot of workmen to the site once to get in the way of him running the dogs."

As if they knew someone spoke about them, barking came suddenly from farther into the gardens. Sabetia jumped, startled by it, and let out a little yip. Darius moved quickly in front of her, his sword glinting in the sunlight, and put an arm out to shield her from whatever might come. "Go back to the house, Lady."

"What is it?" Peering around him, she put a hand to her chest in fright.

He turned, exasperated and annoyed. "The Earl did tell you to follow my orders, didn't he?"

She looked back. The nearest door seemed so far away. "By myself?"

Darius grumbled something unintelligible and probably uncharitable. "Fine, just stay close to me. But don't get in my way. If I tell you to run, do it. Without arguing."

Sabetia gulped and nodded. Staying close, she let him get only two steps ahead as he hurried forward to find the dogs. There was one ahead, barking madly at some azalea bushes. She saw the tail of the other one nearby. Whatever they found, they managed to drive it into the bushes and now had it pinned down from both sides.

As they got close, Darius waved for her to stop. This time, she obeyed. He crept closer and the dogs let him get close enough to see what they found. When he did, he sheathed his sword and rolled his eyes. "Sword, Shield, heel!" There was no amusement in him at all, and he shouted it so forcefully Sabetia took a few steps towards him with the intent to follow the command. The dogs whined and yipped, as if to disagree. Darius, more annoyed now, repeated the command with a growl and they slunk to his sides with their heads and tails down.

Hands clasped together to keep herself from fidgeting, Sabetia tried to get a better look by going up on her toes, but that didn't help. Darius clearly wasn't concerned about the culprit and she took another few steps closer when he told the dogs to go play just as Jason had, pretending to throw something. "Stupid cat," she heard him grouse.

"A cat?" Sabetia had always wanted a cat. Her parents would never let her have one, they didn't want it clawing up their furniture and making a mess. She hurried forward until she saw the pitiful thing huddled up and shaking on the ground. "It must be hurt." That was the only reason she could think of to explain it not running up a tree to escape the dogs. On her knees, she pulled some of the branches apart to get a better look. The poor thing was covered in mud and wood mulch, charcoal gray fur sticking out at odd angles and large yellow eyes staring up fearfully.

"Lady," Darius put a restraining hand on her shoulder, "cats are dangerous things. They claw and bite when they feel threatened. Their claws can cause festering wounds. Be careful." The warning and hand seemed intended to stop her completely, and when she didn't get up or back away because of him, he let go and crossed his arms with a glower. So many unhappy expressions he had at the ready; the man could probably scare off any attackers with nothing more than his unhappiness.

"Hello, Kitty," she said in her most pleasant, soothing coo. "Those mean dogs scared you, didn't they? Did they hurt you?" Its ears faced her and its head lifted, she took both as an encouraging sign. "I'm not going to hurt you, I promise. If you let me, I'll help you. I'll brush all those icky things out of your fur and give you something to eat. I'm sure the cook has something you'll like. Fresh fish, maybe, or a bowl of cream?"

The cat mewled pathetically at her. She took that as an invitation and reached in through the stiff branches to offer it her hand, like she did with the dogs. It sniffed her, then licked her fingers with its rough little tongue. The problem would be getting it out, because she couldn't see a way to do that without hurting it. The cat solved it for her by stepping carefully out of the azalea and proceeding to rub its body on her, brushing half the mud and other debris onto her dress.

"Aren't you a sweetie," she told it, wrapping her arms around the cat and picking it up. Jason didn't seem like he'd whip her or even be upset for getting a dress ruined, so she didn't fret about the muck and mud. The cat started to purr and bumped its head against her chin, making her giggle.

"Lady, I can take it off the grounds." Darius moved to grab it.

Sabetia turned away and carried it to the house. "No, I promised I would take care of it. I meant it."

"One thing I know the Earl won't like is a cat, Lady. He keeps dogs." Darius followed her, more exasperated than before.

"I like cats," she said simply. At the door, she waited for him to open it, but he instead reached out and held it shut so she couldn't.

Looking down at her with all of his looming menace, he scowled. "My Lady, I strongly suggest you reconsider this."

The cat mrowled at him and waved a paw imperiously, as if to tell him to stand aside. Sabetia took strength from that and met his gaze evenly. "Open the door, Darius, or you can explain to my Lord why I am not in his bed later." It was the boldest thing she'd ever done and she braced for him to strike her for her impudence.

To her, it seemed clear he thought very hard about it, but restrained himself admirably, then threw the door open and crossed his arms in a huff. "On your head be it, Lady," he grumbled.

Relieved, she hurried inside before he changed his mind. She went straight to Jason's office, wanting to make sure he wouldn't be angry with her over taking care of the cat, even for a short time. The door was closed, so she knocked.

"Come in," Jason's muffled voice said.

She opened the door to find he had a guest, and both looked at her. The other man – dressed like Jason's guards – was an elf; she'd never seen one before, but knew his race at once. From the pointed tips of his ears to the cant of his green eyes and the near-white yellow of his stick-straight hair, he couldn't be mistaken for human. Sitting in the chair opposite Jason, he smiled pleasantly at her, and it bothered her for no reason she could place.

"My flower, what-" Jason's eyes zeroed in on the cat and he pursed his lips in disapproval. Instead of finishing, he turned to the elf. "I think we're done here?"

"Yes, my Lord Earl," the elf man stood and bowed his head politely, "I believe we are. I'll contact you when I have more." Sabetia stood out of his way, entering the room as he left it with another polite bow of his head. His eyes flicked to her pendant and widened just a trifle. The pause made her squirm, but it was brief and he walked off with a purposeful stride, ignoring her friendly smile as it wilted.

Jason waited until the door closed before giving her his full attention. "Why do you have a cat?"

"He's scared and hungry, I found him and he's so sweet. Can I keep him?" She may have stared down Darius over the cat, but this was Jason, and the house belonged to him.

He leaned back in his chair and rubbed his eyes with a thumb and finger. "Sabetia, I prefer dogs." His movement attracted her attention to a small mirror lying on his desk. He wasn't particularly vain about his appearance, making it an odd addition to the office. It had a strange pattern etched into it, of various lines forming a shape she didn't quite comprehend.

"What's that?" She stopped scratching the cat to point at the mirror. It registered with her that he used her name, which he hadn't yet done since she came to his house, and along with her wish to be able to take those words back, a light blush colored her cheeks.

Jason picked up the mirror and deposited it into a desk drawer. "Nothing of consequence. The cat, Sabetia, why did you bring a cat into my house?"

He used her name again. She gulped and pouted. "You said the dogs won't be nice to me, and I've never had a pet. Please, Jason, can we just try him for a few days, see if he'll be nice?"

He scratched at his beard while he breathed deeply in and out a few times. She held her own breath because of it. Even the cat seemed to grasp the seriousness of the situation and sat still in her arms. "If it makes a mess in this office or destroys anything I actually like-" Sabetia's heart swelled. If Conditions meant he was going to say yes! "-or if it scratches me or anyone else who complains to me about it, then it goes. I mean it, Sabetia. You can have your pet, but not if it causes trouble."

She bounced on her toes and smiled with joy. Leaning over the desk, she gave him a swift peck on his lips, then ran out again. "Thank you, my Lord!" When he next came for her, she'd be ready and willing to do anything he wanted.

Chapter 4

After two months, Sabetia was used to this new mirror. It had a handsome cherry frame with whimsical whorls carved into it. Jason said it belonged to his mother, but refused to speak about the woman, saying the topic didn't interest him. When she pressed, he growled, so she didn't ask again. Now, here she sat with Myra fixing her hair yet again, this time for her wedding. Her mother and her groom devised the dress for her, but Jason let her pick her shoes and her jewelry. There was truly no need for such finery, so he said, except that the High King and Queen would marry them in the Great Hall of the Royal Palace.

Grandmother's blue gemstone necklace lay on her chest, new matching earrings hanging from her ears. Myra's handiwork would see her hair piled atop her head with a subtle blue stone studded tiara, one not bold enough to be a statement about ambition or intent. Caitlin assured her no one would object to it.

How strange they two really would be married on the same day. Sabetia rubbed her belly lightly, as she'd taken to doing idly since she first determined she was truly pregnant two weeks ago. Caitlin, too, was pregnant, with about the same timing. Royal Prince Quinn arrived almost two weeks early, by virtue of having paid a mage to bring him, and they were Handfasted that day – Caitlin told her as much in confidence.

"I'm so happy for you, Love." Myra tucked the last few curls into the confection that made the woman in the mirror look ten years older.

Sabetia scritched the gray cat sitting on the dressing table, licking his paw. “Poor Charcoal, such a good kitty, but you'll have to stay here. There's a party tonight and you can't go.”

“I'll keep him company.” Myra rubbed Charcoal's back lightly. “We'll get some fish and have a grand old time in the kitchen while you're away.”

Charcoal meowed. It always seemed as if he understood what was said around him. The cat never once scratched anything inside, always made his messes outside, and kept away from Jason. Not only that, but when he made noise, it sounded like he participated in the conversation, only lacking the right parts to make the right sounds. Myra often commented he was a remarkable creature, so Sabetia knew this wasn't common for cats, but she didn't care. This time, he seemed to say that was fine with him.

“No making a mess of the bride or her dress,” Myra told him sternly, pointing an accusatory finger at him. The cat licked the finger, then rubbed his face on it to scratch his cheek. “Scoundrel.” She chuckled and picked him up.

“The Earl will be taking tomorrow off,” Sabetia told them as she stood up and paced to the full length mirror to look herself over. Her breasts were larger now, a corset would just be ridiculous even if she wasn't pregnant. The dress held her in place well enough anyway, and her cleavage pleased Jason without any effort being made. This dress was four pieces, and she wore nothing under the least layer, as her soon-to-be husband preferred.

Her dress had a patterned skirt, gold and blue as the dominant colors. With it, she wore a solid blue silk top, the sweetheart neckline and cuffs of the long sleeves edged with lace made from golden thread. Over those, she wore a gown of lighter blue, the skirt split in the front, the bodice low enough she needed the silk top underneath it to preserve decency – it provided all the lift to keep her bosom in place. It also had slit sleeves designed to drape from her elbows. The final layer was that whisperweb overdress, as Jason commanded. For shoes, she chose blue slippers she'd spent the past month embellishing with her own embroidery.

"You're the loveliest bride I've ever seen in my life." Myra almost choked with tears of joy. "He's such a good man to you, even if he is a little rough sometimes."

"It's accidental." Obviously, when she wound up with a random bruise or new sore spot, it wasn't because he meant to hurt her, he just got carried away. They were always in places that shouldn't be left uncovered in public anyway. Certainly, that was why her mother chose her lower back when she whipped or caned her, but that was different. It was on purpose, and punishment for what she did. Jason getting lost in wild abandon, despite the results, warmed her to her toes, because it meant he still wanted her, that he wasn't bored with her.

Myra nodded. "Yes, I can tell from where they are. Even so, I worry a little for you, that he may one day take a liking to it. Like a dog that gets the taste of human flesh."

Sabetia frowned at the comparison. "He's not a dog, and in a few hours, he'll be my husband."

"No, of course not, Love, that's not what I meant."

"Good." Sabetia nodded her satisfaction. "You've made another stranger out of my reflection. That woman is altogether more lovely than me."

Patting Sabetia's hip fondly, Myra shook her head. "No, that's just what you look like when we make the effort to show you off to best effect. You could look like her every day if you wanted to waste two hours on primping and preening."

Sabetia turned and hugged Myra, careful not to get cat hair on her dress. "I'll see you this evening to get all this back off."

Myra snorted and shooed her out of the room. "Assuming his Lordship will wait that long for his Lady. Off with you to go get your title."

The idea she did all of this to get a title made Sabetia laugh all the way down the hall to the stairs. Jason stood at the bottom of the stairs, waiting for her. The moment he saw her, he sucked in a breath. "I swear, every time I see you, you're more desirable than the last."

"My Lord," she said fondly, reaching out her hand for him.

He took it and kissed her palm. "It's only the knowledge that I'll make a mess of these expensive clothes we need to wear for the High King that will keep your skirts down in the carriage." They moved swiftly out of the house to the waiting carriage, Darius and Keric falling in behind them, a few of the other guards Sabetia didn't know yet also joining them.

All but Keric wore armor today beneath their outer layers of finery, even Jason. The weaponry – Darius had a long dagger along with his usual blade, as well as stilettos on his forearms – and armoring was for show and tradition, so Jason said. No one would dare attack them.

Keric rode with them inside the spacious carriage, relaxed and comfortable. For this occasion, he wore a deep, dark green suit with gold trim and carried a mage's staff. The slender length of wood was carved with mysterious runes and topped with a jagged blood red crystal clutched in carved claws. He kept a hand on the staff as if concerned it would wander away on its own.

Sabetia watched out the window with a delighted smile as the carriage trundled through the city, pleased by the warm weight of Jason's hand on her thigh. Very little would actually change today. She'd become his wife, the Lady of Venithys, a role she already played in his household.

"Oh," Keric suddenly said into the silence, "I meant to ask if you want me to stay with you all night?"

"The High King's precautions should be more than enough." Jason waved dismissively. "Enjoy yourself, indulge however you wish. We'll stay a few hours after the ceremonies, at least."

"Thank you, my Lord, that's generous of you."

"The guards may do the same, let them know. You're really only here for the rides to and from, and presentation."

"Of course. Take a moment to adjust to the light when you climb out, my Lord, and I'll be able to secure the carriage in that time."

Curious, Sabetia turned to ask him, "By locking it?"

"In a manner of speaking, Lady." Keric smiled, the kind one turns on a child asking about something she had no way to understand. She'd seen that expression before, many times. It meant the person using it felt she wasn't smart enough to grasp the subject. Usually, they were right, but it still made her feel like she ought to be ashamed for asking. "I'll use magic."

"Oh." Her eyes dropped to her hands in her lap.

Jason squeezed her leg. "Don't worry about these things, my flower. You take care of yourself and my child. I'll take care of everything else."

"Yes, my Lord." He was so very good to her. She shifted to lean her head against his shoulder.

"We'll plan to leave when the clock strikes ten tonight, I think. Check with Prince Quinn's guards to find out when they mean to leave. If it's later than that, we'll have to stay longer."

Keric nodded and had nothing further to say before the carriage stopped at the High King's palace. It was, as befit the home of the supreme authority for four nations, a grand building in white marble, pure gold, and deep maroon. Servants helped Sabetia climb out first, Jason and Keric followed. As he'd been asked to, Jason spent a moment blinking in the light and straightening his jacket. Behind him, Keric touched his the crystal of his staff to the carriage and his lips moved, though Sabetia couldn't hear any sound from his mouth.

Jason offered Sabetia his arm and led her into the palace. A stiff, precise guard opened the door for them. This was Sabetia's first visit to the palace and she gaped all around at the high ceilings, priceless artwork, and numerous magical lights. Darius followed Sabetia just as Keric followed Jason, and the three men's boots clacked on the marble floor. A servant opened a door for them, into a large, lushly appointed sitting room where the High King sat with a glass of amber liquid, regarding a man Sabetia didn't know and High Princess Caitlin, both sitting on a couch opposite him.

Also in the room stood two Disciples of Clynnidh, both dressed in the ceremonial white robes of their order. One was Matron Aila, the other woman was a stranger to Sabetia. Jason walked right in without hesitation, pausing a few steps inside the room to bow to all those assembled. Sabetia didn't him pulling on her hand to curtsy to these people. Darius and Keric followed them, also bowing.

High King Kaidyn raised his glass to acknowledge them all. "Come in, have a seat. I believe the High Princess is already acquainted. Royal Prince Quinn, this is the Earl of Venithys, Jason, and his intended, Miss Sabetia."

Caitlin smiled broadly and only waited until the introduction finished before jumping up to hug Sabetia. "Sit with me," she said excitedly, taking Sabetia's hand and pulling her to one of the couches. The two women sat together, Jason watched with an indulgent grin and sat next to Quinn. Keric and Darius stayed standing, at attention.

Quinn was a plain man, unremarkable in appearance with light brown hair, no beard, and brown eyes. At least he wasn't ugly, for Caitlin's sake. Quinn and Jason shook hands and exchanged pleasantries. The Prince had a higher voice than the Earl – like his narrower frame and lesser muscle mass, it seemed best suited to lofty pursuits like thinking and painting.

"Chiefly, this meeting is to discuss the ceremony itself," the unknown Disciple said. She commanded the attention of the room with her high, nasal voice. "It is unusual for two noble weddings to take place in the same ceremony. Considering this and the relative ranks of the parties involved, we have crafted a unique proceeding.

"Matron Aila will marry the Earl and Miss Sabetia first. Immediately following this, I will marry the Royal Prince and High Princess. The High King will offer his blessings and recognition for both pairs. The specifics are simple, as befits a ceremony performed with no practice. Matron Aila or I will indicate where to stand. Whatever you're told to repeat, do so in as clear and firm a voice as you can manage."

"Mages will ensure your voices carry, but you must still do your part." Matron Aila picked up the instructions seamlessly, as if they'd rehearsed the speech. "Earl Brexler, once we're finished, you and Sabetia will stay where you are, but I will leave the dais. Remain silent and still until the High King tells you to do otherwise. The procession out will be the same as the procession in, merely in the opposite direction. We will arrange everyone shortly. Are there any questions?"

"Where should my men stand?" Jason indicated Keric and Darius with an offhand wave.

The High King said, "My men will go to the right, yours should go to the left. If you have more here with you, bring them, you can have as many as me, which will be six."

"I have four more, yes, Majesty."

"Good." The High King smirked. "It wouldn't do to have uneven lines." No one else said anything, and Sabetia couldn't think of anything to ask. After a few long seconds, the High King stood.

"Very well. Try not to fidget or shift your weight unnecessarily, and don't gape, dear." The last was undoubtedly meant for Sabetia, though he didn't seem unkind.

She blushed bright pink. "Yes, Majesty. Oh, I mean no. Er," she ducked her head as her cheeks turned to scarlet, "I won't."

While all the men laughed at her, Caitlin patted her hand. "She'll be fine." Leaning in closer, she said more quietly, "Just remember that everyone is staring at me, not you. You're so much prettier, but I'm the Princess."

Sabetia nodded at the encouragement and mustered a small smile. "I'm going to miss you."

"I'll miss you, too." She cleared her throat, commanding the attention of the room. "I command that Earl Brexler must bring his Lady to visit us before the baby arrives."

The High King had no interest in such a thing. Prince Quinn nodded amiably. Jason, on the other hand, lifted an eyebrow without smiling. "I'll see what I can do, Highness, but make no promises. My duties do not lend themselves well to vacations of more than a few days at a time."

"Then you can just send your Lady," Caitlin sniffed. "I have commanded it."

"I understand, High Princess." His words were clipped and curt, delivered as if she ordered him to clean her privy.

"Good." Caitlin nodded, either oblivious to Jason's tone or pretending not to notice. "Sabetia is my friend, and I refuse to be deprived of her for very long." She hugged Sabetia, then they were arranged for the procession by the Disciples.

Why didn't Jason want to go? Surely his business matters could be handled by someone else for a few weeks. If they really couldn't, he could afford the services of a mage (assuming Keric couldn't handle teleporting). Distaste for her traveling alone made sense, at least. Such a journey would be made through wild lands and across the water. Even if she went by magic, there would likely still be some travel, and she would stay in an unfamiliar place. He would worry, no doubt, about her safety. And he would miss her. That must be it.

Buoyed by the idea that the mere idea of being parted for more than a day made him surly, she wrapped her arm around his and beamed up at him. He looked down at her, surprised by her sudden closeness, and touched her face lightly with a smile in return. Just when he opened his mouth to say something, the High King threw the doors open and the procession began. Sabetia took a deep breath and walked with him behind the two Disciples.

The Great Hall came by its name honestly, as it was enormous, large enough to hold Jason's spacious manor house and still have room to spare. People stood shoulder to shoulder from the back to a few feet shy of the five wide steps to the dais at the other end. As the High King passed each row, everyone bowed or curtseyed and stayed that way until Caitlin and Quinn passed, affording Sabetia a spectacular view of an ocean of glittering jewels and velvets and silks and brocades in every color imaginable. It took a great deal of effort to keep herself from gawking.

Keric and Darius must have handled the orders for the guards – they already stood at the front, the six of them arrayed according to the High King's wishes. They all looked so stalwart and stony.

Everyone else seemed so confident and at ease. Sabetia's heart raced more than it ever had before. She couldn't recall being this nervous in her entire life, couldn't ever remember being so worried about making a fool of herself (or anyone else) before.

Her mouth went dry as she suddenly realized that everyone in this hall knew, without a doubt, she carried Jason's child. That shouldn't be embarrassing, every marriage in Myredren began in the same circumstance. Yet she couldn't stop thinking they all imagined her naked and judged her, fantasized about her, noticed the size of her thighs and waist. Her mother always said she was too fat. This dress showed it.

She must have fidgeted in her distress without noticing it, because Jason covered her hand on his arm with his own and squeezed. His lips barely moved as he muttered softly, "Calm down."

His words made her straighten again. She brushed her eyebrow with a delicate finger, just needing an excuse to look away from all the faces turned toward her. It helped. A little. She made an effort to slow her breath, to make it smooth, even, deep. What did Caitlin say? Everyone came to see the princess, not the commoner. Jason wanted her, but no one else did. Her father didn't want her around anymore, so Jason said, and he took the first – and only, she assumed – offer he got for her hand.

Jason squeezed her hand again to get her attention when they reached the steps. "Don't trip," he breathed out. No, she mustn't embarrass him like that. Taking up a fistful of her gown, she climbed the steps until Matron Aila stopped them at the third and crouched down with the other Disciple. Caitlin and Quinn stopped behind them, at the base of the steps. The High King stood in front of his ornate golden throne, the High Queen sat in hers, her finery matching her husband's. The only other people she noticed were her parents, sitting in the front row. This was the first (and possibly last) time they would ever have that honor, and her mother had to be reveling in it.

"Lords and ladies, you are here to bear witness to a momentous event in our kingdom." High King Kaidyn spoke only a little louder than normal, yet it carried past Sabetia like a leaf on a swift river. "On this day, the Earl of Venithys weds his chosen bride," he gestured with both hands to the pair, "and my daughter, the High Princess Caitlin weds Royal Prince Quinn.

"Truly, either union on its own is worthy of this hall. Both at once is a joy beyond measure. Let it be known that this has happened because of a serendipitous friendship between two young women, who longed to share this day with each other with enough fiercely loyal passion to move the coldest of hearts."

He directed his attention to Matron Aila, who stood and lifted her hands up. "Blessed be the Mother Goddess, Blessed be the Saint Clynnidh." Here, the reactive intonation of 'Amen' felt stronger, louder, like the very place reverberated with it, like the walls took the word in and expelled it with four times the force. "Only Niwlynys itself is more connected to our Mother Goddess, only that hallowed ground can compare to the Blessings bestowed upon this House of our High King.

"Hear us, Mother Goddess, as we call upon you to join this man and this woman in your eyes, to make them as one." Holding out her hands, she made a tiny gesture to get them to raise theirs. Sabetia let hers be taken just as Jason did. "Jason Brexler has come before me and proclaimed his intent to defend and care for Sabetia Kayles until the day of her death. I bear witness to the truth of Her acceptance of this union, the pledge forged under my guidance and consummated between them. I have confirmed before the Goddess that Sabetia is with child, proving Her acceptance of this union. Entwine these two souls, let them never waver in your eyes, let them be more together than either can be apart, let them be held in your bosom and bring many children into this world as one."

In just a whisper, she told Jason what to say, one phrase at a time, so that the assembly only heard him speak, not the Matron. "I avow that I have chosen Sabetia as my mate in sound mind and without coercion, that this choice is mine and mine alone. I accept the binding placed upon me to take Sabetia into my home for as long as she shall live." As he spoke, a thin cord of light snaked out of the Matron's sleeve to wrap around Jason's wrist twice.

The Matron fixed her intense gaze on Sabetia, making her heart race and her breath quicken. "Calm, child," Matron Aila hissed softly. Then she began telling Sabetia what to say.

"I...avow that I have...pledged myself to...to Jason...as his m-mate." Her tongue seemed to trip over the words. She was so nervous about making a fool of herself that it seemed to be happening, a sort of self-fulfilling prophecy. A second cord snaked out of the Matron's other sleeve, though, and the moment it touched her hand, soothing calm flooded her. Oddly, sorrow came with it, but the cord buoyed her nonetheless. "No other bed have I gone to since I made this pledge, and may the Mother Goddess strike me down if the child I carry is not his."

This was not the first wedding Sabetia ever attended, she'd heard similar words spoken before and seen the binding cord before, but she never understood it to be anything more than a simple invocation for show until now. This was a true binding, one she felt in her core. She had the direct attention of the deity watching over the four kingdoms while she made this vow. Had she gone to another man's bed, the Mother Goddess would truly have struck her down in that moment.

The Matron squeezed her hand and whispered for her to stop speaking as she let go of them both and the loose ends of the cord slipped out of her sleeves. They found each other and joined with a bright flash of white light. "The Mother Goddess has spoken," Matron Aila said aloud, "She gives her approval. What has been joined here cannot be sundered, let it be so. I proclaim this pair Jason and Sabetia Brexler." Normally, such a pronouncement would trigger applause, but the main event had yet to happen, and the other Disciple, standing directly behind Matron Aila, held up her hands to forestall it.

Matron Aila gestured in a rather complicated fashion that Sabetia didn't quite understand, distracted as she was by the strange sensation of the light cord still wrapped around her wrist. It hung warm and heavy, yet oddly chilled her and buoyed her arm. Fortunately, Jason pulled her down to kneel and sit back on their feet while Caitlin and Quinn moved around them to face each other on the top step. Caitlin touched Sabetia's head lightly as she passed by, careful not to muss her hair while affirming her support.

It was done, yet the cord remained, and Sabetia didn't understand why. Wasn't it supposed to fall away? The other Disciple began to speak, but Sabetia didn't pay attention. Had something gone wrong? She turned her head just enough to see Jason. He didn't seem worried and also wasn't paying much attention, just waiting with thinly veiled boredom for this to be done. He did, however, notice her looking at him, and he covered her hand with his own, lacing his fingers with hers.

With this small gesture, the cord faded to leave behind a real cord of gold in its place. Dumbstruck, unable to recall that ever happening before, Sabetia stared at it, oblivious to the rest of the ceremony. She regained her senses when the crowd applauded, Caitlin and Quinn now with their wrists bound by the same kind of cord as hers and Jason's. It was over, then, except for the High King's final pronouncement, which he stepped forward to make.

Kaidyn drew his sword, the legendary blade Alagrenis, and used it to tap Caitlin and Quinn's cord of light, making it fall away. "Behold, the Royal Prince and Princess of Aithemor," he boomed out proudly. The pair parted, no chin holding them fast, and slipped around Jason and Sabetia. At Matron Aila's direction, Jason and Sabetia stood again. "Behold, the Earl and Lady of Venithys." If he was less proud of this, Sabetia could hardly blame him. When the sword tapped their wrists, the golden cord remained and the High King looked at it with a small amount of surprise.

He sheathed the elegant weapon while the crowd applauded more, making enough noise to wake the dead. He leaned forward and spoke into Jason's ear, who nodded and unwrapped the cord from his wrist, leaving it with Sabetia. What this meant, she had no idea, but she took the cord in her hand, assuming it must be important for some reason. They paced out behind Caitlin and Quinn, this time leaving through the front doors of the palace. A large, dark cloud passed over the sun just as they stepped outside, making Caitlin frown.

"That's a bad omen," she said as she looked up.

"Don't be foolish," Quinn chided with amusement. "If it started to rain on us, that would be a bad omen. This is merely the Mother Goddess carrying needed rain to the farmers' fields. That's a blessing for the kingdom."

Sabetia looked down at the cord in her hand and wasn't sure which of them she agreed with. "I don't know what that means," Jason said quietly, taking her hand and lifting it up to brush his lips over her fingers, "but I think you should switch it for the chain of your pendant." The large blue teardrop stone sat safely on her chest. There was no reason to worry about its golden chain, but this cord was more important and she didn't think Grandmother Kayles would be mad at her for swapping it, especially not for this one.

She nodded and gripped the cord tightly, intending to take care of it later. Right now, behind the guards who flowed out to surround their charges, a flood of people clogged the doorways, all of them wishing to tell the two brides and grooms how lovely the ceremony was, and to wish them all well, and to hope they would be remembered later for having shown up. Unlike peasant weddings, no gifts would be given to either couple: this was all about favors, and being seen and noticed. Sabetia, standing beside Caitlin, smiled at people until her cheeks hurt, and took so many hands she was glad not to be wearing any rings that might be lost, either accidentally or on purpose.

The greetings took a very long time, until the High King and Queen finally appeared in the doorway, signaling the end of the line. Her own father shook hands with Jason right then, congratulating him. As expected, he and Angelica both had dressed every bit as well as any noble here. Travin put his hands on Sabetia's shoulders and kissed her forehead. When he pulled away from that, his eyes dropped to her chest, then he gave her a perfunctory smile and moved on to bow to Caitlin and thank her for allowing him to come.

Jason kissed Angelica's hand politely, they exchanged polite words. Sabetia took a deep breath to deal with her mother, only to be ignored. Angelica breezed past to gush all over Caitlin. An elder gentleman that Sabetia presumed to be Quinn's father, King Galver of Aithemor, clapped Jason on the shoulder and kissed her hand politely as she curtseyed. He was more interested in Caitlin and Quinn, understandably so. Actually, Sabetia got the impression King Galver was most interested in Caitlin. He even patted her on the rump, which seemed strange, but Sabetia was too busy to think anything of it. The High King and Queen didn't come by to greet any of the four of them, the pair merely stayed in the doorway.

"And now, it's time to celebrate," the High King boomed out over the grand courtyard. "Lords and ladies, make your way around to the rear gardens, where we will feast and drink and dance until no one is left standing!"

Sabetia took one step in that direction before Jason pulled her back. "No, my flower, this way." They followed Caitlin and Quinn inside, where Caitlin jettisoned decorum immediately and threw her arms around Sabetia. The girl shared a warm, lengthy hug, completely ignoring everyone and everything else.

"I'm so glad we were able to share this," Caitlin whispered. "I'm so happy for us!"

"So am I, on both counts." Sabetia reveled in the embrace, the warmest she'd had since leaving Myra earlier. "I can't believe this finally happened, and now you're going away. It's so unfair."

"Not until tomorrow morning."

"Jason wants to leave at ten tonight."

"What?" Caitlin pulled away and gave the Earl a look full of indignant outrage. "My Lord Earl, I command that you must stay the night in a guest suite at the palace so Lady Sabetia may see me off in the morning."

The men all gave her very similar amused looks. It wasn't just Jason, but also Caitlin's own husband, her father, and her new father-in-law. Sabetia noticed it flickering across the faces of many of the guards, including Keric and Darius, though they all kept it brief, returning to their more proper stoic expressions of vigilance. She then watched while the noblemen apparently communicated through rapid, wordless exchanges of facial expression and small gestures. Sabetia stopped trying follow it all before they stopped doing it.

"You're welcome to a guest suite here anytime, of course," the High King finally said. "Unfortunately, I daresay we don't have any spare rooms right now, considering how many nobles we're hosting from across the kingdom."

"There must be one someplace," Caitlin whined.

Jason bowed to her. "Highness, I regret it would be most prudent for you and my wife to say your goodbyes tonight. I hope you will allow us to be on our way at a decent hour that we may find our bed before we're too tired to use it properly."

Caitlin stamped a foot and stuck her chin out stubbornly. Quinn stared as if he'd never seen her before and now had some small regrets for choosing to marry her. Before she could say anything, he spoke. "That's a shame, my Lord Earl, but we understand. We look forward to the time when you're able to visit. I'll see to it you're able to take your leave at a reasonable hour."

"Thank you, Highness." Jason shook hands with Quinn and the men and the High Queen started walking while the two girls stayed there, ignored by everyone except Darius and one of the palace guards, who both stayed behind.

Sabetia stood there, not sure how to feel. She didn't expect to see Caitlin in the morning, and never thought to ask. Caitlin just showed there was no reason to feel wrong about that, as her outburst gained nothing. Her duty, after all, was to please her husband and bear his children, not to make demands and annoy him. Caitlin didn't seem to realize that, and it would probably irritate the other girl to learn the lesson. She sighed, more out of concern for her friend than anything else.

"Lady, Highness," Darius said, "I respectfully suggest we catch up with them."

Caitlin scowled. “No.” Grabbing Sabetia's hand, she turned and ran into the Great Hall.

Surprised, Sabetia stumbled a few steps before running along behind the princess, lest she be dragged. “Caitlin, what are you doing?”

“Showing them,” Caitlin shouted.

Sabetia looked back to see Darius chasing after them, but only half-heartedly. He *could* catch them, but chose not to. They were, after all, running on marble flooring in slippers, and had to be careful not to slip and fall. When he held out an arm to keep the other guard from charging them down, she knew he was letting them go, just keeping them in sight for their protection.

“Where are we going?”

Caitlin reached the back wall to the left of the dais and fumbled with something. An unnoticed door swung open and the Princess pulled her through it. The last she saw of Darius for now was him being led elsewhere by the guard who must know where this door led. It closed behind them automatically as they tore down a dark passage. Caitlin yanked Sabetia around corners they couldn’t see. At the other end of it, they burst through another door and into the cavernous kitchens, where at least a hundred people worked feverishly on the feast that would begin soon.

They darted through the room, narrowly avoiding a dozen or more mishaps and leaving chaos in their wake. Caitlin snatched up some kind of tart. Sabetia didn't dare try for one of her own. They hit the door only to run straight into Darius and the guardsman. The tart smashed into the guard's uniform and he grabbed Caitlin's wrist. Darius merely caught Sabetia and made sure she didn't fall to the floor.

"My Lady, my apologies for letting you be kidnapped. The attack came from an extremely unexpected source."

Out of breath, Sabetia panted and used his arms to steady herself. "No apologies needed," she puffed out. "Not your fault."

Some of Caitlin's hair came loose as she screamed at the guard to let her go and struggled against his grip. He pulled her in and made a very determined effort to restrain her without getting any of the red fruit tart on her dress. She threw a great deal of energy into trying to free herself, but succeeded only in making a lot of noise and wearing herself out.

Darius pulled Sabetia away from the Princess's tantrum, far enough there was no danger of being accidentally kicked or hit. Softly into her ear, his arm holding her close from behind, he said, "Thank you for not being like that, Lady. I might have to quit if you made my job that unpleasant."

Sabetia wanted to cry, watching her friend so upset by something that seemed so silly. "Caitlin, please. It's okay. I'll come visit sometime, I promise. We can write to each other, too. I'll tell you all about how big my belly gets, you can tell me what your new home is like so I'll know where everything is before I get there."

Whether it was Sabetia's words or simple exhaustion, Caitlin fell into a sobbing heap, held off the floor only by the guard. The man released her and knelt by her side when it seemed clear she wasn't playing a ruse to get away. Darius also let go of Sabetia, and she knelt by her friend's other side, rubbing her back and pushing aside her wild, loose hair to see Caitlin's face.

"What's wrong, Caitlin? I thought you were happy."

The other girl wept, Sabetia hated to listen to it. After looking to the guard, who nodded for her to do whatever she wished, she pulled Caitlin into her lap and held her close, rocking her and stroking her hair.

This had to be about more than just not getting her way. She only saw Caitlin once since her Handfasting. It was at some wealthy man's house, just a bunch of women gabbing for a few hours over tea and cakes. They came up with the notion of marrying on the same day then, and others took care of arranging it. The Princess seemed fine at the time, didn't say a word about anything wrong. Both of them thought they were pregnant already, though neither was sure yet.

"I hate him," Caitlin choked out.

"What? Why? What happened?"

Caitlin looked up at her with her big brown eyes, now red and puffy. "He's taking me away. I want to stay here."

The anguish in her face tugged at Sabetia's heart. What Caitlin wanted to hear, though, she couldn't say. There was no option for Caitlin to stay here while Quinn went home. Likewise, she couldn't move to Aithemor. Their husbands both had titles and responsibilities. "You knew this would happen, Caitlin. You knew you'd go to his home. This isn't a surprise."

"It wasn't real."

Had she really been dancing through the past two months in so much denial? Sabetia sighed and hugged her friend tightly. "We'll write each other. You'll make new friends. I'll come visit when I can.

He's your husband now, Caitlin, you have to do as he says. It's the will of the Mother Goddess."

Caitlin sniffled and wiped her nose with a handkerchief Sabetia got from Darius. "He's lousy in bed."

"Then teach him to be better."

"You saw what he just did. He does that all the time."

"He's a man."

Caitlin didn't like that answer and she pushed Sabetia away, sitting up. "Why are you taking his side?"

"I'm not." Sabetia tried not to feel rejected. Caitlin was just upset. She didn't mean it. "He's your husband, there's no other choice now but to accept him for who and what he is."

"As if I ever had a choice." Her voice was so bitter and angry. "My father chose him, not me. I had to do my duty to the kingdom. 'Nothing comes free', he said. We could have waited another two years, until I was eighteen, but the king of Aithemor started getting difficult about some trade agreements or something. I'm a peace offering."

"I'm sorry." What else could she say to that? Sabetia reached out and brushed Caitlin's hair with her hand. "The baby will be yours, to love and cherish, and he can't take that away from you." Caitlin didn't flinch away or disagree, at least. "When I come to visit, we'll compare our bellies and talk about sex, if that's what you want, but now you'll have to have your hair done again. There are bits of cherry tart in it, and it's all over the place."

Caitlin made a little noise halfway between a laugh and a sob, but she pushed herself up, getting to her feet. Darius helpfully gave each woman a hand with standing. “I'm so tired.”

“We're going to tell everyone,” she said clearly to both men, “including Royal Prince Quinn, that she's had a spell of sickness from the baby. She's fine now, but needs to rest for a little while. It would be best if you carry her, I think.”

“Yes, m'Lady,” the guard said with a little bow of his head. He'd gotten rid of the tart while she wasn't looking, brushed off all but a very little bit of it. Caitlin didn't resist as he picked her up and carried her away.

“We should find my husband.” If she hadn't been practicing saying it to Charcoal for weeks now, the words would feel strange on her tongue.

“I agree, Lady. I hope you don't mind my saying so, but that was a nice thing you just did.” He gestured down the hallway they stood in and started walking.

“Thank you.” She blushed light pink. “All I hope is that the Earl isn't angry.”

Darius nodded his understanding and guided her through the palace. They found Jason with Quinn, the King, and the High King, sipping dark liquid in small glasses, at ease on couches in a sitting room. “My Lords,” Darius said politely after knocking on the open door, “Lady Sabetia.” Jason turned, she could see he was unhappy with her. “Princess Caitlin suffered a bout of womanly sickness, Lady Sabetia stayed behind to assist her. The Princess has taken to her rest for now.”

Both of the younger men stood up. Quinn kept his drink as he excused himself and left the room, Jason set his down on the table and made his own polite excuses. "Good job. You can go enjoy yourself at the party," Jason told Darius as soon as he stepped out into the hallway. He then ignored her guard as the man gave him a bow of his head and walked away quickly, perhaps concerned Jason might change his mind and call him back if he tarried too long.

Jason's eyes stayed fixed on Sabetia, his expression unclear to her. He took her arm and pulled her into the room across the hall, another sitting room with the door standing open. She didn't resist, and felt the tightness of his grip was unnecessary. All but throwing her inside, he shut the door behind them. "You've embarrassed me, Sabetia."

Wishing to placate him, she put up her hands and shook her head. "I didn't mean to. She's my friend, I only wanted to help."

The way he moved closer made her feel like a mouse staring up at a large cat. "Fortunately, Quinn was much more embarrassed than me. You didn't openly defy me like his new wife did."

"I would never do that, my Lord."

"I think a lesson may be order anyway." He picked up her hand and pulled her fingers open to take the gold cord. "Think on this my wife." As he spoke, his hands moved to take off the gold chain she wore, to replace it with the cord. "What you do, what you say reflects on me. I will not tolerate the kind of behavior Caitlin just showed. When we get home tonight, I'll show you how I intend to punish you for doing such things. Not because you deserve it today, but because you have to know what it is you're risking should you ever consider disobeying me."

She gulped and couldn't keep herself from panting with fear. His hands lingered around her neck, settling there so easily she could well imagine him choking her. "I don't need that, my Lord." Her voice, breathy and scared, sounded tiny to her own ears. "I have no wish to disobey you."

"Perhaps." His hands squeezed just a little, for just a moment, before they slid to her shoulders and he pulled her in to hold her tightly. "A bargain, then. If you behave for the rest of the day, then I'll be merciful."

Just a few hours ago, she had the option to run to Matron Aila. No longer. If she bothered the Matron with this now, Aila would tell her to go back to her husband and behave to avoid the worst of it. She belonged to him now. For the rest of her life.

Chapter 5

"Sabetia!"

Between the emotional drain of Caitlin, the celebration that went late into the night, the hyper vigilance Sabetia felt charged to for the duration of it, Jason's vigorous attentions as soon as they got home, and his need this morning, she was exhausted and slept well into the day. His angry shout woke her, and she found herself unexpectedly looking at herself. It took a moment for her to realize it was her reflection in the dressing table mirror. Ordinarily, she wouldn't see that on waking, but somehow, she wound up lying on her belly with her head at the wrong end of the bed, her feet not quite on Jason's pillow.

He'd tossed her around more than usual this morning, been rougher than usual. Because she was looking in the mirror, as she raised her head up and pushed her hair back, she saw a bruise on her shoulder. Did he do that to her, or was it an accident of Caitlin's flight she didn't notice when it happened? She didn't know and had no way to find out.

"Sabetia!" His voice came closer. Why was he angry? She had no idea, but scrambled back to the pillows and covered herself with the sheet in response to it. The sound of his clacking boots moving swiftly up the hallway inspired panic in her belly. She jumped when the doors flew open to let him in, his face a picture of perfect rage she flinched away from. He stopped a few feet into the room and glared at her. "How dare you cover yourself up from me in this room," he snarled.

She blinked, terrified of his temper, and then he was beside her. Pain exploded in her head. It happened so fast, she had no idea what he did, just that she found herself face down on the bed in agony.

Sabetia cradled her head, whimpering and rolling onto her side. "I'm sorry," she managed to get out. As she tried to think of the words to explain, something sharp and hard struck her back and she shrieked with the pain.

"Yes, scream. There's more where that came from, but for now, it's enough." He grabbed her by the hair and pulled, forcing her out of the bed and onto her feet, then down the hallway. "I told you, Sabetia. If the cat ever destroyed anything or made a mess, it would go."

Holding onto his arm to keep from falling, Sabetia whimpered more. "He never has."

"Until today," Jason growled. He hauled her down the stairs by her hair, still naked. She stumbled and fell, rolling down a few stairs before he caught her and dragged her into his office. Throwing her to the floor, he kept his grip on her hair and yanked her head up, putting her eye to eye with four claw marks in the seat of his chair. It wasn't the chair for guests, it was Jason's chair, the one he sat in to do his mysterious work. It stank, too, and he moved her head so she could see the deposit Charcoal left on the floor where his feet belonged. Yanking her back up, he dragged her to the guest chair, where he sat down and bent her over his lap like a child he meant to spank.

"That is no mere accident, Sabetia. After two months, he

deliberately came in here and defiled my office. If it was just a random chair, just a random corner, I would toss the cat out and that would be that. This is *not* random. What did you do to make it do this?" He let go of her hair, but when she lifted her head, he delivered a sharp smack to the back, making her already burgeoning headache worse. "Tell me, or it will get much, much worse."

"I didn't, my Lord." She prayed he would believe her. How could he not believe her? What did he think she could possibly have done?

"I don't believe you, Sabetia. You wanted the cat, I let you have it. I gave you conditions. For two months, it didn't violate them, and I didn't care about your pet. Now, all of a sudden, the day after our wedding, I find this. Explain that to me."

He was insane with rage, not thinking clearly. She had to find a way to calm him before he truly hurt her. "My Lord," she said slowly, thinking as hard as she could through the pain. "I'm sorry. Let me apologize to you properly, upstairs. I know what you like, my Lord, I'll do anything for you." It was true, she would do anything to keep him from striking her again.

His fingers drummed on her back, making her suspect he was thinking, his anger cooling. "If I see the cat again, you'll be punished."

"Yes, my Lord." A measure of relief made her shake.

Finally, after what seemed like an eternity, he picked her up and set her on her feet as he stood himself. "Go back upstairs." A sharp swat to her bottom that also stung her lower back made her yip and hurry. Her head pounded. She wanted to go to Myra and get something for it, but her maid had the day off today and wouldn't be back until tomorrow afternoon. She clung to the railing of the stairs for support as she ran up them. At the top, her steps got more and more unsteady until she reached the doorway to the bedroom and had to hold onto it.

That first blow must have been a slap that knocked her head into the headboard. Downstairs, that new blow to her head must have been in the same place. When she let go of the door frame, it was to collapse into a dizzy heap and throw up bile. How long she lay there, heaving with nothing else coming out, she had no idea, but Jason found her. She could tell he stopped and stared for a few seconds before kneeling down and gently picking her up. "Oh, my flower," he said with a heavy sigh, and he took her to the bathing room.

The tub was large enough for both of them at once, but he didn't climb in with her this time. He laid her carefully inside it and ran warm water to wash her off with a very soft cloth. The heaving stopped, but she still felt dizzy and couldn't think over the pain in her head. Worse, her abdomen started to ripple with agony and soon after, the water ran pink to the drain. Over and over, he brushed her face with the cloth, rinsing it off between. This man who just showed her such incredible rage was so tender when she needed him to be.

"I'm sorry, my Lord," she coughed.

"Hush, my flower. I know." He stayed there with her while she groaned from the cramping that she guessed the meaning of before she pushed the bloody globs out of her body. With the help of a servant, he wrapped her up and carried her back to bed, where he held her close and stroked her hair. "I shouldn't have gotten angry with you about the cat," he told her. "It was your cat, I blamed you. If you hadn't covered yourself against me, though, I wouldn't have hurt you. And now you've lost the baby."

She cried into his chest for a while before falling asleep and woke up alone again in the dim light of evening. A tray of food sat on the bed beside her. She ignored it and just lay there, too many dull aches overwhelmed by how empty she felt on the inside. It was her fault she lost the baby, not Jason's. If she only came when he called, if she only made sure the office door was closed last night, if she only didn't shy away from him, then everything would still be fine. But none of those things happened, and now everything was so very wrong.

The man she married deserved better than her. He deserved someone stronger, someone smarter, someone more thoughtful. All she did was try his patience, test him, make him angry, do the wrong thing. What did she give him in return? She ate his food, brought in a stray animal that ruined his office, and embarrassed him in front of the High King. And now, she bled out the last of his child, too broken by her ineptitude to keep growing inside her. She wouldn't be a good mother anyway. How could anyone as pathetic and hopeless as her ever hope to raise a son as strong as Jason, or a daughter as good and sweet as he deserved?

Her eyes slipped from the sheets to the wall, back to the tray. She wasn't hungry. The last thing she ate was a piece of cake Jason fed to her while she sat on his lap. He used his fingers for the last few bites. She licked them clean for him and he kissed her like he would tear her clothes off there, in full view of hundreds of people. If Keric hadn't been in the carriage with them, he would have done it there. Just a step out of the carriage, he slung her over his shoulder, a hand snaked up under her dress and making her moan before they reached the stairs.

That was before she made him angry, so angry he did things he didn't mean to. It was all her fault for being so troublesome and difficult. He couldn't help being angry when she gave him so much reason to be. She never should have taken the cat in. She never should have let Caitlin pull her away. She never should have covered herself up. This was all her fault, and Jason would be better off without her. He could find some other woman, one that would do everything right and keep him happy.

Didn't she throw up? Yes, but she still wasn't hungry. The idea of food made her stomach churn, which reminded her how empty she was. Jason could move on and find another woman if she died, which didn't seem like such a bad thing right now. The Disciples said everyone was a vessel. A woman filled her vessel by bringing children into the world and taking care of her husband. She failed at both, horribly. Maybe her vessel was damaged and should be thrown away. Her mother tried so hard to mold her into perfection, but she couldn't shape something already so horribly broken.

She was so tired her eyes wouldn't stay open. Drifting back to sleep, she wondered if she could stand to slowly die by inches, and if anyone would care. The next thing she knew, she stood on a street corner, her body insubstantial. People passed through her and didn't react to her. It was strange but freeing, to be here but not in the world. Did she die and come back as a ghost? Before she could ponder this notion, she heard a child coughing nearby. She hurried that way, finding herself gliding a few inches above the street instead of walking.

Soon she found the child, lying on the ground in that park Caitlin pulled her to after that funeral. He was a small thing, tucked out of sight and pale, coughing so softly she couldn't imagine how she heard it from so far away. Dressed in rags and weak, he would die soon if no one did anything. She knew that with so much certainty that it frightened her. But she could do something. If she tried, she could help him. All he needed was a warm blanket, a bowl of soup, a bit of bread, a little love, and she could give it to him, all at once and easily. Swooping in under the shrubs, she tried to touch him, but her hands went right through.

As she watched in horror, trying again and again to help him, his breaths came weaker and weaker, then stopped. She could have prevented this, but she didn't. She'd already done so many things wrong already. This was just one more, and she wanted to weep. A high, piteous cry caught her attention, and she sped to find the source. A girl, just rolled over by a carriage and too far gone for anything but powerful magics to save her, lay on the street, ignored by those passing by. She could save the girl, somehow. Her hands again passed through the girl's body and the girl's cries grew weaker until she, too died.

The next was a man sliced by a scythe during the harvest who bled out while she watched helplessly. Then a woman dying in childbirth. A man bleeding, a woman falling, a girl screaming, a boy whimpering, and more and more. The images whipped around her, a whirlwind of pain and death she could prevent, if only she could touch them. Every face burned into her memory, each a testament to what would be lost on her death. So many lives depended on hers, even if she didn't understand how that could be.

She was no hero, no mage, no one of consequence. Yet, when she woke with a start, sucking in a breath, she knew beyond any shadow of doubt that she had a purpose. To fulfill her purpose, she had to live. And she felt alive, more than ever before. The sorrow for her loss still lurked in her mind, but at a remove, as if something stepped between her and it.

"What is it?" Jason's sleepy voice announced she woke him.

"I'm hungry," she said, trying very hard not to whine about the ravenous hunger gripping her belly.

The bed rocked as he moved. One of the magical lights came on to reveal him in a pair of loose pants, rubbing his eyes and flipping the covers aside to get the food for her. "There's a tray," he said wearily, getting up and fetching it from her dressing table. "Do you need help?"

"No, my Lord, you're very tired. I'll be quick and put the light out when I'm done."

He nodded and set the tray on her lap, rubbing his face again. "If you need more, I'll go get it for you."

"Thank you, my Lord." Enough words. She pulled the covers off the plates and devoured the food, not caring in the slightest what it was. This was the most wonderful food she'd ever tasted. It was so delicious, in fact, she suspected she might be delirious with hunger.

"Slowly, eat it slowly." He sat down on the other side of the bed again. “Eat fast and I'll have to change the sheets when you get sick.”

He was right, of course. Chewing was important. Tasting was important. Savoring was important. Above all, living was important. She had to live. That dream – it was a dream, wasn't it? - hung fresh in her mind, and she remembered it well. The faces, she couldn't picture clearly, but the way it went, she remembered that.

The Mother Goddess wanted her to find ways to help people, especially those less fortunate than herself. In the morning, she would try to figure out a way to do that, something Jason would approve of. There had to be something, and she would find it. No more stray animals, and she doubted he would accept stray people, but there would be something she could do.

Several times, she had to force herself to slow down, the excitement of having a purpose making her want to hurry and get on with it. Jason fell back asleep before she finished the food. She had no desire to wake him again. Trying to sleep more felt wrong. What else could she do at night like this? Getting out of bed, she carried the tray away with a candle. She set the tray in the kitchen and heard a noise like papers shuffling. That was an odd noise to hear in the middle of the night.

Creeping out into the hallway, she stayed as quiet as she could. “Is someone there?” She said it softly, hoping not to rouse the house for nothing. The noise stopped, and she noticed the door to Jason's office was cracked open. Movement made her catch her breath, but instead of running away, she went forward and pushed the door open, a rush of panic surging through her. Charcoal sat on the desk, looking up at her innocently.

She let out a relieved breath and bustled into the room. "Charcoal, you made the Earl very angry with what you did in here. I'm surprised he didn't catch you and wring your neck." Scooping him up, she carried him to the kitchen, shutting the office door behind herself. "You have to leave and never return, Charcoal. If you come back, he'll probably have his guards chop you into bits or give you to his dogs." She set the candle on the counter and held him tightly, scritching under his neck. "Find another place to live, Charcoal, please. I can't bear the thought of what he'll do to you."

If she opened the door now, Keric would be awakened by an alarm, but a small window should be fine. The one over the sink was large enough for the cat. "Go, Charcoal. Be safe. I'll miss you." The cat stared at her for a long moment, then licked her nose and jumped out the window. She shut and locked it behind him and sighed. First Caitlin, then her baby, now the cat. Myra would be next. The thought depressed her and sapped her energy, leaving her feeling she could go back to bed now.

Whatever separated her from her loss drifted away by morning. She awoke when Jason did and cried in his arms for a little while. "My flower, you should get outside." Thankfully, he didn't push his comforting into lovemaking. That would have been too much to bear right now. "Dress warmly, get some fresh air." He brushed her tears away gently, so gently that part of her wondered if at least some of his brutality was her imagination.

"Yes, my Lord." She let go of him and moved gingerly, expecting to feel sore. But there were no aches or pains.

"What is it?" Jason peered at her face, obviously confused by what he saw there.

Shaking her head, she stood up carefully, finding no care was needed. “I feel...fine.”

“Do you?” He pulled a shirt on and moved to her side as he buttoned the cuffs. “That's good. Perhaps we can replace what was lost sooner, rather than later.” Bending down, he kissed her cheek. “Take the carriage, go wherever you like. I'll make sure Darius has some spending money for you.”

“Thank you, my Lord.” Replace what was lost? So soon. Could she handle that so soon? Was she fit for it? Did that matter? It was her duty to give him children, and her fault she lost this one.

He smiled at her, it made her feel loved. “It warms me to the bone to hear you call me that, my flower.”

She returned his smile, though hers felt strained. He kissed her hand and left her alone to dress herself. By the time she'd bundled up against the chill, the carriage stood ready for her, with Darius waiting to help her inside. He climbed in with her and the carriage started moving.

“I'm sorry for your loss, my Lady.” The condolence felt awkward. She didn't blame him for that. “At the Earl's suggestion, we'll go to Brexler Park first, and I'll accompany you for a walk.”

She stared out the window, watching all the people go about their lives as if nothing happened yesterday. How insignificant that made her feel. “Thank you, Darius. That sounds fine to me.”

He nodded. “We could go to the temple afterward, if you like. Matron Aila is always available when anyone wishes to speak with her, so it seems.”

Although the Matron probably knew a great deal about the loss she felt, Sabetia shook her head. “No, I don't think that will be necessary.” Better to keep it to herself than accidentally say something disparaging about Jason.

“As you say, my Lady. Would you like to visit with your parents?”

“No, not at all, ever.”

“I see. How about-”

She cut him off as nicely as she could, with a hand lifted to make him stop. “I appreciate your suggestions, Darius, but I'd like to just go to the park for now and see how I feel before making any decisions about the rest of the day.”

He didn't look offended. “I understand, my Lady. Just trying to help.”

“I know.” The park wasn't very far, they'd arrived already. With his aid, she stepped out and gathered her cloak about herself. It was that very same park, from the funeral, from her dream. As she walked into it, she wondered whatever happened to that boy who helped them. Did he ever come here again after that? Did he actually steal something from Caitlin? It looked like he did at the time, but she didn't really know and Caitlin never said anything was missing.

Darius stayed a few paces behind her, giving her the illusion of privacy. Her feet took her down the stone paths, winding this way and that. Everything was dying with winter upon them, except the evergreens. Stopping at a bench facing the previous Earl's grave, she tumbled into the memory of that afternoon. Before she lost herself in it, a small noise caught her attention. She had no idea what it was, but like last night, couldn't ignore it. When she began peering into the shrubs, Darius moved up.

"What's the matter, my Lady?"

"I think heard something."

"Could be nothing, then."

She gave him a weak glare. "Please look."

"Yes, my Lady. Hopefully, it's not another cat." He picked his way into the bushes and stopped short just a few feet in, making an exclamation of surprise. "It's a boy." He reached down and carefully began to pry the plants apart to reach him. "He's freezing, my Lady, your cloak, please."

Sabetia stared blankly, numb as she handed off her cloak to him. This was exactly like her dream. The trees overhead, the bushes down below, a little boy coughing weakly, everything was the same. She hadn't thought the dream could be literal, didn't imagine for a moment those were specific people that she had to save and the specific circumstances they would be found in. How would she find the little girl in the road? If she went about the city, would her carriage wind up being the one that hit her? What if she couldn't find the girl before it was too late?

Darius pulled the child out, wrapped up in her cloak, and brought him to her. "Sit, my Lady, hold him while I fetch help."

The boy's face hit her like a sharp slap. She remembered it. The moment she laid eyes on him, she knew was supposed to save this boy. "No, wait," she told Darius as she took him in her arms. The child couldn't be more than five years old, and he was scrawny and pale, probably small for his age. Reaching into the bundle, she touched his face and felt a jolt from the contact.

Though she could tell he was sick by looking, something happened in the connection between them and she knew it to be true. The sickness ate him from the inside, and there was nothing to be done for him without magic. He needed a true Healer, but such people were rare and she didn't know where to find one. A Disciple wouldn't be good enough – they only had minor healing talents.

It felt like something pulled out of her through the fingers touching his face and she sat back down heavily on the bench. Darius made some concerned noises and knelt by her side. She ignored him, feeling how the sickness retreated at her command. Her will forced it back, fought with it like clashing armies inside the boy's body. Sweat beaded on her brow and she heard Darius say something about going for help. Her other hand seized his wrist, refusing to let him leave her like this.

Then the sickness was gone and the boy opened his eyes. "Mama?"

"No, child, I'm not your mother. Where is she?" A deep well of anger filled her as she pulled her fingers away. If his mother tucked him away and left him here to die, she didn't deserve to have him back.

"I don't know."

"My Lady...did you...?" Darius sat beside her and took the boy from her.

"Yes, I did." She was tired, so very tired. "I think I can make it to the carriage, Darius. Would you see him safely to the Temple for me?"

"My Lady, we should tell Matron Aila. This is...a gift, it's..."

"No."

"No? But, my Lady, surely-"

"No. Tell no one. No one at all. You're my guard, you keep my secrets. Even from my husband."

Darius went silent for a short time. The little boy seemed content to appreciate how much better he felt for the moment. "My Lady, he's my employer. If he asks me, I'll tell him."

"That's fine. No volunteering information. If he doesn't directly ask whether I can heal or have healed anyone, you don't tell him. I have my reasons. Trust that they're good ones." If only she knew what they were.

They sat in a tense, heavy silence for a short time. Finally, Darius nodded. "Yes, my Lady, as you wish."

Chapter 6

The silver tray in Sabetia's hands was something Jason's mother bought, many years ago. It was smooth, almost like a mirror, and showed her a woman that seemed so much older than a week ago, since the wedding. She had no scars, no bruises, no outward signs of it, she just stared and found herself looking at someone foreign. With a heavy sigh, she set the tray aside and pulled out the next piece of the tea set to unwrap it.

"What are you doing down here, my flower?"

She looked up from her perch on the floor, holding a silver sugar bowl, its protective cotton and paper in her lap. "The housekeeper asked me if I would look through these things and decide what to do with them."

"Did she." His lip curled like he wasn't pleased.

For the past week, he'd been very gentle with her, even moreso than their first night together. She had a keen desire to keep it that way. "I'm sorry, my Lord, I should have asked you first." Hurriedly re-wrapping the bowl, she scrambled to find the right words to soothe this over. "I thought you had no interest in them, as it's all in boxes in the cellar. I still should have asked first."

"Those were my mother's." She flinched at the sharpness in his voice.

"I'm sorry."

He stared at her, except she didn't think he really saw her just then. "She murdered my father in his sleep. A servant found her still stabbing him in the back." How flat his voice sounded, so hard and angry. Sabetia sat very still and quiet, not wanting to focus that anger on herself. "She snapped, shrieked at him. I came running, thinking they were being attacked by some intruder." He took a deep breath and looked away, disturbed and discomfited by the memory. "I was asked to keep her things until after she hanged and must have forgotten about it."

Timidly, Sabetia asked, "What would you like done with it all?"

He scratched his beard and went quiet for a few long moments. "Get rid of it, all of it. I've already saved out what I want to keep of my father's things, so all of that can go, too."

"Yes, my Lord. I'll see to it."

"Good. Don't waste too much time down here." Whatever he wanted when he came looking for her, it must not have been terribly important, as he turned and left without mentioning it.

She sat alone in the cellar with his mother's things again, terribly curious about what really happened. A wife murdering her husband... Such a strange idea. Trying to imagine herself doing the same thing was too distressing for words. In no way could she ever hurt someone on purpose. What she ought to do now, though, was determine which things could be given to the Temple as charity and which things should be sold. The silver could be sold, no poor person would ever use such a thing, and she repacked the bowl and tray without examining the rest of the set.

A few hours later, when Myra came to tell her lunch was ready, she had two separate groups of boxes. On one side, clothes, linens, and similar things which could be donated. On the other, silver, jewelry, and similar things to be sold. She explained which was which to Myra and trusted her to see it taken care of. The matter was finished and she put it out of her mind. They had a dinner party set for tomorrow, she needed to focus on that now. Jason left most of the details in her hands.

She spent the rest of her day and much of the next attending to the preparations for the party, and all seemed as close to perfect as such a thing could get. When the guests began to arrive, she was there at the door to the chosen parlor to greet them. The weather had taken a turn to the frigid or she would be outside. Instead, Jason's guards met them and conducted them inside, where she took over. Jason kissed her forehead and went to the bar, where he would fix drinks for people as they came in, leaving her on her own. His trust in her was warming. And as he trusted her, he also watched over her, able to see should anything go wrong.

Nothing did go wrong, not as people arrived. It was five other men with their wives, all of them the lesser nobles of the area. Sabetia hadn't met any of them yet, this was her first introduction to Jason's friends. She conducted the last of them into the parlor and was given one of Jason's warm smiles of approval when she closed the doors behind herself and sat down quietly, not interrupting the conversation.

Very soon, it became clear the men would spend the time speaking of things none of their wives had any knowledge of or interest in. She and the five other women all sat quietly, patiently, and Sabetia resolved that after the meal, they would sit separately, even though that wasn't part of the plan. Fortunately, the servants called them to the meal before too long, and she sat at the end of the long table, opposite her husband.

As the first course was served, the Baron in the middle nodded politely to Sabetia. "Lady Brexler, I find this is my first opportunity to compliment you on the coup of securing a wedding in the Great Hall of the palace." Agreement ran up and down the table with nodded heads and murmurs. "However did you catch the Princess's eye, my Lady? You were raised a commoner, were you not?"

Sabetia flicked her eyes to Jason, who subtly gestured for her to go ahead without his interference. "I met her at the funeral for the late Earl, my husband's father. We were children and unconcerned with matters of title. Over the years, we met again several times at events such as this one – my parents are wealthy in their own right – and became friends. It was her idea for us to share the day."

"How sweet." The nearest wife smiled. It seemed empty and hollow. "I've heard the Princess is fond of taking in strays of all sorts."

Sabetia blinked, not sure she heard that correctly. It was surely an insult on her and her parents. By extension, it was further an insult to Jason. Not sure what to say in response, she looked to her husband, who had a mouthful of soup just then. From his expression, he heard what was said just fine, and didn't care for it, but wanted to see how she handled it. "I'm not sure I know what you mean, Countess. Are you suggesting the Earl's tastes run to the common?"

Her husband, seated across from her, quickly stepped in. "No, of course not," he said with a nervous chuckle. "There was a story about a dog and Princess Caitlin, wasn't there?"

"Not one I've heard." Jason wiped his mouth with his napkin, pushing his half-eaten bowl of soup away, causing a servant to swoop in and remove it. "Please, do tell it."

The Count stumbled over a story Sabetia knew wasn't true, about Caitlin adopting a dog that wandered onto the palace grounds. She wasn't sure about the wisdom to interrupting him, and chose not to, letting his story ramble to completion. Jason gave the man his undivided, rapt attention, and when he finished, her husband looked at her. "It sounds as if she truly loved that dog. Sabetia, surely you must have met it or heard about it?"

"No, not that I can remember." She looked down, feeling strangely bold. Jason didn't want to let this Count get away with covering for his wife, that was clear, and she felt honor bound to do what she could to help him. That would please him, which was a good thing. "It's an odd tale, in fact, as I understand she takes ill in the presence of dogs and cats both. Being near them makes her prone to horrendous fits of sneezing. Pity the High King, who had to lose his daughter to have hunting dogs!"

Her last statement caused amusement to run down the table, though the Count glared at his wife instead.

The woman's nostrils flared and her eyes narrowed. "All the same, our household has no need to put things up for sale like beggars with a collecting tin. My husband has the sense to keep his wealth secure."

"Excuse me?" Jason wasn't amused anymore. He stared hard at the woman, who looked very pleased with herself.

"Didn't you know, my Lord Earl?" She turned and fixed Sabetia with a venomous smile. "It must be your wife collecting pocket money, then, to spend behind your back on-"

"Elesse," the Count hissed, cutting his wife off before she could finish. The rest of the table went silent, all watching Sabetia.

She stared, confused and frantic to defuse this. What would Jason do if she didn't? "I wasn't aware that contributing to the household by disposing of unwanted items was somehow shameful."

Jason's expression flashed on a glower just for Sabetia, but he dropped it quickly in favor of a broad grin for the table. "A wise woman knows that coppers falling between the cracks are a leak that should be plugged, lest the household sink by inches."

"Of course, my Lord," the Count quickly agreed. His wife didn't look shamed or mollified, but she didn't say anything else through the meal, and conversation turned to safer topics. Sabetia caught Jason glancing at her every so often as the evening wore on. After the meal, the men decamped back to the parlor while Sabetia led the women to another sitting room. It wasn't prepared specifically for tonight, but had everything it needed already. Letting everyone enter before her, she turned to the servant woman that followed them out and beckoned discreetly for her to follow.

"Can I interest anyone in coffee or tea?" To her relief, the servant understood her part to play and bobbed a light curtsy with a pleasant smile. She took the requests, along with Sabetia's for tea, and left the room to fetch it all. Pacing around to sit in one of the two chairs left vacant by the couches, she had no idea what to talk about. These women were all strangers, one of them was hostile, and she had no idea what they made of the insults traded at the table.

Before she even opened her mouth, the Baron's wife smiled pleasantly at her and asked, “How are you feeling, Sabetia? I hope an evening like this doesn't put too much strain on you. I remember when I was pregnant with my first, we had a party like this in my third month, and I had to leave early to lie down.”

What was she supposed to say? Sabetia's face fell and she sat back in the chair. “I lost it.”

Her news was greeted with sharp intakes of breath from everyone but the Count's wife, who seemed intrigued. “Oh, how awful. You poor thing.” The Baron's wife squeezed her knee gently. “How did it happen?”

Sabetia's eyes glistened with tears that she didn't want to shed right now. Instead of answering, she shook her head. There was no way she would explain the whole incident to these women. “I don't know.” As lies went, this one was probably easy to swallow. It happened all the time, so Myra said. Her sister suffered through two before being blessed with her son. The sympathy in the room told her she was convincing.

“Perhaps you're not old enough yet.” The Count's wife said it with an air of expertise. She alone had no sympathy at all, and struck Sabetia as being like a vulture waiting for her prey to die so she could pick at the carcass. “I've heard it's common with girls your age, to not have the strength for it. Even the Disciples wait until sixteen.”

“I've never heard that,” The Baron's wife sniffed. “Rather the opposite. But it could be something you ate, or an animal you were close to.”

One of the other two women said, "When I had those awful pains with my second, my maid suggested there were herbs that could be used to end it, that's what the commoners do when they can't afford another child. Maybe they were accidentally in your food."

The Baron's wife nodded with authority. "That makes sense. I'm sure the servants know which ones they are, and just forgot. You should speak to them, Sabetia. Perhaps even fire one. I've found that makes quite a statement about mistakes."

Charade accepted, it needed to be carried through now, and Sabetia nodded. "That's good to know, thank you. I'll be sure to speak with the kitchen staff in the morning."

"I hope that's all it is." The Count's wife clearly didn't hope any such thing, but the other three women acted like she did and agreed with it.

Sabetia gave them a brave smile. "So do I. But we barely know each other, I'd love to hear about your children." With the conversation turned, she regained control over herself and enjoyed the tea that arrived within a few minutes. The other women all had children, ranging in age from two to eleven, and they all had advice and stories for each other. A servant appeared an hour or so later to inform them that the men were ready to leave, prompting the women to all get up and wish each other well.

Jason bade her stay inside while he went out to see them off. She took the initiative to go upstairs and undress for him. He wasn't gone long enough for her to do more than remove her blue pendant necklace, pull out the sticks and combs that held her hair up, and wipe the powder off her face before the front door opened and shut again. His boots announced him moving upstairs and down the hall swiftly. Given how close he was when she rose to begin taking her clothes off, she didn't bother, just stood where he could see her through the half-open door.

"My flower." Neither his expression nor his tone offered hints about his mood. It wasn't until he stood so close she could feel the cold still clinging to his jacket that she guessed he was unhappy with her. One arm snaked around her back and slipped up to grab a fistful of her hair, which he used to draw her head back. This wasn't so strange, he appreciated her neck. "You embarrassed me again tonight." Like this, she couldn't speak well, so she remained silent. "The Countess will be a thorn in my side for some time to come. I told you to get rid of those things, not to sell them."

He wanted an answer, because he pushed her head up to look at him. "I'm sorry, my Lord, I thought it best-"

"You do not think," he growled. "It is not your duty to think, it is not your place to think. I think, not you. When I told you to get rid of those things, all you needed to do was tell the housekeeper to get rid of it all."

"I don't understand. You said-"

Yanking her head back again cut her off again. "I said that to save face. We are not poor, we are not close to being poor, and we do not need to do things like sell our possessions. Is that clear?" Frightened of what else this night might hold, she nodded as well as she could. "Let's make sure this lesson is remembered. I won't have you repeating these mistakes, any of them." He tore her dress off and slapped her across the face so hard she was knocked to the floor. "Get on the bed, Sabetia."

She looked up, terror overwhelming the ache in her cheek, to see him pulling his belt off. "No, my Lord, please. I'm sorry. I didn't mean to embarrass you." Torn between shying away and throwing herself on his feet, she stayed where she was.

"It's too late, Sabetia. Get on the bed."

Maybe if she tried to make amends here on the floor, he would change his mind. She crawled quickly back to him, getting on her knees and putting her hands on his hips. "Please, Jason, please. Don't do this. I'll do anything you want."

The belt hung from his right hand, the slim gold buckle dangling an inch from the floor. He stood there for a few seconds in stony silence, then grabbed her hair and pulled her to the bed, tossing her onto it. "I didn't think you needed this sort of thing, Sabetia. I thought you wanted to please me already, but I see that was wishful thinking. Lie still, woman." He let her go and watched impassively as she failed to stop herself from scrambling away. With a surprised squeal, she fell off the other side of the bed.

On the floor, she crawled away from him. When she reached the end of the bed, she got up and ran for the door, hysterical and sobbing. Behind her, Jason still stood there, watching, now with his arms crossed. She hurried down the stairs and ran into the front door with her shoulder, hysterical panic driving her to open it and plunge into a light snowstorm. The frigid air hit her like a new slap, making her stop and remember she was naked.

Panting, she stood on the front step, staring out into the

darkness. With the guests gone, the lanterns by the door had been extinguished and she stood in shadow. Why did she run? There was nowhere to go. Jason was her husband, he alone held claim over her. It didn't seem to her she'd done anything so wrong at dinner that she deserved to be punished for it, but she surely had now. Had she merely done what he said, it might have been short and minor. Now, it would be much, much worse, and she earned it. If it was her mother in his place, she would be caned until she bled for this. She had no idea what Jason would do.

"My Lady, you'll freeze to death." Keric's voice came from behind her. "Darius, bring a blanket," he called back into the house. An arm wrapped around her waist and pulled her back in, Keric shut the door firmly. She must have set off the alarm. His body radiated warmth as he held her close from behind.

"What happened?" Darius looked confused and concerned as he threw a blanket over Sabetia from the front. She stared at him blankly, numb and scared, too frightened of her husband for words.

"She's still a child in some ways." Jason's voice came from the top of the stairs, he sounded amused. "Children can sometimes do foolish things. Bring her back to my bed."

A look passed between Darius and Keric, she didn't understand it. Keric said, "Yes, my Lord. I'll bring her directly." Darius looked down and walked away. Sabetia saw him rub his forehead wearily as he went. She didn't struggle against Keric when he bent down and picked her up. There was no reason to treat him poorly for doing nothing more than what she should have done: obey their master. That's what Jason was: the master of this house and all who lived within it. She was just a special kind of servant, like Keric and Darius.

Jason walked in front of Keric, stopping at the bed while his mage laid her on it and took the blanket with him. Keric looked down at her as she rolled limply onto her side, the shock wearing off and turning to tears. It looked like he wanted to say something, but Jason's voice made him step away.

"Shut the doors on your way out."

"Yes, my Lord."

"We're not to be disturbed, no matter what."

Keric paused for a moment. Sabetia could see him look at Jason like he meant to protest, but the Earl turned and gave him an upraised eyebrow, a look that dared him to speak freely. "Yes, my Lord," Keric finally said, sounding defeated. He walked away just like Darius had, without looking back, and shut the doors with a very final clang.

It was a very long night. She woke alone in the morning to aching pain from her neck to her knees, mostly on her back. The sheets would need to be cleaned of her spattered blood. A tray of food sat beside the bed. Someone came this morning and saw her condition. A noise off to the side made her stir, sending prickles of agony rippling across her body. "Who's there?" It hurt to speak, even, and her voice came out as a harsh croak.

"You're awake," Myra's voice said with relief. "Don't move, Love. I've put a dressing on the worst of it. Should draw down the pain and keep it from scarring too badly." She knelt by the bed, putting herself not far from Sabetia's face, and smiled at her with pity. "Let me help you drink and eat."

Her maid fed her slowly with a spoon, keeping her from making a mess on her pillow. "You can't let him do that to you again, Love. He'll kill you."

"No, he won't. It's alright. I'll be fine."

Myra pursed her lips and frowned. "Not if he does this all the time, Love."

"I just need to take more care not to upset him." Myra bit something back, she could tell, but Sabetia was too hurt to draw it out of her. "This is my fault. I ran from him. I don't know why, but I mustn't do it again. I'll be fine with a day of rest, I'm sure."

Myra sighed heavily and shook her head. "You should rest tomorrow, also."

"I'll try to."

"In the meantime, shall I read to you like I used to?"

Where her mother's canings were dark spots in her childhood, Myra reading to her the next morning after each was a silver lining. "Yes, please, that would be nice."

She pulled a book out, proving she expected that, and opened it, but didn't start right away. She looked at the page without speaking, without her eyes seeing the words. "You're ten years younger than me, Sabetia, but you're the best friend I've ever had. I swear that a day will come when you never have to endure anything like this again."

Sabetia closed her eyes and let the tears flow freely. "I love you, too, Myra."

Myra kissed her lightly on the forehead and read aloud about talking mice facing the great dangers of cats and owls stalking them.

Chapter 7

Ten lives, that's how many Sabetia was able to find and save over the next two years. She stared at her reflection in the carriage window, wondering if she had to make this journey to find more of them. The seventeen year old woman staring back at her didn't smile, she only brooded. Ten was also the number of miscarriages she had in that time. After the third, she stopped telling anyone about her pregnancies, aside from Myra. After the fifth, she felt almost nothing about it anymore, just a vague sadness for a lost opportunity. The most recent one happened a few days ago, and the reason why she finally made this long overdue journey to Aithemor.

The chill of the late winter air was a blessing that made it possible for her to be bundled up enough to cover all the bruising and whip marks, even gave her enough cushioning to make it all not hurt quite so much. Myra sat beside her, also bundled up, but making the most of the traveling by doing some embroidery on a handkerchief for her sister. Darius sat opposite them both, taking up the whole other bench and reading a book. So many secrets in this carriage.

They weren't going the whole way like this, just to Ar-Toriess, where they'd pick up a delicacy for Caitlin and use a charm Keric made to get them the rest of the way. His skill grew with time, and he now made such charms for sale when he wished to, but still stayed with the Earl. Sabetia suspected some kind of debt between them, like Jason having saved his life somehow, or perhaps Keric was a half-brother. The loyalty made no sense otherwise.

She held the letter from the Princess in her hand, the one where she agreed to the visit and asked for the seeds. It only arrived a few days ago, yet the creases in it were already worn and the edges rough. Sabetia had read it so many times since it arrived that she could recite it from memory.

Dear Sabetia,

I would love for you to come visit. Delia is just now thirteen months old, so you just missed her first birthday. I should have written, but I heard you lost yours, and I am ever so sorry about that. I did not know what to put in writing. Things are fine here, as you will see when you come. Everything is fine with Quinn. ~~*His father is*~~ *I am looking forward to seeing you after all this time. If you could bring me some tescher seeds from Ar-Toriess when you come, I would be grateful. I miss the little joys.*

Love, Caitlin

She didn't quite know what to make of the last sentence, or the crossed out part. Caitlin's pen blotted it in strange places, too. As the carriage trundled along the road, she opened the letter once again and rubbed her finger over the grit crusted ink, wondering if Caitlin sanded it because she was in a hurry or out of habit. Sighing, she folded the page up again and tucked it up her sleeve, turning to staring out the window.

An hour later, they left the city. Myra looked up and out the window every so often from there like she expected to see something, but had no conversation to make. Sabetia was in no mood for chatter anyway. Another hour after that, they were halfway to Ar-Toriess when Myra looked up and put her sewing away like she expected to be getting out soon. Sabetia considered asking her why, but the carriage stopped abruptly and rocked back. She heard the sounds of horses panicking. Dull thuds against the wood sounded like small things hitting it.

Darius dropped his book and leaped out of the carriage, sword drawn before he hit the ground in a tumbling roll. Myra reached out and pulled the door shut again, then held onto Sabetia. "Just stay put," she said. "We'll be fine."

"Fine," Sabetia echoed faintly, wondering how anything to come of this could possibly qualify for any version of the word 'fine'. She was used to being beaten regularly, but only by a man she knew would always restrain himself from disfiguring her, lest she appear anything other than perfect for his guests. At this moment, she thought of the Countess who gleefully took the news of each miscarriage and was almost certainly the source of the embarrassing rumors that Sabetia was physically incapable of carrying a child to term, that Jason was duped into marrying her and would never have heirs.

Men grunted outside, more of those thuds came. It was a frightening thing to live through, even with Myra's hand clutched in her own and knowing Darius was out there, defending her. Two more guards rode with them – Jason didn't want to chance anyone thinking the carriage was an easy target. It sounded as if they may have ridden into an ambush, though, which probably meant three men were no match for their attackers.

When the carriage door opened, an unfamiliar male voice called, “Come out, Lady, and you won't be harmed.”

“No, don't-” Darius's voice was cut off by a sound Sabetia knew well enough as someone being hit.

Myra tugged on her hand and pulled her out of the carriage. “We're unarmed,” the maid called out, quite calm. Sabetia saw one of her guards was dead, the other bleeding to death. Darius was in poor shape, but alive on his knees and with his hands bound in front of him. An elf man – one she felt certain she'd seen someplace before, but couldn't remember where – held a sword to his neck from behind. Another man knelt over the bleeding guard, checking him over. Ten more men stood about, three of them had minor injuries, and two others lay on the ground, dead already.

These men were armed and armored, but unclean, unshaven. From what she knew of the subject, they had the look of brigands. It was strange one well equipped elf should be found in the company of humans such as this, but that was hardly her greatest concern at the moment. Myra walked right up to the one man that seemed to be the leader from the way he stood and held himself while the others all looked to him.

“You promised no one would die,” the maid said accusingly.

Sabetia stared in shock. “What?”

The leader shrugged, unconcerned. “They fought back harder than expected, and two of my men are dead.”

“You could have used nonlethal weapons,” Myra protested.

The leader rolled his eyes. Reaching out, he grabbed her and shoved her into the waiting arms of two of his men. His eyes stayed on Sabetia as he said, "Do as you please with her. This one, I have plans for."

"What? Wait," Myra shrieked, "we had an agreement! I paid you to set us free!"

A cold, icy hand of dread clutched Sabetia's heart. Myra paid men to rescue her from from her husband, and they decided it wasn't enough, or they had no honor in them, or something. Now, good men were dead and she would be worse off than before. Myra might not survive this. She might not, either, depending on what this one had in mind. She took a deep breath and stood straight, meaning to meet her fate with as much strength as she could muster. If Jason had taught her anything, it was how powerful fear could be.

"Do you understand who I am and who my husband is?"

"Aye, Lady," he grinned, "we know all about your Earl and how he beats you."

Courage. Strength. Determination. It was a prayer to the Mother Goddess to give her these things she knew she didn't have. "That is what he does to the one thing he values above all else. What do you think he will do to the men who have taken it from him?"

A stiff breeze blew a dead leaf into her field of view, rustled the leader's unkempt hair. His eyes contracted a tiny bit, just enough for her to see he got her message. He lifted a hand, beckoned some of his men with his fingers. "Tie her up. Take these two for the market. Be swift, they'll be hunted. Use the carriage."

"What about the driver?"

"Tie him up and take him along. Waste not, want not."

"And this one?" The man checking over the bleeding guard

pointed to him. “With care, he'll live.”

The leader paused and looked that way, then waved the matter off. “Too much effort. Kill him. Let's go.”

Sabetia paled as the brigand nodded and stabbed a dagger through the man's throat as if he was nothing more than a downed animal. Two men hauled Myra away, shrieking until one struck her in the face. Understanding these men had no compunctions about violence, Sabetia didn't resist as they bound her hands and herded her back into the carriage.

Darius had to know a losing battle when he saw one and climbed into the carriage willingly, too. Right behind him, the elf stepped into the carriage and punched Darius in the gut. He grabbed Sabetia's bound hands and pulled her close, smirking as she flinched away from him. His hand dove down the front of her dress. She expected him to grope her, but he did something much worse. Pulling the blue pendant out, he stared at it, eyes glittering with greed.

“No, please don't take that,” she whimpered.

“Poor thing.” He closed his hand around it and yanked, breaking the clasp and taking the stone. “You have more important things to worry your pretty little head about.” Stuffing the stone in his pocket, he backed out of the carriage. A brigand shoved the unconscious driver in at their feet and warned them to be good before slamming the door shut. They were under way within a minute.

Darius sat with his head in his hands. “I'm sorry, my Lady.”

She leaned against the wall of the carriage, tears rolling down her cheeks. Myra was gone. Worse, the one thing she cared about in all the world, the one thing she ever had that mattered, that she promised to keep safe and secure, and he took it with so little effort. "There were too many of them. You couldn't have done anything more than you did." Jason never once tried to take her pendant away. It was a line he never crossed. Once, he asked her if she'd like a new one, something in a different color. All she had to do was say it was a family heirloom, and he never asked again. He respected what her grandmother charged her with. These people respected nothing, except perhaps money.

"I know, my Lady. That's not what I'm sorry for." He lifted his head slowly. A wince spoke of injury and she reached for his hands, taking them in her own as best she could under the circumstances. That pulling sensation began and he sighed as her healing took his pain away. "I don't deserve that." Though he protested, he didn't pull away to make her stop.

It wasn't as exhausting now as it had been the first few times. Her body, or her mind, or whatever it was, slowly adjusted to this power and she found herself able to handle it better. Not that it mattered right now. What Myra faced filled her mind. It would be terrible, and her best friend was only trying to help. If she was lucky, they would kill her quickly, but she very much doubted Myra would get that kind of mercy. "We have nothing but time, Darius, and an uncertain future. If you have something to say, this may be your only chance."

Two deep breaths later, he started talking, staring at his bound hands, one thumb idly rubbing the other in discomfort. "I saw what happened the first time. He went berserk because of that cat, and I saw him haul you down the stairs and back up them. The next time I heard your screams. The time after that..." He shook his head. "There are too many times to count. I shut the door, I put a pillow over my head. I told myself I had no power there. He's my employer, I work for him, not for you. Even if I did work for you, he's your husband. What was I going to do? Tell the carriage driver to just keep going instead of stopping at a park or a row of shops?

"I'm a coward, my Lady. Not in the usual way – I can face down a man or beast that wants to kill me. But I can't protect a woman from her husband because I can't bring myself to call him out for hurting you. I should have said something that first time, suggested he get help for his temper. I tried to get you to go to Matron Aila, but not hard enough. She would have told him off for doing those things to you. Just show her one bruise or scar, and she'd get righteous in his face, I guarantee it. But you refused and you held your tongue and it went on, and on, and on.

"Sometimes, I hear your screams in my sleep, they invade my dreams, turn them to nightmares. I chase a dark creature, the thing making you scream, and when I catch it, I fail in pathetic weakness, overcome by it and thrown into silence. And that's the thing, it's the silence. If you'd just say something, my Lady, just tell someone." He seemed spent by the confession and sagged where he sat.

Sabetia stared straight ahead, listening but not understanding. Darius's words made no sense. "I deserved those punishments."

"No, Lady." He took her hands and held them tightly, shifted until he met her eyes with his own, demanding she not look away. "No one deserves that, not even a misbehaving child. No one deserves to be hit with a belt, or a cane, or a whip. No one deserves to be slapped so hard you fall at his feet. No one deserves-" He choked, unable to put the rest into words. "Any of it. No one, Lady, not you, not anyone else."

"A man has needs."

"Jason Brexler isn't a man," Darius growled, his eyes taking on an almost frightening intensity. "He's a bully. He's a coward and an ass, and the next time I see him if he so much as lays a finger on you, I'll kill him and feel no remorse." He looked away, scowling. "What you deserve, Sabetia, is to be loved. Not punished, not trained into obedience, not any of the damned things he's shown you."

She had no idea how to respond to that. Sabetia sat back and said nothing, her mind busily refuting everything he said, but the words not coming out of her mouth. Over the past two years, she made up excuses, wore high necked gowns, sent her regrets when she couldn't cover up the bruises, and lost ten different potential children. She gained and lost weight with each one, she was exhausted most of the time. She hid her gift from everyone but Darius without knowing why. All of that for what? Why did she hide it, why was she so ashamed of it? Shouldn't the cuts and bruises have been worn with pride?

Sinking into these thoughts, she dozed off, not quite asleep and not quite awake. Darius stayed quiet, brooding on his side of the carriage. At some point, she noticed him trying to undo the ropes around his wrists with his strength and his teeth, but he gave up after a while. They were secured with magic, she saw it happen herself, and nothing so simple as brute force would break them. Until he struggled, of course, she didn't even consider doing so, but his failure meant that once she did realize it was an option, she still didn't bother trying.

The carriage stopped. It jolted Sabetia awake and made Darius sit up. He didn't have his sword anymore, but he could probably still fight. "Whatever happens, my Lady, I will come for you."

She smiled sadly, touched by the sentiment. "Don't make promises like that. Save your strength and save yourself."

"You're worth ten of me."

The door flew open and a hand grabbed his wrists before she could even try to answer that. They hauled her out into a large, dim room right behind him. The driver, just now regaining his senses, came last. A man dragged her through doors and hallways, down stairs and more hallways that seemed to be complicated just for the sake of being complicated. If their goal was to confuse her enough to prevent escape, it worked.

Eventually, Darius and the driver were taken in one direction and she in another, then she was tossed into a room, the man following in behind her and shutting the door. "You have a choice, princess." He touched a stone to her binding and it fell away to be tucked into his pocket. "Either you strip yourself, or I do it for you."

"I'm not a princess." Even so, she pulled her cloak off and offered it to him.

He didn't take it, instead pointing to the floor, where she dropped it. "I don't really care."

She pulled off her scarf and dropped it onto the cloak, then stepped out of her shoes. "What do you mean to do with me?"

"Me? Nothing. I don't get to sample the goods."

Her fingers flicked over the buttons of her dress. "Will I be forced to go about naked for long?"

"A while, yes."

There was no point to struggling or resisting. Jason taught her that much. She turned around and pulled the dress off, letting it fall to the floor. Showing him her back felt less violating than facing him.

"Not virgin territory, I see," he sneered. "Maybe we will cover you up after all, or maybe we won't. Not my decision." He took her clothes and left her in the small cell. She crumpled to the floor weeping, the silence and solitude too much to bear. If she was 'the goods', she could only assume she was being sold to the highest bidder. Slavery was illegal under the High King and had been for a long time, but that didn't mean people didn't do it.

Sometime later, when she was past tears for herself, for Myra, for the pendant, the only thing she had left to think about was what Darius said in the carriage. She deserved love, he said. What did that even mean? Love was something in storybooks, it didn't happen to real people. In the tales, the hero felt something when he first saw his lady love, and the woman gazed at him adoringly and jumped into his arms. Then he rescued her from a dragon or a manticore, or angry kobolds, or whatever the story featured as the enemy. They lived happily ever after.

With Jason, she thought she found her hero. At her party, he took her breath away. She thought it was love. Surely, no one else but her one true love could make her feel so helpless and wanted and wanting all at once. It wasn't all happiness and joy from there, and if she was honest with herself, the first bruises hadn't been won with pleasure. He hurt her almost from the beginning. Why didn't she tell Matron Aila when she had the chance? She knew the answer, of course. Jason was an Earl, and if there was any one thing her mother was very firm about, it was that marrying a title should be her first priority in life, doubly so for a wealthy one. Managing to botch that would have meant worse than what she was getting at the time.

And now, her best friend tried to help, but couldn't think of anything other than paying someone unscrupulous to kidnap her. Myra was surely dead by now, or wishing she was, and Sabetia mourned the only real friend she'd had by her side for nearly ten years. Caitlin was dear to her, but far enough away to be irrelevant. Besides, she was an awful friend to the princess. Not once had Sabetia written to her like she promised. After that first miscarriage, she couldn't bring herself to put the words on paper.

Another beating and another, and soon enough, he didn't bother making up reasons to blame her for his need to hurt her in his bed. After two years, she didn't think he could enjoy sex anymore without hearing her whimper and seeing her bleed. If Darius was right, that made Jason a monster. What if he was right? What did that make her? She had no idea how to answer, and was saved from trying by the door opening again.

"On your feet, princess." The man was back, and threw a thin piece of cloth at her. "It's everybody's lucky day. Come on. Put that on and let's get this going." When she didn't move fast enough, he grabbed a fistful of hair and yanked her up. It reminded her forcefully of Jason, and she quickly pulled the skimpy little dress over hear head. The rough fabric was see-through with a handful of cheap flecks of glass scattered across it.

His hand clamped around her wrist and yanked her out of the cell. They didn't go far before he handled her up some steps and shoved her out onto a small stage. Bright lights shone in her face, making it difficult to see beyond them, and she stopped trying because it hurt. Her jailor spoke quietly with someone else, then stood behind her.

A new male voice said, "Gentlemen, this one is a little old and not fresh." Rough hands turned her around to display her back. "She's been disciplined quite a bit and is now docile." She was turned again and he pulled her chin up again. "Has not been sampled since acquisition, was raised in a clean, well financed environment. Soft and not used to hard work, really only good for one thing, but an excellent specimen for that purpose. I think we'll start the bidding at two hundred."

"Two hundred," a male voice called out.

"Two-fifty."

"Three hundred."

After a short silence, the auctioneer said, "We have a bid of three hundred. Anyone else?"

"Three and a quarter."

"Three-fifty."

"How about everyone fail to resist while I kill you all?"

This question, delivered by a dry female voice, caused a stunned silence. A strange gurgle came from behind Sabetia, and the hands holding her in place fell away. She didn't react until the auctioneer fell back with an arrow sticking out of his left eye socket. At that point, she squeaked in shock and dropped to the floor, not knowing if she would be shot next. It put her face to face with her jailor, swiftly bleeding out from a slit throat.

The room erupted into chaos. Sabetia scrambled to get away from the dying men, feeling no impulse to heal either of them at all. She heard a light tenor voice say, "That was the best you could do?"

"It felt like it struck the right cord." The female voice sounded more like she concentrated more than the man. Backed out of the harsh lights now, Sabetia made out the pair of them standing in the middle of a group and fighting them. The woman had a dark wooden bow with brass pieces on it. She stabbed one man with the end of the bow, he fell to the floor. The man at her back had two daggers, one thick and dark, the other thin and silvery. While she watched, he slashed at three different men facing him, one screaming and scrambling away, another falling to the floor with blood spurting from an open wound, the third barely scratched.

"Next time, I'll do the talking," the man said as he danced gracefully around the blades his opponents tried to stab him with. "You have no panache."

"You waste too much time talking." The woman stabbed another man with her her bow, then fired it at one fleeing the room.

"Don't bother, gentlemen, we've taken the precaution of sealing the doors to keep any of you from escaping justice." Sabetia got a good look at his face and knew him immediately, just like she always did when she met the people she was supposed to heal. He had short red hair, a thin scar down the line of his jaw, and otherwise was the kind of handsome that brought to mind the word 'scoundrel'.

The woman snorted. “Honestly, buying people isn't really worse than selling them.”

“Oh, that one is Count Marster. A pity. So you know,” the man called out towards one small group of men approaching with the intent to fight, “I slept with your daughter, and when she fell asleep, I stole the books you keep in the wall safe behind your mother's portrait.”

“You did what?” This obviously enraged one of the men, and he charged the man with the two daggers.

“I doubt there was much sleeping,” the woman snorted. The pair of them both easily sidestepped the charging man, moving in tandem like partners and both stabbing him as he flew past them.

“Well, no. Give me a little credit. Oh, and you,” the man pointed at another member of the audience, “your wife is delightful. When I was done making her cry out in joy, I took your business files as payment for services rendered.”

“Goddess bless, Connor. I swear you're an alley cat.” These two didn't seem to be taking the whole situation very seriously, but they were skilled enough to not have to. Sabetia turned her back on them, hoping for a way out, and spotted a gray cat with some kind of cloth in its mouth, running straight towards her. It looked just like Charcoal, actually. She got to her feet and met it halfway. The cloth was her own cloak, and the cat offered it to her. Throwing it over her shoulders, she got the feeling it wanted her to follow it.

She hurried after the cat, but stopped at the open door, not wanting to leave her rescuers behind. The Mother Goddess charged her with healing the man, and she wasn't going to ignore that. The cat mewled impatiently at her, but she ignored it, staying there and trying not to watch the fight. It was a chaotic mess, with bodies moving and blades flashing in the meager light. She heard grunts and groans, clangs and clatters.

As she waited, huddled on herself by the door, she wondered at the serendipity of the moment, at how they'd attacked just as she was being sold instead of after it was too late for her. She was the first one offered, after all. A few more minutes and she would have been gone forever, given to some unknown master for who knows what kind of treatment. This man wouldn't be like Jason, who loved her and wanted her. He, at least, treated her well most of the time. Did it make up for the parts when he didn't? She wasn't sure.

Lost in her thoughts and far enough away from the fighting to avoid harm, she didn't notice it ended until the man put his hand on her arm. In that moment, she knew he had several minor injuries, all of which would add up to him realizing he needed attention as soon as the rush of the fight wore off. She gave him what she had to offer, healing the wounds over.

"Whoa." Crouching beside her, he sucked in a breath. "You're a healer?"

"Yes."

"I guess they didn't know that. Can you take care of Rae, too?" He pointed to the woman, just now stabbing a body with a thin sword.

"Yes. Are you going to release the others?"

"That's part of the plan." He turned and beckoned to Rae.

She jogged over, favoring her left leg. Rae was a relatively plain woman, with long brown hair in a thick braid down her back, brown eyes, and an air of competence. The moment Sabetia got a good look at her face, she knew Rae was one of the people she was supposed to heal, too. "You say that like there actually is some kind of grand plan."

"There is," the man gave her a bright smile, "we've just exhausted most of it already."

Rae rolled her eyes and crouched down to give Sabetia her attention. "Are you okay?"

Instead of answering, Sabetia put her hand on Rae's, forcing the healing energy to knit the deep gash in her leg, and a handful of more minor cuts here and there. If anyone else needed healing, she wouldn't be able to do it right now, as this exhausted her.

While she did that, the cat rooted around the nearest dead body and pulled a set of keys out of a pocket. The cat deposited the keys into the man's hand, and he scratched under its chin, in exactly the same way Charcoal liked. Was it the same cat?

"Charcoal," she said, making it sound just the way she used to say it when he rubbed on her legs to get her attention.

The cat turned to look at her, then hung his head. "Now you've done it," the man chuckled and bapped the cat lightly on his head. "Yes, he's the same cat, his name is actually Shadow. We know exactly who you are, Lady Brexler. It's thanks to you we found this place, actually, because of your husband's carriage."

"Been trying to crack this for months," Rae confirmed.

The man sighed with disappointment. "I admit I thought he was going to be a bidder."

"She called you Connor?"

"Yes, m'Lady, that's my name."

Sabetia peered at him. "I know you from someplace."

"I hope it's not from when I broke into your house."

Rae rolled her eyes again. "Did you sleep with *her*, too?"

"No." Sabetia answered it for him, not particularly wanting to get into this. "I've only been seduced by one man, thank you." Where did she know those blue eyes and that light red hair from? His coloring wasn't terribly unusual, though she couldn't say she'd met many redheaded men, certainly none since she was married. Wait, did she meet him as a man? She'd surely recognize him if she did. His name... "At the funeral. That was you in the park, wasn't it? The boy who helped us. Caitlin and me. We were running and she slipped into the grave and twisted her ankle."

Connor opened his mouth and shut it, going thoughtful.

"Quite a feat you've accomplished, Lady Brexler – he's speechless." Rae helped her back to her feet. "Interesting they chose to sell you first. I thought they saved the prettiest ones for last."

"They go oldest to youngest."

"Thank you. I think it was this way to get back to the cells." Sabetia pointed and pulled away from Rae, not really needing help to walk here with walls handy for support. It seemed best if the archer had both her hands free. "There could be other guards, couldn't there?"

"Yes. By the way," Rae said grimly, "don't look back, it's pretty ugly. We don't usually leave survivors to squirm out of jail time when the Guard shows up."

"You're vigilantes."

"Something like that." Connor sighed like this actually weighed on his mind. "I assure you, everyone here deserved some kind of justice and most of them would never have gotten it. Just the idea of buying and selling human beings is bad enough, but most of them have been under our scrutiny for other dealings for a while."

"I heard." Sabetia wasn't sure what to think of these people. "What will you do with me?"

Connor shrugged. "Swear you to secrecy, then take you home."

Now she had until they finished going through the place to decide if that was what she wanted or not. She turned to watching her feet and making sure she didn't stumble or fall over while her strength returned. The cat followed along by her side, staying quiet. Rae let Connor get a few steps ahead with her bow ready. Sabetia and the cat stayed behind her.

Connor put up a hand to stop them and disappeared around a corner. While the two women waited, Sabetia heard awful sounds, ones that would probably invade her nightmares. These two people were very efficient killers, and it didn't seem to bother them at all. Connor's hand appeared again, beckoning them forward. Sabetia turned the corner to see him kicking a new corpse to the side of the hall, out of the way.

A few more men had to die as they moved through the halls, then they finally found the other cells. Connor used the keys to unlock the doors, leaving Rae to step in and tell the naked occupants they needed to get up and get out of here. It fell to Sabetia to try to keep them calm. She took one hand, then another, and another, gathering them around herself, telling them everything would be okay. It was a bunch of boys and girls, aside from herself. No wonder they called her 'a little old'; some of these children had to be eight or nine at most. The driver was the oldest prisoner here.

Connor unlocked the last door and opened it himself, only to back out again with strong hands wrapped around his neck. The heavily muscled occupant thumped him against the wall. Sabetia looked up and for just a moment, had to appreciate what fine condition Darius was in. He was only the second man she ever saw without clothes, and he compared favorably to Jason. Then she realized what was happening and called out.

“Darius, no, they're rescuing us!”

Her guard stopped and blinked. He glanced back at Sabetia, surrounded by children. He saw Rae, then looked back at Connor. Letting go, he stepped back. “Sorry. I thought this was my one chance.”

Connor coughed and rubbed at his neck. “Turns out, it is. Just not the kind of chance you mean.”

“Right. Are you alright, my Lady?”

It seemed to Sabetia he was embarrassed, though she couldn't say if it was because of his nudity, his mistake with Connor, that he wasn't the one to free her, or something else. “Yes, I'm well enough.” She turned to Rae. “Any chance we can find some clothes down here?”

The cat meowed insistently and Sabetia followed, the children huddling together. Rae, she noticed as she slipped around the corner, was very uncomfortable in their midst. But that wasn't important right now. The cat led her to a crate full of cloth. She recognized her own dress and changed into it, then grabbed up an armful of the rest of the clothing.

"How did you get my cloak?" The cat wouldn't answer, of course, but he did reach up on his hind legs and tap the corner of the chest near the top. "Oh, was a bit of it hanging out?"

Charcoal – no, his name was Shadow – meowed and nodded his head.

"You're a very strange cat, Shadow." In a manner that seemed proud, he meowed at her again while she hurried back to the others with it and handed out small dresses and pants. When she found a large pair of pants, she wadded it up and threw it at Darius. The driver's pants were also there, and a shirt for both men.

Darius didn't look any happier for having clothes, but the rest seemed to be. "What will you do with these children?" Sabetia held a particularly small boy in her arms. He wouldn't stop crying into her shoulder.

Connor shrugged. "We'll leave them here with some food and water, alert the City Guard to the location, and let them handle it."

She gaped in outraged shock. "You're just going to leave them down here?"

Rae edged away from the group, back towards the way they came. "We don't really have the resources to handle this."

Sabetia blinked several times. "Is that all you do? Swoop in, pass judgment, open the door, and walk away?" She hefted the child onto her hip and gathered her cloak about herself as if it were her dignity. "So be it. Come, children, I'll take you someplace warm, with good food and clean water." She began walking, having no true idea where the exit was, with the group of children following her. They passed by Rae, who watched her with something akin to awe. Darius followed without comment, taking up the rear. The driver also followed, holding a few small hands.

She'd gone perhaps twenty paces before Connor said, "Wait." He sounded grudging and unhappy. "We can at least show you the way out."

"And escort you to the City Guard," Rae added.

"Yes, and escort you to the Guard." Connor sighed and made his way to the front to lead them all.

"What city is this?" In the darkness of a moonless night, she couldn't see much and recognized nothing. The air here had a peculiar smell she didn't know the source of, something acrid and unpleasant.

"Rennsen, the industrial district. North side."

Sabetia almost laughed out loud. Myra paid someone to take her far away, and after everything that happened, she wound up just miles from Jason's house. But Myra wasn't here, and the laugh died in her throat, tasting like acid. If she told a guardsmen her name, they would take her home and everything would be like it was before, except without Myra. She would have her fine clothes, everything she could possibly want to eat, a roof, a bed, servants. So long as she allowed herself to be used by her husband, she could have all the finest things, all the time.

Her other choice? Freedom with uncertainty. Never in her life had she needed to find ways to survive on the streets, to get by without money. She had nothing to offer but her healing gift, and that wasn't something she could sell, not ever. It would be worse than selling her body, more like selling her soul. Such a gift was meant to be shared freely, and she tried to before. Now, with this freedom, she had a chance – a bright, shining chance – to give this gift to as many people as she could. All she had to do was find a way to eat, and sleep in safety. All she had to do was push past the fear.

Connor seemed content to lead the way as they all walked, so she turned a let some of the children pass her, waving to her guard. "Darius," she called back, and he nodded, moving up to meet her in the middle. It looked like she interrupted a conversation between him and Rae.

"Yes, my Lady?"

"I'm not going home."

For once, he smiled at her. "Good."

"You should stop calling me 'my Lady'."

"As you wish," he nodded.

"In fact, we should probably not use my name."

"That seems prudent. What should I call you?"

"Darius, you don't work for me. You're free to go at any time."

"And yet, I'm staying." He looked around like he was considering which piece of real estate to purchase. "I won't let you go alone into the streets. This is at least partly my fault. You won't bear the brunt of my mistakes alone." Fixing her now with a pointed stare, he said, "I pledge my life to yours, no matter what name you go by. It's the penance I set myself to right the wrong I've done to you. You can refuse, deny, cajole, whatever, but you can't relieve my shame with mere words. It runs too deep. For two years, I was paid to protect you, and I failed. I now pledge to do it properly, for so long as I live, with no expectation of payment on your part. I so swear it in the eyes of the Goddess."

Taken aback by such an oath, Sabetia said nothing at first. She turned her attention to the ground under her bare feet. "Thank you." What she did to inspire such loyalty, she had no idea.

"It's my pleasure," he said, bowing his head respectfully.

"Betsy." The name came out of nowhere, she just blurted it out.

He bowed his head again. "It's my pleasure, Betsy."

"That's it," Connor said from the front, pointing at an imposing stone edifice. "North side Rennsen City Guard post. Rae and I can't go in with you, but-"

"You mean that you won't." Sabetia gave Connor a stern look, one she hoped adequately expressed disappointment and scorn. "It's alright. None of us needs your help anymore. You did your part, right?" She led the children inside, Darius and the driver herding them along.

This post probably wasn't used to the kind of sight the two dozen of them presented. A pair of guardsmen sitting at the front desk stared blankly at the assembled group. One was young, probably very recently into his tenure with the Guard. The other had the look of a grizzled veteran deemed to old to walk the streets anymore.

"We were held prisoner nearby," she told the two men, "they tried to sell us all. Everyone there is dead, I know nothing about how any of it happened, we just found the doors unlocked as if by magic and escaped."

The two guards blinked at her. "Uh, yes, miss. Are you alright?"

"We could use some food and water, perhaps blankets. These children need to be seen to their homes, and this man also," she indicated the driver. "My friend and I will be fine to make our own way."

"S-sure," the younger of the two guards stammered. "We don't really have, um, I can take you to the cells, that's all we really have..."

"They're warm," the older one offered.

"Cells?" Was this really the best the Guard could do? "We were all just held in cells, waiting to be sold to men who would do unspeakable things to us, and you want to put us back into cells?" She squared her shoulders and glared at him. "This is unacceptable. Call for a wagon of some sort and take us to the nearest Temple. The Disciple there will be able to help us. While we wait, find something for them to eat. Who knows when they were last fed."

Whether it was her stern, commanding words or the sea of children staring at them with their big, wide eyes, or Darius standing with his arms crossed and ready to use violence, the younger guardsmen hopped to comply. The older one sighed and nodded, then also got to work on the matter. He took the information about where to find all the corpses and got some crackers and water – all they had on hand to eat.

They piled into a wagon with the younger guardsman driving. Connor and Rae were nowhere to be seen as it trundled down the street. "Lady," the driver said softly to avoid being overheard, "what should I tell the Earl?"

She frowned and tried to think of something that wouldn't earn the man anything undeserved. Darius answered before she could see a way through it. "Tell him the truth, keep it simple. The carriage was attacked, you were knocked unconscious. When you woke up, you were a prisoner. Some strangers came and released you with all these children. Just leave out anything about the Lady. You didn't see what happened to her and have no idea where she is. Her guards were probably all killed, likewise with the maid."

The driver nodded, rubbing his face wearily. "He'll look for you, Lady. He'll turn over every stone until you're found."

"I know." She stared off into the darkness, not sure what to do.

"Let him come." Darius cracked his knuckles, glowering at them. "I'll be waiting for him."

The driver gulped. "I wish you good fortune, Lady, Darius."

"Thank you. To you as well." She fingered the cloth of her cloak, pulling it closer. Her name was Betsy now, and it would be for so long as she needed to hide from Jason. Provided Darius didn't go murder her husband in his sleep, they could be hiding from him for years. And he would think she'd been taken by kidnappers, which would make him search all the harder. He had Keric, who could probably find her, and if he couldn't, there was more than enough money to pay another mage to do it. Holy ground might protect her, but she couldn't just stay in a Temple for the rest of her life.

Was it time to tell a Disciple? The woman might send her home, or she might bear her secret and help her flee. No matter how sacred the marriage bond was, the Disciples were still women. She sat and pondered how to tell this unknown Disciple everything while the wagon bumped and bounced on its way. The guardsman stopped in front of a Temple less ornate and grand than the ones she was used to, then helped them climb out the back. She took pity on him and let him leave without speaking to the Disciple inside. He fled with her well wishes.

They walked inside to find a building in need of repairs and fresh paint. No artwork graced the walls, and half the windows were boarded up, the other half filled with small panes of thick, bubbly glass. It had no benches at all, and just the stone altar in the center. She directed the children to sit near the altar and went for the inside doors, knocking on them until someone answered. An old woman, hands gnarled, face creased and lined, long hair wild and white, finally shuffled out with the help of a cane.

"I'm Elder Vanora." Her voice crackled and resonated with age. "How can I serve you, miss?"

"Guardsmen brought us here." She explained what happened as succinctly as she could, finishing with, "We really just need a place to stay, perhaps some blankets if you can spare them, food and water, and help to get these children home."

"All are welcome in the Mother Goddess's house," Elder Vanora said. "I don't have much, but it's all here to be shared. Come, bring them, we can sleep together, all of us. It's better for warmth. There's some soup we can heat up, and cheese, apples, and a little bit of bread."

Sabetia almost cried with relief. Finally, someone who not only could, but would help with what they really needed, not just pass them off on someone else. "Oh, thank you so much. Let's save the soup for morning, though. We're all very tired." By the time they herded all the children into the small room Elder Vanora offered, it was hard to move around. Sabetia and Vanora handed out the cheese and apples and bread. The children ate like they'd had nothing of the sort for a while.

She wasn't entirely certain where to settle herself. Vanora waded into the sea of children and curled up among them, not minding in the slightest that they snuggled up and accepted her as easily as they took the food. Darius, sitting in one of the corners, gestured for her to join him, so she picked her way there. When he pulled her close to lean on him, she stiffened, imagining Jason's reaction and remembering Myra's comfort. He let go without a word.

Chapter 8

"What happened to this place?" Her own needs and problems seemed small and unimportant compared to the state of the Temple and the plight of these children. Betsy sat next to Darius, surrounded by the kids, all of them eating a thin vegetable soup with a handful of stale crackers each. The driver had left already, at first light. She and Darius couldn't stay long, not if they wanted to evade Jason. As soon as he knew where the driver spent the night, he'd come looking to try to find her.

"The same thing that happens to all of us: time passed." Elder Vanora refilled water cups from a pitcher, insisting upon doing it herself. "It was first built about two hundred years ago. Back then, this area wasn't part of Rennsen; it was a small village to the north. Trappers provided animal skins that were turned into fur and leather goods. That's the smell, you know. It's the chemicals and such they use for the leather, which they still do around here. A nice place to live then, so I've heard. At the time, this was the largest building around. It was plain because the people it served were simple, common folk.

"But time marched on. Rennsen grew, so did demand for the goods. The leatherworkers banded together and made innovations that increased output. Land was freed up, but with such concentrated leatherworking, the stench was too much for people to live nearby. Even the leatherworkers moved far enough away to not smell it at home. No one wanted to live nearby, so other businesses took over. People don't live here anymore, they just work here. It was already a dying Temple when I took it over, oh, some thirty years ago now.

“It was a punishment, of sorts, for being too obnoxious.” Vanora grinned. It was infectious enough to make her grin back. “When I pass on, I expect they'll finally tear it down and put up something more 'useful'. Until then, I stubbornly remain at the post I was assigned, ministering to the occasional lost soul.” Her gesture indicated everyone in the room. “This is quite a bit more than I'm accustomed to taking in at once, but I'll manage. Goddess willing, I always do, somehow.”

Such a sad tale. Betsy looked around the room and wondered what would be put in its place when they tore it down. Another warehouse or factory of some sort, probably. She forsake the ability to do anything about that when she decided not to be a Lady anymore. “When the Earl of Venithys comes to question you about his missing wife, you should see about prevailing upon his generosity for the benefit of these children.”

“And what makes you think he'll do that?”

“That other man was her driver.”

Darius reached over and covered Betsy's hand with his own. “We beg you to say nothing to him, Elder Vanora, about either of us.”

Vanora raised an eyebrow. “Run off and found yourself a new man, did you?”

“No.” It was her imagination that Darius actually looked a little crestfallen at that answer. “I'm tired of what he does to me, Elder. I've miscarried ten times under his care and lied about it to protect him. The truth is..." She took a deep breath and shut her eyes, unable to say this while she could see the old woman's face, or worse, Darius's. "He hit me. He whipped me. He dragged me by the hair, used his belt, a cane, even a knife. I bear the scars of what he's done to me, and will for the rest of my life, but I don't have to let him keep doing it, not anymore."

She opened her eyes when Darius squeezed her hand. Vanora wasn't looking at her anymore, rather at something behind her: Connor and Rae with their clothes clean and changed, both well rested and now staring at her. Betsy immediately blushed scarlet and faced her bowl instead of their two saviors.

"Don't be ashamed to tell that tale, girl." Vanora said, patting her shoulder. "I might have known this was your handiwork. Did you at least bring bread?"

Betsy didn't see what happened until the child next to her scooted away and Connor sat down, offering torn pieces of bread to both her and the child. "I had no idea. He wasn't doing that when Shadow uninvited himself. Had I known then..."

"You would have done nothing." She took the bread and dipped it into her soup, not feeling particularly charitable at the moment. Here, under Vanora's watchful eyes, she didn't fear him, though her mind supplied ideas of what he could do to her in a dark alley. He proved himself deadly and merciless last night.

"No, not nothing." Connor ran a hand through his hair. It looked like a nervous gesture. "I'm not what you think I am."

"I think you're a cad and a vigilante who's forgotten why he's doing what he's doing."

He pursed his lips and didn't look at her. “We saved your life last night. But you saved ours right back. Either of us might have bled out before we realized we were going to. I've had close scrapes before, I know what they look and feel like.”

“Why are you here?”

Rae made a space for herself across from Betsy and sat. “We need your help.”

“I won't help you run about executing people you feel deserve it.” Unwilling to budge on this point, she ate the now soggy bread, savoring the flavor in a way she hadn't done since Jason fed her for the first few times.

Shadow jumped into Connor's lap and put an insistent paw on Betsy's arm, meowing plaintively. “He's sorry he didn't realize what was going on, too,” Connor said.

“It wasn't, not then. It happened later.”

“He blamed her for the cat's actions.” Darius's spoke in a low, dangerous rumble. “Used it as an excuse-”

“Darius.” Betsy didn't want to put that kind of guilt onto Connor, it wasn't really his fault. “It's not important. What is important is that I won't be the person you can run to when you get hurt who won't ask questions or ignore what you did to need healing.”

Connor opened his mouth, but stopped before he said anything. “Look,” Rae said, “this isn't really about that. You didn't wind up in that market by walking there, and we need to know who grabbed you and how.”

Vanora coughed. It might have been just to get their attention, or it might have been a genuine cough of sickness. "You should stop pussyfooting around and just tell her the truth, children. All of it. She's a worthy soul."

Rae and Connor both looked dutifully chastised. Connor tapped his fingers on the table, Rae brushed at an imperfection on the surface with the side of her thumb. Betsy finished her soup and was about to get up when Connor finally spoke. "We work for an organization that's a little less legal and proper than the Guard. We do the dirty work they can't or won't to clean up the city. Rennsen isn't a nice place to live unless you have a lot of money, but it's getting better because of what we do. We're half of the field agents active in Rennsen. Our group operates at least one agent in every major city in the four kingdoms.

"Along with our resources, we have an extensive network in the underbelly of the city, and we've been tracking a ring of child traffickers for a while now, years. They've been crafty and their customers have a lot of money, enough to cover all of this up and keep it quiet. Shadow was looking into the Earl two years ago because I thought he was involved. He's not, but you should know some of his business dealings are a little less than savory. Nothing I was interested in at the time, but he's on my list of people to get into when this is taken care of.

"All I want right now is to shut the whole thing down. Every man there last night was doing one of three things." He held up his hand and ticked each one off as he said it. "Buying, selling, or guarding those doing the buying and selling with full knowledge of what was going on. We happened to be out and recognized the Earl's carriage going someplace unexpected, so we followed it and made our way through the tunnels. When we got there, I was genuinely surprised to see you up for sale. But the point is, it was a big break, a chance to crack the whole thing wide open."

Rae laced her hands together on the table. "If there's one thing we can't just let anyone get away with, it's selling people, especially kids. That's not right. Maybe everyone who died last night didn't deserve to, but they set down that path of their own free will. Every man there last night had a choice, and he made it. I understand how you feel, I really do, especially knowing what you've been through. Ask yourself this, though: if you could kill the Earl for each of the potential children he beat out of you, would you?"

Betsy looked down at her empty bowl and spoon and thought about that, really thought about it. She knew how Darius would answer, he'd made that clear. Why did killing have to be the only answer, though? "What about repentance? Forgiveness? Isn't it the Mother Goddess's place to judge us?"

"I don't think there's forgiveness for what he's done, but you should have become a Disciple, girl." Vanora's warm voice wrapped around her, offering comfort. "Everyone can't live up to and doesn't deserve those ideals, sadly. I don't precisely approve of what these ruffians do," she ruffled a wizened hand through Connor's hair, "but it's hard to deny the results." That hand gestured around at the children. "Maybe what they need is a younger person, still full of life and with two strong arms and legs to chase them around like an angry goose, forcing them to be better than they are."

Connor ran a hand through his hair to fix it and ducked down to avoid further gestures of affection. Shadow climbed out of Connor's lap and onto the table to brush against Sabetia's face, meowing plaintively, begging her to not be mad. She closed her eyes and let him do it, the softness reminding her of the best things in life: warmth, affection, companionship. Pulling him into her lap, she nodded. "Alright, I'll come with you. All I'm committing to, though, is helping with this particular thing. After that, if I'm not willing, you let me walk away and leave me alone."

"I accept." Connor stood up and looked her over with mild bemusement. "You can keep the cat for now. He's nothing but trouble anyway."

"She's not going without me." Darius stood up and offered Betsy a hand up.

Rae cracked a grin and let her eyes drift downwards. "Wouldn't dream of leaving you behind, big fella."

"Go with the grace of the Goddess, Children." Vanora hugged Betsy around the shoulders. "They need you, Betsy. Remember that. You might just need them, too." Louder, she said, "Bring money next time, you miscreants."

Connor pulled a small pouch out of his pocket and tossed it to her with a grin. "I'm wounded you think I didn't this time."

She caught the pouch and chuckled as she shooed them all out. Betsy gave the old woman a little wave and followed Connor, not sure she should ask where the money came from. He probably looted it from those men last night, which meant she really didn't want to know. There was something else she wanted to know, though. "What did you take from Caitlin that day?"

Connor thumped the door open and shrugged. “I don't remember.”

“You're lying.”

Rae sniggered behind her. “I reckon she's sharp, Connor.”

Giving the archer a fleeting glare, he shrugged again. “It's not important. I didn't start my life of crime by stealing from the High Princess, I was already a lawless little urchin by then.”

Betsy rolled her eyes. “You're mocking me.”

He gave her a smarmy grin full of teeth. “Maybe a little.”

“Can we banter somewhere else?” Darius loomed behind her, and she could tell he'd like to finish strangling Connor. “We need to be long gone before the Earl arrives.”

“Of course.” Connor bowed with a flourish of his hand and looked them both up and down. “You'll need proper clothes and shoes. I'm guessing a sword might be useful, and perhaps some armor. Fortunately, I happen to have access to funds for resupply, and expected at least some of this. To shopping!” He strode off up the street. Betsy, still carrying the cat, had to hurry to keep up.

“Joy,” Rae said, full of sarcasm. “At least I get to take the rear so I can watch Darius's in those tight pants.”

Darius huffed out a mildly annoyed breath and kept up with Betsy, helping her when Connor cut down an alley and she needed to evade debris. They went down side streets and more alleys, eventually coming out onto a major street Betsy wouldn't ordinarily be caught dead on. It was better than a slum, but not by much. Shops lined both sides of the street, with apartments over them. Everything here was probably perfectly fine, just not like she was used to.

The shop he took them into was exactly what she expected from the outside. Betsy was accustomed to being measured, selecting fabrics she liked in colors that flattered her, and giving basic instructions to the seamstress. In a week or so, she would have a new dress made just for her. This place sold rather plain, pre-made garments of linen, wool, and cotton, some in hideous patterns, most in drab colors. She sighed and leafed through a rack.

"Really? That bad?" Connor gave her an amused sort of chiding look. "I can't afford what you're used to, Betsy. This is kinda how it has to be. Or you can go back to your asshole and ask him for pocket money. You're probably not going to be on that level, ever again. We don't exactly do high paying, glamorous work here. You want something that won't get in the way while you run, hide, and dodge arrows."

Betsy flinched and looked away. "What exactly are you expecting me to do?"

Darius picked out some pants and a shirt without complaint, barely paying attention to what he was grabbing aside from the sizes. "She shouldn't have to do any of that. I'll be protecting her."

"Yeah, sure." Connor crossed his arms and leaned against the wall casually. "We'll see how that goes. All I'm saying is, you might want pants instead of a dress." He nodded his head towards Rae, who still wore dark leathers like she had last night. "Not just for mobility, of course. We can put you in armor if you wear pants."

"Armor." Betsy took a deep breath and rolled the word around in her head, trying to imagine herself wearing it. She didn't want to braid her hair back like Rae did and wasn't comfortable with the idea of armor in itself. It was something a person wore with an expectation of being involved in fighting. The only fighting she felt equipped to handle was verbal, with other women, and she hadn't yet come out strictly on top in that arena. The mere idea of wielding some kind of a weapon and using it to actually hit someone made her a little nauseous.

She frowned and picked out a lavender wool dress. "I don't want to wear armor." She took it to the back to try it on, ignoring both Connor and Rae. They could dress however they wished, but she was done being told what to wear or not wear. Two long years, she wore a thin robe in the house because Jason told her to. She wore nothing in the bedroom because Jason told her to. She wore blue, all the time, because Jason told her to. Maybe not wearing armor would cause her some problems, but she wasn't comfortable with it, and she wasn't going to do it.

Two hours and three shops later, she wore the wool dress and had two spares, along with wool socks, leather boots, a brown oilskin and wool cloak, white gloves and a white hat. They walked out of a smithy, Darius still settling into his new chainmail and his own wool clothes and heavy boots. Connor and Rae knew where they were going now, Betsy just followed along with Darius as a hulking shadow beside her.

This part of the city was wholly unfamiliar, and she didn't have a clue where they were. It was full of four story buildings all crammed together with no gardens or grass to speak of. Some stretches had a tavern or shops for the ground floors. None of it looked terribly reputable to Betsy. She was helpless to stop herself from making a face of distaste when Connor and Rae walked up to one of these taverns and went inside. At least they didn't go to the bar. She and Darius followed them straight out the back, to a stables. Connor dropped a few coins onto the table next to the man tending the place, who looked like he could use a very long bath and a lot of coffee.

"I've never ridden before." Betsy looked up at the horses Connor and Rae busily saddled. They were beautiful creatures, she could tell that even though she knew very little about such beasts. The ones Jason had were all for pulling carriages – he didn't ride, neither did she. Or rather, if he did ride, he didn't say anything about it and never did it while she was watching.

"Are we taking two horses or three?" Darius crossed his arms skeptically.

Connor shrugged. "You can take one if you like. The stableman won't notice, and we'll likely have it back before its owner notices."

Betsy goggled at him. "Are you stealing these horses?"

"These two?" Connor patted his gray stallion on the neck. "No, not at all. They're ours. We keep them here because it's tucked out of the way and no one who knows us would ever expect us to use this place. It's a risk, keeping quality horses here, but one that hasn't proven wrong yet."

"Also," Rae added cheerfully, "the bartender has a nice ass."

"I'll take your word for it," Darius grumbled.

"You should ride with me, Darius." Rae cinched the strap on her roan mare and checked it. "You're a big guy, and Clover can take it.

Betsy can ride with Connor – Bonbon is a big baby."

Betsy giggled. "Bonbon?"

Connor stuck his tongue out at Rae. "I didn't name the horse, he came that way."

"Just like his master." Rae led Clover the horse out through the big stable doors, then swung up into the saddle once outside.

"Wench." Connor followed her and held out a hand for Betsy once he sat in his own saddle.

Darius frowned and led Betsy to Connor's horse. "She's right. This is the best option. Just relax and-" He gritted his teeth as he glanced at Connor. "-hold on."

"I'll be fine," Betsy assured him. It took both men to get her settled behind Connor. Thank goodness she picked the dress with the full skirt and had drawers under it for warmth. The cat slunk around Connor to sit in front of him. Darius had no trouble getting up behind Rae, showing some measure of experience with riding. She put her hands on Connor's waist, he grabbed and pulled them together in front of himself.

"Hold your own hands or you'll be exhausted in no time," he told her over his shoulder. "The goal is to not fall off, and I promise not to read anything into you having your arms wrapped around me."

A light blush colored Betsy's cheeks. "You already know more about me than my husband did when I was Handfasted to him." She squeaked as the horse started walking, the unfamiliar movement startling her.

Connor put one of his gloved hands over hers. "Relax. So long as you hold onto me, you won't fall." He paused for a moment. "That sounds awful. I can't imagine what that must be like."

"Was it just bluster when you told those men you slept with their daughters and wives?"

"No, but that was just a night of fun without commitment. I never promised them anything and asked nothing in return."

While she had known sex to be enjoyable, she didn't quite understand this idea of bedding women for 'fun'. "I was taught that sex is about children and pleasing my husband."

"No doubt." The way he said it, he didn't approve.

"What do you mean?"

"Let me guess. Your goal in life was to be pretty and attract a wealthy man."

"What else would it be?"

Connor clucked his tongue. "Rae's goal is nothing like that. She wants to make her world a better place and avoid being killed while doing so. I know another woman whose goal is to suck the marrow out of each and every moment of her life. My boss is a woman, too, and I'm not completely sure what her goals are, but they have nothing to do with her looks or getting married."

"I am aware that not every woman can be like that. I have- Had. I had servants. My best friend is my maid." She sighed. "Was. She's probably dead by now, or will be soon."

"Oh?" It was only fair that if he was going to help her, she should tell him as much as she knew. Betsy related what happened, how she wound up where he found her. "That explains a lot. I must admit, I was having trouble figuring it. If she's still alive, we might be able to get her free. But, you're right to be prepared for the worst. Given what happened, I think we should change our plans. Do you think you could find where the carriage was attacked?"

A thrill of hope sang in Betsy's veins, for Myra. "We were on the main road. Unless they cleaned everything up, there's likely something left of the attack. Four men were killed there."

Connor goaded the horse up to walk beside Clover and told them what he wanted to do. Rae and Darius agreed with the plan. Betsy noted Darius was brooding again, but couldn't do anything about it, because Connor spurred Bonbon to go faster and they took the lead. Though she couldn't help but wonder where they were going before she explained all of this, the gait of the horse kept her from doing anything but holding on for dear life. Trying to talk would be an exercise in teeth chattering, mostly.

They rode for a while, long enough that Betsy felt she needed to get off the horse soon. Just when she thought she'd figured out how to properly phrase that without whining, Connor reined Bonbon in, making him stop. "We may have found the spot."

Rae stopped beside him and snorted. "Ya think?"

Betsy leaned far enough to see and sucked in her breath. They didn't try to hide anything at all. The two guards had been speared in place like grotesque scarecrows, posed with their hands out towards the road, either reaching for help or hoping to grab someone and pull them in to be devoured. Large black birds tore at the bluish flesh.

"I knew those men." Darius said it quietly, with enough intensity to make Rae flinch.

Connor's head tilted back and forth as he regarded the scene.

They didn't get close enough to make out faces. "It's an ambush."

Rae shrugged. "Looks more like a message to me."

"No," Darius said, "it's a challenge."

Connor and Rae seemed to agree with this assessment, but Betsy didn't really understand. "For who?"

"The local lord, most likely," Connor said. "Challenging the High King would be stupid."

"It was a particularly large band." Darius stared at the two figures in the distance, his expression cold and hard. "I can't say for sure that the archers moved up, and I counted fifteen. Could be as many as twenty-five or more. A fair number to turn against a Count or Baron."

"These people mean business," Rae observed.

"Why would they want to challenge him?"

Connor turned to regard Betsy. "He has something they want. Land, power, money, cattle, a pretty daughter, whatever. These men were paid to take you. They might have wanted the money to prepare for this somehow. Who knows how your maid contacted them, but it hardly matters."

"Probably through those slavers." Rae turned to fiddling with the bracers on her arms, tightening the cinches. "Trolling in taverns would have gotten her there."

Connor looked around. "They'll have a base near here. Someplace in the shadows."

"Left," Darius said. "I saw them come from that way at the beginning." He pointed off towards the tree covered hills. "They'd more likely stage where they came from than making the effort to do it across the road. Besides, the trees are close enough for decent archers. The shape of the land hid the ones who shot the drugged darts that knocked out the driver. He pulled the reins with him when he fell, making the horses rear and stop." He rubbed his chin, scanning the area. "There. The rest of the men hid there. They knew we were coming, and must have had a way to stop the horses if the driver didn't."

"Just get on the road in their way would be enough," Rae said, "with no driver to direct them. That's a lot of men for just the two of us."

Darius corrected her. "Three. I wasn't hired as a bodyguard because I look pretty."

"It probably helped, though." Connor grinned as he turned Bonbon to walk through the grasses.

Alarmed, Betsy watched Rae bring Clover to walk beside them. "What are you doing?"

Connor shrugged. "We need information, which we're only going to get by going in, and if we're going in, we might as well do an assault on the place. And here I thought today would be boring after last night."

Rae snorted. "I hope I brought enough arrows."

"Wait a minute." Betsy grabbed a fistful of Connor's sleeve and pulled enough to be sure she had his attention. "You mean to just go in there, wherever 'there' is, and kill everyone?"

"What would you prefer? That we leave them to do as they please to anyone traveling down this road? How about the local lord, just let his people be slaughtered?"

"Stop the horse."

"What? Why?"

"I'm getting off."

"I wish you were," Connor said very quietly, probably not expecting her to hear it.

Not sure how he meant that, she let go and pushed herself down without bothering to wait for him to stop. Her landing was less than ideal, but they weren't going very fast and she didn't hit her head. In reaction to it, Darius jumped off Rae's horse and ran to her side. She got to her feet and waved him off, marching back to the road.

"My Lady, what are you doing?" Darius grabbed her arm, stopping her.

"I'm not going to just be carried into a killing spree, and those men deserve better than to be on display like trophies." She yanked her arm away and he let go, like she knew he would. "They died to save me."

Darius rubbed his forehead in exasperation and followed her as she moved swiftly down the road. "There's nothing you can do for them, and there could be traps on the ground. You could be killed."

"Then I'll be killed!" She ran towards them, intent on doing something for them, anything at all. If the only thing she could do was to pull them down to at least lie on the ground, on the Mother Goddess's womb, then that's what she would do. They weren't worth less than her, they didn't deserve to die because of her. No one should ever face that. It wasn't right, it wasn't fair, and she couldn't live with herself if she just walked away from them now.

"I gave you my word. I meant it." Darius caught up and grabbed her from behind. “If protecting you means protecting you from yourself, then so be it.”

“Let me go!”

“My Lady, stop.” He was far too strong for her, but she struggled anyway, trying to break free. “Lady. Betsy. Please.” He picked her up so her feet didn't touch the ground anymore, and she kicked and squirmed. “Stop, listen to me.”

“We can't just leave them there!”

“Yes, we can. I knew them, Betsy. I know their names. Before the Earl brought you to his house, I was one of them. We drank together, played cards, went wenching. Those men,” he pointed at the corpses without releasing her, “were my friends. There's nothing I can do for them. The lord's men will come and pull them down, see them respected. I know you, Betsy, I know this is hard for you. I've watched you with the people you heal, I've seen how it wounds you to watch them suffer.”

She couldn't help it, she was crying now. All she wanted... She didn't even know what she wanted or why she was so upset, this was just all so wrong. “I'm sorry.”

“I know. But that's not enough. Regret won't bring them back, nothing can. We can prevent these men from taking any more lives, that's what we mean to do. That's why Connor and Rae do what they do. It's not about revenge, or even about justice, not as much as they say or think it is. It's about making the world a place where an Earl's wife can walk down the street safely if she so chooses, wearing her finery and not worrying about someone snatching her off the street and selling her to the highest bidder.”

"How are they better? Aren't they murderers too?"

Darius breathed in slowly, deeply. Although very little changed, the embrace felt more intimate all of a sudden, like a warm, safe place she could stay forever. "The world is hard and cold and brutal where they live."

She sagged into him, letting his strength buoy her. "What about forgiveness?"

"Some of us can never be forgiven for what we've done, we just try to use what we have to protect the rest. Knowing they'll be hunted like the dogs they are, the men whose hearts hold this kind of darkness take pause and turn away from it. The ones who can be saved will save themselves if only the punishment is clear and harsh enough. I wish everyone could be rescued from himself, Betsy, but they just can't. Not in the world I live in." He let go and started walking back to Connor and Rae. "Stay or come along as you prefer, Betsy. I imagine the lord's men will be along sooner rather than later, and they'll take you in if you ask."

"Wait." Was it really like that? She was taught the Mother Goddess watched over all Her children, kept them safe and warm. Yet, how could that be, if children were sold like cattle in the shadows of the city she called her home? People like Rae and Connor struggled to stop them, and now Darius, too. "What is it you can't be forgiven for?"

Darius stopped with his back to her. Over his shoulder, he said, "It's my burden to bear, Lady, not yours."

"If I don't come along-" She didn't know how to finish the question, or if it even was a question.

Darius started walking again, his only answer a shake of his head.

Her mouth went dry as she guessed what he wouldn't say. Such a wretched choice. Go along and keep them safe while they killed perhaps two dozen men, or stay here and know that if they never came back, it was her fault for letting them go to their deaths in the name of the greater good. Her cheeks burned with shame. How could she possibly look at herself in a mirror again if she let her morality – which seemed to be too stark and bright for this cold, dreary world – be the only reason she didn't help when they asked?

With Connor and Rae, it was even worse. She'd been charged by the Mother Goddess to keep them safe. Maybe it wasn't about last night. If they were going to go about throwing themselves into danger over and over, she needed to be there in case this time was *the* time. Whatever reason they'd been chosen and Darius hadn't, she was charged with their protection, and had to take that seriously. Elder Vanora was right, maybe even speaking for the Goddess.

Hurrying after Darius, she took his arm and found him looking down at her with relief. "I'm sorry. You deserve better than this from me."

"I'm sorry, too." His gloved hand patted hers. "You deserve better than this from the world." Nothing else needed to be said, and he lifted her back onto the horse behind Connor, where she wrapped her arms around him.

"May we go now? I'd hate to miss our appointment for tea with these gentlemen."

Rae rolled her eyes at Connor and spurred her horse into a trot instead of answering him.

Chapter 9

"That's probably the place." Rae looked up from the ground where she crouched to point at a small stone building off in the distance, just visible through the trees. It was built up against the side of a hill, perhaps into it. "The tracks go that way."

Darius landed a few feet away, dropping down from the tree he climbed to get a better look. "There's nothing else around and I saw two sentries up in the trees. I saw at least one shape go past the window, but no one else is standing guard outside."

Connor nodded, staring at the little house. "There's another way in, no doubt, but it'll take us too long to find it. We'll have to get close before you take out the archers," he told Rae.

"Unless we use them to get the door open."

Darius shook his head. "Nothing they've done suggests they'll react stupidly. If they see the sentries go down, they'll barricade. We need to get in without them realizing until it's too late."

"Surprise is my favorite element." Connor peered off towards the house again, reaching over to pet Shadow briefly where he sat on a rock nearby, also looking that way.

Betsy had an idea, and she blushed bright pink. It was probably a very bad idea, and they all had so much more experience with this sort of thing. "What if I go knock on the door, demanding to see Myra?"

The four of them stared at her blankly. Connor was the first to find something to say. "You're supposed to have been sold last night.

And, how did you find the place?"

Now with solid proof she had nothing to contribute, Betsy's blush turned scarlet.

"Well, she's got a point." Rae stood up and shrugged. "Sometimes, the best infiltration is the distraction. I'll go find a perch, you boys slink in close. Betsy walks up to the front door in plain sight. She'll have their attention. Just need to pretend like you're someone else. Pull your hood up, make sure all your hair is tucked away, and claim to be here to negotiate."

"It's too dangerous." Darius crossed his arms and scowled.

Connor looked Betsy over, then shrugged. "If anyone has a better idea, let's hear it."

Lying, she'd done that before. Often, even. She kept everyone guessing for two years, never knowing what Jason did to her. They whispered she was too weak, or had bad blood. No one suspected Jason for even a moment, only her. Come to think of it, why did they never feel it was reasonable to lay the blame for his lack of heirs at his feet? Always, they assumed it was her, something about her or her family. At any rate, this didn't sound too difficult. "Is there anything special I should do?"

Rae patted her shoulder. "Just don't act nervous. They'll know something is up too soon." She turned her attention upwards.

"You don't have to do this." Darius touched her arm and looked her in the eyes.

"I know, but I can."

Connor offered her a small knife, hilt first. "Take it. In case you need it."

She held up a hand, refusing it. "No, I can't. I couldn't ever."

Darius shook his head. "That's why this is a mistake."

The knife flipped in Connor's fingers and disappeared. "You still haven't explained your brilliant alternative plan." He reached over and pulled the hood of her cloak up, arranging it carefully around her face and tucking a lock of stray hair inside it. His eyes lingered on her mouth for a second or two, then flicked away abruptly. "Give us about five minutes to get into place, then walk into plain sight. Go all the way to the door, look around like you're scared. Knock and say you have a message from your Lord."

"What message is that?"

He smirked. "Two men with blades and an archer."

"This will work." She told both of them as much as herself.

"Yes, it will. Unless Soldier Boy here trips over his own feet." Connor flashed a cheeky grin at Darius, who scowled again and made a fist he probably wanted to smash into Connor's face. "He won't, though. He's a professional, and he knows your life is on the line." With that, he tapped the end of her nose playfully and moved away.

The nickname confused Betsy, and she didn't understand the cool glare Darius gave Connor's back. He shook his head and huffed a little. His mouth opened to say something to her, but nothing came out and he followed after Connor. They both disappeared around a tree. Five minutes, she had to wait five minutes. Rae was gone now, too, up in the trees someplace. Shadow disappeared while they were talking, leaving her alone here. This was about Myra more than anything, she had to remember that.

This was the most frightening thing she'd ever... Actually, no, it wasn't. This didn't compare to that night she ran out naked into the snow. Then, she was alone, truly alone. Now, there were three people and a cat backing her up. Rae had incredible aim, she saw that last night. Darius was stronger than anyone she knew. Connor was more competent than he acted. Shadow was smarter than he looked. All of them would protect her while they did this horrible thing that had to be done, because the world she grew up in wasn't real.

It wasn't scary after all. The worst thing that could happen wasn't as bad as what Jason did to her. Looking back, she knew Darius was right. Her husband terrorized her, forced her into submission, made her afraid of him. Before that, her mother crafted her into someone susceptible to him. Was that why he chose her? Did he see it in her, even then? He must have. Why else would he have been so enamored with her? Certainly, she knew she was attractive, desirable physically, but someone like him didn't want just a pretty face, he wanted an obedient slave to dominate.

Act scared, Connor told her. When he said it, she didn't think it would be hard. Yet, as she stood here, thinking about these things, she wasn't scared. There was no reason to be afraid. Death would free her from him forever. Pain was fleeting. She probably still could act scared if she wanted to, but she didn't. He was wrong anyway. Showing fear showed weakness, and the kind of man who would kill in cold blood for money or power fed on fear

She squared her shoulders and walked confidently to the door, every fiber of her being announcing to the wood that she was the Lady here. Because she was. Jason didn't make her a Lady, he didn't make her anything but a pet. Being a Lady, she did that all on her own, when she healed those with no hope and set them on a new path. That was nobility, that was using power wisely, that was something Jason would never understand, and it lived in her core. She stood with confidence and rapped on the door with the back of her hand.

In the time it took for someone to open the door, she felt no doubts creeping in. She was meant to be here right now, doing this. The man who answered – opening the door about halfway and looking unconcerned abut any threat she might present – didn't recognize her, he just looked her over skeptically and suspiciously. "What d'you want?"

"I have a message for your leader." Her voice was as clear and calm as she felt.

"Oh, yeah? What's that, then?"

Two thuds behind her, happening in quick succession, made her feel even bolder. No matter how little she liked the killing, those two sounds meant she truly had nothing at all to fear. One of her hands reached out and pushed the door open farther. "Challenge accepted." The words formed of their own accord; she didn't know what they'd be until they were out of her mouth, and the callousness of them horrified her.

An arrow whistled past her head to plunge into the man's neck. He gasped and fell back, hands pawing at the arrow. Connor and Shadow darted inside, Darius right behind them. Betsy stepped aside, putting her back to the wall in case anyone in there decided to throw or shoot anything at her.

She heard the men scuffling inside and didn't want to see any of it. That one man being shot right in front of her face was burned into her memory; she wouldn't forget it for a very long time. The way his eyes went wide with panic, the way he flailed and gagged, it was awful. Looking out this way, she saw the two men lying on the ground, one of them quite still. The other coughed and gurgled and gasped and reached for something.

Rae jogged past on her way to the door, thoughtlessly stabbing him in the chest with her thin blade, the effort not causing her to miss even half a step. “Good work.” She patted Betsy's arm, also without stopping, and went inside.

Trying to block out the sounds of battle and death, Betsy watched the one man give up and go limp. Right now wasn't the time to be worried about whether they deserved this fate or not. Perhaps she should simply be grateful these three were inclined to hand out quick deaths instead of making them suffer for long. That was what Rae did with her sword, really: she put the man out of his misery. If they had to die, it would be swift and with as little pain as possible.

Someone touched her arm, she turned to see Connor checking her over, pulling one of his thin gloves off with his teeth. He gently took her chin in his bare hand and brushed her cheek lightly with his thumb. It came away with a tiny smear of blood. “You did great.” He wiped his hand on his pants and stuffed it back into the glove. “We're moving in. Keep your eyes up, on us. Stay close and quiet.” He disappeared back inside without waiting for a response.

Keep her eyes up, yes, that sounded like a very good idea. She took a deep breath and stepped into the small house. Resisting the impulse to look all around the room, she focused on Darius and moved towards him. She tried not to think about the coppery smell of blood hanging in the air while dodging the upturned and broken furniture. Connor stood at the back, holding a finger to his lips while the cat pushed a spot on the wall. A hidden door swung open.

It opened into a dark, rough-cut stone tunnel with a mild downward slope. The light failed a short distance in, making it a gaping black void. Connor lifted a hand and mumbled something, then his glove glowed with a soft blue light. He and the cat ducked into the tunnel – it wasn't quite tall enough for him to walk upright. Betsy could probably manage it. Darius went to follow directly, but Rae put out a hand to stop him.

"He's checking for traps and alarms. Give him about ten paces before following and stay that far back. When he stops, you stop. I'll take the rear. Betsy, you go after Darius."

Darius nodded and peered down the tunnel. When it seemed Connor had gone far enough, he started in and had to walk almost doubled over. Betsy followed him, only just having to duck her head. She barely heard Rae's soft footfalls behind her. With Darius leading, Betsy saw nothing but his hulking form filling the passageway. They stopped three times. After the first time, she had to step carefully over a plate on the floor outlined in white chalk. The second time, she saw nothing.

The third time they stopped, Darius reached back and pushed her against the tunnel wall. "Door," he whispered, then she understood. Whoever or whatever lay on the other side of it, she'd only be in the way. Pressing herself against the wall and side stepping, she changed places with Rae and covered her eyes. A few long, tense seconds later, she heard the door swing open and boots hurry away from her. The smell of chicken soup filled the air.

A scuffle happened not far from the door, someone shouted. The call cut off abruptly. “I suppose this was a little too easy so far,” Connor said.

Darius growled at him. “Is this all just a game to you?”

“Yes. It's the 'let's not get killed' game. Come on. Speed will help us here.”

“Betsy, let's move,” Rae hissed. “Stay close to me.”

She pulled her hands down to see firelight. The tunnel emptied into a kitchen – the light and the smell came from the hearth where a large pot steamed over an open fire. Her eyes skipped over the two bloody bodies and fixed firmly on Rae's back as they all hurried out into the next room. She stopped when Rae did, and watched wide-eyed while the woman fired off three arrows in quick succession.

Only now, standing so close and in enough light, did she notice the bow had no string and Rae carried no quiver. She put her hand where it would be if she'd pulled a string back, an arrow appeared, she let go, it was fired. Rae had an enchanted bow.

The men fought, she heard it all, then they moved to the next room and fought more. Rae followed them, staying in the back and firing into what must be a mess. Sabetia heard Connor grunt. It sounded like pain and her feet carried her out there, past Rae and into chaos. That first man's shout must have alerted these people to something, they came to see what it was, and now they fought for their lives. Darius and Connor stood side by side, backs to Rae and

Betsy, as they wielded their blades with skill. There were so many of these brigands, at least eight of them. None fell to just one blow – it took three or four strikes for each brigand.

Connor clenched his jaw and moved stiffly. Whatever injuries he took, they were serious. While she moved towards him, determined to help, she saw one sword get through Darius's guard and plunge deeply into his leg, then get yanked back out. He staggered back a step, favoring the leg, but kept fighting, his sword flashing in the light provided by a fireplace.

She reached out for Connor and put her hand on his back, willing the wounds to close, demanding that her power, wherever it came from, heal him now. There was no time. It needed to flow swiftly and smoothly, because Darius couldn't wait for her to get to him. At her call, it came in a flood, rushing through her and into Connor, surprising them both. Darius limped to her protectively, keeping her from having to go to him, and she put her hand on his back next. Again, the power slammed into him, his wounds disappearing in a blink.

All of a sudden, she became very aware of the fighting all around her. The brigands regarded her as the greater threat now. There were so many – it seemed two more joined the fight with each one cut down. She may not have been afraid outside, but this situation terrified her. She ran back to Rae, dropped to the ground to get out of her line of sight, and crawled behind her. There, what she saw made her scream to get Rae's attention.

Three men crept down the hallway with blades out. One was that elf she remembered holding that very blade to Darius's throat. They hadn't attracted Rae's attention yet, but thanks to Betsy, the archer turned and fired at them. She missed the elf in front, he dove and rolled across the floor, pulling a smaller blade and throwing it at her. Rae was hit in the chest, the knife sank in just a short way and threw off her next shot. The elf slid down the hallway, taking Rae's attention.

That left the other man running up. Still on all fours, Betsy scrambled out of the way. The man hit Rae in the back, knocking her into the opposite door frame with a grunt. Betsy watched impotently while the woman yanked the elf's blade from her chest, flipped it around, and stabbed it into her attacker's thigh even as she reeled from the impact. More movement turned her head. She saw the elf get to his feet and hesitate for a moment before deciding to run for it.

He had her pendant, or could tell her who he sold it to.

Betsy clambered to her feet and chased after him. It was her responsibility to keep the pendant safe. She had no idea if the story her grandmother told her was true or not, but she wasn't going to be the one that let it slip through her fingers. Not after so many generations of her family managed to hold onto it.

He turned a corner, she followed. Just around it, a sharp pain and a pair of cruel, canted eyes told her she'd run right into his blade. Twisting it hurt horribly and made her groan, which he liked. “Fancy meeting you here, Lady Brexler. I have half a mind to take you with me right now.” He yanked the blade out. She squeaked in pain and grabbed for the wall as she slid slowly down it. “You're worth a lot, you know. Your husband would pay dearly for his little toy.”

"You have...mine," she gasped, one hand doing nothing more useful than pawing at his leg while the other clutched at her wound. "Give it back."

"Oh, the pendant? Yes, I know." He crouched to be face to face with her again, his voice smooth and dark and cold. Now she remembered where she saw him before. This was the same elf man she met in Jason's office, when she brought Shadow in. Jason knew this man and had dealings with him. "Silly and stupid to make a little girl the guardian of something so precious. These idiots have no real idea what your husband is up to. You don't, either. That's for the best."

While he spoke, he pulled the stone out, still on the gold chain, and dangled it in front of her face. She tried to grab for the pendant, but he batted her hand away easily. "Of course, he didn't even notice what was right under his nose. Humans. You all have the perceptive capabilities of blind thistles."

He shoved the pendant at the knife wound, and she groaned with the fresh new pain. Did he wedge it inside her? When he pulled it away again, her blood covered the stone. "I'm going to leave you here, I think, because you'd slow me down like this, and your friends will take care of you. We'll meet again, though, I promise. And when we do, if I understand the legends properly, it'll be to watch you die. Sleep well tonight, Lady, and enjoy what time you have left."

With that, he grinned and hurried away. She couldn't breathe, it was hard to think. All the things he just said, she had to remember them to tell the others. It was important. He had her pendant and said things that made her think he had to be stopped. They had to find him again. He would be long gone before they searched the hideout. Even now, he was probably already out a back way and running for it.

"Betsy!" Darius's deep voice boomed, echoing around so she couldn't tell where from.

Almost hyperventilating from a type of pain she wasn't used to, she tried to heal it, but nothing happened. She couldn't heal herself. That was incredibly unfair. "I'm here." Her voice was too soft and breathy, and she thought she might faint soon.

"Here she is." Rae's voice was distant but firm, then she knelt by Betsy's side. "Heal yourself, Betsy."

"I can't. It won't."

Rae took her hand and the power flowed out of her without even trying, wiping away Rae's wounds. The woman made a noise of surprise. "Seriously, you can heal me, but not you? That's all kinds of messed up."

Betsy nodded and managed a weak smile. "It's okay. Looks worse than it is."

"Right." She straightened and shouted, "Connor! Over here! You need to do your thing!"

"What thing?"

Rae squeezed her hand. "Damned if I understand it, but he can maybe heal you."

Darius got there first, dropping beside her and laying her out on the floor. The moment he touched her, she healed him, too. He didn't pause for a moment, didn't say anything, just tossed her cloak open and lifted her dress up to see how bad the wound was. He sucked in a sharp breath, which she took to mean he didn't like what he saw. Again, she was grateful to be wearing drawers under the dress. "You're going to be fine," he said.

"You're lying." It still hurt, so much.

"Try to calm down," Rae said, "take longer breaths. It'll hurt less. We're not going to let you bleed out like this."

"You'd let me bleed out...some other way?" Her eyes fluttered and she had a hard time focusing.

Darius made a strangled noise. "*Now* she jokes."

Connor skidded to a halt and took it all in quickly. He bent down and yanked his glove off with his teeth again, pressed that hand to the wound, making her squeal from renewed pain. And, of course, she healed him. It was such a gross insult. Something unexpected happened along with it, though. The power went into him, that was normal. Instead of just flowing like it usually did, he grabbed it and pulled, like instead of water, her power was a rope. When he got to the end of the rope, he turned it around and fed it back into her, pushing warmth on her, flooding her body with it. The pain left her – it couldn't stand up to that kind of an assault.

He sat back on his heels and looked like he'd just made a significant effort, but smiled with relief at her anyway. "How incredibly rude, you tried to leave without saying 'goodbye'."

"I'm sorry," she said as Darius helped her sit up. She felt weak like she always did after healing. "I had no idea that's how it feels to be healed. How did you do that?"

Connor's smile turned to a smirk. "I have a special talent I've squandered on being a shiftless layabout, if you ask my father. I can take the power others command and use it myself. It's not without risk, I can burn myself, and probably would have just now if it wasn't healing power I took from you. You're a lot stronger than I thought from last night."

Betsy didn't really understand, but she nodded anyway. "Are they all dead? Did you find Myra?"

Darius's mouth went thin. "Myra's body is in a back room. The men are all dead or fled. How did you get hurt?"

"One of them got past me." Rae stood up, pointed her short sword down the hall. "They flanked us." It was for the best that Rae answered, because Betsy was too busy trying not to cry to answer. Certainly, she expected Myra to be dead, but having it confirmed was horrible.

"It was that elf. The one that held you yesterday and took my pendant. I saw him at the house once, too."

Darius scowled. He really did have an impressive scowl. There must have been a time in his life when he found himself with reasons to scowl often before she met him. "He's more of a bastard than other elves I've met."

Betsy sniffled. "I want to see her."

The three of them traded looks, giving her the impression they all thought that would be a mistake. "Betsy," Darius said. He offered her a hand to help her up while searching for words.

She pushed his hand aside and got to her feet herself, tears still sliding down her cheeks. "I'm not leaving her here." Wiping a hand across her face, she looked around to try to figure out which way to go. The back was probably that way. She hurried off to find her best friend, not caring about whatever they thought she shouldn't see. Behind her, she heard Darius call her name again and ignored it.

The doors were all thrown open already. She peeked into the rooms as she went by, and stopped dead the last one. It was awful. Stopping in the doorway, she leaned against it and wept for Myra. Darius brushed past her to pull her friend down and wrap her in a blanket.

"I'll carry her."

"We should bury her."

Darius sighed. "It would be better for her family if we leave her where the local lord will find her. He'll see to her properly."

He was right and she knew it. Nodding, she followed him as he led the way back out. All she could think about was how gentle Myra was with her, how she tended to her misery. When Myra needed that in return, where was Betsy? Sleeping safely in a temple and buying new clothes. Connor and Rae said nothing and didn't get in her way as she knelt beside the body to say goodbye. Words clung to the back of her throat, and all she wound up doing was kissing her friend's cold forehead.

"Betsy," Connor said gently as she settled behind him again on the horse, "I don't want to press right now, but we aren't sure where to go from here. If we're going to find that elf, we need you to tell us what you know about him."

She wiped her face again and took a few deep breaths to calm herself. Tears wouldn't bring Myra back, nothing could. "He had my pendant and said he knew it was special. Made it sound like Jason knew something about it, but never realized the pendant was part of it. I don't understand any of this." If she told them the elf threatened her, Darius would probably have some kind of fit or need to hit something. She just left that off, it wasn't necessary. He already stabbed her, they could figure out he meant to kill her eventually.

Connor twisted in his saddle. "I know the Earl is into something, I just couldn't ever figure out what it is. He uses a code or abbreviations I can't figure out in his papers. What do you know about the pendant?"

"Only the story my grandmother told me when she gave it to me. She said it held the spirit of a demon and made me promise to protect it. If the sword it came from is ever reassembled, the demon will be set free."

"Sounds like we need to visit a lorekeeper." Rae's voice was too light for Betsy to bear right now. She buried her face in Connor's back, trying to block it out.

Connor slumped in the saddle. "Please, no, by the Mother Goddess, don't make me go to her."

"Oh," Rae laughed, "you like her and you know it. You'd jump her if she shut up long enough with her nose not in a book."

"Since that'll never happen," Connor grumbled, "it's not really a concern."

"We should get going." Darius said, his voice sharp.

The horses started moving and Betsy turned enough to watch the land go by. The boring repetition of rolling hills and trees and farmland in the distance soothed her. She remembered Myra sewing a tear in a doll's dress so Angelica didn't notice, washing and kissing her knee when she scraped it, dressing the cuts on her back to make them heal swifter. All that time, the only thing she did in return was...nothing. She was never going to do nothing again.

Straightening in her seat, she wiped her face again and patted Connor's shoulder. "Who's this lorekeeper?"

Riding beside them, Rae grinned. "Her name is Evi. She's sweet, but Connor can't stand her." (Connor huffed an annoyed little snort.) "She remembers everything, and I mean *everything*. If she's heard it, read it, seen it, or thought it, she knows it. Some folks call her the Archive because of it. Talks a lot, easily distracted by cats and chocolate."

"I've never heard of her," Darius said skeptically.

Rae shrugged. "I've never been to Aithemor. What's your point?"

"That's where we were going. Caitlin must be terribly upset that I didn't show up." Betsy frowned, reflecting she'd done nothing for Caitlin, too. There was nothing she could do about that right now, though. "Do you think the sword is real?"

"The elf does. It sounds like your husband does, too." Connor shrugged. "If they're willing to kill for it, then it's at least that real."

"Good point," Darius said. "If they've been working on it for a while, I wonder how much progress they've made."

"Enough for the elf to know about the pendant," Rae said.

How could he have learned about that? "You know, Myra was there when my grandmother told me the story. She was fixing my hair."

Rae and Darius both stared at her with very similar expressions of contemplation. They looked at each other, then at Connor, and Darius spoke first. "It may have come up while she was hiring them.

I don't think they had time to torture information out of her and get the pendant here. The elf must have had people watching for it to appear. Makes me think he was slumming it with these men, just hanging around until he could get what he wanted. And he's apparently been working on it for a while, if you saw him first two years ago."

"With that much time to work, he may already have the other pieces of the sword." Connor reached over and patted Betsy's leg, which she didn't like, but said nothing about. "This is sounding more and more like it's up our alley." As it turned out, Evi would be found in Ar-Toriess, so they ran no real risk of encountering the Earl's men on the way. It was an odd coincidence, being the place Betsy was headed when those men attacked her carriage.

Ar-Toriess was not the same type of city as Rennsen. Originally founded by the first Middyn, a man who actually bore the name, it was envisioned as a haven for scholars and sages. As time passed, it grew and attracted the best and brightest of those who sought knowledge as their passion. Long ago, the High King determined it would be charged with holding as many of the scrolls and books and papers of knowledge as could be transported there, available to all those willing to make the journey and treat them with respect and care.

Here, among this cluster of tall and wide buildings stuck in the middle of nothing, young mages with patronage or wealth traveled to study with masters in their gleaming towers. Scholars flocked in to immerse themselves in the grand stone library vault, among the words written an age or more ago. It was a place where the roads were paved with a strange, smooth and seamless black material, not cobblestones or bricks (or gravel like the main road they took to get here).

Little space was wasted on anything but knowledge. Who knew how these people fed themselves. The only animals Betsy saw were horses. Shadow even seemed strange as Bonbon and Clover's hooves clopped down the streets; Betsy saw no birds, no cats, no dogs, nothing, not even the squirrels she sometimes spooked in the gardens. Greenery was notably absent, as well, which probably explained the lack of animals.

In place of trees and shrubs and grass and parks, Ar-Toriess had sculptures. Some were statues of people or animals, others had more opaque shapes, things Betsy didn't know how to interpret. The people themselves didn't seem especially unusual, though none of them wore the clothing of laborers or the poor. Many went about in uniforms that spoke of working as servants, a few wore clothes Betsy would associate with moderate wealth – finely woven cottons, silk blends, and furs with gold and lace trims. Like the rest of the four kingdoms, Ar-Toriess appeared to be inhabited by all humans.

Save that one elf man. It gnawed on her mind, that an elf should come this far. The stories all painted them as in love with their own land, Myveshar, so much they rarely ventured from it. Why did that one man come here? Was it because of the sword? Had he discovered the legend and somehow found Jason as a willing patron in the search for it? She had no idea how such clandestine matches were made, whether it was about finding an artifact or selling children, or anything else. Myra, poor, sweet Myra knew enough to find someone who could attack a carriage. Maybe it was that elf who found her.

"This is the place." Connor's voice stirred Betsy from her thoughts. She discovered they were in front of a stables as impressive as anything else around here. It had unusual lines and curves that spoke of someone designing for form as well as function, and with enough money to make it happen. A pity Jason never got anyone to do such things for him. But then, he probably preferred the squared nature of his mansion.

Connor helped her down from the horse and led the group into the building attached to the stables while a young man tended to their mounts. The floors were not marble or stone as Betsy expected, but warm, honey brown wood that made the place feel homey despite its vast size. Even this small entry chamber was large enough for twenty or thirty people to stand comfortably. A pleasant man sat at a large desk, Connor asked him for Evi and was directed to someplace called 'the Rotunda'.

As they walked through wide hallways and up wide stairs lined with paintings and sculptures of all sorts, Betsy tried to see everything. She finally found plants in the form of hanging baskets overflowing with small flowers and tiny ivies, and boxes of herbs filling the corridors with their sweet or savory scents.

Finally, they came to the place that must be the Rotunda, a large round room with a dome overhead made of thick panes of yellow glass. The outer walls were covered with books and scrolls on shelves, another ring in the center had the same. The shelves went up high enough they had rolling ladders hung in several places. In the ring between them, numerous armchairs had been scattered about, all of them upholstered in muted shades of brown, with polished wooden tables between.

The room had several occupants, all dressed differently than the two types outside. Some wore very plain tunics and trews, in shades of brown and white. These were all young people, in their teens, working hard at one thing or another, surrounded with papers and scribbling furiously. The others had a red-brown robe over similar clothes, with no sign of taking notes about them. These people looked over the materials in a way that seemed more idle.

And then there was one woman, probably near twenty years old, in a lavender shirt and brown leather pants, both fitting her snugly enough to see she was fit and trim without being muscled. Her light brown hair was braided in a complicated fashion atop her head, like a crown. At the moment, her slightly elongated nose was buried in a thick tome held just far enough from her face so she could turn the pages, which she did at an alarmingly speedy rate as the group of them approached. Her hazel eyes darted across and down the page so fast Betsy couldn't imagine how she got anything out of it.

Connor cleared his throat when he stood close enough to not bother too many other people by attracting her attention. "Miss Evi, I wonder if we could have a little of your time, please?"

She looked up, curiosity plain on her face, then broke into a wide, pleased smile. "Connor!" Dropping the book on the nearest table, she jumped up to wrap her arms around him in a warm, enthusiastic embrace. "It's been ages, and you brought Rae!" She let go of him before he really had a chance to return the hug, which seemed to suit him just fine, and hugged Rae, who was much more amused by it and returned the embrace. “How have you been? You know, I've run across so many things you might be interested in, like the history of the kobold warren of-”

“Evi.” Connor said her name impatiently to cut her off. “We're here about something specific. It's important and time sensitive.”

“Of course it is,” Evi said with a little wave, not at all offended by his curtness. “And who is this? Oh my, such a tall, strong man you've brought along, and a lovely lady. I'm Evi. Of course, he won't bother to introduce anyone to anyone - that would be polite.” She put a small emphasis on the last word, probably meaning it as teasing.

Betsy blinked a few times and looked around, surprised no one tried to shush Evi. They all seemed to be trying very hard to ignore her. One young man at a table held his head as if the sound of her voice caused him agony. “Betsy,” she said quietly as an introduction. “This is Darius.” Along with her gesture, she noticed Darius was faintly amused by the woman.

“I'm so pleased to meet you!” She took Betsy's hand in both of hers and squeezed it in a friendly, familiar way. “Connor hardly ever stops by, and when he does, he so rarely brings new friends.” Letting go, she took Betsy's arm by looping her own through it and led them out of the Rotunda, back to the stairs. “All he ever wants is information, the greedy cad.” She leaned conspiratorially towards Betsy and lowered her voice. “I think he secretly wants me to write down his exploits so everyone will someday know exactly how much dashing and daring he's accomplished for Myredren. I haven't decided if I'm going to or not. We'll see. But you're new, you have to tell me everything about yourself. Where are you from?"

Evi said all of this swiftly, with what seemed an abnormally small amount of breath behind it. Betsy waited a few seconds before saying anything, not sure if the question was actually one to be answered or not. "Rennsen, and we came because something has happened that we don't understand. We were hoping you might know something about the subject." Sensing she might not get another chance to explain for a while, she delved directly into it. "My grandmother told me a story about a pendant several years ago, and it seems like it might actually have some truth to it." Without a pause, she dove into the story, relating it as well as she could remember.

They went down one floor and wandered into an indoor garden full of flowers and butterflies and ladybugs. Evi sat them down on a stone bench and looked thoughtful for a short time after the story was finished. "It sounds a lot like the legends about Kailesce, who was a woman, not a man. She lived a very long time ago, before Clynnidh, when the four kingdoms were still full of petty warlords squabbling over women and land. There are very few stories from that time; most of them only written down after the Order of Middyn began spreading literacy throughout the lands, so it's hard to say what's true and what's fiction. However, this tale is close enough to that of Kailesce that I'm thinking there might be at least some truth to it."

Betsy nodded, a little in awe of Evi. "That name is so close to my father's, Kayles. Can it be coincidence?"

"Probably not." Evi's eyes lit up with excitement. "In fact, it's probable that your family was given stewardship of this, and it passed from woman to woman since then, along with the story. They probably changed the gender on purpose, so the women who married into your family, the only ones that would've kept the name, didn't get any wild ideas about running off to be heroes or anything. You know how men can be." Evi gave a little roll of her eyes. "Can't have girls wishing for that.

"Anyway, giving it to the wives was brilliant, really. Put a jewel like that in a man's hand and he tries to protect it by locking it away. There's always someone like Connor who will find it. Give it to a woman? She'll put it in her jewelry box and wear it openly. Hide it in plain sight. Brilliant." She sighed wistfully. "You have it, then?"

Betsy looked down and shook her head. "It was taken from me, by someone who knew what it was."

"Oh no!" Evi bounced to her feet, truly upset by the notion. "We have to get it back!"

"We?" Connor sounded tired. "No, Evi, you're not coming with us."

She pouted at him. "But you have to let me see it! I need to see it, Connor, and record what happens. I've never seen anything like that outside of a book. All I'm asking for is to come along so my new friend Betsy and I can talk about her family and discover clues!" Betsy smiled at being referred to that way, it was sweet.

Connor narrowed his eyes and slumped his shoulders. "Evi. You're a sage, a bookworm. You don't have any idea how to handle what we do."

"Knowledge is a useful tool." Rae barely suppressed a grin.

Glancing over his shoulder, Connor gave her a glare of pure

venom. "We already have our hands full protecting Betsy, which we're happy to do because she's not useless."

"I'm not useless! I know all kinds of things about camping and cooking and anatomy and geography. I know all the maps for the entire world, and you know I do."

"We only have two horses," Connor said smugly. "And there aren't horses for sale here. Even if there were, I don't have enough money on hand to get one that can keep up with ours."

Evi smiled brightly. "Your father has one. It's a fine specimen, and I even know how to ride it." She took Betsy's hand and pulled her up to stand. "Come on, let's go see Moralan." Before Connor could protest (which he definitely intended to do from the look of sheer agony Evi just inspired in him), she ran off, Betsy in tow. She found herself as helpless to resist this time as she had been with Caitlin and hurried along behind. Darius missed when he tried to grab one of them. It looked like Rae was too busy laughing now to care about the two women dashing away.

They practically flew down the stairs and out through the grand double doors. Betsy got the distinct impression everyone was used to Evi doing odd things and just accepted it. They hurried down the street, turned a corner, went up another, and did this a few more times with no sign of Evi slowing down or getting winded. Betsy kept up as best she could. She was tremendously grateful when Evi stopped and went to a door.

Although the city appeared to be made of grand edifices and towers, this entire street had more normal houses, all of them nice and with small gardens behind fences. More than half had signs on those fences, proclaiming what she assumed were specialties. Moralan Rovito's listed several things she didn't recognize the names of, but one stuck out: tescher seeds, the very thing Caitlin wanted her to bring. Was he the man she was supposed to see about that? What an odd coincidence.

Not pausing to knock, Evi opened the door and walked right in, pulling Betsy along behind her. “Moralan!” Evi finally let go of Betsy's hand and started wandering around the house, calling the name out a few times. Inclined to be a good guest, Betsy shut the door behind herself and waited, panting from the run, in the entry. It was a small room with hooks to leave cloaks and coats, a thin rug for wiping off shoes and boots, and another door standing open in Evi's wake.

Connor had to know where this place was and she felt certain that, even if Evi forgot about her, the others would be along soon. She heard voices deeper in the house, Evi's high pitched one and a lower one that sounded a lot like Connor, but couldn't make out what they said. After a short time, boots ran back towards her, it sounded like they came downstairs. Evi appeared in the doorway, excited and a little breathless.

“Betsy, I'm so sorry! I didn't mean to leave you here.” She offered Betsy a hand and pulled her along again, taking her up a flight of quiet wooden stairs. This house belonged to a man in the same way Jason's house belonged to him. All the decorating was minimal and had a masculine feel to it, in wood and black and dark blue with white trim. At the top of the stairs, a man stood watching them. He was strikingly handsome and a near copy of Connor. This version had gray hair that made him look distinguished and stately, and something about him spoke of power, where Connor felt more like danger.

"This is Betsy," Evi said proudly, like she presented a puppy in the hopes of being able to keep her. "Betsy, this is Moralan. He's very nice, and my sponsor here."

"A pleasure, Betsy." Moralan took her hand and kissed the back in such a perfect rendition of the courtly gesture she reacted to it, offering him a smile and a light bow of her head. He seemed to notice and returned the smile.

"We're going on our adventure together. She's ever so sweet, and her family has a secret, a long history they've been protecting for ages. It's all so wonderfully exciting. I can't believe I get to be part of this! But someone has to write it all down afterward. After all, those who come after us are doomed to repeat our mistakes if no one ever documents them, and I'm sure that with Connor around, there will be lots of mistakes, of all kinds."

"Probably spectacular ones," Moralan observed dryly. How he managed to get a word in when Evi hadn't stopped to breathe yet was a mystery, but perhaps knowing her for a while afforded such insights. "I expect he'll be along soon to collect you ladies?"

"Oh, I'm sure. You know how he is." Evi kept smiling cheerfully through all of this and pointed down the hall. "Will you keep Betsy from being all alone while I get my things? We're going to be traveling, I mustn't go unprepared. Anything could happen."

Moralan chuckled. "Of course. Take your time."

Evi squealed with glee and ran down the hall, disappearing

through a door.

“I take it she lives here with you?” Betsy followed Moralan into a sitting room with books lining one wall and three well-worn chairs.

He gestured for her to take what looked to be the most comfortable of his chairs and sat in one facing her. “Originally, I claimed she was my daughter to get her into the school here. Now there's no need but she still keeps her room anyway. A creature of habit, our Evi, no matter how enthralled she is by the idea of change.”

“I expect you're Connor's father?”

Moralan sighed heavily. “Yes, for all that means to him. I expect you're his new conquest?”

Betsy blushed light pink. “No, not at all. I'm married.” She left him, but no matter how much she wished it wasn't true, in the eyes of the Mother Goddess, they were still one.

He snorted. “I wasn't aware that ever stopped him before.”

Her blush darkened to a dusky pink. “It stops me.”

“I commend you for your restraint. Very few women seem to have any of it around him.”

“You don't have a very high opinion of him?”

Moralan pursed his lips, he thought about that for a short time. “How well do you know him?”

“Not very. We just met yesterday. He's- I...” Betsy thought over everything that happened since then and wasn't sure what she actually knew of him. “He rescued me by accident. I've dragged him into something I didn't mean to.”

He laughed. “Imagine, that boy suckered into some mad quest by a beautiful woman."

Betsy didn't quite know how to respond to that, so she left it alone. "Are you a scholar like Evi?"

"No one is like Evi, but no. I'm a mage. We – Evi and I, that is – came here a few years after Connor's mother died, when he was, oh, thirteen, I think, in the hopes I could get him to pursue magery by surrounding him with books and such things." Moralan's face fell into a mild scowl. "It didn't work, obviously. I couldn't even get him to join us here, let alone listen or learn. Said he'd rather live on the street than put up with me. Since then, he's wasted what talent he has on cheap parlor tricks to impress women not worth impressing."

Either Moralan didn't know everything Connor was up to, or he'd been asked not to discuss it. Whichever it was, Betsy still didn't know what to say. Her own path was laid out before her a long time ago, and she never questioned it until yesterday. Connor was clearly a very different sort of person than her. "Maybe you can help, then. Have you ever heard of an object being used to imprison a demon somehow? It was done through some sort of dying curse, as far as I know."

Moralan looked at her curiously. The expression reminded her of Connor. "Do you know anything about demons?"

"No."

"Most people don't." He sat back and went pensive. "Unfortunately, they aren't known for being trustworthy, so it's difficult to know what's fact and what isn't, but the basics have been confirmed. Our world sits in a vast sea of something called Aether. Some of us are born with the ability to manipulate it – that's all it takes to make a mage. That's another subject entirely, though. Suffice to say it is the source of our power. It is also the source of other things. It's very likely the various gods are manifestations of the Aether. But, I see I'm confusing you, so I'll stick to the subject at hand.

"As near as we can tell, the stars you see when you look up at night are the lights of souls between lives. When your soul leaves you body at death, it passes out of our realm and into a place *between*, where it waits. They cluster together for some reason, and bigger clusters make brighter lights. Now, the Aether lies between our world and the stars, like a great ocean. Most make it to the other side, but a few get stuck. These ones that get stuck go mad, and are what we call 'demons'. They're not of the world, and have no place. Their motivations vary, depending on what mattered to them in life, but all despise mortals, for we've managed to hold onto what matters most of all, which is our sanity.

"Getting back to your question, yes, it is quite possible for a demon to be bound to an object, or even a person. They've been stuck once and are susceptible to it again and again. Destroying a soul, even a damaged one, is impossible so far as I know, so this is really the only way to stop them once they've managed to return to the world."

Betsy didn't really understand all of this, but the main point was that the legend had a good chance of being true. "Does it happen a lot?"

"I suppose that depends on how you define 'a lot'." Moralan shrugged. "Evi probably knows dozens of tales of demons being defeated, and each defeat would have to correspond to a demon being imprisoned one way or another. Logically, we would be drowning in such objects by now, though, so someone must have figured something better out at some point."

Now she knew it was possible, only one other question needed to be answered. "How would a person free one of them?"

Moralan pursed his lips and gave Betsy a speculative look. "It would be specific to the prison itself, and the method used to bind the demon to it. Blood is usually involved somehow." The man had more to say, but stopped when the front door opened, loudly enough to be heard upstairs.

Connor's voice rang out, sounding unenthusiastic and perhaps sarcastic. "Hi, Dad, I'm home. Just stopping to pick up my women, and I'll be out of your way again."

Blood. The elf man took her blood. Betsy stood up, pale. "I'm not 'his'." Why she felt it was important to be clear on that with Moralan, she had no idea, it just was.

"He said it that way for my benefit, not yours." Raising his voice, he answered his son, "They're here and safe." He then pointed down the hallway. "Evi's room is the second on the left. It was nice to meet you, Betsy." Picking up a book from his desk, he offered it to her. "Give this to Evi, it's for emergencies. Please do your part to bring Evi home when this thing is over, whatever it is."

"It was nice to meet you, Moralan. Thank you for your time and the information. I understand Evi is like a daughter to you, and I'll do my best for her." Taking the book with a small curtsy, she went for the door he said and found a room she liked a great deal. Unlike the rest of the house, the dominant color was purple, leaning towards the lighter shades. Evi's things were neatly arranged, yet still somehow chaotic. She had books and books and more books, bins full of clothing and things, all of it scattered in a manner that seemed haphazard, but Evi navigated it with ease.

As she was about to knock on the open door to announce herself, Evi straightened and hefted up a backpack straining to hold everything she'd crammed into it. A scrollcase stuck out of the top at an odd angle and a beige shirt sleeve hung out the other side. A pouch dangled from the bottom. "This will be the most exciting thing to ever happen to me, except for all the things before we came here." Her eyes bright and cheeks flushed, she reminded Betsy of herself following in Jason's wake at her party for that first night. Such a foreboding thought.

Chapter 10

"I don't know the specifics of the curse, no one knows that, just that the demon was supposed to be bound to the gemstone." Evi rode happily on her horse, a small bay gelding the slim sage rode alone. Connor rode beside her with Betsy, Darius and Rae followed a few paces behind. "But, I can tell you that the sword itself wasn't just a sword, it was an enchanted blade. Kailesce was a swordswoman of exceptional skill, and some accounts claim she had enough power of her own to be regarded as a god, of sorts. One of the stories recounts her part in the raising of the Freistfell Mountains, though the tale conflicts with dwarven accounts of their god Thurenir's creation of them, so who can really say? Maybe she made the original range and Thurenir made them as grand and majestic as they are today."

"The sword, Evi." Connor jammed the words in when the sage paused to take a breath.

"The sword," Evi echoed after sticking her tongue out at Connor, "broke into six pieces that flew across the world. So the stories say. Let me tell you something strange about it, though. The original scroll of the story is a basic outline, just a two foot long parchment, cracked on the edges, probably written not long after it actually happened, maybe even by an eyewitness. Along with those notes, there were scribbles on the side, just a handful of words: 'reflections of her soul' with a question mark and 'flashing in the sun'. These were written at the end, probably meant to refer to the the pieces of the sword itself."

"Delightful." Connor didn't sound remotely delighted. "Notes about how to poetically refer to them. How does that help us?"

Evi smiled like a cat with cream. "Curiously, neither of those descriptions were used in any of the tales, not even the one done by the same hand as the outline."

"And this means...?"

"Connor," Evi said like she was disappointed in him, "those are both the types of turn of phrase poets and epic writers use a lot. There's no reason not to use them from the writer's point of view."

"Does it have to be a guessing game?" Connor rolled his eyes and harrumphed. "If you have something to say, spit it out. We haven't even decided where to go next yet, and we're almost to the city's edge."

"Isn't it obvious?" Evi pouted at him.

Betsy squinted a little and had a thought. "You think he decided not to use them...because...they were too descriptive? Would lead someone to them too easily and thus lead to the demon being freed?"

"Yes, exactly!" Evi gave Betsy a pleased smile of pure joy. "I knew you were going to be a good friend, Betsy. Don't you see, those are clues about the sword pieces!"

"Why would we need clues about that?" Betsy frowned and tried to puzzle it out for herself, but she really had no other ideas now. "Aren't they pieces of a sword? Clues about where they might be found would be more helpful."

"There are clues to the locations, of course. It would help if we knew which ones have already been found. But, more importantly, I don't think they *are* just pieces of a sword. It was enchanted, remember. It could do all sorts of things." Evi bounced more than the horse's gait should cause. "That much magic in one place being destroyed would have to have some sort of side effect. So they aren't just hunks of metal, they have to be something else, something that could reflect a soul and flash in the sun, but not like steel!"

Connor didn't respond to Evi, though she looked eagerly at him. Betsy thought she wanted validation or agreement from him. "That's very clever, Evi. What could they be, though? What can reflect a soul?" She thought of what Moralan said, but didn't know of anything that reflected stars, specifically. A mirror could reflect them, of course, but it could reflect anything. Even a soul?

"Well, I don't know, but it's still all so exciting!" Evi sat back in her seat, still smiling brightly.

Betsy frowned more, thinking about mirrors. They always surrounded her at the two places she'd called home, so she could be sure to look her best for her parents, then for her suitors, then for her husband. None of them were special, though, and she shook her head. It was probably a stupid idea anyway. "What will we do now?"

They reached the edge of the city, where they had the choice to go east, west, or south. Connor stopped and looked out over the land, though there wasn't much to see. "Back to Rennsen," he finally said, and started his horse that way. "That's where Rae and I are based. We have a place to stay there, and people we can ask to look into things for us. We'll put the word out about the pendant and get some sleep and decent food while that churns. Maybe someone will know something, or have heard of this Kailesce legend thing. Worst case, that elf comes looking for us and we kill him. Problem solved."

Betsy frowned, but this didn't seem like a good time to argue about killing again. Not after what Darius said earlier. She didn't like it, but this world didn't seem to be a place that cared very much what she liked or didn't like.

Hours later, most of it spent with Evi chattering idly about things Betsy didn't really understand or care about, they rode in through the gates of Rennsen. Darius covered his face with a scarf and hood to hide his identity. Betsy only had to face Connor with her hood up to keep from being recognized. They went for another half an hour or so, then dropped the horses off at that inn again and stopped inside for dinner (Rae paid). After that, Connor and Rae left Betsy, Darius, and Evi in a small apartment with one bedroom while they went out.

"You must tell me everything," Evi demanded gleefully as soon as the door was shut. She took Betsy's arm and pulled her to the couch to sit beside her. "Why are you mixed up with Connor? What do you know about all this? Who's he," she pointed at Darius without leaving time for the questions to be answered. "What's the story? I must know if I'm going to help, and I want to help, so you have to tell me or I'll be forced to come up with my own ideas and then who knows where we'll wind up?" There, she stopped and looked expectantly at Betsy.

With a little nod, Betsy began. "Darius is my...friend." If she was going to stay away from Jason, she needed to act like it, and the first step was not to call Darius a 'bodyguard'. From there, she related the story of how she was taken and Connor and Rae rescued her, and they went to that stronghold, all of which Evi listened to raptly, not interrupting with even a single little sound. Somewhere in there, Darius heated water and made tea from what Connor kept in the little kitchen. "Moralan told me that it's actually possible the pendant could have a demon bound to it."

"If anyone would know, it's him." Evi nodded with an air of authority. "He's a very smart man and Connor is stupid for not listening to him. Then again, Moralan is dumb for not listening to his son, so it goes both ways. They're such men. No offense to you, Darius."

The big man shrugged from his perch at the small kitchen table. "None taken. What I really want to know is how the Earl got mixed up in this. I don't remember seeing the elf before, so I don't know how long he's been involved, and I certainly have no idea why he got into it. I can say the Earl does have a varied collection of business partners, so I suppose it could have happened through them. The elf is a strange piece of the puzzle, though."

"He is," Evi agreed. "Everything I've read about elves paints them as devoted to their own lands and uninterested in anything outside it, except what threatens them. A demon stored away safely doesn't seem like much of a threat. All the tales suggest that an elf, upon finding such a thing, would try to persuade the owner to part with the object in order to better safeguard it, but not to unleash the demon, not to use it."

"Is it so impossible to believe one elf might be different from the rest," Betsy said, "that one man might be despicable?"

"Well, no, of course not." Evi took a sip of her tea and stared off at nothing. "The stories are naturally full of people who were evil despite their natural tendencies, so I suppose it's not so strange after all. There's probably an elven angle to his madness, though. Maybe he has revenge on his mind for something, and thinks he needs the sword to exact it. There's a tale just like that, actually, now that I think about it, only it was a dwarf who felt he had to prove himself worthy of his father's anvil because of all the horrible things the father told him about how pathetic he was, and then an earthquake killed him and the son went on a quest to find a way to bring his father back from the dead, which, of course, only happens in epic tales of redemption. In the end, his efforts turned his father into a revenant and the son unleashed the demon to fight the revenant for him. It's a tragic story and the hero is really an anti-hero."

"How does that relate to this?" Darius drummed his fingers on the table, staring at Evi.

"Never mind," Betsy said hastily, not wanting to deal with a tense silence for the rest of the night. "What matters right now is that we don't know what the pieces of the sword look like or how the demon in the pendant will get free. I can't believe it's just simple to do, or it would have happened by accident by now."

"Well," Evi said, her attention on Betsy now, "It was supposed to have killed Kailesce by puncturing her heart. Whether that's what actually happened or it's metaphorical, the point is that it was bathed in blood to form the binding in the first place, so blood would be a necessary component of the unbinding. So, putting the sword together would only be part of it. The pendant itself would probably have to be primed with blood of some kind, and then the sword, once put together, might have to pierce someone's heart. That's a guess, mind you."

Betsy went pale as Evi spoke, and one hand went to clutch her side where the elf stabbed her. That was what he meant. It had to be. He bathed the pendant in her blood, then he said he would kill her later. How many pieces of the sword did they have? How much longer did she have before an elf, maybe bent on revenge, came to stab her through the heart with a sword belonging to her own ancestor? A shiver ran down her spine.

Darius noticed, she was sure of it. "I keep wondering why he stabbed you, Betsy. There was no reason to. He could have grabbed you and dragged you along, or killed you, or even just thrown you into the wall. He's a strong man, and you're not very difficult to overpower physically. There was no need to stab you, none at all, especially not like that."

"He stabbed you? You didn't say that!" Evi, alarmed, gripped Betsy's arm and pulled until their eyes met. "Oh my goodness, you're Kailesce's descendent, her blood runs through your veins! Did he take any of it?"

Betsy looked down at the mug in her hands and didn't want to answer. Darius said, "I see." He looked down at his own mug. "So, we can be sure that one of the steps is complete."

Evi's face went through several expressions rapidly until it seemed she understood. "If that works..." She gave Betsy a sympathetic look. "We'll stop him from hurting you again."

"Yes," Darius said firmly, "we will."

Such a promise struck Betsy as foolish, but she mustered a smile and said, "Thank you." Evi hugged her tightly and there wasn't much else to say. The scholar got up and washed their mugs. Darius made them take the bedroom while he laid himself out on the couch. Betsy fell asleep listening to Evi's breathing, warmed by her new friend snuggled up to her and haunted by the idea of being stabbed through the heart.

She opened her eyes to find herself walking down a road shrouded in silvery mist. Nothing marked it as being any particular one, it was just a well-used packed earth path edged with tall grasses. Though the grass was green, the air carried enough of a chill to be late winter. Her breath came out in white puffs of vapor, and she felt the cold to her bones. Looking down, she discovered she wore only that blue robe Jason made her parade around the house in. Hugging herself, she started moving to warm up.

Hurrying through the mist, she kept going forward, hoping to find someplace warm, or at least something to bundle up in. A thin piece of satin wasn't much better than nothing at all. She pushed herself to a jog in the hopes it would help. The scenery didn't change at all, it remained shrouded in fog and silent save for her footfalls. This went on until she had a sudden inspiration to run off the path. It might hurt her feet, but it felt like the right thing to do.

A sharp turn took her into the bank of fog where she could see nothing at all. Her feet squelched in thin mud, grass blades brushed against her legs and robe, and she smelled damp earth. Soon, her feet splashed in warm water and plunged onward, going until she could only reach the bottom with the tips of her toes, her face the only part of her above the surface. She didn't know how to swim; she'd never been in water outside of a bathtub.

After taking a deep breath, she ducked under and pushed her way forward as quickly as she could, knowing she needed to reach the other side. Her feet dug into the silt at the bottom, propelling her forward. Her body felt the press of the water, the need to surface and take in air. Still she pressed on, not knowing how to get up there, up to the light. Just when she thought she might explode, the bottom sloped up and she burst out, into warm air, into summer.

Soft, low grass met the water's edge. Tall oaks and maples swayed in a light breeze with hints of buildings farther up the shallow slope. She looked back and saw it was an island or peninsula – no, she knew it was an island – surrounded by a lake covered with mist about thirty feet from the shore. The mist went up as far as she could see, impossibly high, and there was only one place she could be where that made any kind of sense: Niwlynys. Somehow, she got through the mist surrounding the mysterious island of the Disciples, who were supposed to be the only ones able to manage such a thing.

What did this mean? Was she called to become a Disciple? No, that couldn't be, she was married in the eyes of the Mother Goddess, and the Disciples weren't allowed to ever marry any man. They were chosen no older than the age of twelve, and there was no such thing as coming to the path later in life. Confused, she found her eyes drawn down to see something glitter in the bright sunlight. A golden cord lay in the grass, just like the one that appeared at her wedding. The wire basket for the stone hung from it, empty. She crouched down and picked it up.

Intent on finding something to explain all of this, she stood again and walked away from the water. The trees were beautiful, so much moreso than she ever remembered any being before. Each tree was an expression of a perfect specimen of its type, each leaf a perfect leaf. No two looked the same, yet they all somehow seemed to be the epitome of their type. The grass, too, was strangely surreal, as were the tiny white flowers dotting it here and there.

She stumbled into a clearing filled by an open-air smithy, one with no smith to be seen. The forge sat silent and cold, the tools all hung or placed neatly on racks and shelves. Except for one hammer. Betsy walked up and hefted the hammer in her empty hand, not sure what to do with it until she spied a spike braced in the ground, sharp end up. Thinking of the answer put her next to the spike and she draped the cord over it.

With the hammer in her hand, she wasn't sure what she wanted. Here was a chance to break this bond in the eyes of the Mother Goddess. She knew that's what this was, but was that right? Was it her choice? More importantly, how would this change anything? He wasn't going to just ignore her if he saw her again because she broke the cord. The second she fell under his control again, he would treat her as his wife. This wasn't even the real cord – she was dreaming.

With that realization, she found her courage and swung the hammer, smashing it into the spike and cutting the cord in two. Both pieces fell to the ground and she stepped back, away from them. He only had what hold over her she allowed him to have. That was true, had to be true. A flash of light caught her eye. She turned to look, but the gleam was too strong for her eyes. Whatever it was, she had to get it, had to have the source of that blinding flash in her hands. It was important.

She blinked and blinked and couldn't fight past the glare until her eyes opened to show her a wall in dim light. Evi still lay snuggled up to her, and Rae slept on the edge of the bed with them. Connor must be back, too. Betsy, now wide awake, slipped off the bed as carefully as she could to avoid waking the other two women. Padding softly out into the other room, she found Darius sprawled across the couch and Connor lying on the floor, using some kind of wadded up cloth for a pillow. Shadow was curled up on the blanket covering him next to his feet. He and Rae must have been out very late, so she didn't want to wake either of them.

She faced the kitchen, unsure where to begin on the subject of making breakfast. Last night, Darius used a fire in the hearth to heat water for tea. The kettle sat out, upside down to dry, but the fire was dead now and she had no idea how to get it started. It wasn't the first time she ever ventured into a kitchen, it was just the first time she ever tried to accomplish anything in one. All she could manage without help was filling the kettle with water.

Something soft brushed against her legs. She looked down to see Shadow rubbing himself on her and looking up. The second she noticed him, he started purring. It was a distraction, one she indulged in willingly. Bending down, she scooped him up and started petting him, scratching behind his ears and under his chin how she knew he liked it. Connor sighed and shifted in his sleep, making her stop for fear of disturbing him. The cat rubbed his head to get her to start again, so she did. Within a few moments, Connor sighed again. The man and the cat had some kind of link.

Quite content in her arms, the cat kept purring at her, bumping his head against her chin and leaning into her ministrations. A few minutes into this, he meowed loudly. Connor groaned, waking up. “It's too damned early, Shadow. Go back to sleep.” The cat jumped down and laid himself across Connor's face, forcing him to wake up. After spitting cat fur, Connor grabbed the cat and yanked him aside as he sat up. “Alright, alright, I'm up.”

Connor's grumbling woke Darius with a start. He lurched to his feet, blade in hand, blinking owlishly in the brightening morning light. “Who's attacking?”

“No one.” Betsy gulped and backed away from both men, not sure what they'd do in this condition. Her back hit the kitchen counter with just a few steps. “It's morning. I'm sorry for waking you.”

Darius sat back down heavily and set the sword aside, rubbing his eyes. “It's fine.”

“Shadow's fault, not yours.” Connor stood up and stretched. “We got something last night, hopefully Evi can narrow it down for us.” He pulled things out of cabinets, getting them together for breakfast. “We'll need to get moving as soon as we can, but Rae and I were too tired to do anything other than sleep when we got back.” Betsy sat down on the couch with Darius, watching Connor work. She didn't see him do anything in particular to light the hearth fire, it just sprang into life with what seemed to be nothing more than his touch.

“Did you sleep well?” Darius reached for his boots and pulled them on.

"I suppose so."

"Nightmares?"

"No, nothing like that." Betsy frowned and looked down at her hands in her lap. "I think I need to go to Niwlynys, at some point, but I don't know why."

"Good to know. If Connor and Rae got a solid lead, we should probably take care of that first."

"Of course." Whatever they found would obviously be more important than some dream she had that might or might not be about this whole sword thing.

"Connor, can't you even try to be quiet?" Rae shuffled out yawning. "How much sleep did we get? Half past none?"

"No, it was at least quarter to some." Connor set a bowl of something light brown and lumpy into Betsy's hands with a spoon.

She was accustomed to pastries, or eggs, fruit, meat, bread with butter, all kinds of things, but not this. Asking questions felt like it would be taken as rude, so she lifted the spoon and tried it. It had a mild apple flavor, overwhelmed by sweetness. "Breakfast soup?"

"Oatmeal," Darius said. "That's what it is."

Connor stuck a bowl into Darius's hands. "I'm sorry that my table is not as fine as you're used to, m'Lady." She couldn't tell if he was being sarcastic or genuinely offended by her reaction.

"It's fine," she told him hurriedly. "I've just never had it before."

"You'll have plenty of experience with it soon enough. Ah, Evi, good morning."

The scholar smiled, bright-eyed and wide awake, her steps bouncing and energetic. "Oh, Connor's cooking! I can tell by the smell. That means lots of sugar and hardly any flavoring. Just the way I like it."

"Very funny." Connor handed her a bowl and went back to get one for himself.

Rae served herself and sat on the floor. "Here's what we found out. There was an elf going around yesterday, not long after we raided that stronghold. Even in those parts of the city, elves are rare, so when one comes through, people notice. This one sounded like our guy, too."

Connor nodded along as she spoke. "He hired people to go on a trip to the Freistfell Mountains, for some, and I quote: 'semi-dangerous, authority-avoiding spelunking'. Probably, he meant to take those guys at the stronghold, and had to replace them on short notice, thanks to us. They left yesterday afternoon."

"It means we're about half a day behind them already." Rae looked at Evi. "But, the Freistfell is big."

"Freistfell covers thousands of miles," Evi nodded. "The piece of the sword that is allegedly in the mountains is near the part where Keryth and Endrisinore share a border, about the middle of the range."

Connor scowled. "I hate Endrisinore."

Rae sighed and stared at her oatmeal. "Not my favorite place, either."

All Betsy knew of Endrisinore was what everyone said. The Prelate was supposedly a god, she'd ruled the land for several hundred years now without aging. Her armies invaded Myredren and Liath Moor every five or ten years, causing bloody conflicts and necessitating a robust border guard. Those were the facts. The rumors spoke of dark, fell things happening there, of consorting with demons and children taken away in the dead of night to serve the Prelate.

Darius didn't look like he found the prospect pleasant, either. "Do we need to go into Endrisinore, or just get near it?"

"Just get near it. Skirt around a kobold warren, too." Evi ate as swiftly as she spoke and was almost finished already. "The peak we'll want to investigate is called Praghlorgil. Don't you just love dwarven names? They're so full of garbley sounds that get strung together to make something wondrous. Prah-glor-uh-gill." The second time, she stretched out the syllables, rolling the word around in her mouth.

"Yes," Connor said wearily, "they're wonderful. Can you narrow it down any more than that?"

"Oh, hm." Evi squinted at the wall. "It mentions the sun, so I would guess the western face, but it could be south. Hard to say without seeing it in person. The maps aren't complete enough to know for sure. I wonder if the elf has a better idea somehow. He seems to know what he's looking for already, so maybe we can follow him. It might be for the best he's got a head start on us."

Rae nodded. "Using mercenaries cobbled together from the underbelly of Rennsen should make them easier to track. They won't be highly skilled at group stealth. If they're actually going to Praghlorgil, we should be able to follow their trail to find the right way up and in."

"This is so exciting!" Evi jumped off the couch, knocking her now-empty bowl and spoon to the floor. "I've never been on a genuine adventure before, and this one just keeps getting more and more wonderful! I can hardly wait to write it all down and tell Moralan everything!" She dashed into the bedroom and reappeared just a few seconds later with her pack. "I'm ready to go. What are all of you waiting for? It'll take us a week to get there on horses!"

They rode out of the city on the south trade road. A chilly rain threatened to fall; the day was cold and overcast. Betsy was grateful for the need to keep close to Connor, because she felt certain she would freeze without his warmth to share.

It felt like the day passed slowly. They stopped for breaks every two or three hours, had a cold, bland lunch in the saddle, and saw nothing terribly interesting. Farmland and small villages surrounded Rennsen, then gave way to grassy rolling hills between small towns. People passed by in the other direction and they passed other people in wagons and carriages, but no one stopped to chat or waved as they went by. Betsy passed the time by falling into a numb fog, just letting the world go by without paying much attention to anything.

As the sun slid towards the horizon, they rode into a small town. The inn was full and the tavern was busy, but the town had an area set aside for camping with stone fire pits and pickets for horses. Betsy and Evi stood by, useless, while Darius and Rae set up blankets and a fire, and Connor went to fetch them all hot food for the night. Soon, they all sat bundled up around the small fire, enjoying a thick stew in bowls made of bread with small fruit pies, all of middling quality.

About halfway through the meal, Connor looked up at Darius. "How do you know Endrisinore?"

Darius paused with his spoon halfway to his mouth and sighed.

"I was in the Army."

For Connor, Rae, and Evi, this seemed a satisfactory explanation. Betsy, though, was now curious about this man she knew so little of. "What happened there?"

Darius gave his attention back to his food. "Unpleasant things I'd rather not speak of. You're better off not knowing."

Betsy blushed light pink and looked down. "I'm sorry, I don't mean to pry or bring up unpleasant memories."

"It's alright. Suffice to say we were needed there." Darius glanced at Connor. "I trust your experience was also unpleasant?"

Connor nodded, so did Rae and Evi. "Connor and I grew up near the border. It hadn't been attacked in a long time, that's why people lived there. Then it was." Evi shook her head sadly. "There's no town there anymore. Villages have been abandoned even though they were never attacked. Our current High King decreed a no man's land buffer zone, it's patrolled by soldiers and no one lives there. Which, if you ask me, is really the same as ceding the land to Endrisinore, just worded differently. However, in his defense, that decree has been tried before, and it did reduce the number of deaths each time. It's just fertile land there, so after the Prelate has been quiet for a while, people forget and want to farm there again, and they're allowed to, and so it goes. "

"My older brothers and father were in the Army." Rae tore a bit of her bowl off and toasted it over the fire. "None of 'em came back from the border."

Darius's eyes flicked from Evi to Connor and then to Rae. "How long ago was that?"

Connor stared into the fire. "Ten years, three months, and sixteen days. I was ten."

Betsy stared, finding the precision to be unnerving. What exactly happened?

"About ten years for me, too," Rae agreed. "Don't know exactly when like that, we just got a notice it happened."

"Ten years ago," Darius said, "I'd been in the Army for a little over a year, just a dumb seventeen year old rookie. I was stationed at the outpost near Eolin."

"Oh my gosh." Evi whispered harshly, like she was suddenly concerned about being overheard but couldn't contain herself enough to not get excited. "We grew up in Eolin!"

Ten years ago, Betsy was just a little girl who hadn't met Caitlin yet. She knew her mother demanded obedience. That was all she really understood about the world. "I'm sorry." The woefully inadequate statement fell out of her mouth. Part of her wanted to know what really happened there, the rest was unwilling to ask such a thing. Darius was brooding already, she didn't need to make that worse. Connor and Rae both stared into the fire, attesting to their own preoccupation with the subject.

"Don't be sorry. This is fascinating. I never knew that about you, Rae, and who would've guessed we'd meet one of the soldiers that helped us escape those horrors while on an adventure to save the world from a demon! This world is truly a magical place, to bring people together like this."

"Evi," Connor snapped. "There is nothing 'magical' about that."

"There's nothing magical about meeting a sweet woman skilled in healing who wants to keep from letting her madman of a husband hurt people? There's nothing magical in finally finding one of the men who made it so we were able to live that day even though my parents and your mother didn't? There's nothing magical in learning that us coming together now, like this, is part of something greater than any of us? It was a long time ago, Connor, you need to accept she's dead and that it wasn't your father's fault."

Now Betsy blushed, aware she'd caused something she didn't intend to. "I'm sorry, this is my fault. I shouldn't have asked."

Connor scowled and got up. His jaw moved like he wanted to say something but held it back. After a few tense seconds of that, he turned and stalked away. Evi jumped up to go after him, but Darius stopped her by grabbing her arm. In her place, Betsy got up and hurried after Connor, terribly ashamed of herself and wanting to make amends somehow. She followed him as he headed into the darkness, then kept going when she couldn't see or hear him anymore, expecting him to still be moving.

"Why are you following me?" Coming out of a shadow so black she walked right past it, his voice startled her. He sounded so angry she fought the urge to run away from him, from what he might do to her.

"This is my fault." Even knowing he was there, she still couldn't see him.

"Exactly how do you figure that?"

Not sure how to answer the question, she wrung her hands together. "It just is."

Connor sighed heavily. "No, Betsy, it's not your fault that Evi thinks she can fix everything with enough words filling the air."

No, that probably wasn't her fault, but she didn't want to argue about it. She peered into the shadows as hard as she could, but still couldn't see anything. "How do you do that, hiding in the dark so completely?"

"Practice." He emerged from it to stand at her back, his hands placed lightly on her shoulders. The suddenness and forced intimacy of his new position made her flinch. He squeezed her shoulders lightly, probably intending that to be reassuring. It only made her uncomfortable. "Lots of practice."

She didn't squirm, it didn't occur to her to try to get away from him. "Should I have left you alone?"

"Probably not." His hands dropped away and he stepped back to lean against the nearby wall where she could see him, arms crossed. Before he said anything else, a pair of men stumbled into the narrow path between two buildings, laughing like drunks. Connor's attention immediately went to them, watching like a predator. Betsy stepped closer to him, certain she didn't want them to think she was alone. Connor reached out and pulled her close.

The two men were in a good mood. One gave Connor an extremely obvious and lascivious wink. The other pointed at Connor and slurred out, "Nice night for a piece of that. You sharing?"

Connor gave them an amiable grin as he shook his head. "I would, but we're recently Handfasted." On hearing this, Betsy recognized his intent and played her part, leaning into him and resting her head on his chest.

"Lucky bastard." They didn't seem put off, and continued on

their way without incident.

Standing there with Connor's arms around her felt safe, but in the same way Jason's arms did. It was difficult to push him away, even harder not to. "Thank you."

"For what? Not leaving you standing there to fend for yourself? I realize your husband is an awful, but he must be some kind of depraved ass for you to think I need to be thanked for this."

She pulled away, enough so he let go. "He wouldn't have left me to fend for myself, he didn't even let me go into the back garden without Darius."

Connor snorted. "He sounds like such a wonderful person. Truly, I must meet this man. I'd like to introduce him to the sharp, pointy ends of my blades."

Betsy sighed and shook her head. What was she supposed to say? This situation reminded her rather forcefully of how Jason was when they first met, how he said all the right things and did all the right things. That version of Jason gave her whatever she asked for, even a cat when he didn't want one. He made her feel safe and wanted without being loved or free. The worst thing he ever did was giving her that version of him back after the other one showed himself. "He's not all bad," she heard herself say. It was true, just not right. "It doesn't matter."

Connor's mouth tightened at the corners and he looked away. "No, of course not." He took her hand and rubbed her palm with his thumb. The contact felt intimate in a way she couldn't explain – it was just her hand. "You're not like Rae or the other women in our line of work. No one is like Evi, and she's practically my sister on top of that. All the other woman I've se-" He definitely changed his mind about the word he was going to use there, but the pause and stumble were subtle. "-en and spent any amount of time with were older, weary of their lives. Bored noble wives, mostly. A few unhappily unmarried daughters here and there."

She had a feeling she knew what word he almost said, and didn't really approve. Worse, it sounded like he meant he was trying to seduce *her.* "The ones you slept with. Coaxing them into breaking their oath to the Mother Goddess for...it was 'fun', wasn't it?" It came out more harshly than she really meant, and she looked down at her hands on his chest. "I'm sorry, that was rude."

"I do it to gain access to their husbands' offices and papers." He snorted and shook his head. "Which makes it sound so much better."

Betsy tried to imagine herself in ten years, if none of this happened and she was still Jason's toy. Already, she was used to it. At some point, he would have to admit he was causing the miscarriages and find some way to satisfy himself long enough for her to bear him at least one child, just as his father did with his mother. Then it would be muted, perhaps. He'd find some other target and be happy with that, maybe even ignore her in favor of a series of young women he brutalized in her stead. Over time, she would become a shadow of herself, starved for something she didn't even know she needed.

Someone like Connor would sweep into her life, showering her with affection and attention. She'd be so taken with him, maybe even feel so much more alive than ever before. He'd steal into her bed and steal out again, perhaps insert himself into her walks or meet her furtively. Darius would know and keep her secrets, just as he did with the healing. Jason would never know, because he didn't care anymore.

"I understand," she said after a long pause.

He lifted her chin with one finger to look into her eyes. "Yes, I think you do. I sent Shadow in because you were so young and so new to the Earl's life. We're both very sorry you were hurt because of it. I never intend to cause real problems for the wives I target. It's supposed to be good for both of us." His eyes slipped down to her lips. She could tell he wanted to kiss her. What did she want? It never really mattered before.

It felt like a very long time that they stood there, poised on a cliff and ready to dive into the uncertain waters below. Then he jumped. She hadn't been kissed like this is a long time. It was enough to make her dizzy and breathless, flushed and weak-kneed. He wanted her, it was in how his hand slid down to press on the small of her back, pushing her closer to him, then slid just a little farther, and it was in how his other hand cupped her cheek and chin.

He reminded her of Jason so much it hurt. Why couldn't he be different? Why couldn't he stay this way? But he wouldn't. He told her with his own mouth that he would walk away. Unless... Maybe...

"Connor? You've been gone a...ah." Rae's voice wasn't very far away, Betsy saw her over his shoulder when Connor reluctantly broke the lingering kiss off. "Right, should've guessed. Never mind."

Connor pulled his hands away and held them up for Rae to see, like he'd been caught doing something wrong. "Go ahead, go back with her. Darius is probably in a froth or something because you haven't come back yet."

Betsy nodded, not sure how she felt, and walked away from him to go with Rae. She glanced back to see him watching over his shoulder, standing like he was embarrassed or ashamed (she couldn't tell which for sure in the dim light). Her body felt warm all over, and she touched her mouth hesitantly, trying to keep the sensation. If only...

They were out of earshot without being in sight of the camp yet when Rae said, "Be really, really careful, Betsy."

"What do you mean?"

"Connor isn't- He's not used to... Look." Rae stopped and faced her. "He's my partner, we work together. What happens to him happens to me because it affects how well he does his job. You're not like the women he usually goes for, and I've seen him watching you. His instinct is to take what he wants, which, right now, is you. He's not going to do it by making you fear him like your ass of a husband does, he's going to do it by making you want him. He'll do everything right, say what you want to hear, and when he gets bored, he'll leave. He's a not the kind of man you want to get attached to like that."

Half-formed fantasies faded, slapped in the face by reality. "What if-"

Rae cut her off. "There is no 'what if', not with him. He doesn't know how."

"People can learn, they can change." She knew it wasn't really true and cringed at her own begging.

"Don't plead with me about this, Betsy. I'm not in charge of him." Rae put a hand on Betsy's upper arm, giving her a muted smile. "All I'm saying is to be careful. You're really nice and you've suffered a lot, and I don't want to watch you get hurt by my partner, that's all."

Betsy nodded, she understood. For a few wild minutes, she imagined Connor sweeping her off her feet and being everything Jason wasn't. It all crumbled to ash, leaving grit in her mouth. "Thank you."

"We should get back, Darius is in a fair fit. He'd be looking for you, but I convinced him he was better off staying in case you wandered back on your own."

"Thank you for that, too." Betsy sighed. "I suspect if he was the one who found us, he'd have choked Connor to death by now."

Rae laughed, "Aye, probably."

Chapter 11

The next day was a repeat of the first, with gradually lessening numbers of people on the road. Towns and villages appeared less frequently, and the land grew wilder. At Evi's direction, they turned down a smaller road to the east just after midday, one with unchecked grasses and young trees growing into it and along the middle. The horses desperately wanted to sample the greenery.

Connor yanked Bonbon's head away from the grass yet again and turned to the scholar. "Are you sure this is the right way to go, Evi? No one's been along here in at least a year, maybe more."

"This road connects with another one about a hundred miles down, it's going to save us half a day of travel. I think that's important, isn't it? Since we were about that far behind the elf and his people?"

Grudgingly, Connor nodded. "Fine, but we need to go faster than this or the horse will drive me nuts. Are there any villages along this road?"

"No, it's just a bypass for merchants. It goes through a swamp, and there are dire wolves in the forest it cuts through."

Everyone turned to look at Evi, who seemed blissfully unaware of the sudden attention. Betsy asked, "What are dire wolves?"

"Picture a wolf." Rae waited a beat, Betsy nodded. "Now imagine it's as big as a horse and thinks you're about the same to it as a bunny rabbit is to a regular wolf. And, for some insane reason," she looked back at Evi, "we're going through a forest known to have these things. On purpose. To save time."

"You know, Evi," Connor said, "we have a saying in our line of work: Enemies make a short road long."

"They don't patrol the road and demand sacrifices," Evi said with a little huff of annoyance. "Accounts of the area simply mention the beasts have been encountered in the wooded portions of this particular road. Only two lives lost."

Darius rubbed his eyes like weariness crashed over him. "That anyone knows about. Who knows how many were just never heard from again."

Evi rolled her eyes. "You're all making much too big a fuss about this. The swamp is much worse."

"Excuse me?" Connor stopped Bonbon and pulled him to block the road so everyone else had to stop, too. "We haven't gone that far down this road, we can still turn around."

"Oh, honestly, Connor. You're such an alarmist."

"I prefer to think of myself as a specialist in the art of not getting dead."

"Come on, Connor, you're not afraid, are you? We can't really afford to lose time like this. If we move faster down the road, we should be fine. When we reach the swamp, we just get through it as fast as we can and don't let the horses follow the lights. It's not that big a deal." She goaded her horse around Bonbon and into a canter, leaving everyone behind.

"We could just let her go," Rae observed dryly.

Connor bared his teeth and glared at her. "It was your idea to go to her in the first place, you know. I haven't forgotten that."

Rae snorted. "And I'm sure you never will."

"Let's just get this over with," Darius said as he rubbed his whole face.

Betsy couldn't think of any way in which she was at fault here, which felt very strange. Except for the part where they wouldn't be here in the first place if it wasn't for her. "She's just trying to help."

"Yes, and it's going spectacularly." Connor got his horse to follow after Evi's, Rae did the same. They caught up quickly and kept going, with Connor, Rae, and Darius watching the sides of the road apprehensively. Betsy watched, too, but wasn't really sure what she was looking for. For all she knew, they could turn invisible or blend with the landscape or run faster than the horses. If that was the case, they wouldn't get much warning before terrible things she didn't want to think about started happening.

Time passed, the hyper vigilance faded. Stiff and uncomfortable, Betsy focused on not complaining. No one wanted to hear that, no one needed to hear that. Only Connor would hear it anyway, and she didn't want to annoy or bother him with something so unimportant. Eventually, she got hungry and still said nothing. It wasn't until the horses slowed down of their own accord that they paused for a break.

Connor climbed down and helped Betsy do the same. It was funny how she didn't really notice where his hands were yesterday as he did this, but today, she felt like he must have placed them purposely to remind her of his touch. "We shouldn't stop long," he said. "Walk around, keep moving. It'll help." He handed her bread and cheese. "Eat."

She took it with a grateful nod and found Darius next to her. "Are you alright?"

"Yes," she said with a nod, "I think so."

Darius looked her over like he didn't quite believe that. "Move around, bend your knees a lot. Eat."

Betsy looked from him to Connor, now stretching his arms above his head, and back. The two men traded looks she didn't know how to decipher, but they didn't seem friendly. Instead of saying anything, she ripped off a piece of her bread and pushed it into her mouth. That act seemed to satisfy both of them and she paced a short distance away, intent on following their directions. If she didn't, they'd probably compete for who got to hover over her until she did.

Halfway through the meal, Rae said, "Did anyone else hear that?" The archer grabbed her bow and turned around in a slow circle, holding it ready to fire while she scanned the trees on both sides of the road. Connor pulled his daggers, Darius put a hand on his sword hilt. Betsy hurried back to all of them and noticed Evi take a book out of her saddlebag. This didn't seem like the right time or place for reading material to Betsy, it seemed like the time to get on the horses and get out of here. The horses stamped and snorted like they agreed.

Everyone was so tense, she didn't dare speak. What she did do was tuck the rest of her food into a pocket to eat later, when her stomach wasn't tied in knots anymore. Why didn't they just mount up and go? If these dire wolf things were watching, why didn't they just attack? She opened her mouth to say something, to ask what was going on, but that seemed to be taken as a signal of some sort. Four giant wolves flew out of the trees, racing to the group so quickly she almost missed it by blinking.

Bonbon reared with a scream of challenge. Clover stood her ground and kicked out with her hind hooves at the first dire wolf to reach her, knocking it sideways with a blow to the head. Momentum carried the giant wolf farther, crashing into the horse and knocking them both down. Rae hopped aside and sent an arrow into another wolf's skull. Connor rolled to the side and stuck both daggers into another of the beasts as it tore past him. Darius faced the final wolf as it came straight for him, putting his blade up to meet it at the last possible moment. The sword went down its throat along with his hands and arms, all scored by the wolf's exceptionally large fangs.

Evi spoke, but Betsy was too frightened by all of this to really understand any of it. She stayed where she was, rooted to the spot, and watched the pages of Evi's book fly free of the binding to wrap around the head of the wolf Connor cut but didn't kill. It all happened so fast, and Betsy had no idea knew what to do. Nothing she could do would hurt anything, ever. She was happy with it that way. The very idea of standing there and letting an enemy rush her was terrifying. What Darius did, what Connor did, what Rae did, she couldn't do those things and never would be able to.

Darius's wolf slammed into him just as the first had, also knocking him down with a crunch that sounded bad. Rae's target staggered and waved its head drunkenly, she danced out of its way and put an arrow into the wolf on her horse. The pages covering the front half of Connor's wolf refused to come off when it shook itself.

Connor took advantage of that and stabbed it again. It whined and fell to the ground.

Just like that, it was over. Darius roared with the effort as he rolled to get the wolf off his body and pulled to get his arms out of its mouth. He stayed on the ground, clutching one arm with the other, jaws clenched. That was something Betsy could deal with. She rushed to his side and felt the healing start immediately. Behind her, grunts of effort by both Connor and Rae announced them heaving the wolf off the horse. Clover made soft, weak noises.

"Oh, Goddess, no." Rae choked on the words.

"Betsy, can you heal a horse?"

Her power flowed into Darius, straightening his arm and healing the cuts and cracked ribs and bruises. "I don't know, I've never tried."

"Go." Darius waved her off. "Take care of it first so we can get moving."

She hesitated for a moment, but jumped to her feet when she heard Rae's distressed sob. The archer knelt by Clover's head, stubbornly refusing to cry while she comforted the horse by petting her neck. Her heart broke at the sight, and she hurried over. Putting her hands on the horse's back, she closed her eyes and whispered, "Please work." Nothing happened.

"This horse doesn't deserve to die in pain like this. She fought bravely and nobly to protect us when she could have run to save herself. I don't understand where my power to heal comes from, but if I must spill my own blood to ease Clover's pain, then I will, gladly and with reservation." There, she stopped, because the power flowed out of her and into the horse. Clover made a queer noise, a whinny that might have been confused.

"Oh, thank the Goddess," Evi said breathlessly.

"This," Connor said angrily, pointing at the horse. "This is why we take the longer, safer road."

Rae made a strangled noise and wiped her face. "Shut up, Connor. You've messed up worse before."

He scowled. "I learn from my mistakes. It doesn't do me any good if no one else does."

Evi made a face that was half pout, half determination. "We can afford to take this kind of risk because we have Betsy." She waved a hand over her empty binding and the pages flew off the wolf to reattach themselves and remake the book.

Connor rolled his eyes and went for his horse, climbing up without a word.

On his feet now and still cradling his arm, Darius moved with care, his face pinched with pain. Even so, he managed to be gentler than Connor with his rebuke. "A healer should never be used as an excuse to rush headlong into battle. We were lucky. Betsy can't undo death, remember that."

The horse neighed and rolled to its feet. Rae threw her arms around Clover's neck. Betsy went back to Darius and finished healing him, eyes bright with tears for the horse and Rae. Up to now, she had no idea the archer was sentimental over anything. "There was no need to be so selfless after all."

"It's always better to conserve than to waste."

"Says the man who threw his body in the way of a giant wolf."

Darius's mouth twitched with amusement. "You may have a point. It seemed like the right way to go at the time." He put an arm around her and kissed the top of her head. "Thank you. Make sure you eat the rest of what you have. If you want to switch horses, you can. Evi's can bear the both of you."

Betsy looked over at Connor. He watched her right back, and it seemed like his anger cooled as he sat there on Bonbon's back, staring at her. "No, it's fine. He could probably use the company. Maybe you should ride with Evi. So she doesn't feel rejected."

"Maybe." Darius lost all traces of amusement and walked her to Connor's horse. After helping her up, he went to Evi and spoke with her briefly. She didn't hear the conversation, but they wound up with Darius riding Evi's horse alone and Evi riding behind Rae. The moment they were ready to go, Connor snapped Bonbon's reins. Betsy kept herself close to Connor, ready to listen whenever he wanted to talk.

They moved through forest for a while longer before it gave way to a gentle downward slope of meadow, then to marshes. Betsy didn't see what was bad about the swamp. It had trees and grasses just like the rest of the land, only more sparse and with water visible here and there. Some of the spots of water had dots of brightly colored flowers in yellow and red and pink. Nothing odd lurked in the midst of it so far as she could see, and the road ran high enough to not flood, though it was dark and soft.

After a short time of this, more trees lined the road, plunging them into a gloom where the ground grew softer. Soon, they had to slow down because the road no longer stayed consistently above the level of the water. Bonbon's hooves squelched in mud and splashed in brackish standing water. Flying insects buzzed around them. Betsy huddled against Connor, the cat sitting between them now, and holding the hood of her cloak tight against his back to protect her face. Bonbon's tail swished back and forth, hitting her legs. She did what she could to spread her cloak and dress around to cover as much as possible, but that still left plenty of horse for the bugs to bite at.

Connor made little noises of annoyance, she felt his body twisting as he swatted around himself. "This-" Instead of finishing, he made a gagging sound and spat something to the side. Some must have flown into his mouth.

"Can't we go faster?"

Evi's muffled voice shouted from behind them. "The bites won't kill you, just itch. The real danger is the big ones!"

Betsy didn't want to know what 'the big ones' were like if these weren't them. She held onto Connor's side with one gloved hand and her hood with the other and tried not to imagine how things could get worse. Within minutes, she didn't have to imagine it, because every hoof fell into water and they slowed more. The horses must have been motivated, because even though each hoof beat came with a slurp of thick mud, they still managed to go faster than a plain walk.

Connor tensed, Rae made an alarmed noise without opening her mouth, Darius grunted. Betsy didn't look; she didn't want to know. It was probably the bigger ones. The horse turned and slowed down, Connor leaned back while also grunting with effort and waving an arm around. Whatever was going on, he was busy, and she felt horribly guilty for not helping.

Holding her hood as tightly as she could, she pulled back to look around. To the left, the side where his arm slashed a dagger indiscriminately through the air, large skinny insects buzzed around them both, each about the size of Shadow. One darted at Shadow, now exposed, and the cat swiped at it. His paw whapped it aside and his claws scratched it, but it didn't give up. Betsy covered the cat up, preventing the bug from getting to him again. To the right, blurry lights danced in the distance. The horse tried to go that way, Connor had to haul his head back to the road.

How he even knew where the road was, Betsy had no idea. As far as she could see, it was all just brown and black water with so many gray trees they blocked out the sun. That's why the horse wanted to go towards the light. There was nothing she could see to do to help. Behind them, pages from the scholar's book surrounded Evi and Rae and repelled the bugs from them. Darius still brought up the rear – she could make out his dark shape, but she couldn't tell how well he fared. The horses all had their heads down and plodded along, probably as fast as they could.

Connor groaned, coughed, and spat, and his body swayed like he might fall out of the saddle. Betsy saw one of the bugs, now fat and well rounded, flutter away drunkenly. At the same time, another fell to the water, sliced in half. She pushed herself up against his back again, and felt it as she healed him. Then she started healing the horse. It was a slow trickle of power from her to Bonbon, and seemed as if it would never end. These things must be sucking their blood out. With her here, Connor and Bonbon would be fine, but Darius could be in serious trouble.

Real light started to shine ahead, where a break in the trees signaled the end of this miserable swamp. Bonbon saw it, too. She could tell because he made more effort to go faster and snapped at the big bugs coming close enough to his head. As they got closer and closer, the bugs thinned out. Finally, they broke out into sunshine and the water receded until it was just mud. Bonbon sped up and hurried away from the dark place.

Betsy turned around. Clover was quite a bit farther back than before, Evi's papers returning to their book when they reached the sunlight. All three of them looked haggard and nearly ready to drop. "Connor, stop." She patted his shoulder to get his attention. "I have to help the others."

Pulling the horse around, Connor took them back to Rae and Evi, where Betsy leaned over and put a hand on Clover first. The horse had to have taken the worst of it, and needed to bear her riders. "Where's Darius?"

Betsy peered back into the gloom and couldn't see him or Evi's horse. Power flowed steadily from her to Clover. "If he's in there all by himself, he may not make it out." And it would be her fault for bringing him along, and for suggesting they change how everyone was riding. Evi could have defended herself with her book. Darius only had a sword.

Rae waved wearily to shoo Betsy off. "We're not going to fall off. Go get him."

Snapping the reins, Connor leaned forward, expecting the horse to plunge back into the swamp. Bonbon didn't move. When he wiggled in the saddle a little, the horse backed up several steps. "I'm supposed to be the one in charge here, Bonbon."

They didn't have time for this. Betsy jumped off the horse and ran into the swamp, ignoring the shouts and meows to stop. She already knew this was a bad idea. "Darius!" The buzzing around her grew louder; the bugs seemed to be attracted by the noise. Not far in, the water already reached halfway up her calves and her boots squished in the mud. It took great effort to move, but she kept going as fast as she could. "Dari-" Bugs flew into her mouth and up her nose. She kept going as she coughed and hacked them out. This wasn't going to work if neither of them could make any noise.

Swiping her hands through the air to try to carve a path through the thick cloud of insects didn't help. If anything, it made them more interested in her. Was that dark shape him? No, that was a tree. There was no choice but to keep going, and she did, getting more and more panicked and frustrated. This was a stupid way for someone to die. It was like slipping on nothing and cracking your skull open, or...letting your husband beat you to death because... Right now wasn't the time to think about that. Right now was a time to get through this.

All these stupid bugs! She could barely see where she was going, then her foot stuck in the muck and she fell forward, splashing into the murky water, some of it going into her mouth as she gasped with surprise. It stung her eyes and soaked her completely, plastering her hair to her head. Coughing and spitting again, she sat back on her heels and held a hand in front of her mouth. "Darius!"

He wasn't much farther, she heard him groan and it sounded close. Strength renewed by the sound, she struggled to her feet and slogged through the muck. Just a few more steps, then a few more, then another few more. She nearly tripped right over him as he knelt in the water, holding the horse's head up so it wouldn't drown. He caught her in arms weaker than they should be, putting her immediately into contact with both him and the horse.

So much healing in such a short time, combined with the struggling to get here, took its toll. Betsy swayed and collapsed into him, still conscious, still healing them both, but unable to hold herself up anymore. Through the wet cloak he draped over her face to protect it, she said, "I don't think we're going to make it back out".

He stood up and started to walk with her in his arms, she heard the horse struggling to move with him. "You came back for me," he told her with his mouth very close to her ear. "Hold on as tightly as you can." She clung to him, though she was far too exhausted for such an effort. Now that the initial rush of healing had put them back on their feet, it turned to a slow, steady trickle from her to them, just as it had been with Connor and Bonbon. It seemed to take such a long time to get out of there, long enough that she lost track of it.

A chill woke her up. For a moment, she thought she was on some kind of boat, a rolling motion rocking her gently from side to side. Coming more awake, she realized she was on a moving horse, something holding her tightly in place. "Good," Connor's voice said, "you're awake." She found she was positioned in front of him on

Bonbon, leaning against him with his arms around her.

"What happened?" Her gloves and cloak were gone, replaced by a blanket Shadow sat on to keep in place. Everything else was still damp, including her hair.

"You passed out. Since you're the healer, we figured you're not likely to get sick from being wet, or we would've gotten you dried all off before getting under way again. Darius wanted to wait until you woke up, but we're pressed for time. He also wanted to be the one to carry you, but we determined that he's just too big for the horse to bear you both. It was probably hard on Clover to carry both him and Rae at the same time."

Looking all around, she found the path was back to being hard packed, well used road. Darius rode alongside Rae and Evi, just a few paces behind. She smiled and gave all three a weary wave. As expected, Evi's return wave was the most enthusiastic. Darius perked up when he saw her, his brooding scowl turning to a warm smile and a hand held up to acknowledge her.

She rubbed her eyes and yawned. "How long was I out?"

"Several hours. We're off that side road of doom and back onto a normal one. Just now looking for a decent spot to stop for the night. Haven't seen a town since we turned onto this road, so it'll probably be a rough camp."

"Which means what?"

Connor chuckled. "Which means we'll have to be more careful with our fire and there won't be anyone else nearby for safety. We'll have to set watches, but you don't need to worry about that. Darius, Rae, and I know what to do. You just sleep tonight."

She wasn't really sure what he meant by 'set watches', but it didn't seem important. Other things were on her mind. “I'm sorry you had to carry me like that for so long.”

“No trouble at all.” He cracked a grin. “There are worse things than being forced to keep my arms around a beautiful woman for several hours.” A dark pink blush crept across Betsy's face. It got darker when he pulled her closer. With his lips right next to her ear, she whispered, “Unfortunately, there won't be any sort of privacy at all tonight, and probably not for the rest of the nights until we get back to Rennsen.”

Betsy's blush went fully crimson. “You know I'm still married.”

“Why, my Lady,” he said innocently, “whatever do you think I mean?”

“I-I don't know.” Fully flustered, she covered her face with her hands even though no one but Shadow could see it. “I'm sorry, I didn't mean-”

He chuckled in her ear. “It's alright. I'd like nothing better than you, Betsy. The timing just isn't terribly good.”

It felt to Betsy that if she blushed any harder, her head might explode. “Um, thank you?”

“You're welcome.” Thankfully, he didn't say anything else, he just held her close. The sun slid down to the horizon not long after, and they stopped without finding a better place to camp than the low grasses along the side of the road. Darius set up a small fire, Connor threw a few things together for a sketchy meal, Rae walked with Betsy to a short distance away where she was finally able to change into dry clothes. The whole time, Evi stayed quiet, throwing occasional glances at Connor that he ignored. Connor and Darius also ignored each other except what they really needed to communicate.

Betsy tried to strike up a conversation once, but it fell flat and she gave up quickly. She settled into the blankets, sharing with Evi to keep them both warm. Shadow curled up at their feet. The last thing Betsy saw before she fell asleep was Darius poking the fire and giving her a very small smile. The first thing she saw in the morning was Rae pushing a bowl of oatmeal into her hands. Everyone else was already awake and nearly packed up. Mumbling her apologies for sleeping so long, she ate the oatmeal as fast she could.

They mounted up – Betsy riding behind Connor again – as soon as she was done and got back underway. That one stretch of road seemed to be the extent of the dangers for a group such as them. Every so often, Connor adjusted his cloak and his daggers. It was obvious and odd enough that Betsy finally just asked about it. "Should we stop more often? You seem uncomfortable."

"No, I'm fine. The only thing that'll make anything better at this point is getting there."

"Then why do you keep squirming around? I don't mean to annoy you, it's just...you didn't do that before. On the other road, I mean."

Connor left a long pause before answering. She was about to apologize for mentioning it when he said, "The other road was well traveled. That side road was something no one uses anymore. On this road, we've hardly seen anyone else. It's traveled, but sparsely. This is a perfect road for an ambush."

"Ambush?" She knew what the word meant and lived through one, but still didn't understand. That one was set up to catch her carriage. "Why would anyone ambush us here? No one is expecting us to come along this way."

"Not that kind of ambush. The kind that a band of men set up to spring on unwary travelers to take whatever money and goods they can. Sometimes, they kill the victims and hide the bodies. Other times, they let the victims live with stories of hunting them down and killing them if they tell anyone. Still other times, the victims get away with minimal losses."

Betsy blinked and found her eyes drawn to the sides of the road. "Why would they do that?"

"Money."

She frowned. "Why don't they just take up a trade? Wouldn't that be easier?"

Connor turned around too look at her, somewhat amused. "You really have no idea how the world works, do you?" Shaking his head, he laughed. "Suffice to say that desperation is the most common reason I know of. Some of the people who wind up doing that are wrong in the head and just like killing or having power over other people, but most of them fall into it through circumstance and can't figure a way out."

"That's awful. What should I do if we're attacked?"

"Don't worry about it. Unless the band is large, we're not really in danger. Three horses for five people, no clanking saddlebags fat with coins, and none of us is dressed in rich clothes. Add to that two well armed men, and Rae, and we're not worth the trouble."

"We're not?"

"All they might get out of us is a few weapons and some cheap jewelry, plus the horses if they aren't injured in the attack. What they'll see when they watch us ride past is a waste of energy. Because we'll likely take down at least a few of them before they can neutralize us. Even if they're all archers."

So, they were safe. But not the ordinary people who happened to travel this road. "Why don't the local lords do something about it?"

"Like what? Endlessly patrol the road with men needed to protect the towns and villages? Send those same men to escort every traveler who happens along? Your husband is a very wealthy man, Betsy, but the lesser nobles aren't. The Earl spends his days managing businesses he has stakes in and deals he's gotten into. The other nobles have lands and people to manage. They get what comes from collecting taxes and have to use it to pay their guardsmen and to keep up roads and bridges and everything else. Most Counts barely have enough money to keep more than a handful of servants and eat and dress like their vassals. Barons are a little better off – they might have time to handle a few business ventures."

Betsy didn't really know any of this. The Counts and Barons she'd met were from the area around Rennsen and seemed well enough off. Then again, the ones she knew were all Jason's business partners. He probably managed everything for them. At this point, any questions she could think of to ask seemed stupid or redundant, so she went quiet again. A little more time passed before Connor slowed the horse.

"There are some people walking towards us." He called it back so the others could hear him.

"What's strange about that?"

"Betsy, no one *walks* down a road like this."

She peeked out from behind him to see two people waving to get their attention. Connor tensed and drew a dagger. Behind them, Rae gave the reins to Evi and readied her bow. "I don't understand."

"They were either just robbed recently or are trying to distract us so we can be attacked." He only sounded a little irritated by having to explain. "Shadow, pay attention."

She stared at the two people hard, trying to see details. "The man is injured, look at the way he's walking. And their clothes, they can't be just bait. Connor, we have to help them."

"Betsy, it could all be fake."

People would go so far as to fake injuries for a ruse? Betsy didn't understand any of this. It was so wrong. Why would they do that? She knew that beggars weren't to be trusted, her mother told her that repeatedly. They just sat on the street, though, with cups out. This was an altogether different situation. If Connor was right, this was more like the beggar getting in your way while another one clubbed you from behind. "I'll be able to tell if I can touch him."

"Don't get off the horse unless he's really hurt."

The precaution seemed unnecessary, but Betsy nodded. "I understand." She did, really. He wanted to be able to get them away quickly if he needed to. The closer they got, though, the more she thought that kind of paranoia was excessive. Both had real blood smudged on their clothes, the woman cried and carried a bundle that might be a baby. The man waved his one good arm at them, face pinched with pain. That face crystallized in her memory from her dream. She knew him and needed to save him.

Connor snapped the reins to get the horse to go faster past them. "We're not stopping."

"What? Connor, we have to! They're hurt. Stop the horse or I'm jumping off."

"I don't like it. There's too much cover from those trees and the dip of the land." Unable to believe how he could be so callous, Betsy pushed away from him and slid off the side of Bonbon. "Betsy, dammit." He grabbed her. "I'm trying to protect you."

Yanking her arm away, she found herself falling onto her backside. The two people weren't much farther away, she clambered to her feet and ran to them before Connor could jump down and stop her. Their expressions went from despair to hope at the sight of her. "What happened," she called out.

"It was men on the side of the road," the man said. He looked about ready to fall over. "They attacked and took our horse, our wagon, even our son."

"Can you help her, please?" The woman, still crying, held out the bundle. Betsy took the baby in her arms and wanted to cry, too. She wasn't sure how old the girl was, but that didn't matter, because she wasn't moving. No force could bring back the dead, but if there was even a spark of the child still left, she could coax it out. Pushing the blankets aside, she put two fingers on the baby's cold cheek, brushing it gently. The hair peeking out from under the blanket was golden blonde, just like Betsy's own.

If any of her children had been born, would they have looked like this? Probably. There was nothing she could do to stop them slipping away from her, but she could do something about this one. She had to. Closing her eyes, she wished and hoped and prayed and begged and searched for something, anything, just a the merest hint of life still in this shell. Just when she was ready to collapse and weep for this child she couldn't save, there it was, a tiny little mote of something too weak to pull her in. She grabbed it and force-fed it. Someone stood behind her, braced her so she didn't fall over.

The baby made a tiny noise and still she fed it everything she had, until the tiny body was whole and lusty cries filled the air. She opened her eyes again as she was hugged and found her power being drawn again by the man. His injuries were serious – he would eventually have bled to death without some kind of care. The woman sobbed her gratitude, the man hugged his wife. Betsy leaned against Darius, thankful no one else needed her care right now.

"Tell us what happened," Connor said. "The whole story."

"We're moving to Doverton. Everything we own was in that wagon. We hit a bump and I heard a crack, so I stopped to check the wheels. Men jumped out of nowhere. It happened really fast. They roughed us up and took the wagon, took our little boy."

"He's only three years old," the woman said through tears. "I can still hear his screams. Goddess bless, they're going to beat him and turn him into their little slave. He's just a boy."

"We'll get him back." Rae said this, the statement firm and matter-of-fact. "How far back did this happen?"

"I don't know." The man looked back the way they came. "We've been walking for a little bit. I just don't know."

"With those injuries," Betsy said, "it wasn't more than a quarter of an hour."

Rae nodded. "Do you remember any landmarks? Anything that made the spot look different from anywhere else?"

"No, I don't think so. Wait, actually, yes. The trees were closer to the road. There was a bit that came almost to it. That's probably where they jumped out from. Are you really going to get our boy back?"

"Yes." Darius sounded just as determined as Rae. "Evi, get them some water. We'll be back with your son."

Evi already had a waterskin in her hands, she hurried over and gave it to them. Along with it, she also gave them a blanket. "Stay here and keep warm."

"Thank you. We have no way to repay you at all."

Betsy already felt her strength returning. She must be getting used to using so much power at once. "Words are enough." She turned away, too confused about her feelings to say or do anything more than get up on the horse behind Connor again and hold on while they rode ahead to find the spot the wagon must have been taken from.

"If you ever do that again-"

"What? You'll beat me?" Connor stiffened and she immediately regretted saying it. "I'm sorry, I didn't mean that."

"No," he said, the word clipped. He took a deep breath. "I deserved that. You were right. I was going to pass them by because... Because I thought there wasn't any way they could honestly be victims. I said it before, and I mean it now more than I did then: I've never met anyone like you before, Betsy. You make me want to be a better man."

She squeezed him tightly, warmed by his admission. "That baby, it reminds me of what I've lost. She was so close to dead, only someone like me could tell the difference. I couldn't let her go, not for anything. When her mother took her out of my arms, I..." Finishing the thought was too hard.

He didn't answer right away, not until he reined the horse in to stop. On the ground, he checked the buckles for the saddle as he said, "There will be other chances for you, Betsy." After that, he still didn't look at her. "We need to move quickly. Not only is the boy in danger, but we can't afford to delay too long here. We're still behind the elf and his men, and if we want to catch them, we have to do this fast and efficient. Rae and I have a lot of experience with this sort of thing. I'll go in with Shadow, Rae will cover me. Darius, you go with Rae in case anyone tries to rush the archer. Evi and Betsy, stick together and stay with the horses."

No one disagreed, though Darius glanced at Betsy like he thought about it. Rae took the lead, finding where the wagon was pulled off the road and following the tracks through the grasses and shrubs and trees. Evi and Betsy followed from a distance, stopping when Connor put up a hand for them to. The pair of them sat down with the horses, pulling out food and water to have a small meal. Evi started talking about some group of heroes who chased down a monster terrorizing a village, stealing their children in the night. Betsy didn't really find the story engrossing, but it was a way to pass the time, and it kept Evi from asking questions or talking about things she didn't want to talk about. For a while, at least.

"Betsy, what do you think of Connor?"

The question came on the tail of the story, seemingly out of nowhere. Broadsided by it, Betsy blinked several times and froze. "What do you mean?"

"He's my brother, you know. Not by blood, of course, but he's always looked out for me, even before my parents were killed that awful night. We lived near to each other and Moralan was well respected in Eolin. Everyone wanted to be his friend. My parents actually were. Sometimes, I wonder if my mother wasn't having an affair with him, but it was so long ago and his wife was such a lovely woman, it seems like a blasphemy of sorts to get into the subject or think very much about it.

"I can remember Connor doing things like telling off bullies who thought I was an easy target because I was a little girl that carried around books. When Eolin was attacked, he was only a boy, but he ran to our house and pulled me out of the rubble. Moralan went straight to the fighting, he helped defend us. But Connor, he came for me. He found my parents and didn't let me see them, then he took me to their house, protected by spells and wards and things. We waited in the basement together, hiding in the dark. Moralan came back at some point and we fled to Rennsen with what little he could pack up in a short time.

"So I've known him for a long time. I watched him grow up just like he watched me. Even though he stayed in Rennsen when we moved to Ar-Toriess, I still saw him at least once a month for years. He's told me a lot of his stories, and about the women he's spent time with. None of them have ever inspired anything like his behavior towards you. He watches you a lot, probably a lot more than you've noticed. There's something in the way he does it, too. Clearly, he wants you, quite a bit. At the same time, it's like he's fighting himself over it. Betsy, I think he's trying to keep himself from seducing you."

The flood of information rolled over Betsy. She didn't know what to think about it all. This came on top of the muddled feelings about babies and his queer statements about it. She covered her face and started to cry. There was too much right now, it was too confusing and conflicting. Evi put an arm around her shoulders, Betsy leaned into it. The uncomplicated comfort Evi offered was welcome even as it reminded her of Myra.

"Oh, Betsy, you poor thing. I guess your life was really simple and predictable before all of this. Even if it was kind of awful. I can't imagine what it was like, but I know what mine was like, and I understand it can all be so overwhelming, and however you feel, that's okay."

Through the weeping, she managed to say, "I don't know how I feel."

"Well, that's okay, too. Sometimes you just need to let it all kind of settle out on its own and work in the back of your head while you get things done so you don't starve to death or sit in a dark room for a long time without doing anything more than grunting when people talk to you." Evi stopped for a long breath. "It took me a long time to get over losing my parents. They were such wonderful people, and I loved them very much and they understood me.

Connor does, too, but he didn't then. Kind of, but not really. I think he accepted more than he understood. Moralan, too. They're both very good men, but they're just men, you know? Connecting with their feelings can be difficult.

"Someday, I'm going to make them sit down together and talk about Moira – that's Connor's mother. They'll sit there and talk and neither one will be allowed to get up until they've both cried. Or something like that. Until that day, they're just going to keep being like...like...like two burrs under a saddle, competing for how much they can annoy the horse. No, that's not quite right, but you see the point, I think."

The chatter, only somewhat relevant to her, had a calming effect on Betsy. Evi's voice and the concern she obviously felt combined to soothe the tears away. If anyone was going to take Myra's place for her, it was probably Evi. "Yes, I think so." She wiped her face, actually letting out a tiny little bit of laughter at the idea of the two burrs. After a moment's hesitation, she wiped her nose on her cloak. Her mother would smack her for that, but her mother wasn't here. "Thank you."

Evi hugged her and held on until she pulled away first. "You're welcome. I hope we can be very dear friends, Betsy, because you're so sweet. All I ever meet anymore are students who don't know anything about anything but think they know everything about something and stuffy librarians who get upset if you touch books the wrong way. As if you can touch books wrong! Books are meant to be read, not to be left on shelves to collect dust the keepers have to brush off. I like to pull down random books sometimes just because they look so sad and neglected. I've found so many fascinating things that way. Come to think of it, that's how I found that scroll about Kailesce. It was referenced in a lonely book."

"I'm not sure if it's good that you did."

"Yes, this has certainly been harrowing, as experiences go. But without all of this, I would never have met you. I think it's at least a little worth it because of that." She nodded firmly. "Besides, something awful would happen without anyone understanding why until it's much too late. We're going to stop it somehow, and that's what's important here. We're doing something that matters."

Evi was right, of course. Betsy nodded and took a drink from the waterskin, now with even more to mull over. She still didn't know what to think or feel, but at least she wasn't wound up anymore. Somehow, all of this would come into focus and make sense, at some point. In the meantime, there were going to be people who needed her help whether she understood it all or not.

Chapter 12

Connor had a few minor injuries when the three of them returned, stony-faced, with the little boy, the horse and wagon, and at least some of the family's possessions. It didn't take long to get all of it back to the couple. Betsy wished she could stay with them to make sure they reached the next town, but didn't need Connor's reminder to know they couldn't. She waved to the little boy from the back of Connor's horse, all mentions of reward having been turned down repeatedly.

It felt good to be back to helping people for no reason other than the fact they needed help. Going back for Darius was different. She did that out of...out of a need to help someone for no other reason than that he needed help. Regardless, it was still different. He wouldn't have been in that position if she hadn't put him there. It changed how she looked at the whole situation.

Darius still rode beside Rae and Evi, the three of them chatted on and off throughout the day. And here she was with her arms around Connor, not sure how to talk to him anymore. If what Evi said was true, then she just didn't know what to say. Everything she could think of seemed uncomfortable, or pushy, or annoying, or stupid.

They pushed the horses to make up time, taking several very brief breaks instead of fewer long pauses. Connor said nothing but what was absolutely necessary and didn't look at her all day. They camped on the side of the road again, choosing to get as far as they could before full dark over staying in the safety of a town. The next day was more of the same dull, hurried riding. On the sixth day, they reached the foothills and headed straight for the western face of Praghlorgil. That was also when Connor finally spoke more than a handful of words to her.

"There's something I want to say. I'm just not quite sure how to put it."

The sudden words startled her from a doze. Betsy looked around, taking in the surroundings while she grasped his words. "Alright. Just ramble until you find it, then, I suppose. That seems to work for Evi."

He huffed in amusement. "Evi doesn't need to have a reason to throw words at things." There was a long pause before he took a deep breath and started again. "I like you, quite a bit. You're a very attractive woman, and that's more than enough for me, but there's more to you than that. I usually don't look to find it. All I ever do is look for a particular type and use what I know already works. I listen to them talk, but not really. When I do it, it's to find out how to manipulate them more so I can get what I want and so I can try not to leave too much disaster behind when I leave."

When he explained all of this before, it sounded reprehensible, but not like this. It was hard to reconcile something so despicable with the man she thought he was from watching him and listening to him. Then she thought about how he wanted to ride right past that couple, and it actually wasn't so difficult after all. Rae did warn her.

"My goal has always been to get information by any means necessary. Rae is better with people motivated by self-preservation,

I'm better with schmoozing. I clean up nicer." He coughed. "I don't want to leave you thinking I'm a monster, Betsy. What I do, I do it for kids like the ones we saved with you. That's always what it's about. Stopping people too slippery to get caught by traditional justice. I've never doubted that was the right thing for me to be doing, not in all the years I've been doing it. I still don't. It's right, and it needs to be done, and I have the skills and motivation to do it.

"What you *have* made me doubt is my methods. I would have ridden right by that couple, just because I assumed it was a ruse. And it wasn't, not even close. It was a symptom of the very thing I despise most in this world, of the thing I swore to work as hard as I can to put a stop to. That wasn't the first time those men attacked travelers, and it wouldn't have been the last. I would have left it in my wake, which is the worst sin I can imagine. Turning a blind eye to suffering. Caring more about perceptions than reality.

"You jumped off a moving horse to help them. And I just can't face you anymore because of it. I want you, I do, I can imagine...all sorts of things. But you're worth so much more than me. I don't deserve you, not in any way. I kissed you. I shouldn't have. I didn't realize it at the time, but you're something truly special, Betsy, and you deserve to be actually happy. All I could ever give you is an illusion."

Betsy swallowed past a lump in her throat. She was something special? Perhaps for her gift, but not for herself. Surely, that's not really what he meant. More importantly, she hadn't yet really worked everything else out yet, and here he was telling her to look elsewhere because he wasn't good enough. She wondered if he ever chased off Evi's suitors, and now felt he needed to do the same for her. Only he was the suitor and he was chasing himself off.

"I'm sorry." It just came out of her mouth. What else could she possibly say?

"Stop saying that," he growled. "Everything isn't your fault. This is not at all your fault. I'm telling you that I can't handle the kind of person you are, you're too..." He gestured with his hand. She couldn't see it, but thought it was an expression of him groping for the right word. "Perfect."

Of all the things she thought he might put there, 'perfect' wasn't even a consideration. "What?"

He rubbed his face. "I can't think of any other word that fits. The only thing wrong with you, Betsy, is that you've been treated so poorly you don't think you're worth anything at all."

Flabbergasted, her mouth opened and shut a few times. "That's not true."

"No? Please do catalog every flaw you think you have."

She sat there and stared at his back with no idea how to answer. It wasn't that she couldn't come up with a ready list of everything wrong with her. Her mother and Jason spent all her life telling her exactly what was on that list, she knew it well. No, the problem was that she didn't understand how someone else couldn't see it. All of it was so obvious they could both see these things without thinking. Here was Connor, unable to supply even one. It made no sense. How could he spend all this time with her and not notice?

He turned to look at her and snorted. "Right, of course you're stunned. Because that's what a person like you would be."

"What's that supposed to mean?"

"Betsy, if I had it in me to love someone, it would be you. I would hold you close and never let you go, because that's what you should have. I'm not that man and I can never be that man. I'll make you think you love me then slip out in the night and leave you alone."

She was not going to cry, not now, not over this. "Why can't you change? Are you so dead set on being horrible that you can't do anything about it, even if you want to?" If she stood facing him, she would slap him. Or try very hard to. He could probably dodge it without a problem. "You talk a lot about yourself. I this, I that, I the other. Maybe you should stop talking so much about yourself and try thinking about who you want to be instead of how awful you are."

He went quiet for a long time, and she was too busy wrestling with everything in her head to force him to talk more. Some time later, he said, "Would it make you feel better to hit me?"

"No."

"I'll stand still. Let you get a good one in."

"I don't want your pity."

"How about my blood? A pound of flesh?"

"That's not funny."

"It's a little funny."

"Oh!" Evi's shout interrupted them. "Look!" Betsy turned to see Evi pointing up at the mountainside. A group of horses stood just close enough to be recognized for what they were.

"It could be a random herd," Rae said.

"No," Betsy said, glad for the distraction. "I can see the reins hanging down from their heads."

"She's right." Darius nodded. "It has to be their mounts. We don't have to get in and get them before they find it, we just have to take it from them. We can do that outside, since we know where they're coming back to."

"I count twenty," Connor said, "that's a lot."

"We'll have to take them by stealth. There's no way we'll beat them in a fair fight."

Connor snorted at Darius. "We don't do fair fights. Let's get up there and see what we can find to set up with. Might have to go into the mountain after all, if only to pick some of them off."

Betsy held her tongue about the casual talk of murdering these men. She would just get the same lecture about self-defense and justice and the rest. At this point, she knew all the arguments already and didn't want to hear them again. What had these men really done to deserve having such judgment passed on them? They took money to follow the elf into the mountains to retrieve something that ought to stay buried. That's it. No, she couldn't just let it go.

"They're not doing anything wrong. Only the elf is. The rest of them were just hired to protect him and do his dirty work. You can't preemptively kill them for that. It's wrong. You said that you kill those who try to kill you first, but I think sometimes you use that as an excuse to take down people who are just defending themselves from you.

"All those men at that market weren't trying to kill you until you started killing them. Some of them weren't really doing anything wrong, other than not following their conscience. Is that somehow worse than Darius standing by all those nights, knowing he should do something, but not doing it because he valued his life and livelihood?"

Everyone stared at her. As soon as she noticed, she blushed scarlet.

Rae was the first to say something, she looked thoughtful. "My bow can actually do arrows without killing points, I just don't normally use it that way."

Darius nodded, shame and guilt weighing his shoulders down. "I'm trained in using the flat of my blade and my hilt. So long as I don't go overboard, it knocks them out without causing serious injury."

"My pages don't actually hurt anyone! Except I can suffocate someone. It happened by accident once, and I got them back off in time."

That left Connor, who gazed off at the horses still. Several long, empty seconds later, he sighed and said, "I have a few things I can do that aren't lethal." He snapped the reins and goaded Bonbon into a gallop. There was no time to waste now. The horses climbed up the trail that became a series of switchbacks. When they reached the herd, Connor jumped down and reached up to help Betsy down.

"We should go in until it branches." Rae pulled out her bow as she pointed to a nearby cleft in the mountainside.

"I'm coming this time." Betsy started walking. Before anyone could object, she added, "If you're not trying to kill them, but they're trying to kill you, there's a much greater chance you'll get hurt."

Connor caught up and put an arm out in front of her. "That's fine, I'm not going to argue with my healer. I'm still going in first.

Stay back with Evi." He grinned. "You can keep her quiet."

Evi wrapped her arm around Betsy's and stuck her tongue out at Connor. At least he didn't refuse. She nodded and watched him go, then Darius and Rae. The two women followed a few paces behind and found themselves in a narrow cave with an uneven floor. They had to walk in single file – Evi went first before Betsy took the initiative to do it herself. The going was slow but steady. It widened and turned and narrowed again and twisted. They stopped where it crossed a second crevasse, leaving three directions to choose from.

Connor backed them up to the last turn in the passage, perching himself and Shadow just around the corner and everyone else father back. There, they waited. Betsy sat down. Whatever happened, she didn't need to be on her feet at the beginning, she only had to be ready to run or heal someone after it started. Dim light, enough to see movement and tell who was who, filtered in from a crack overhead. Even so, Connor and Shadow were invisible so far as she could tell.

Everyone tensed at the noises echoing up the passage just a few minutes later. It was the sound of boots on stone and chain links jangling and men chatting idly. They took so long to reach Connor and Shadow. How could anyone stand doing this? Being the subject of an ambush was awful, but at least there was none of this standing around and waiting.

The first two men walked past Connor, then it all began with Darius punching one in the face with his sword hilt and Rae shooting the other with a ball tipped arrow. When it hit the man in the chest, it thumped him and knocked him back, but didn't dig in past his armor. The next man was dragged into the darkness by nothing that had to be Connor. The fourth, fifth and sixth men didn't realize what was happening until it was too late and they were on the ground or reeling, but the rest stopped and backed off. With the trap now sprung, Evi's pages flew out of her book to encircle one man.

"Ambush!" The cry rang out, echoing off the walls.

A different voice, one Betsy recognized, said, "This is what I hired you for, idiots." At least they could be sure this was the right place.

"Right. You want us, come and get us." The rest of the men backed off, out of sight.

Between Rae, Darius, and Connor, three more men found their way to unconsciousness while all that talking happened.

"Rae," Darius hissed softly, "cover me."

"I'll be there shortly," Connor's voice said.

Darius nodded and moved to the corner with Rae. Evi tiptoed up behind them and sent her pages flying around the corner. Rae gave her a sly grin, showing approval for the move, then leaned out and fired two arrows in quick succession. Darius took a deep breath and ducked round the corner. Rae fired more arrows. Evi peeked around the corner, watching, her face set in concentration. There was a lot of shouting all of a sudden, and grunting, and metal hitting metal, and Betsy got to her feet.

She could well imagine the scene. It would be a mess of men all surrounding Darius, trying to kill him, and him making an effort to just knock them out. Soon enough, they'd figure it out and somehow take advantage of it. Connor needed to get out there and help him. Slipping up behind Evi, she stuck her foot into the dark space she last saw him go into, intending to nudge him into action. He wasn't there. Somehow, he left without being seen. Just like the night he kissed her.

Moving up close to Evi, she whispered, "How is it going?"

"They're really outnumbered," Evi whispered back.

"We knew that."

"Darius is pretty amazing."

She took a step and peeked out for herself. Darius had a gash bleeding freely on his arm, but it didn't hamper him. Connor fought on the other side of them. He looked alright for now, though his black clothes made it hard to tell for sure. She spotted the elf, he stood in the wider part of the passage, leaning against the wall casually and watching the battle.

Through all of this, he noticed her and a cruel grin curled one side of his mouth. Launching himself into the group around Connor, he lunged in and slammed a dagger into Connor's back. Betsy shrieked. Even without touching him, she could tell that was a devastating injury. The noise made many heads turn towards her. Darius caught two different men on the jaw at the same time because they weren't looking.

She couldn't help herself. Betsy ran out, intent on one thing and one thing only: getting to Connor and healing him. The number of other people out here that might want to hurt her didn't matter, just that he was hurt badly enough it would kill him without her help. Vaguely, she registered Evi's pages creating a path for her, and Darius turning to follow her, and Rae's arrows hitting a man who leaped into her path.

Reaching for Connor, she put her hands on him and felt a rush leaving her. It had to be fast, there wasn't time to wait. Someone moved from the side, ducking past the pages, and curled an arm around her waist. The arm picked her up off her feet and took her away from Connor, then something pulled at her belly and twisted. Everything went so white she couldn't see anything at all. The world stayed like that for just a second, then she stood in a tended, manicured garden.

Dogs began barking. Two dogs. Jason's dogs. These were her flower beds, they stood on a path between them. "Welcome home, Lady Brexler," the elf's voice said very close to her ear.

Stunned, she turned her head, pale and shivering. "How did you do that?"

The elf laughed and held up a charm, just like the one Keric gave her a lifetime ago. "It's amazing what you can get mages to do when you have the money for it. This time, I'm not going to hurt you, I'm just going to give you to your husband. He'll see you're...taken care of."

"No." She burst into a frenzy of resisting, trying everything she could to get away from him, and he tossed her to the ground. Sword and Shield reached her and stopped just a few feet away, growling. Betsy froze, staring at them. She didn't doubt they'd rip her throat out if she made a sudden movement.

"Aw, good doggies." The elf grabbed her hair and hauled her to her feet, waving off the two dogs. They did what he wanted, which surprised her. "Try it again, Lady, I dare you."

She whimpered and went with him, covering her face. “What do you want now?”

“Don't worry your pretty little head over it.” He tossed the door open and only took a few steps inside when Keric walked in. “Oh, good.” Letting go of her, he shoved her at the mage, who caught her in his arms. “Tell the Earl he needs to keep better track of his wife. There's just one piece left now, I'll be back when I have it. She better be here then.”

Keric nodded. “I understand. Close the door, Inderion. I seem to have my hands full now.”

Inderion the elf smirked. “No kidding.” He left, shutting the door behind him as requested.

The mage sighed and squeezed her. It was an entirely unexpected embrace from a man she never knew to be sympathetic to her. “My Lord, the Lady is returned!” He put a hand on her back to guide her further inside. “My Lady, when there was no ransom demand, we thought you were lost.”

“Please.” That was all she got out before Jason appeared in the hallway, looking at her like he wasn't sure she was real. It was almost heartbreaking to see him like this. He clearly thought he lost her and now was stunned to have her back. But no, she had to remember everything he'd ever done to her, all of it, every night. It might be wonderful tonight, and maybe tomorrow and the next day, but at some point, he would start all over again. It would be the same, only worse for having been free.

“Sabetia?” Before anything else could be said, he was there, holding her close like she was made of spun glass. “I thought-” He stopped talking and focused on her cheek. His finger touched her skin delicately and nudged her chin up so he could see her face better. "Why is there blood here?"

She didn't resist him, she couldn't. "It's nothing." It must have happened as she ran through the fight, but she felt nothing when he touched it.

He stared for another long moment, then let her chin go and looked into her eyes. Habit made her look away and down, flush with embarrassment that he should have worried over her so much. "Are you alright?"

"Yes, I think so."

For another long moment, he stood there, holding her close, looking at her. "Are you hungry? You must be. Keric, take her upstairs and see she's fed." He kissed the top of her head and brushed her cheek with a finger. "I'm glad you're home safe."

"My Lord, Inderion says there's just one piece left and he'll have it soon. He made a point to remind us that she's necessary for the final ritual."

Jason nodded and handed her back to Keric. "Did he leave anything else?"

"No, my Lord."

"I'll be up shortly, I need to finish in my office."

Betsy watched him walk away, then her eyes settled on Keric. "Please," she said again, begging, "I can't do this anymore. Please help me."

Keric looked away and made a face, showing his discomfort. "I can't." He gestured and put a hand on her back to get her to go to the stairs and up them.

No matter how much she didn't want to go with him, her body refused to resist him. "You don't have to do anything, just say I ran off as soon as your back was turned."

"Lady, I can't."

Tears formed, she didn't know what else to do. Against Jason, she was helpless. Someone else would have to help her or she'd never be free. He was bigger and stronger, he had money and power, he was respected and trusted. She was just his wife. "Why won't you do something?"

Keric said nothing as he walked her up the stairs and down the hall to the bedroom. At the door to that room, he paused for a moment, just long enough for her to know he was conflicted, but still turned the knob and pushed the door open. Taking her cloak, he said, "Just go inside. Everything will be fine."

"No, it won't." This was the last stand she could make, the last chance she had to get away. That made no sense, but it still felt true. The moment she crossed this threshold was the moment she gave up. Her eyes burned and tears slid down her cheeks. Even so, she made fists at her sides and held her chin up. "Help me, you're the only one who can."

"Just go inside," he repeated, also begging. "I'm sorry, my Lady, I truly am, but there's nothing I can do."

"Just look away."

"My Lady, I'm a mage." He pointed into the room more insistently as he pleaded with her. "No matter what I do, if you're not here when he returns, he'll know I let you go." That was it, then.

Keric held his oaths or debts, or whatever compelled him to serve her husband as higher than anything. Against that, she had no hope whatsoever and stopped trying. He sighed with relief when she shuffled dispiritedly into the room. "I'll have something sent up, my Lady."

"Don't bother." There was no point. It would be days or weeks or months before Darius was able to figure out what happened to her and find a way to get her out. By then, she wouldn't be worth saving anymore. Maybe she could find a way to get a message to Matron Aila, but nothing came to mind. Jason wasn't going to let her out of the house unescorted now, not even for a moment, and he would find a way to keep her from going to see the Matron privately. It would sound very reasonable, and she would agree with him. She could see it all unfolding in her mind, along with more pregnancies that failed, more knowing and pitying looks, more conversations where she had to dance around the truth.

As the door shut behind her, the soft click felt like the clang of a prison cell. The Mother Goddess made her a promise, she thought, and broke it already. She sank onto the edge of the bed and buried her face in her hands, weeping. In that dream, she broke the cord. Why was she so naïve as to think she could end something like this so simply, so easily? It was just her two hands, and... Pulling her hands away, she looked at them. It was her own two hands. She broke the cord with her own two hands. There was a hammer and a spike, but she had to pick up the hammer, she had to lay the cord on the spike, she had to strike it. All of those things, she did herself, for herself. No one helped her, no one did it for her.

There was a way out of this, she just had to find it and take it and not wait like a mewling kitten for someone to come along and pick her up. Keric couldn't save her, Darius couldn't save her, Connor, Rae, and Evi couldn't save her, no Disciple could save her. This was her problem, and she was going to fix it. All she needed was a plan. Wiping her face, she got up and paced back and forth, thinking furiously. The room had a window, a pane of glass that didn't open. There were things in the room that could be used as weapons, but she couldn't possibly actually harm anyone, not even him.

The door opened, and one of the servants paced in with a tray and a nervous smile. "Welcome home, m'Lady."

As if this place was really a home. It was a house, a place she lived because there was no other option. Yet, there was another option. If she asked, Evi would convince Moralan to let her stay in his home. Connor would to let her use his apartment, Rae probably would too. Darius had skills that could earn him a living anywhere, and he would provide for her until she could figure something out for herself. Without Jason, she was no longer wealthy. That's all he gave her: money. Everything else that happened here was him taking from her. He took her freedom, her dignity, her children, everything, and in return, he expected her to be satisfied with fine clothes and food.

None of this, though, was the servant's fault. "Thank you." If it sounded stiff and distant, that was unintentional. Girding herself to face Jason would take time. She couldn't afford to be soft right now, not for anyone. The woman scurried out and shut the door again, leaving Betsy to ignore the food and pace more. Every time she reached the wall, she reaffirmed her commitment to stand tall, to tell him what she really thought, to save herself from a lifetime of... Torture, that's what he did to her, he tortured her.

She stopped in mid-pace, catching her reflection in the mirror and staring at herself. Mostly, she saw her hair, the corkscrew curls all around her face that her mother always said were her best feature. Myra loved playing with it, arranging it in new, different ways. When people complimented her, that was the part they always mentioned first. Most importantly, Jason used it to control her. He grabbed it, over and over, to get a solid grip on her. If it wasn't there, he couldn't control her with it.

The knives he liked to cut her with were in that drawer, over there. He was so confident of how cowed she was, he didn't even bother finding a way to lock it. Hurrying over, suddenly resolute and determined, she yanked the drawer open and picked the smallest one. Back at the mirror, she took a handful of hair and held it out, putting the knife close to her head and staring, wide-eyed at what she was about to do. All her life, it had been long enough to reach past her shoulders. This was nearly like cutting off a hand or a foot.

"You don't own me," she said, voice small and breathy. If she could tell herself, she could tell him. "I'm not here to be pretty for you to look at. What I want matters." She gained confidence as she spoke, her voice firming with each word. "I'm a person, not a, a-" What was she to him? "A toy." Cringing away from what she saw in the mirror, she yanked the blade through her hair, shearing off a handful. It was a sharp blade and took only one tug to leave her standing there, shaking like a leaf and staring dumbly at her hand, full of her own hair.

She opened her mouth to say something, but the sound wouldn't come out, so she closed it again and gulped. "This is what I want," she whispered. Then she said it again, louder, and again. The fourth time, it was nearly a shout and she threw the hank of hair at the mirror. "I am not a toy!" She cut off another handful and threw that at the mirror, too, then another and another until there was nothing left to cut off this way. Her reflection was strange, an angry woman with odd and uneven short hair, panting from more than just the frenzy of activity. That pile of hair lying on the dressing table was Jason's, he could have that. Nothing else was for him.

The door opened, Jason walked in through it and went straight for her, but he stopped just a few steps in and stared at her, blinking. "Sabetia, my flower, what have you done?"

"I am not your flower, not now, not ever again." Saying that felt so wrong and so right at the same time. It went against everything she was taught. It also came from her heart. The knife still gripped in her hand, she stayed where she was, staring him down.

Taken aback was the only proper description for how he looked. For a few very long seconds, he stood there dumbstruck and she glared at him, terrified and exhilarated at the same time. Then he moved very fast, slapping her hard enough to make her stagger backwards. She held up the knife, but he smacked her hand and she dropped it. He shoved hard enough to be knocked to the floor. When she caught sight of his expression, it chilled her to the bone.

He enjoyed this. That grin was gleeful and malicious, taking great pleasure from her fighting back for once. "I knew you were strong, Sabetia, from the moment I saw you at the funeral." He kicked her in the belly, knocking the wind out of her. “When I saw you at that party, I also knew you were weak. You did exactly what I knew you'd do. Today, you've surprised me for the first time.” Picking her up roughly, he shoved her against the post of the bed, pinning her there with his body behind hers. Her head hit the post as part of it, keeping her too stunned to react properly. “I like it.”

The pain wasn't the worst she'd ever felt; he'd done worse. This time was still different. She reeled and tried to push back against him, tried to resist while he grabbed her hands in one of his, but he was too strong for her. Never before had she felt so trapped and helpless, never before had she understood she had a choice. He tied up her hands to keep her there and moved away while she struggled, squirmed, and scrabbled to find some way to get free.

“Stop, Sabetia, you'll hurt yourself.” Yes, that was his job. “I wish I'd known this was still inside you, my flower.”

“I'm not your flower,” she screamed at him. “Let me go!”

He laughed at her. The sound made her stop and hang limply from the shirt binding her wrists to the top of the post. “Yes, there's really no point to all this effort. It's adorable and delightful, but you're not getting away. Where did you get these clothes?”

What should she answer? Betsy thought about it, she had nothing better to do. If she enraged him enough, would he make a mistake? She could take whatever he could give and felt certain he wouldn't kill her, no matter what. He knew what happened to his mother, and couldn’t expect to fare much better. Even an Earl couldn’t get away with killing his wife in their bedroom. He might be able to frame a guard somehow, but it would be a great deal of effort, and when it was done, he would be without his favorite toy. Thinking she was dead surely made him appreciate what he had when she was returned to him.

She took a deep breath. "I paid a man with sex for them. It was the best I've ever had."

Jason went silent and still.

"There was another man, too. He freed me from the attackers, and I repaid him with sex, also. Both were better men than you, more interested in pleasing me than themselves despite the arrangement. Who knows, the next child I carry may be one of theirs. There was also a woman, I gave her what satisfaction she wanted to hide me away for the day. Had I not needed to go out for food, I wouldn't have been found and I would never have come back, because even she was more capable than you."

She couldn't see him, couldn't imagine what he must be thinking. A tug on her dress was followed by ripping and a line of sharp pain drawn down her spine. "You know what I noticed, Sabetia?" His voice was cold and hard, flatter than she'd ever heard it before. His rage would be quiet, sharp, and painful. All she had to do was endure it and keep her wits about her. There would be a chance, she had to believe that, had to hold onto that hope. "This bruise I just gave you is already yellow."

Ice filled her. She healed herself without trying, and he noticed. It didn't happen yesterday when the elf stabbed her, but it did today. Something about the dream, maybe. Did the Mother Goddess give her what she needed to survive today, knowing it would be brutal? Was all of this destined to happen, and she would have wound up here sooner or later, in this position, no matter what? Her first thought about that was to bemoan the unfairness of it, but that wasn't right. The world wasn't 'fair', it just was. All she could do was make the best of what she had.

Taking a deep breath, she did what she could to brace for what was to come. He would push to see how far he could go, then push again and again and again. This time, there would be no fake apologies, no reassurances it would never happen again so long as she didn't anger him. No, this time, it would be unending and unapologetic. He would never trust her, not for a moment. But somehow, in all of that, if she just endured, a moment would come and she would seize it, even if she had to drag herself across the floor with bloody hands.

Chapter 13

The mirror was right there to keep her company when she woke up lying on her side and groaned. At some point during his efforts, she passed out, unable to stay conscious through what he did. However long she slept, it wasn't enough to undo everything he did, and along with the aches everywhere, she felt a strange tightness in her belly and back. The mirror only showed her face, the rest of her was out of sight from it. Her hair, her beautiful hair, was gone.

Looking down to survey herself, she immediately discovered the source of the queer sensation. A sword stuck through her, the hilt pressing against her belly and the blade sticking out her back. It didn't hurt until she looked, then it felt unpleasant without being unbearable or even especially troubling. How was that even possible? A sword stuck through her ought to hurt, horribly, like when the elf stabbed her.

"My Lady, his Lordship asked me to tend to you as soon as you wake." Keric walked in briskly, coming to her side before he stopped and stared at her.

She looked up at him, accusation as heavy on her face as she could make it. "You could have prevented this."

"Let's get that out," he said stiffly. Pulling the small dagger he kept at his waist, he leaned over her to take a look. "It's healed into you, my Lady."

"Then you'll have to cut it out."

"Yes, I will." At least there was one man in this world who got no enjoyment from hurting her. “I'll be as quick as I can.” He swallowed audibly and gripped the sword hilt with one hand, using the dagger to separate her flesh from it. She could tell he winced with every little gasp she made trying to hold back screams. “I'm sorry, my Lady.” With that, he pulled on the blade to free it, making her shriek as it ripped away gobs of flesh from her stomach where his dagger missed cutting it free.

She panted, trying to handle the pain that lessened minutely with every passing second, while he sat back on his feet and watched her with awe. His eyes went from the blade to her naked body and back. The last thing on his mind had to be the fact she wore no clothes, but she felt exposed all the same and pulled the sheet over herself. “Go. If you can't do anything else, leave me alone.”

“His orders-” He choked on the words.

“Why do you do what he tells you to?” As the seconds slipped by, she got stronger, her body repaired itself more. Her voice reflected that, steadying and gaining volume until she was speaking normally. “What does he have over you that you can't just go to Ar-Toriess and work for yourself? What are you afraid of?”

Keric frowned at the floor. “He saved my life once, my Lady. In a peculiar way that bound me to him by more than just words or deeds. I'm really just as much of a prisoner here as you are. I'm sorry, I truly am. Before, I thought-” He shook his head. “This is beyond anything I ever imagined he was capable of. He's always been rough with his women, but nothing like this.” Setting the blade down as if it was suddenly too hot to handle, he shook his head. “The servants all know, of course, everyone in the house knows. If they didn't before, they do now.

"No one will quit and no one will help you, they're all too concerned about their jobs. I'm sure you don't really understand, but it's perilous to be unemployed, especially with the kind of reference the Earl would give for someone who quit over his treatment of his wife. Keeping your employer's secrets close, he values that in his people."

"He needs to die, for both of us." It was awful to realize this truth. She couldn't do it, she knew that. All she could do was get away.

He wiped his hands, spattered with blood, on his pants. "I can't help you with that. I can suggest that you behave as if this takes you far longer to recover from than it actually seems to. I'll tell him that he almost killed you, at the least. I doubt that's much of a lie, even."

Betsy closed her eyes. "I can't do this anymore."

Keric sighed, she heard him get up and walk a short distance away, then come back. "There's food here, you should eat. I don't know what your gift truly is, but using magic takes energy. What you do probably does, also. Stay in bed as much as you can for the rest of the day. At least you can have peace for this one night." He didn't wait for her to respond before he left her alone.

She could handle pretending to be more of an invalid than she really was. It would be so easy to just fall back asleep right now, but he was right, she needed to eat. Even before she came here, she was hungry, and who knew how much time passed since then. The tray on the nightstand had little bites of waffle already drenched in syrup, with strawberries and a glob of sweet cheese. It was the kind of meal

Jason used to have made when she first came here, so he could feed it to her. The memories made the food revolting. She forced herself to eat it anyway. It was delicious.

Not long after she licked her fingers, the meal finished, she started to perk up. No one bothered her, not even a servant, so Keric must have convinced Jason she was too weak to do anything but lie here. This could be her one chance to get away again. It was cold outside, but the important part was escaping, not being warm when she did. If she went to the Temple, she could be safe there. Aila would protect her, at least for a few hours, and might be able to help her find Darius or Connor. She hurried to the closet and threw a dress on, stepped into a pair of slippers.

She was still covered in blood, but didn't care. It was much more important to get out now than to worry about things like that. At the stairs, she perched low and listened. The house was quiet enough, she thought. She'd be exposed on the stairs, and if Jason stepped out of his office, he'd see her. No servant stairwell meant this was the only way out. She took a deep breath and forced herself down those stairs, one step at a time, as slowly and silently as she could. They were, at least, sturdy enough not to squeak.

No servants were about, and Jason's office door was closed. If he wasn't inside there, he was probably out of the house, tending to business while she recovered. That was what he usually did. Or, at least, that was what he said he did. For all she knew, he was off engaging prostitutes all those times he left her alone to heal what he did to her. She paused at the bottom of the stairs and breathed a few times, then briskly walked to the back door. The front door was in plain view of the gate guards. The back yard had no such things.

Only now did she discover it was a few hours after midday already. If he was out, Jason would return soon. If he was in his office, he might come out anytime. Fortune smiled upon her as she crept to the back door – no servants crossed her path at all. Keric's alarms weren't active during daylight hours, so she wouldn't be caught that way, either. Just when she stepped outside, she remembered the dogs. They roamed freely in the back and would bark the moment they saw her. In this soft blue dress, she didn't blend with the scenery and wouldn't go unnoticed. The only thing for it was to hurry around the house, ducking under the windows.

The two guards stood at their post. Her heart pounded at the sight of them. Something needed to distract them, something that would let her slip out through the front gate. The walls were too high for her to climb, and she thought Keric probably set some kind of alarm up there. After all, someone like Connor could just hop over the wall and stroll right inside if he timed it right and was prepared. Whatever Keric was, it didn't include being a fool.

If Jason arrived or left, the guards would be distracted by him. One would go to open the carriage door for him, the other would hold the gate open. She couldn't imagine a way to use that to her advantage. They had to have orders to prevent her from leaving unescorted, and if Jason knew she tried to leave, he would do something to prevent such attempts in the future. She crouched down behind a line of shrubs to think, blood pumping too fast with fear and a determined sort of panic for her to feel the chill in the air. Maybe she could go back, find the dogs, and get them to froth about something other than her. The only thing they ever did at her command was chase a stick and not bring it back.

Sticks were handy here, the gardeners didn't generally bother raking them up in the less used parts of the yard. Her fingers curled around two and she flitted back to find the two dogs. Both of them lay stretched out in the sun. She picked up a rock and threw it so it landed near them, getting their attention perked, then she hurled the two sticks, one after the other, as hard as she could into the back. That done, she ran back to hide in the shrubs again.

It was the worst plan imaginable. Somehow, it worked. Perhaps the Mother Goddess watched over her, aiding her in this dark time when she made such an effort to help herself. Whatever the reason, the dogs didn't notice her and started barking madly, like they had when she found Shadow. It went on for long enough that the two guards took notice of it and one ran off to deal with it. The other stayed. She wasn't sure what to do about that until Keric's voice shouted from the front door.

"Guard, go check around the back, it seems like there's someone about." She saw him jog to the front gate and didn't hear anything else he said, but the guard nodded to him and ran off to the back. This still wasn't ideal, but it was a better chance than she was likely to ever get again. As soon as the guard was out of sight, she stood up and tore across the grounds as fast as she could. Keric didn't see her until she slowed down to avoid running into him, and he was plainly surprised by her presence. "My Lady, you should be inside, resting."

"No, I needed the fresh air. I think I saw someone coming around the side of the house. The guards missed him completely."

She could tell he knew she was making this up. There was no possible way that, after their earlier conversation, he wouldn't see right through this shallow ploy. “I'll investigate it immediately, my Lady. You should return inside for your own safety.” He gave her a respectful bow of his head, turned his back on her, and walked away.

The moment he went out of her sight, she yanked the gate open and ran as fast as her feet could manage. She didn't care what the neighbors' guards and servants saw or didn't see, she didn't care about the gentleman walking down the street, and she didn't care about the two carriages trundling along. What mattered was freedom. Fear of being caught out by Jason returning in his carriage pushed her to keep going even when she thought her chest would explode. The Temple was in sight, then it was right before her, then she hit the door with a little squeak rather than slow down and yanked it open.

Betsy peered into the main chamber, moving cautiously in case someone present might recognize her, but it was empty. She remembered coming here that first time, how Jason looked standing up there. At the time, he was genuinely mourning for his father. Their relationship must have been close. He probably learned everything he knew from his father. Including how to treat his wife? Her feet took her to the platform, where she stepped up and went to the altar, running both hands over the smooth stone surface. Was that why his mother killed his father? After just one day spent away from him, feeling truly free, she wished Jason was dead. If his mother endured that sort of treatment for more than twenty years, it was a miracle she waited that long.

"Betsy?" Darius's voice surprised her, she turned and smiled at him.

Remembering what she did to her hair made her understand why he sounded so uncertain of her identity, and she reached up to rub it sheepishly. "You came for me."

"Did he cut off your hair?" He jogged to her, hopping up onto the platform, and wrapped his arms around her, holding her close.

"No, I did it. I thought...I was trying to make him angry." Leaning into him, she returned the embrace. "It worked a little better than I expected."

"I only stopped in to check with Matron Aila, if she'd seen you. The others are taking a walk past the estate to check the security. Rumor has it you returned unexpectedly this morning."

"Rumor is surprisingly true." She breathed in his scent, it felt more like home than anywhere else she'd ever been. "How did you get back so quickly?"

"Evi. She's apparently got a book that she can use to send messages to Moralan."

Betsy nodded, remembering him giving it to her. Standing here, enveloped in safety, she recalled the dream from the other night. Was the Mother Goddess trying to tell her something? That blinding flash, it was important and... She pulled away enough to look up at him. "Darius, I think there's a piece of the sword on Niwlynys."

He frowned in thought. "Only Disciples are allowed there."

If Jason and the elf were the only ones actively looking for the sword, they'd never be able to get that piece, which meant it was safe where it was, and this whole scheme was fruitless. Except that assumed neither of them could charm, con, or otherwise convince a Disciple to get it and bring it out. When he made an effort, Jason could be quite disarming. No, they would have to get it somehow, before Jason or the elf managed the same trick. If it could be destroyed, all the better. She didn't have an answer for the question of how, though, and shrugged.

"I might be able to go there. Because of my gift. I could...ask a Disciple to be trained." Yes, that would work. Betsy didn't know how she knew it would work, she just did. "But not Matron Aila." Who knew what Aila would or wouldn't tell Jason. She didn't want to find out the hard way.

Darius nodded. "Yes, we should go." He kept an arm around her shoulders and they walked quickly out of the building. The cat sat outside, waiting for them. Upon seeing Betsy, he ran off down the street, towards Jason's estate. "The cat apparently can communicate with Connor somehow, like a mage's familiar. They'll come for us." Guiding her into a nearby alley, he pulled her in close again for another embrace, then held her at arm's length by the shoulders to look into her eyes. "What did he do?"

His gaze was too intense for her, she looked away. What she was powerless to stop Jason from doing embarrassed her too much. "It's not important."

"Just by you saying that, I know it was bad. Tell me."

She shook her head. "Not now. His security will be on extra guard as soon as they notice I've gone missing. There's nothing you can do about it anyway. I just want to leave the city and never return."

"Promise to to tell me another time. You can't hold it all inside forever, Betsy, it'll eat you up. It's not noble to carry that. My father-" Darius pressed his lips together and clenched his jaw. "He wasn't much better than the Earl. He murdered my mother and escaped justice, and I've done everything I could to try to find him, except look for him myself. Maybe I will someday. But listen to me. I joined the Army for a lot of reasons. What I found there were a lot of other men with their own stories. We shared them with each other. Having spoken of it, at length and several times, the anger is less than it once was. I can live with it better for having talked it out. You will, too. I swear it on my life. So, please, just promise you'll speak of it at some point."

All this time, she never thought to ask him about his life, not even about his family or friends, or anything. He would have given his life to protect hers, because that's what Jason paid him to do, and she had no idea he carried this burden around. Betsy blushed, ashamed she'd been so self-centered, focused on her own problems and suffering, oblivious to those around her. Her head began nodding of its own accord. "Yes, I promise. Just not now."

He moved like he meant to touch her cheek, but thought better of it and dropped the hand awkwardly. "Good." Whatever else he intended to say was cut off by the cat showing up again, Connor, Rae, and Evi right behind him. "We need a Disciple," Darius told them without preamble, "just not this one."

"Vanora will help." Connor took a moment to catch his breath, then Betsy found herself being hugged by him. "I'm glad you're alright. We heard what happened, more or less." Letting go, he gestured for everyone to follow, and they did. Darius glared at Connor, Betsy wasn't sure exactly why.

Evi took up Betsy's arm as they hurried along in his wake. “Here, take my hat, it'll hide your face some.” The large white knitted hat got stuffed onto her head. “Your hair, such a shame, we'll have to fix it. Her voice lowered to keep from being overheard. “You should have seen them. Connor went nuts. Darius, too. Both of them yelled at each other, it was something. I think if Rae didn't get in the middle of it, they might have come to blows. Never, in all my years of being either avoided or big brothered by Connor have I ever seen him so invested in the well-being of a woman other than myself. Or Rae. He cares about Rae, too, quite a bit, but not like that. She's another sister to him.”

Betsy frowned and her eyes found Connor's back, leading her mind to considering how she actually felt. Gratitude, she certainly had that – he saved her from a fate potentially worse than her marriage. Then he saved her again, from dying. Now, she saved herself, but he was clearly prepared to break into the house and get her out, and he had a way forward. Connor was handsome in her opinion. He also liked women, a lot, or so everyone suggested, including Connor himself. He kissed her, and it was wonderful, except for how it reminded her of Jason.

As she watched the one man, the other glanced back. His gaze flicked to where she was looking, and before she could do more than notice, he turned away again. “And Darius, too, he's definitely got something for you, Betsy, it's just hard to say what, exactly.”

“He's been my personal guard for two years.”

Evi gave a happy little sigh. "Oh, you have two men ready to stab each other over you, that's so incredible. I don't have even one. But then, that's not really so very important to me. I like books much better. If you don't like it, you can just close it and walk away. And if you do, it'll be there whenever you need it, forever."

Betsy didn't think Connor and Darius would actually hurt each other over her. Both clearly cared for her, she just wasn't so sure how deep it went for either. There was, however, one man who would definitely stab anyone he thought wanted her. She glanced back in the direction they came, half expecting to see him charging down the way, sword bared, face set in a snarl of rage. If he ever found out that Darius wasn't dead and was helping her stay away, Jason would kill him. They were really in the same position, and he stayed with her out of guilt. Connor might be helping her out of guilt, too, because of Shadow, or he might genuinely care about the demon in the sword.

The possibility either of them did this out of nothing more than attraction to her was so ridiculously preposterous she had to laugh on the inside. Who would want a woman with a husband like Jason? Even if the marriage was fully and officially dissolved somehow, Jason would never stop wanting her, specifically. Some other woman wouldn't do, he had to have her. Before this, she might have suggested all he wanted was a pretty girl. Now that he knew she could heal herself, there would never be anyone else for him.

These thoughts occupied her as they moved through the city, even with Evi prattling on about stories of love and romance. It was a long way. The only reason she didn't need to stop and take a break for a few minutes was the persistent fear he already scoured the city for her. He might even get the City Guard to help and tell them she was driven mad by her ordeal, or something along those lines. By the time they reached Vanora's Temple, her dress itched from sweat mixing with dried blood and Evi had gone quiet.

Betsy and Evi sat down on one of the benches close to the door, both worn out by the hike. Darius stayed with them, vigilant at the door. Connor and Rae went farther in, looking for Vanora. The three of them stayed quiet until the old woman was brought to them. She walked straight to Betsy and offered her a gnarled hand. "I know why you're here, child. Come with me."

Standing, Betsy took the hand without question and didn't look at the others. This was about her, not them. It was for her, not them. "Did you have a dream?"

"No, nothing like that." Vanora led her to the altar. "Sit."

It was a strange place to be asked to do this, and she hesitated. Wasn't it a disrespectful thing to do? "Here?" Her finger tapped the stone, it felt so real and solid. Like stone should, of course, but more than that. Somehow, the altar felt more weighty and significant than mere rock could be. She didn't remember noticing that in Aila's temple.

"Yes, girl," Vanora chuckled, "put your rear on the stone. You won't be struck down for it."

"Why?"

The Elder put her hands on her hips and gave Betsy a stern look. "Why are you here?"

Although she could probably lie quite convincingly, Betsy felt this woman would see right through her, with or without the altar. “I need to go to Niwlynys.”

“Only Disciples and Acolytes can get to Niwlynys. You're not the first and too old to become the second. Ass on the altar.”

“It's important.” Taking the choice of words as a sign the old woman's temper wouldn't tolerate her continuing to not obey, Betsy got on the altar, sitting up straight.

“How so?” Vanora pulled the hat off Betsy's head and examined the aftermath of the impromptu haircut with an unreadable expression.

“Can you imagine there are Disciples who would, if paid a great deal of money, go there and bring something back for someone?”

“Of course. We aren't saints or gods ourselves, just women willing to further Clynnidh's work.” A pair of scissors came from a pocket and she began snipping at Betsy's hair.

“I need to go there first and find something. And destroy it before it allows someone to release a demon.”

“Mmhmmm.”

“I dreamed about it. The Mother Goddess sent me a vision, like the one she sent to tell me I'm a Healer. I have to go to Niwlynys and do this.”

Hair fell from her head, drifting down all around her. “What makes you so sure you have to do it? Why not Rae or the other woman, or just any Disciple?”

For maybe a minute, Betsy sat there in silence, watching the others watch her from across the room. They looked like a band of able warriors from a tale, ready to tackle any challenge before them.

She didn't feel like she fit into such a group. “It's my responsibility. My grandmother charged me with protecting the stone the demon was bound into, and I failed. I can't get that back, but I can do this.”

A brush came out of another pocket, Vanora used it to sweep the hair off her neck and shoulders and back. “If you need to go to Niwlynys and the Mother Goddess finds you worthy of the trip, the mist will let you through. If not, it will devour you. It doesn't actually matter if you're devoted to her or not. What matters is your certainty and worth.”

Betsy picked the hat back up and still sat there. “I'm not worth that much.”

“Nonsense.” Vanora smacked her in the back of the head with the brush, but so lightly she barely felt it. “Go face the mist, girl. It's something you'll have to do alone, but you need to do it.”

“Can you tell us the way?”

“No.” Vanora put her hands on the altar and looked almost apologetic. “It's not that kind of place.” A bright flash of light blinded Betsy momentarily, then she blinked and found herself staring up at the bright blue sky. She lay on sand, water lapping gently beside her, and no other people around. Sitting up slowly, she saw she'd been deposited right where she needed to be: on the shore of Mist Lake. Silvery fog sat on the surface of the lake just twenty feet in, and it extended up into infinity. On the other side of that fog, she'd find the Isle of Clynnidh, Niwlynys, where she needed to go.

Vanora was clearly more than she seemed. Right about now, she probably had to deal with four shocked, unhappy people. There was nothing she could do about that. Likewise, the question of how to get back wasn't important. Looking around, she saw no boats or rafts of any kind. Her dream had her trying to swim – she took that as an instruction.

As it was in the dream, the water felt warm and pleasant. When she couldn't reach the bottom anymore, she tried to move her arms and legs enough to keep her head above the surface. It was a lot of work. The dress was heavy, it seemed to be part of the problem. She turned around and kicked her way back to where she could still touch the bottom. There, she rested for a short time and pulled the dress off. An island full of women devoted to Clynnidh's path weren't going to be troubled by a naked woman in their midst.

Leaving the cloth there, she gave all the effort she had to trying to swim across the lake without knowing how. She managed to keep her face above the surface this time, and watched the mist swallow her up. Warmer than the air, it filled her with cloying dampness as she breathed it in. Suddenly, it was impossible to tell which way she needed to go. All around, she saw nothing but mist. In the dream, she was underwater and just knew which way to go. Should she duck under now? If she did, would she be able to break the surface again before she ran out of air?

This was a test, if what Vanora said was true; she was being tested by the Mother Goddess. Either she would find her way through it, or she wouldn't. Taking as deep a breath as she could, she let herself sink below the surface and looked around. Her eyes stung in the murky water, but she kept them open. Pain was nothing more than a passing trial to be endured. A dark shape in the distance pulled her that way.

As she got closer, it resolved into Jason, hanging from a chain secured around his calves, a weight on the other end. His eyes bulged, he was starting to drown. Her first impulse was to turn around and swim away. There was the man she knew had to die for her to be free, and for Keric to be free. Darius could be free, too – with Jason dead, she wouldn't need the protection he offered and he could feel his debt to her was repaid. But he was a person, too. No matter how horrible and despicable he was, no matter how awful the things he did were, was she really qualified to judge him for it?

It was a test. She didn't know the answer. Killing someone was so horrible, so awful, but Jason was horrible and awful, too. What was she supposed to choose? Was one wrong worse than the other? Was Connor's approach acceptable? He wasn't a bad person, he didn't do awful things that she knew about, he just happened to kill people instead of bringing them to the Guard for trial. If she set aside that part of him, everything she saw so far pointed to a decent man. And Rae was a decent woman. So was Darius, who would have choked Connor to death if given the chance, and wanted to kill Jason for her.

Her lungs started to burn, she just didn't know what to do. He reached out to her imploringly, and she just stayed where she was, frozen, paralyzed by the decision. Not doing anything was going to kill them both. The moment that thought entered her head, she kicked for the surface, staying out of his reach. She didn't sneak out of his house just to sacrifice herself for him. He shoved a blade through her and walked away, then sent Keric to help her.

Breaking the surface was the most wonderful thing imaginable. She sucked in a lungful of air in warm sunshine with a grassy slope not far from her. The mist lay behind her, the Isle in front. She moved as quickly as she could for the shore, crawled up on it and collapsed, panting. Was that tacit approval for killing Jason? Wiping water off her face, she didn't want to think about it. Given the choice between her life or his, she chose her own. Was that the test? Maybe there was someone here who could explain it, because she didn't really understand what point was being made.

"Are you alright?"

Betsy rolled enough to sit up partway and see the owner of that high pitched voice. It was a girl of thirteen or fourteen, wearing a plain, simple dress of white cotton. "I don't know." It was the most honest answer possible.

The girl blinked a few times, then hurried closer. "How did you-Did you *swim* here?"

"Yes, through the mist." Betsy let the girl help her up – she felt a little unsteady on her feet and rather worn out. "I need help and the Mother Goddess guided me here." That wasn't quite so honest, but didn't feel like a lie, exactly.

"Oh, my. I've never heard of anyone doing that before. I mean, not successfully. There are stories..." The girl helped her up the gentle slope and into the trees. It was lovely here, the colors all seemed brighter than normal and the weather was an indulgence after a long winter back home that hadn't lifted enough for the plants to come back yet. The sun felt warm without being hot, the light breeze was probably just right for someone wearing clothes. For Betsy, still sopping wet and quite naked, it made her shiver.

"I've heard the stories, too. I wasn't honestly sure I wouldn't wind up one of them."

"That's the bravest thing I can imagine."

Brave? Her? Betsy didn't consider herself brave, she just did what she had to, trying to right the wrongs she was responsible for. "I need to find something that I think is here, and maybe talk to someone about a strange gift I seem to have." No, she wasn't brave at all. If she was brave, she would tell the girl she needed to talk to someone about Jason, about putting him behind her.

"I'll take you to the temple." They walked at the pace Betsy set, slow and careful. This place was far from deserted, and she started to see other women and girls doing various tasks and activities. That group of girls washed laundry, a mixed group over there used looms and spinning wheels, others tended gardens, worked with food, sewed, and more. The island must be self-sufficient, which made sense now that she thought about it.

No one was bothered by her nudity so far as she could tell, though it certainly marked her as an outsider of some kind. By the time they wound through the small wood buildings nestled among the trees to reach the grand stone temple, several of the women and girls followed, presumably curious. The inside of the temple was just like the ones in Rennsen, if a little more ornate. The decorations, however, weren't opulent, merely plentiful. Carvings of myriad images and runes covered nearly every inch of the walls, much of it painted or inlaid with other stones or metals. This building had been here for a long time, and many, many women left their mark.

In the center, a woman in a white gown finer and better fitting than the girl's knelt, head bowed. "I know who you are," the woman's crackling voice whispered. It felt like that voice went straight to her mind, bypassing her ears. "Sabetia Kayles."

Betsy sucked in a breath, surprised. Should she correct the woman? "I'm using Betsy these days."

"For good reason." The woman stood slowly and waved a thin, wrinkled hand to beckon her closer. Lines of age creased her face, and her movements betrayed frailty. "Come, child, come before the Mother Goddess in this, Her holiest place, as you are, bared for Her."

The girl ducked out from under Betsy's arm and backed away. Betsy walked with care, her body protesting the effort with nothing to use as a crutch. "I don't mean to interrupt-"

"Oh, hush," the woman snapped, but not unkindly. Accustomed to being silenced, Betsy went quiet immediately. "Don't apologize for living, it's unbecoming. You're here exactly when you're supposed to be, and you shouldn't take any guilt for it not being when I was expecting you. Now, you're here for a reason. Let's talk about it." She gestured for Betsy to go to the altar, just as Vanora had, and already reassured that wouldn't be asked if it wasn't acceptable, she sat on the cool stone. "Lie down, relax, and tell me why you came."

For some reason, lying down felt more like exposing herself, but Betsy did as she was told. Why would she resist? She never resisted anyone or anything. Not successfully, anyway. "I need to find a piece of a sword before the men trying to assemble it do. If I don't stop them, they'll release the demon bound in one of the pieces."

The woman stood beside the altar, looking down at her. Those eyes were a faded blue, almost gray, and traveled down her body until they rested on her stomach. “I see.” She reached out a warm hand and placed it lightly just below her belly button. “You're sure that's the reason you came?”

Betsy gulped. The contact made her want to squirm for how intimate it felt. So many years of being punished for not sitting still had a tight grip on her and kept her frozen in place. “It's the most important one.”

“By what measure?”

“I'm just one person. I can only affect so many others. A demon can do much more harm than I could ever do good.”

“Are you sure about that?”

Betsy frowned, not comprehending. “Yes, of course. I'm not important.”

“And yet, you're the one looking for the piece of the sword.”

“It's my responsibility. I promised to keep it safe.”

The woman's gaze seemed to hold pity. “Do you know the greatest challenge men face?”

“The Disciples teach it is to master their inner demons, the darker impulses that yearn to make war instead of peace.” This change of subject confused Betsy. What did it have to do with anything?

“I find it ironic that men would seek to loose actual demons when they have their own to contend with, don't you? But then, the Earl of Venithys has never bothered to even try to master his own demons, so why shouldn't he seek to throw the bonds off a true one?”

With every question, Betsy understood this conversation less. “I don't know why he's doing it."

"Don't you? Think, child, think. Imagine, for a moment, that everything in your life happened to bring you here, now." The hand on her abdomen pressed firmly without being uncomfortable. "How did you meet him?"

"At the funeral. His mother murdered his father." Except that maybe wasn't the right way to see it. "I think...I think his father hurt his mother and she finally couldn't take it anymore and killed him to make it stop."

"I'm glad to hear you made that connection. Do you know anything about her?"

"Just that her name was Evelyn."

"Yes. She was my daughter. I wanted her to be a Disciple, like me, but that wasn't the life for her." The woman pulled her hand away and sighed. "I didn't like that man, he was an ass. She would never admit to what was going on. I knew anyway. Such things can only be hidden so well for so long. You know that already, you know they whisper about you, about him, about what might be really going on. But you can't bear it anymore and he's crossed a line."

"Are you saying that your daughter killed her husband so Jason would remember me when I got older? That everything I've been through in the past two years was...some kind of grand plan to make this moment possible?" Betsy wasn't sure whether she was more angry or horrified by the thought. Everything she was taught about the Mother Goddess painted Her as a benevolent mother figure, one far more pleasant than her own, one with arms that would hold you when you needed it. And yet, where was the Mother Goddess through all of her pain? Standing by and watching to see how much she could take?

"That's an overly simplistic way to explain it." The old woman's eyes glittered with something Betsy didn't much care for. It felt like being watched by her mother.

"But that doesn't mean it's wrong." She sat up, not caring about the instructions she was given, and turned to show the woman her back. "This was about preparing me for something? He branded me with a hot iron, he used everything I can imagine to make me bleed, he killed his own children just because he couldn't contain himself. He revels in my pain, takes pleasure from my screams and whimpers." Tears now streaming down her face, she glared at the woman and didn't know when she started shouting. It happened somewhere in there, her voice raising until that was the only word for it, and she didn't stop. "He stabbed me with a sword just because he could!"

If he stood before her right now, she would tell him, but it wouldn't do any good, because he was bigger and stronger, and loved to watch her cry and bleed for him. Without him here, she could shout and not be hit for it, she could say anything and not be hit for it, she could feel anything and not be hit for it. "I thought he was everything, and then men came and showed me that he wasn't. They weren't nice to me, but they were nicer than him. They put me up for sale, and they were still nicer than him. I don't know what my buyer would have done, but I might have liked it if it was any gentler than him."

Myra was the only person who knew all of this, and here she sat, telling a complete stranger. "They took away the only friend I ever really had, but that was still gentler than what he did to me. He..." She buried her face in her hands, rage leaking away. It was so unnatural to feel so much anger, it couldn't possibly stay long. "He did the worst thing imaginable. He gave me hope for the future, and then took it away. Over and over, until I was dead inside."

The woman hugged her tightly. "You're not dead inside, Betsy. You never were. Just hiding. Waiting for someone to take your hand and bring you back into the light. You can live, you don't need to cower in the darkness. He has no hold over you here, there is nothing he can do to you here. Out there, you have friends, they'll help you protect yourself if you let them. Above all, you have never deserved and will never deserve anything he did to you. I swear to you it's true, Betsy. None of it was ever your fault. Not even for a moment. You're not to blame for any of it."

"He always said-" Betsy hiccuped as she wept into the other woman's arms, frantic for the comfort.

"Forget every word he ever said. Not a single one was true or right. His hands are his responsibility, so are his words. Blaming you for him hitting you is like blaming a pig for rolling in the mud you made by watering his sty or a dog for chewing the slippers you told him to fetch. It's not your fault, it has never been your fault, it will never be your fault." She rocked Betsy as she held her, and turned to repeating herself as Betsy cried hysterically into her shoulder.

Chapter 14

The blanket covering her when she woke was made of something soft Betsy didn't have a name for. It was some sort of animal hair, probably, and it made her feel warm and cared for to have it. She lay on a bed in a small room, one with nothing else in it, aside from a small table holding a wooden cup. The cup proved to have water in it, which she drank down. A plain white dress like she'd seen the younger girls wearing here was draped over the foot of the bed. She picked it up and put it on without hesitation. No footwear was left for her, so she padded out barefoot to find what there was to be found.

In the bright sunshine, colors struck her as brighter, even moreso than before. The grass was so green, the sky was so blue, the flowers were so red and yellow and orange it almost ached. Even the white and gray and black felt more like white and gray and black. Standing in the doorway, she breathed in and out and it filled her with enough joy to put a smile on her face.

"The Lady Of Niwlynys says you are to be taken to the smithy, then escorted off the island." It was the same girl as before. "She says your task is urgent and you must return to the world soon. She also says if you want to come back, use a boat next time."

Betsy laughed, it sounded strange coming from herself. When was the last time she truly laughed? Before the wedding, probably. None of what came after sat so heavy on her shoulders and her heart just now. This place was truly magical, a refuge from the harshness of the world. Staying here for a while would do her much good. “Yes, of course. I'll bring my own clothes, too.”

The girl grinned in response and offered Betsy her hand, which she took gladly. They went through the village, still full of women working at various chores. Now, Betsy noticed they did their tasks with smiles on their faces and chatter on their lips, full of companionship and happiness. How did she not notice it before? When she came, she truly was dead to the world, so much that she couldn't see what was right in front of her.

They stopped at an outdoor smithy, laid out just as she saw in her dream. A woman with thick arms and wearing a leather apron and gloves pounded bits of metal with a large hammer. She stopped when she saw Betsy and the girl, stepping out of the way and gesturing for Betsy to do whatever she needed to do. There was the spike, she was drawn to it for the familiarity. This time, she didn't have the gold cord, but she would get it back and bring it here. Yes, that's what she would do. That's why the cord became real, so she could do that very thing here, not just in a dream.

A flash of light drew her attention, also just like in her dream. The table held tools, metal ingots, and partially worked pieces. Along with those things, she saw a mirror, etched with lines her mind couldn't comprehend. She recognized it. Jason had one just like it, one he hid from her. One she saw when she met the elf man for the first time. This was it, the piece of the sword kept safe on Niwlynys. Two years ago, Jason had at least one. Now, the elf had the pendant. By now, they might have everything but this piece.

She picked it up, it felt just like a small mirror should. Really looking at the lines, she could make out the shape of a sword hilt if she squinted. Not sure what to do with it, she figured it would be simpler if she had the actual piece and smashed it against the table. Except nothing happened. It hit the table and the impact reverberated up her arm, but the mirror was undamaged.

"Don't waste your energy," the smith said. "I've hit it with a sledgehammer and it didn't even get a scratch. Needs something else to break it."

Her blood, that's what it needed. Jason never realized he had the key under his nose all this time. Clenching her teeth together against the sharp sting, she scraped a shallow cut across her arm with the edge of the mirror and smeared her blood all over it. Light flashed so bright it hurt her eyes, and when it faded, she had a hilt in her hand. Her blood would also reforge the blade, she knew it to be true. The elf knew that, too. He knew what to do and had every intention of doing it.

The girl rushed to her side, grabbing her arm to help with the cut, but it had already stopped bleeding. "Oh my," she said, breathless with wonder. "I've never seen anyone heal like that, not even the Elder Healers."

"My gift is to take pain."

"Wow." The girl used her own sleeve to wipe the blood away, heedless of the tiny spatters marring Betsy's dress already.

"I need to go. How can I get back to Rennsen?"

"The forest around the lake is an eerie place," the smith said. "Trust it."

Betsy nodded. "I need a boat, then." The girl bobbed her head, eyes wide in awe, and led her to a small dock with small boats, then rowed her away from the shore. They passed through the mist with nothing more than a chill settling around Betsy. Would she only be tested the one time, or was it always safe to leave the Isle? They glided to the beach, where the girl whose name she never even asked for smiled at her and wished her well. Betsy helped her turn the boat and gave it a push towards the mist.

She stood on the beach again, alone in the cold, drab world. It seemed darker here somehow, though the sun was still overhead, the sky still clear. Colors didn't look the same, either. Niwlynys was truly a place apart from the world in more ways than just one. If only she could have stayed longer, but she had to get back to Rennsen. Resolute and with the hilt gripped in her hand, she turned her back on the mist and walked quickly to the trees. Trust them, the smith said, and trust them she would.

None of what happened was her fault. If she took nothing else with her from this time on the Isle, this one thing was important. Everything Jason did happened because Jason did it, not because she did something that forced him to do it. He told her that she made him angry and that's why he punished her, but that was a lie. He did those things because he wanted to, and the cat was just the first excuse of many, designed to keep her silent and obedient. Darius told her that, but she didn't really grasp it until the Isle. Nothing would ever be the same after the Isle.

The trees slept here. She moved through them with as much care as she could, worried about waking and offending them. When she started to feel hungry, she hastened her steps, expecting the trees weren't going to provide. Quite suddenly, she stepped out of the trees to find herself in a place she knew well, Brexler Park. It was cold; she immediately hugged herself and wished she at least had boots.

"Betsy!" Darius found her again, he was good at that. Before she took another step, he wrapped his arms around her, warming her with his own heat. "Vanora said you'd wind up here somehow."

"The Disciples know more than they let on," she said with a little smirk.

"Are you alright?" He pulled away to look her in the eyes again. She could see how worried he was, how much fretting he did, how strongly he felt for her. If only she'd been looking, she would have seen it before. Evi said it, but she didn't believe it. Except she didn't feel that for him. At least, she didn't think she did. What did that feel like?

"Yes, I'm fine." She held up the hilt. "I found the piece. It was there, just like I thought. Jason has at least two of the other pieces. I have to go back to the house and get however many there are."

"You're not going back into that house."

"I agree." Connor and Rae arrived with Evi right behind them, probably having heard Darius's shout.

Evi ran right into her and hugged her. "I'm so glad you're okay." She stepped back and looked over the new dress. "You're really hard on clothes."

Betsy laughed and had a feeling she'd be doing it a lot more. "Yes, I certainly am." Taking Evi's hand, she ran off, pulling the other woman up the street with her. The men would to try to argue about whether she should do what she needed to do in the hopes of talking her out of it, but she wasn't going to have any of that. They could grump to their hearts' content later, when this was done. Right now, she had pieces of a sword to collect so she could properly destroy them.

They reached the gate to find the guards surprised to see her there. "Let me in," she said with an air of authority she never once displayed before. The two men blinked, glanced at each other, then hurried to comply. "Is the Earl on the premises?"

"Yes, my Lady, he is. Inside the house."

"Of course he is." The last thing she really wanted right now was to confront him, but it would have to happen sooner or later. She heard boots and jangling behind her and knew who it was. "These three other people are here with me. Let them through." With that, she swept past them and up the drive, her dignity intact so far. So what if she was barefoot and wearing less than half of what she really needed for the weather? She walked like she owned the estate and everyone inside it, pushing away the icy pit of fear gnawing at her belly. He was going to do what he always did, and she couldn't stop him.

"Betsy," Darius pleaded from right behind her, "let us go in first."

"No." This, right now, was her one real chance. The one before, that was fake. It was a temporary escape. She had this one chance to stand up to him before her nerves failed her and she chose to hide and flee again. That path was attractive, but it made everything her problem. This was his fault, his problem, his responsibility, and she wasn't going to shoulder it for him anymore, never again. She let go of Evi and marched herself up to the front door, tossing it open confidently. The cat came with her, able to do so whether she wished it or not.

"Jason," she shouted into the house, surprising herself with how much she sounded like her mother. This time, she wasn't going to try, she was going to succeed. She crossed her arms while she waited, letting the chilled air into the house all around her.

He stepped out of his office, expression coolly annoyed to see her standing there. "Sabetia," he said, careful and calculating.

"Give me the mirrors." How demanding she sounded.

She didn't know what the others did behind her, but could guess from the way Jason crossed his arms and set his chin. "I don't know what you're talking about, Sabetia."

"Yes, you do. Hand them over."

"This is a new side of you, my flower. We saw a little bit of it yesterday, didn't we? But this is full force." He took one step towards her, but stopped and put his hands up, perhaps in response to Rae. "Had I known your mother was locked inside you, I would have done things a little differently."

"Is there a problem, my Lord?" Keric's voice drifted down the hallway as the mage walked up behind his master.

"Uninvited guests on the property. Deal with it."

The doors slammed shut behind Betsy, obviously Keric's doing. The sound was loud and final and followed by a thud on the wood. Those four weren't going to be kept out by magic. She wasn't alone and needed to remember that. "If you would remove yourself upstairs, my Lord, the guests will be handled."

"You won't be able to deal with them so easily."

"It doesn't matter." Jason looked back into the office. "Inderion, if you're right, it's time."

The elf stepped out of the office, looking at her like she was the answer to all his dearest wishes. If those wishes included something to terrorize, that is. "I've got them. Get her and let's do this."

"I won't be 'gotten'." She held up the hilt like she could use it to defend herself.

Inderion the elf's face lit up with greedy delight. "Just as I said, your Lordship. She has the last piece."

Betsy's heart stopped. How could she have been so stupid? All she had to do was get the smith to smash this hilt to oblivion, or melt it in the forge, or destroy it some other way. Instead, she brought it here, where it could be joined with the rest of the pieces. Her zeal to put a stop to this all at once made it possible for them to do exactly what she intended to prevent.

Jason was suddenly in her face. He shoved her against the doors so hard she dropped the hilt and stared blankly at him. There was no hair for him to grab, but that didn't stop him. He seized her wrists while she was still stunned and wrenched then together in one hand. That was all he needed to haul her up the stairs, stumbling and cracking her knees and chin on the steps. She fell at the top and he dragged her across the floor to the bedroom.

This wasn't supposed to happen. Behind them, Inderion followed with a stack of five mirrors, a disturbing grin on his face. "You're going to release the demon."

"Bravo, little girl. Congratulations on figuring it out." Inderion watched with undisguised glee as Jason slammed her head against the floor. The contact drove all thoughts from her, all she could do was lie there while Jason picked up one of her arms and sliced it open. Inderion smeared the blood over the first mirror, it flashed into a piece of the sword. Jason put a knee on her back and held her down with all his weight while they did it over and over, five times for five pieces.

"Jason, please." He had a grip on her hands even as he leaned on her back, keeping her from doing anything more than ineffectually kicking her feet.

"Don't worry, Sabetia, it'll all be over soon."

"Why are you doing this?" She whimpered as Inderion stabbed her in the arm again to dip the end of one piece in her blood and fuse it to the next.

Jason chuckled. "It's funny, actually. You gave me that flower the first time we met. I was going to just toss it on the casket, but something stopped me, I don't know what. I kept it, held onto it all the way out of the Temple and for the walk home. Could have ridden in a carriage, but I walked. On the way, I was so absorbed in my thoughts, I tripped over an old beggar. The man was dead, just lying there on the side of the road in a nice part of town.

"If I hadn't had the flower, I would have just stepped over him and alerted the next Guard I saw to him there. But I did have it. I paused long enough to drop the flower on him. In so doing, I noticed a glint of light on something tucked into his jacket. It was one of the mirrors. I'd been searching for them for over a year already with no luck, and I just stumbled over one. Because of you."

"Blah blah blah," Inderion said with a roll of his eyes. "He originally wanted glory, but now he also wants revenge on his mother's soul for killing his father, and I want money. That's all there is to it, little girl. Nothing deeper than that." Out in the hallway, she saw movement and recognized Keric, busy doing something. "And, of course, the mage, who owes your dear husband his life, wants his freedom, which he will get for doing this."

If Keric was up here, he wasn't defending the house. Was that because he thought it secure, or because the others were dead already? "My Lord, the circle is ready." Keric stood up and avoided Betsy's eyes. "Bring everything here. Take care not to mar the circle." Was it her imagination, or did he place special emphasis on that instruction?

Inderion stood and brought the sword, complete except for the pendant. Jason took his knee off her back and pulled her up by her hands, still both pinned in his one larger one. "Jason, this is madness. She killed him because she couldn't take it anymore. You know that, you wanted me because you thought I would never do it to you. You learned how to treat your wife from how he treated his, and hate her for winning when she fought back. How do you expect a demon to punish her soul anyway? She's in the stars."

Jason held her close so he could kiss her ear. She felt his moist, hot breath on her neck. "I like you without the hair, Sabetia. If you survive this, and I think you might, I'll show you how much." He set her on her feet inside the circle of silvery dust.

Inderion pulled her pendant out, crusted in blood and still on the golden cord. No, that was only half of the cord. It was broken already. “Yes, yes, I'm happy you get to keep your toy even though we're going to stab her through the heart.” He bent the wire basket to extract the pendant and clicked it into the pommel, then there was another bright flash of light. Turning to Betsy, he smiled with pure malice. “Which it is now time to do.”

Betsy saw movement at the head of the stairs, something small and gray and feline. If Shadow was in the house, Connor couldn’t be far behind. Just as she opened her mouth to try to stall them a little longer, Jason swept her feet out from under her and she fell, hitting the floor hard enough to make her cry out. Inderion put a boot on her neck, Jason sat on her legs. The sword was positioned over her chest. Inderion slammed it through her.

It hurt so much she couldn’t make a sound. Someone else screamed instead. She heard Keric shout in a mild panic, “Keep it in the circle!”

A dark red glow seeped up the runes on the blade, from her chest to the hilt, as if it drank her blood. The world started to fade away, it was hard to keep her eyes open. Her body bowed with the pain when Jason wrenched the blade out of her, then she fell back to the floor, still not making a sound. She turned her head and saw everything happening in slow motion. Darius hit something in the empty air as he rushed towards the men, rage on his face. One of Rae's arrows hit the same barrier, Connor followed Darius more cautiously. Evi shouted something from behind them.

“Break the circle,” she gasped, hoping one of them would hear her and do it.

She blinked and it seemed like more than a half-second passed.

The circle was broken, and the cat was covered with silver dust. Jason faced Darius, holding his own against his former guard with the newly forged sword. Inderion sparred with Connor, the elf seemed frantic as he fought for his life. Rae shot an arrow through them, at a dark cloud crackling with blood red lightning – the shaft passed through ineffectually to thunk into the wall behind it. Keric crawled towards Betsy. Evi held a book with the pages flying out of it, streaking through the air at the dark cloud. Unlike before, the paper had no effect, diving through the cloud and coming out the other side.

Evi's pages flew back into her book. A crackling boom echoed around the hallway, coming from the cloud. The men all flinched away from it, and Betsy felt it in her bones. While she watched, hurting too much to do anything, she saw the cloud start to take shape, like a twisted, gnarled man. In the moment when Darius's eyes flicked to the dark shape over Jason's shoulder, Jason thrust the sword into the larger man's belly, forcing it out through Darius's back and yanking it out again triumphantly. Darius dropped to the ground, still alive but clutching his stomach and gasping for air. At the same time, Rae let out a deep breath and sent an arrow straight into Inderion's eye. The elf staggered and fell to the floor. Connor gulped at the sight of the dark form, but pounced on Keric's back as he kept moving towards Betsy, landing daggers first into the mage's back.

Jason raised the sword, blade down to deliver a killing blow to Darius. "That one," a strange, deep voice said. The dark shape flew at Jason before he could lower the sword, surrounding him and disappearing. From the shock on Darius's face, Betsy guessed this wasn't making things better. Ignoring Darius now, Jason looked at his hands. "Yes." The one word was long and drawn out, full of wonder and pleasure and profane joy.

"No," Betsy moaned. Connor leaped up at Jason, blades first and pouncing like a cat. Jason the demon caught him in midair on the blade and flung him against the wall, a harsh crack announcing Connor wouldn't be getting up again soon, if ever. Keric lay on the floor, his body still. Evi's book spilled its pages again. They plastered all over Jason's body, giving Rae a chance to put an arrow in his shoulder.

"Evi, get back," Rae hissed out as she pulled the string of her bow back again and fired. The new arrow hit Jason's chest off center as he ripped a page from his face and stalked towards the two women. "Evi, go now, get out!"

"I'm not leaving you here alone." The scholar pulled another book out and threw it at Jason. He batted it aside with the sword. The book tried to lodge itself on the sword, but the blood runes flared and burned right through it. "Fire," she whimpered.

Rae backed up to the head of the stairs, Jason stalking towards her. She bumped into Evi, sending her shot wide. Jason swung a fist at Rae's face, she ducked. The blow landed on Evi's shoulder instead, knocking the scholar off balance enough that she fell down the stairs. It was awful to watch, Betsy turned away only to hear Rae grunt in pain. Where her eyes went was right to Darius as he heaved himself to his feet, stumbling and barely conscious, and went at Jason. Betsy shut her eyes. She couldn't bear to watch him die.

If only the gaping hole in her chest would heal over, she could do something. What, she wasn't sure, she just felt so helpless and hopeless. She couldn't do anything to Jason, he proved that over and over. Even when she wanted to fight him, she couldn't. Someone else always had to step in to save her. Someone else always had to do something so she could get away. If it wasn't one thing, it was another, and she was never going to be free. Not until one of them was dead.

She opened her eyes to see Rae lying on the ground at Jason's feet, her bow gone. Darius sat in the corner at the top of the stairs like a discarded rag doll, bleeding to death. Jason stood poised with a boot on Rae's neck, ready to deliver the killing blow to her back. "Jason!" She screamed it out as loudly as she could, distracting him enough that he looked up at her instead of stabbing Rae through the heart. "I'm the one you want. Not them. Once you have me, they won't be able to touch you. Why waste your time on them when you could just have me?"

There was no possible way she could stop him, all she could do was give Rae a chance to stop him somehow, one small chance to kill or be killed. She watched with horrified triumph as he smiled at her, a smile so much more cruel and evil than anything he'd ever shown her before. The demon pushed him over the edge, beyond where he was ready to go on his own, and whatever he chose to do, it would be long and drawn out and worse than anything that came before.

Jason dropped the sword in a gesture of what looked like pure arrogance. Every step he took felt like one step closer to doom, and yet Betsy watched, determined. "Yes, you're the one I want. You're mine." Crouching down over her legs, he grinned with delight. "Are you finally willing, my flower?"

No, she was not willing at all. But she had to pretend, for just a minute. Even so, she didn't have to and wasn't going to say it out loud. For all she knew, that would create some kind of binding contract. Instead, she lifted her hand. It took so much effort. Panting, she shut her eyes away from the greedy, satisfied look on Jason's face as he watched her offer herself in such a small way.

Considering the circumstances, he took her hand surprisingly gently in both of his. She felt something unexpected at the contact, and opened her eyes to see if he noticed. He didn't. It was as if her power worked in reverse on them. Something trickled into her through her hand, a tiny little flow of fire making its way straight to her heart. Something was happening, and it gave her strength. The ache in her chest eased minutely, more than it was doing on its own. Instead of healing him, she drew power from him to heal herself. Her blood freed the demon, and her blood could destroy it.

She put her other hand on top of his and gave him a pained smile. "Your flower, always," she whispered, hoping to keep him distracted long enough not to notice what she was doing. If she could just make it flow faster, she could drain him dry of whatever fed her. Wild fantasies of saving Darius, Rae, even Keric flashed through her mind. Tightening her grip suddenly, she *pulled.* The floodgates opened and sent power coursing into her, burning her up with its intensity. Her mouth fell open in shock.

Jason's eyes went wide, flashing with panic. "What are you doing?" He pulled at his hands, but for once, her grip was too strong. Scrabbling back away from her, all he did was pull her up, the hole in her chest closing over, healing from the inside out. "Stop it! Let go! I'm the one in control here! Why is this happening?"

"No, not now, and not ever again. Never!" Betsy held on with all her might, pulling and pulling and pulling so hard her hands blistered. The power was too much, she couldn't contain it. Flares of white light streaked away from her body like shooting stars, seeking out the bodies of those who didn't deserve to die here today. One hit Connor, another hit Rae, and Darius, and Keric. One more flew down the stairs to where Evi lay. "You have no power here," she told Jason, unafraid of him. "I am not your anything, and you will never control anyone or anything again!"

White fire erupted from her hands. Jason screamed, his body spasmed. Betsy gritted her teeth against the pain as she, too, was burned. But she wasn't going to let go. Pain was something to be endured, not to be afraid of. It wasn't even that bad compared to being stabbed in the heart or slowly cut over and over, or being whipped until she bled. This flame was almost as much ecstasy as it was agony.

The blood rune blade caught her attention as it rattled on the floor, rocked by all the power coursing through the room. If she just reached for it, she could grab it. Never, ever did she want to raise a blade to hurt another person with it. But Jason wasn't really a person anymore, he was a vessel being used by that thing. And her dreams already showed her that this man had to die; it was the Mother Goddess's will. She kept a tight grip on him with one hand while she grabbed for the sword with the other.

It was an awkward thing, something she had no idea how to use, but the light guided her. The blade nearly moved of its own accord, plunging into his chest and seeking his heart. Jason's eyes bugged out and his mouth fell open. Dark smoke roiled out and up. "No you don't," Betsy breathed. She let go of Jason with her charred hand, sticking it into the cloud. The dark cloud sparked and roiled with colors, burning with white flames as it was pulled into her hand. Betsy felt an oily stain course through her and the blade flared with searing heat until she had to throw her head back and scream. Out of her mouth poured white-gold light, shooting straight up. It hit the ceiling and blasted through, disappearing into the sky.

Betsy swayed on the spot for a moment, then collapsed into darkness.

Chapter 15

"I'm so glad you're awake." Evi's voice was the next thing Betsy heard, and it made her smile. "She's awake!"

Betsy opened her eyes to find herself lying in Jason's bed. Her arms lay outside the covers, both wrapped in white bandages up to her elbows. Evi perched in a chair beside her, just setting a book on the nightstand. Betsy opened her mouth to say something, but only a harsh croak came out.

"I'm sorry we put you in this particular bed, but it was closest." Evi picked up a glass and helped her drink cool water from it. "Everyone is fine, except that your husband is dead, and so is that awful elf man."

Darius hurried into the room from the hallway, stopping just behind Evi. His hands moved awkwardly, like he wanted to reach out and touch her but didn't dare. His eyes, though, filled with relief. "Welcome back." Both of them looked clean and had changed clothes.

Her throat now less raw, she tried speaking again. "How long?" All she could really manage was a whisper. Evi helped her drink more.

"Almost two days," Darius said. "Once we were sure you were alive, Connor and Rae left. They didn't want to get mixed up with any guardsmen."

Evi bobbed her head in agreement. "Connor said you can come see him any time you want. So did Rae." She picked up a folded piece of paper off the tray and set it on the bed next to Betsy. "He said you should have this." Betsy recognized Caitlin's letter. He must have found it in that awful marketplace.

Darius cleared his throat. "Regardless, everything is cleaned up. Keric explained a lot." He sat on the edge of the bed, taking care not to get in the way as Evi fed her oatmeal that soothed her throat. "I wish he'd told me some of those things sooner. We could maybe have done something less...destructive. Still, it turned out for the best. Matron Aila was here. She said there were no traces of the demon left, and affirmed for the High King that Jason's death was his own fault. No one is being arrested for it. The house and Jason's accounts are yours. Keric left, but said he'd be back after he takes care of a few things. It's been years since he saw his family, or really been anywhere but under Jason's thumb. When he comes back, he wants to make amends with you."

Betsy nodded (Evi kept her mouth full so she couldn't speak), knowing she could forgive him, easily. All this time, he wanted to help, but couldn't do more than keep her from freezing to death or looking the other way when she escaped. When he did come back, she wouldn't even need to hear him apologize.

"He told us the story of how he wound up bound to Jason, and how Inderion got involved. I'll let him explain to you when he returns. He took the sword, saying he wanted to study it, especially the runes." The sound of boots on the stairs made Darius stop and turn to see who was coming.

Betsy's attention went there, too, her pulse quickening as she imagined Jason coming for her. Maybe he'd bring flowers to try to woo her again. But when the person came into sight, she knew it wasn't him. It couldn't be him anyway, because Jason was dead. She had to get away from this house. The memories in it would kill her if she let them.

"I came as soon as I heard." Caitlin hurried up the hall, carrying a small toddler and smiling. The sight of her was hard to take in some ways. It was the baby, she thought. "I'm so sorry, Sabetia, from what people are saying, it was awful for you here." She sat down on the other side of the bed and leaned over to put a hand on Betsy's arm.

Evi stopped feeding her and sat back with her tray. Darius kept his mouth shut, somehow managing to fade into the background despite being a large person sitting on her bed. "You're here just for me?"

"For a few hours, at least." Caitlin's smile faded around the edges. "I have to be home for bedtime or Delia will go crazy." She lifted the little girl up and rubbed noses with her.

Betsy smiled as much as she could. It wasn't very impressive. Hopefully, Caitlin would think she was too tired to do better. "She's cute. How have you been?"

"Oh, you know." Caitlin's smile faltered more and she held the baby out like the little girl was some kind of shield to hide behind. "Busy, busy, busy. Delia is a handful, even with her nanny helping, and I've got another one on the way already. We'll have a brood at this rate." She giggled. The sound struck Betsy as being off somehow. It was subtle, but Betsy knew that light, tittering laugh well enough from using it herself.

Holding up her bandaged hands to show she couldn't take the

child, Betsy searched what little she could see of Caitlin's face, trying to figure out what prompted her behavior. There hadn't been many letters, and none of them hinted at anything wrong. Or did they? That letter, the last one she got, it wasn't just an empty statement. She remembered a few crossed out words, and then recalled a hand someplace it didn't belong. "Caitlin, is Delia Quinn's daughter?" The moment the words left her mouth, she wanted to take them back, but only because they were so blunt.

Caitlin's eyes went wide and she sucked in a breath. The reaction was short, quickly smoothed over and tucked away. "Of course she is. How could you think of accusing me of that?"

A few days ago, Betsy would have left it be. Not today. "Are you sure its not Galver's?" She watched Caitlin try and fail to suppress surprise. Instead of waiting for her to answer or deny it more, she pressed on. "He's been forcing you." This made so much sense. "He made you uncomfortable before the wedding, and that's why you ran. I remember, you told me Quinn was lousy in bed, but he wasn't the real problem. Did he force himself on you that night, or did he wait a day or two?"

The little girl was silent, somehow sensing this was important. Caitlin stared at Betsy, unable to look away. "It was...the next night." Her breaths came out in short, sharp heaves as she started to panic. "You can't tell anyone, you just can't. He'll die soon enough, it's fine."

"Caitlin," she fixed her friend with a stern, pointed look, "silence is how they get away with it. If I'd just once stood up and said what Jason did to me, I could have stopped it, I know it. And what will you do anyway, if he doesn't die before he starts looking at your daughter the way he looks at you? Tell Quinn, Caitlin. You have to tell him. Right now. Make it stop before you lose your mind and kill him like Jason's mother killed his father. Remember? She was hanged for that, and he was only an Earl. Think of Delia and tell Quinn and your father both."

"They'll never believe me."

"Then tell a Disciple."

Caitlin opened her mouth to protest again, but shut it without saying anything. She sat there, pulling Delia into her lap and hugging her tightly. Tears leaked out of the corners of her eyes. "He said if I told Quinn, he'd tell Quinn I came to him and asked for it."

"A Disciple will listen, Caitlin, I promise." Betsy reached out and put a hand on Caitlin's arm.

Nodding, Caitlin wiped her face. "I should go. There's a Disciple here, isn't there?"

"Matron Aila. Anyone around here can direct you. I wish I could take you there myself."

"You're the best friend I've ever had." Caitlin set her daughter down and hugged Betsy, then scooped Delia up and fled the room.

Darius scratched his chin when she reached the stairs, finally moving after being so still for so long. "It's a lucky thing this bed is so large and ornate."

Evi nodded. "Poor girl. I wanted to hug her, but I was afraid she'd notice me and fall into pieces."

Betsy looked down at her hands. "If we'd only talked to each other, instead of pretending-"

"It's not your fault." Evi patted her leg.

Betsy wished she could take Evi's hand and squeeze it, but settled for smiling fondly. She was right, it would just take her some time to get used to the idea. "Are you going back to Ar-Toriess?"

The scholar fell into a pout. "I'd rather stay, but I do have ever so much to write about all of this, and I want to look up everything there is to know about Kailesce, and about the sword and the demon. I adored having an adventure, but I think perhaps one was enough for me. Probably." She leaned over and hugged Betsy tightly. "I'll come back for lots of visits! You should visit me, too! It's not that far, really, and I think I could come once a month or so."

"I'd like that. I'll write to you when I'm ready to start visiting."

Evi beamed and got up, her eyes darting from Betsy to Darius and back several times. "I look forward to that. Until then, I should get back to Moralan before he forgets to not be a grumpy old mage. I'm so glad you're okay." She kissed Betsy's forehead and bounced away, off down the hall and the stairs.

Betsy pulled at the bandages on her hands, wanting to see what the damage was. "She's very pretty."

Darius turned back after watching Evi go. "Yes, but she spends too much time with books. And talks more than I'm comfortable with." He scooted closer so he could loosen the bandages and help her unwrap them.

"You know, I'm not a damsel in distress anymore, I don't need to be rescued." Her skin must have nearly burned off – it was all pink and raw under the bandages. Once she saw that, she wrapped it back up. They'd need another few days, probably.

"That's very true." He helped her straighten the bandages and looked serious while doing it. "You saved yourself. You also saved my life. I'm indebted to you for that."

"The Mother Goddess did that. She decided you were worthy and gave you back your life. I was just a vessel. Darius," she put her hand on his as he pulled them away. He took it gently and met her eyes. "I won't have you staying with me out of guilt or debt or honor, or whatever else. I value you, you're very dear to me now. But I want you to live your own life, whatever that is. Don't follow me around just because you feel you ought to. I especially don't want you to feel like you're competing with Connor for my attentions. Or anyone else, for that matter."

He lifted her hand and kissed the bandage covering it so lightly she barely felt it. She had the distinct feeling it was something he did to give himself a way to avoid the subject. "What are you going to do now?"

She relaxed and closed her eyes, feeling tired enough to fall asleep again already. If he didn't want to talk about it right now, she wouldn't press. Besides, it was a good question. There were so many things she could do with Jason's money. One answer sprang to mind, and she knew it was the right one. "I'm going to sell the house and never return to it. Then I think I'm going back to Niwlynys for a while. They said I'm welcome, and it's what I want to do. For me. I'll be able to learn more about my gift, and when I come back, I can help Vanora keep them from tearing that old temple down. We can turn it into a refuge for lost souls. Put Jason's wealth to good use."

He made a soft little noise like a muffled laugh. "Of course you will. Leave it to a healer to use her hard-won freedom and money to help others. I guess I can't follow you to Niwlynys, so you win."

She took a deep breath and thought of Myra, of how happy she'd be to see Betsy finally free. No one was ever going to harm her again. "I want to see the stars tonight, Darius. She needs to know she didn't die in vain."

"With your hands still hurt, it might be best if I carry you."

Opening her eyes again, she could see he only wanted to help. "No. I might need an arm to lean on, but I don't want to be carried anyplace, not ever again. I need to walk on my own two feet."

He cocked his head to one side and smiled at her. "Does that mean you don't like riding horses or taking carriages?"

Betsy laughed, hoping she'd be doing it a lot in the future.

Also By Lee French

The Maze Beset Trilogy

Dragons In Pieces

At The Farm (short story companion)

Dragons In Chains

Dragons In Flight

The Greatest Sin

(Co-authored with Erik Kort)

The Fallen

About the Author

Lee French lives in Worcester, MA with two kids, two bicycles, and too much stuff. She has written several books, including the Maze Beset superhero novel trilogy. In addition, she is an avid gamer and active member of the Myth-Weavers online RPG community, where she is infamous for finding unexpected ways to use squirrels. She also trains year-round for the one-week of glorious madness that is RAGBRAI, has a nice flower garden with absolutely no lawn gnomes, and tries in vain every year to grow vegetables that don't get devoured by neighborhood wildlife.

Lee can be found online under the name AuthorLeeFrench on Facebook, Twitter, Goodreads, Pinterest, tumblr, and Wordpress.

If you liked this book, please take a minute to review it on www.Goodreads.com, or wherever you purchase your books online.

Made in the USA
San Bernardino, CA
04 January 2015